THE CUFFLINK

Susan Bass Bolch

DEDICATION

We are all familiar with the concept of the Big Hero, someone whose very name evokes instant recognition for his acts of valor or admirable and inspiring deeds. This book, however, is dedicated to someone whose heroism, with a small "h," profoundly affected my world. He is a hero not for a single or even a series of memorable episodes that by definition marks the Big Hero, but rather for having lived a life that by its very humanity helped me discover its true heroism. Many of us are paralyzed into inaction by perpetually waiting for the big idea or the divine inspiration. We diminish or even overlook the concept of everyday heroism because, cloaked in seemingly small events, it appears trivial or less compelling for its impact on our own lives or the world. Yet, there are heroes all around us who deserve celebration because in their lives of festival and folly they define the human experience; such a man was my father.

Even now, he is with me. He no longer pulls his thread through the fabric of existence, yet like fine silk, he remains a human treasure. It has been a year since his passing. I no longer grieve with tears. Instead, I realize that he continues.

His is the genesis of this story. He is why I write it.

How much of what we think we know about someone is fact as opposed to invention, not just ours but theirs? I knew my father for nearly half a century. I know what I observed of him, what he shared with me, and what some others have said about him. Yet, there is much that I do not know. At one time, he was a benevolent giant in whose shadow I dwelled. I was both the beneficiary of his largesse and an intermittent thorn in his big toe as he trod the path of his self-defined and often declared righteousness and sought to keep me in lockstep. Later, when I learned of his more serious wounds, he was augmented rather than diminished in my estimation not only because of the grace with which he bore them, but also because, by then, I carried my own. He is interesting to me because he is not perfect, and he has become more accessible because of his flaws. He has changed the way I think about heroes, becoming one by experiencing and surviving, by succeeding and failing, and sometimes by just carrying on.

It no longer matters whether I can separate fact from invention. Perhaps in describing a life, they are inseparable.

What is your money-making now? What can it do now?

What is your respectability now?

What are your theology, tuition, society, traditions, statute-books, now?

Where are your jibes of being now?

Where are your cavils about the soul now?

Walt Whitman, Leaves of Grass, Book 12, Paragraph 6

CHAPTER 1

FRED SPUN HIS WOODEN top on the parquet floor in the hallway outside the front room where his sister and brother practiced their instruments. He had lost count of how many times the stripes of yellow and red expanded and contracted like a kaleidoscope each time he set the top in motion, but he watched again as it wobbled and then gyrated, the circular motion causing it to remain precisely balanced on its iron tip. When the top finally toppled in a last violent thrash, Fred yawned, a look of boredom creasing his young face. Harmonious piano and violin riffs engulfed him, as he twirled the top again.

From the beginning, Fred was on the outside of their circle. Only one year separated his sister, Lorraine, and his brother, Will, but it was a dozen years before Fred joined them in the already crowded row house. Lorraine played the piano, her long, delicate fingers evincing everything from the heart-stopping emotion of the classics to the foot-stomping rhythms of ragtime and jazz. She was a tall, curvaceous beauty with an easy laugh and smoldering magnetism. Will was her alter ego. Aesthetic by nature, he walked with the stoop of the serious and a perpetual look of wonder on his spectacled face. He was more than an accomplished violinist; for while Lorraine's playing had an undercurrent of mischief, his was almost celestial. Lorraine attacked her instrument with abandon; Will seemed to merge with his.

To Fred, it was like being caught between fire and water, essential elements that both attracted and repelled him. Music was their common language, words he could not speak. He was air, beloved and needed by both of his siblings, yet invisible to them.

Sometimes he would sit for hours in a corner of the front room, his head resting against the wall and his eyes shut, listening, transported. The music surrounded him, and he disappeared in a melodic haze of love and awe for his sister and brother.

But other times, he just wanted to be in a regular family. "Freddy, can't you keep the noise down?" his mother, Ruth, would entreat him almost daily throughout his childhood. "Can't you see that your sister and brother are practicing? Don't you hear the music?" For hours a day, their practice would fill the house. *That's all anyone can hear,* he whined to himself.

One afternoon, when he was ten, Freddy was working steadily on his homework when Lorraine called loudly from the other room. "Freddy," she fumed, "stop tapping your foot. You're breaking my concentration, and you're messing up the beat."

Freddy ached for silence. *I hate you,* he raged to himself.

"Where am I supposed to go, I'd like to know," he huffed. "This is my house too, you know. Just because you're older and can play your stupid instruments doesn't make you better than me!" Fred stomped his foot and sang dissonantly. "I can make as much noise as I want to."

As he capered around the room, Lorraine brought both hands down discordantly on the keys of the Steinway grand piano that dominated the spare furnishings of the small front room and yelled, "You're such a baby. We don't have time for this. Get out of here before I make you sorry." Her dark eyes seemed to spit particles of light as she rose from the piano bench and lunged toward Fred, almost felling the ornate silver menorah that had belonged to her great grandmother, her empty hand crashing down on the mahogany sideboard.

Their mother, Ruth, having heard the commotion, rushed from the kitchen in the rear of the house, trailing the aromas of roast chicken and noodle kugel. Momentarily distracted by a picture frame that angled imperfectly on the hallway wall, she straightened the sepia-toned photographs of her father, Rabbi Yitzhak Bloom, and grandfather, Avram, a rabbi before him. "Such learned men," she whispered reverentially. Ruth pulled the dust cloth from the pocket of her starched apron, breathed on the glass, and wiped away her fingerprint before focusing her attention on her warring children. She turned to Lorraine, neatly pocketing the cleaning rag next to the library book that never was out of reach and cajoled her, "He's just a little boy. He just wants to be around his big sister and brother. He doesn't mean anything."

Lorraine resumed her seat and sighed deeply. "Well, he's annoying us, and we can't get any practicing done."

Fred began to sing and dance again defiantly. "I don't care," he grumbled. "I can be in here if I want to."

His mother caught him by the elbow and shook him hard. "Frederick, either go outside or go up to your room. Here," she said, grabbing a book from the overstuffed shelves that lined the walls and thrusting it into her son's hands, "read this and improve your mind. And you two," she continued, turning to Lorraine and Will, "get back to your practicing. You're just looking for an excuse." She dragged Fred from the room despite his protestations and warned him not to interfere again.

Looking back over his shoulder, Fred saw Lorraine and Will reluctantly take up their instruments and resume their practice, repeating the same music again and again. "See," he exclaimed in a self-satisfied tone to his mother, "They're not so perfect. They don't even want to practice. They're only playing because you're making them!" Their mother kept the beat with the flat of her hand as she plumped the pillows in the corners of the sofa. She cast a warning, narrow-eyed glance at Fred as she made her way back to the kitchen.

Fred dropped the book on the semicircular table under the mirror in the tiny foyer. "Find something to do with yourself besides being a pest," his mother admonished. Fred went out the front door and sat on the concrete stoop. He could see Lorraine and Will through the window, but he could hear only the muffled sound of the music. Mesmerized by the tableau, he saw his sister, seated at the piano, her head moving in time to the music, her auburn hair flying around her face. She looked like an avenging angel come to earth. Will stood behind her pointing to the sheet music with his bow, his lithe body swaying to the same cadences. Fred fidgeted, and his anger swelled. He reached into the soft earth of the small flowerbed next to the stoop and contemplated the clod of dirt in his hand, the embodiment of his rage and isolation. He hurled it at the window. The hideously satisfying splat of the ugly, brown tentacles of mud as they radiated from the center of the glass like a monstrous spider caused Lorraine and Will to turn their heads in his direction, aborting the music just before it reached its crescendo. A simultaneous rush of surprised gratification and horror propelled Fred around the side of the house where he crouched on the small strip of evenly mowed grass in the shade of the lone, leafy pin oak tree. He swiped at his eyes with his smudged hand and felt the hot tears cake in the mud on his cheek even as he grinned.

Ruth shot out of the house like a poison arrow and grabbed Fred by the collar. "You will wash that window until it gleams," she cried, "and you will not play with anyone or anything until you do!"

Fred shamefacedly marched into the house, followed by his mother, who handed him a bucket of soapy water and a sponge, pointing angrily at the filthy window. When he finished restoring the window to a sparkling clean, he went to his room and stretched out on his bed. He eyed the sketch pad and colored pencils on his nightstand and soon began drawing a picture depicting Lorraine and Will on stage playing their instruments to a packed Carnegie Hall-like auditorium. When he finished, he took the stairs two at a time and ran into the front room. Thrusting the drawing into his sister's hand, he said, "I made this for you."

A smile spread across Lorraine's face, and she turned to Will with a look of appreciation. "Look what Freddy made," she exclaimed. "Will, you should keep it. You're the one headed for the big time."

Will grinned modestly, but he took the picture and focused on his little brother. "Freddy, you've got real talent," he praised. "Can I keep this?"

"Sure," Fred agreed, basking in their attention. "It's yours."

Later that evening after Fred had gone to bed, Will brought the drawing to his parents, his voice uncharacteristically firm and determined. Laying it in front of them, he urged, "Look at this picture Freddy made. He shows genuine artistic talent, and he hasn't had the first bit of instruction. I know you want him to play the cello, but he never practices and really shows no interest. I talked it over with Lorraine, and we agree that you shouldn't force him and instead should encourage him to spend some time with Uncle Julius so he can get even better at what he really loves." Julius, his father's younger brother, was an artist and sculptor of some renown who had received acclaim for sculpting the marble lions that flanked the entry steps to the Philadelphia public library. These majestic, lifelike felines, the personification of strength and courage, were revered throughout the city and beyond. Tourists and art aficionados made pilgrimages to the expansive sweep of steps that led to the two massive white limestone plinths on which the lions, with their regal heads swathed in luxurious manes and their sinewy bodies rippling in muscular splendor, kept their perpetual vigil.

His parents looked from Fred's drawing to their sensitive older son and then at each other. As was typical, it was his father, Walter, who spoke. Gently lifting the drawing by the corners so as not to wrinkle or smear it, he replied, "This is really quite good. We've got plenty of music in this house already. Let's see if we can help Freddy develop his artistic talent."

Will accepted the drawing from his father's outstretched hand and took it back to his room where he carefully taped it to his dresser mirror. He couldn't wait to tell Fred that he soon would begin art lessons.

Most Saturdays, Fred's siblings would go off, arm in arm, their heads together wreathed in shared whispers and smiles to enjoy an afternoon together. He would beg to come along, but even when they let him, he felt left out. The chasm of years was too wide to bridge, and he would quickly grow impatient and brusque. "Don't you want to hear about my school?" he needled. "How come you two aren't talking to me? Don't you ever stop talking to each other?"

On one memorable Saturday, however, it was different. It was an overcast day; and while Will was talking to Lorraine, Fred snatched his brother's hat, basking in their momentary yet undivided attention, as he snaked his way through a city crowd laughing and waving the stolen property high above his head. It was one of the few times he'd ever stopped them mid-sentence. When they caught up to him, Lorraine twisted his arm until he relinquished his grip on the hat. "You're being a brat," she yelled. "You let go of that hat right now."

Will mussed Fred's hair and calmed Lorraine with a bemused grin. "It's all right, Lorraine," he said placating her. "Our kid brother was just being funny. Like this," he joked as he suddenly grabbed Fred by the waist and turned him upside down. All three of them laughed uproariously.

"Let's go for some ice cream," Lorraine pronounced after catching her breath.

"Sure," Will agreed, "we three Musketeers deserve a break. Race you to the corner!" he yelled taking off at a run with Lorraine and Fred speeding behind him.

"Winner buys," Lorraine screamed into the gap between them. When they caught up with Will at the corner, he had already placed his coins on the counter. "You better have ordered three vanilla cones," she admonished with mock menace.

"Yeah, three!" Fred chorused.

By the time Fred was thirteen, Will's musical talent was recognized throughout Philadelphia. Neighbors stopped his parents on the street and said, "We heard Will play last night. It was like listening to the angels."

Appearing to grow physically taller, his parents proudly accepted these accolades. Turning to Frederick, they would make the dreaded comparison. "Will has set such a fine example for you, Frederick. You should strive to be like him. Maybe you can excel at something like your brother," his mother, Ruth, repeated as a mantra.

"Your brother is on his way to becoming the best violinist in the city," his father, Walter, would affirm. "Don't you want to achieve something like that?"

Will was like the horizon at sea. No matter how hard Fred labored to reach him, he kept receding in the distance. "Maybe I don't want to be like him," he said angrily. "Maybe I'd rather have a brother my own age who liked to play with me instead of spending all of his time with his stupid violin!"

Walter's words were a stinging slap: "You're jealous of your own brother, Frederick. That's a pathetic excuse for your own shortcomings."

Now, Fred's anger was overt. "Jealous?" he jeered. "Why should I be jealous of a pantywaist? I don't ever want to be like him!" Only after the words had escaped his lips did Fred see Will leaning against the doorframe. His hands were buried deep in his pockets, and his thin frame was even more bowed than usual.

CHAPTER 2

T HAT SAME YEAR, Will auditioned for the Philadelphia Symphony Orchestra. Excitement permeated the house the day Will received their letter of reply. His hands, usually so careful, ripped open the envelope with anticipation. Four pairs of eyes were upon him as he unfolded the heavy parchment page embossed with the symphony's letterhead. Lorraine, who always wore her emotions like a fresh corsage pinned to her shoulder, succumbed to her anxiety.

"Are you just going to stand there and keep us in suspense?" she exploded into the tense silence. "Tell us what it says, or I'll read it myself." Lorraine sprang toward the letter, but Will sidestepped her and, raising his eyes from the page, he encircled her waist and swung her around in a wide arc.

"I've been accepted," he exclaimed. Lorraine shrieked with joy, and Ruth and Walter enveloped them.

Fred stood off to the side like an outsider, watching his family embrace. His emotions surged within him, a cacophony of discordant notes: pride and resentment, love and fear. He had hoped with youthful vanity that his parents would compare his flawless recitation of the Torah at his recent bar mitzvah favorably with his brother's acceptance into the Symphony. His desire for that level of recognition was an omnipresent refrain that echoed hollowly in his head, drowning out the acclamations for his brother that filled the room. He left the room without so much as an offer of congratulations.

He thought back to a story his mother had told him so many times that it was etched in his memory as if he had been there. She had argued with his father about giving Will violin lessons, insisting that a man of letters and culture knows music. She had found a violin teacher just down the street who was willing to accept Will as a pupil for just twenty-five cents a lesson.

Her husband spoke seven languages fluently, but he harbored a secret shame that his still subtly accented English marked him as an immigrant even after so many years. He was proud of his American-born wife, the elegance of her speech and the scholarly family into which he had married. Walter thought it was fine for Lorraine to take piano lessons but believed that Will would have no use for the violin in the real world. He believed his son needed to learn something practical so that he could make a buck, not waste his time on music. After all, hadn't he provided for his family for years as an insurance salesman?

Nevertheless, Ruth had convinced him that the violin teacher believed Will had talent and could become a real musician based on a few lessons that she had given him for free just because he seemed promising. Walter conceded, and Will had developed his gift at almost a prodigy's pace.

For as long as Fred could remember, the house was always filled with music. Will communicated through the violin as if it were his voice. His music was laughter and anguish, beauty and sorrow. Even their father became convinced that Will's music was soul-speech. Will's body swayed and his eyes closed, as his supple fingers plied the bow, caressing the strings, until he and his instrument were one. And the music, oh, the music.

Then came the illness. At first, it seemed an ordinary cough. Tea with lemon was the cure, his mother urged. She instructed Will to wear a scarf around his neck and to change his damp shoes immediately upon returning home throughout that cold winter. The cough persisted and worsened until it was a deep and constant hacking. There were many doctors, each with a different diagnosis and prescription, until the last doctor confirmed with one word what they had all feared: "Tuberculosis."

Still, they hoped. Walter heard that spending time in a dry climate was the cure. He talked of moving to Arizona where Will could recuperate at a sanatorium. Ruth made soups and tried to tempt Will with all of his favorite foods, insisting that by keeping up his strength, he would recover. He grew weaker daily, spending his days cooped up in his bedroom, row upon row of medicine bottles on his bedside table and the stale smell of disease.

But always there was the violin. At first, Will continued to play, seeming to have an almost frenzied desire to vanquish his illness with the beauty of music. Later, when he was too weak to lift it, the violin remained at his side like a talisman against evil.

Fred realized that he finally had a purpose in his brother's life, and even more importantly, a way to show Will that he cared about him. He had spent so many years resenting Will's success. Now, he could do something for his brother.

Since Will couldn't leave the house, Fred became his brother's barometer of the outside world. Every day after school, he bounded up the stairs to tell Will about the day's events. As Will lay quietly in bed, wheezing and coughing, Fred would talk about school, about the weather, about what was happening on the block. It was the most time the brothers had ever spent together.

One day, though, when Fred came up the stairs, his father was waiting, blocking the door to Will's room. Placing his hand on Fred's shoulder, he lowered his head and moaned, "He's gone." Unbelieving, Fred tried to push his way past Walter into the room; but his father held him steadfastly. It was only then that Fred heard the muffled sobs coming from his parents' room. At that moment, his mother uttered a single, wrenching cry that was primal in its agony.

Fred broke free and ran in his shirtsleeves long and hard into the icy wind and away from the death grip that clutched his family. His lungs burned with the searing recognition that Will's music had been hushed. His hot tears fell on the frozen sidewalk. The ice did not melt, nor did the frozen manacle of guilt that encased his heart. *Oh, God,* he agonized, *How could I ever have been jealous of him?*

Strains of Will's music, like a resident apparition, seemed to occupy the house as his family continued to mourn him. As adored as he had been in life, Will had been beatified in death. Death, particularly premature death, blurred the sharp edges of memories until they appeared perfect. What few chances Fred had to truly know his brother were gone, and even his childhood memories had been sanitized to the point that only the canonized icon of Will's achievements remained.

Fred remembered throwing the mud at the window, interrupting his sister and brother as they practiced their instruments. He recalled the drawing he had made that Will had kept. Importantly, it was due to his brother's encouragement that he had been able to take a weekly art lesson with Uncle Julius. He regretted calling his brother a pantywaist and looked back fondly upon their all too few trips to the ice cream parlor. Mostly, he was sad that he would never get to know his very talented brother now that their age gap had at last begun to close. In place of having a real brother, both talented and flawed, he and Lorraine had joined their parents in a silent, strict pact to glorify Will's memory. The narrow parameters of any discussion mentioning Will were clearly drawn. He was the smartest, the most talented, the most handsome. He was a model son, student, and musician. He exceeded every expectation and never faltered.

Fred's life now had a dual purpose; he was not only a keeper of the flame of Will's brief but stellar life, but also, he was the remaining, primary repository of all of the hopes that his parents had invested in Will. While Will was alive, Fred had fought desperately for his parents' attention. Now, he had gotten his wish, but in a nightmarish incarnation. He was cosseted and over-protected, and carried the impossible burden of living up to a saint.

On this, the first anniversary of Will's death, the yahrzeit candle flickered in its glass, casting a shadowy pall across the kitchen counter where it stood in silent memorial to Will. The animation of the flame was the sole movement in the otherwise empty room. It danced across the ceiling belying the crushing loss of which it was stark reminder.

Fred took a seat at the kitchen table. Staring deep into the candle's flame, the yahrzeit candle blinked intermittently. Fred held it in his hand and peered into its waxy, opaque surface. Since his brother's passing, Fred kept the flame. *After all*, he realized, *hope may flicker, but it still burns.*

CHAPTER 3

SINCE WILL HAD PREVAILED upon his parents, Fred had gone to his Uncle Julius' art studio every Friday after school. Uncle Julius recognized early his nephew's artistic talent; and at seventeen, Fred had become adept at drawing and was beginning to make his first tentative forays into the art of sculpture. He was in awe of the virgin blocks of stone, the tools, and even the smell of oil-based paints. His uncle's sable-tipped paint brushes were always arrayed in meticulous order from smallest, those with merely a few hairs that were to be used for the tiniest detail, to largest, those with wide, flat bristles that could slash a canvas with color in just one stroke. The palette knives also had been disciplined into size order, as had the pristine canvases neatly stacked against one wall. The paint tubes and pastel crayons each were arranged in a perfect rainbow commencing with the palest shades of violet, through a seemingly endless progression of blues, greens, yellows, oranges, and reds, and then disappearing into the abyss of browns and finally blacks.

Fred felt a keen anticipation on the days that he left school and headed toward his uncle's home. He tried to think only of the escape that an hour immersed in his art would provide. When he was painting or drawing, he could forget about everything: school, friends, the memory of his brother, and even the awkward Shabbat dinner he'd have to endure later that evening with his aunt and uncle who made him feel like a slide under the microscope as they scrutinized his every move in a way unique to the childless.

In spite of Uncle Julius's talent and the impressive acknowledgement he received in the limited sphere of the art world, he and his wife, Pauline, were most vocal about the fact that she had graduated from college. Uncle Julius seemed to grow visibly taller when speaking about his wife's academic achievement, and she never lost an opportunity to laud it over most everyone else whom she regarded as less accomplished, including her husband.

"Julius's classroom is only the natural world or the details of someone's face," Aunt Pauline always said with a dismissive wave of her arthritic hands. "After all, he is merely an artist. I, however, have always had the need for books to feed my intellect."

She was a large, thickly-built woman with a demonstrably unshakeable belief in her own superiority. She looked like an upended tortoise, her sizable bosom protruding like a calcified shelf on which rested the beaky profile of her face. Fred pictured her disdain as something tangible. He imagined that her heavy-footed gait was caused by her having been condemned to drag a shackle of officiousness along with her, much as the Greek gods had cursed Sisyphus to perpetually push his rock.

Returning home from the studio for a quick bath and change of clothes, Fred assumed a pleasant expression to mask his unhappiness at the prospect of yet another evening of his aunt and uncle's barely veiled arrogance and his parents' placid acceptance of their presumed inferiority. Walter did not own a car, so Fred and his parents made this weekly pilgrimage on the elevated train. After having endured these weekly dinners for many years, Will was gone; and Lorraine, who since Will's death filled her nights with jazz clubs and the company of strangers, could no longer be compelled to attend this painful ritual. Reduced to a threesome, only Fred, Walter, and Ruth felt sentenced to attend.

Uncle Julius had told them the previous week that he was going to purchase a used 1929 silver anniversary Buick. After the stock market crash, very few people had money to spend on such luxuries. When Fred and his parents walked from the el to his uncle's house, they saw the car gleaming at the curb, a behemoth of shiny green paint, chrome and glass. The family skirted the curve of the fender as they walked up the path to the door. As if he had been awaiting their arrival, Uncle Julius swung the door open and exclaimed, "Isn't she a beauty? Have you ever seen a prettier automobile than that?"

"It's lovely, Julius," Fred's mother dutifully replied. Her eyes were cast down at her feet, as if the worn leather of her shoes commanded her gaze. Fred linked his arm through his mother's, gently pulling her into the house and brushing past his uncle who filled the doorway.

Walter brought up the rear. He gave a backward glance at the car and muttered, "That must have set you back." Uncle Julius's silent smile was almost a sneer. The door closed like an eyelid, blinding Fred's view of the street; but already having seen the car at the curb, he recognized once again that the road that his father was on was patently different from Uncle Julius's.

Dinner was an hour of clinking glasses and silver scraping against china interrupted only occasionally by required conversation. "Wait until you see the interior of that automobile, Ruthie," Julius crooned. "It's all leather and as comfortable as your favorite chair!"

Ruth looked up from her plate and locked eyes with Fred. They shared a brief, surreptitious look of annoyance, knowing that she hated any diminutive of her given name. Julius was the only person who insisted on calling her Ruthie and the only one who had ever gotten away with it. Emboldened, Fred jabbed, "Maybe you'll give us a ride home so we can see the inside of the car. I'm sure we'd all like to see it since we never rode in your old car." His mother kicked him under the table, a silent reproach.

"Oh, Fred. No need to take your uncle out of his way. He's a busy man, and his time is valuable. Anyway, we have an easy ride on the el," Ruth intoned. Turning to Julius, she added, "I wish we could afford such a treasure." There was a momentary pause in the conversation, and Pauline emitted the only sounds, as she consumed large bites of chicken fricassee. Ruth searched out Julius' eyes at the head of the table. "Well," she continued, gaining confidence, "We chose to invest in our children. Will was a virtuoso who would have been the youngest member of the Philadelphia Symphony if he were still with us, and Fred is such a stellar student that he's been recommended for the Jeffers scholarship for 1932 by his high school principal." As she spoke, her back became straighter, and she lifted her chin higher.

As if he had suddenly awakened from the torpor of the meal, Walter snapped, "Frederick will win that scholarship. Just you wait and see." Fred felt his face redden, but he sat more erect in his chair. Looking at both of his parents, who sat beaming at him across the food-laden table, he recognized that they had the same expression in their eyes that Uncle Julius and Aunt Pauline had when they were talking about their automobile. Instantly, he knew that he no longer lived outside the circumference of Will's estimable spotlight; he had become his parents' shiny bauble. His chest expanded with pride even as he felt the weight of this new burden press down upon him.

After the dishes were cleared, Walter, Ruth, and Fred wasted no time putting on their coats and hats and tightening their scarves against the cold. "It was a delicious dinner," Ruth said to Pauline, lightly kissing the loose skin of her cheek. Walter echoed her goodbye, and Fred stood wrapped in his uncle's embrace.

"Say, how about I give you that ride home in the new car?" Julius said as he grabbed his coat and hat from the hall closet. "No time like the present to see that interior I was telling you about." He pushed past them and hurried down the sidewalk purposefully, as if he routinely drove them home from Friday night dinner. "Fred, you ride up front with me," he said over his shoulder as he slid into the driver's seat.

Walter and Ruth leaned back against the soft glove leather of the back seat of the five passenger touring sedan. Fred stared at the gleaming controls on the dashboard, as his uncle pulled away from the curb. Julius regaled them about the features of the car all the way home, sounding more like an automobile salesman than a close relative. "This baby is powered by a 331 cubic-inch six cylinder engine that produces 91 horsepower," he enthused. "Notice that the interior is fully carpeted, and she's equipped with a Fisher Vision & Ventilating windshield, internal-expanding four-wheel mechanical brakes and Lovejoy two-way shock absorbers!" His incomprehensible monologue, sounding like he had memorized the sales brochure, was broken only by scant syllables of affirmation emitted by his three passengers. Fred tried to understand the car's features, but his parents' eyes had glazed over.

"Ruthie, don't you just feel like a queen?" Julius demanded as they reached their destination. Fred stole a glance at his father, who looked like he had been sucker punched, his expression crumpled by inadequacy and his complexion ashen from standing too long in his brother's shadow.

Fred said nothing as he opened the rear door for his parents.

"Why, I suppose so," was all his mother could manage as she uncurled from the backseat onto the sidewalk, joining her husband and son. "Goodnight, then. Thank you for the ride," she whispered before hurrying inside after her husband. Fred stood alone in the faint moonlight watching his uncle's taillights recede into the distance.

The following Friday, Fred again returned to Julius' studio. Taking care to keep to the path that knifed through the immaculate front lawn, he turned toward the studio at the rear corner of the house. He knocked lightly and called out. Although he knew that the door would be unlocked, Fred waited to be granted admission. Nephew or not, Fred knew that Uncle Julius regarded him as a guest.

"Come in," was the distracted, muffled greeting that emanated from behind the door. "Don't track in any mud, and shut the door before you let all the heat out."

Fred scraped his feet back and forth on the doormat, shutting the door as quickly as he could without allowing it to slam. "Hi, Uncle Julius. I came to work on my painting."

Fred unpacked his pastels as he spoke, and eyed the composition that he had begun several weeks ago. It was of a group of men playing cards, a scene that he had witnessed most Thursday evenings when his father hosted a pinochle game for a few close friends.

Fred looked over his shoulder at his uncle who was concentrating on chiseling a piece of marble. He considered asking him to evaluate his painting, but he had begun to question Uncle Julius' genuine interest in his talent.

Sometimes, he thought, even as he gazed lovingly at his unfinished canvas, *I wonder why I come here at all.* He could not forget that only a few months earlier before his sixteenth birthday, his uncle had promised him a watch. Fred was certain that he could not have mistaken his uncle's intention because he had repeated it several times. The hollow din of Uncle Julius's words still rang, "When you have your next birthday, you are going to be ready for a modern man's timepiece, Frederick, not an old-fashioned pocket watch, mind you, but an instrument worthy of an artist and a gentleman of intellect. Yes, you shall have yourself an Omega wristwatch, a chronograph that tells the time and date, and I shall give it to you." *Surely*, Fred reassured himself bitterly, *there could have been no mistake.*

But when his birthday finally arrived last April, he waited all day and late into the night with no word from his uncle. Later that week, he came to the studio for his lesson, having convinced himself that Uncle Julius was deliberately waiting to see him alone to make his presentation of the long-awaited gift. Fred left that afternoon without so much as a "Happy Birthday," and he had to face the fact that there would be no watch.

Uncle Julius just said things. In fact, he said things all the time—things that made Fred feel like he had discovered a shiny penny imbued with extraordinary properties, one with all the good fortune of a talisman. Then, the penny turned out to be just a penny after all.

Fred rolled a pastel between his fingers. He liked the solid feel and the richness of the color. After having tried his hand at sculpting, he decided that stone was cold. Pastels turned the pristine canvas into a vibrant, animate entity. He cast a critical eye on his card players, and added a quick, sure stroke with the crimson pastel. The man's jacket he was working on, a bright red doublet, leapt to life under his steady hand. Fred surveyed his work with satisfaction.

Fred sensed Uncle Julius at his left shoulder. His uncle pulled at the corner of his lip and narrowed his eyes. "Well, Freddy," Uncle Julius said condescendingly, "your technique is improving. Your use of color in this painting is vastly superior to your last one." He said nothing further, and Fred watched him return to the block of marble that occupied most of the rear of the studio, circling it with his chisel in hand like a matador determining when and where to strike.

Fred applied the color with increased confidence and vigor. The figures began to assume dimension and character, a result of improved texture and more sophisticated use of light and shade. Fred smiled to himself. He stepped back from the easel to achieve more perspective, pushed his hands deep into his pockets and cocked his head to one side in the waning sunlight. His fingers closed around a small, round object lodged in the lining of his neatly pressed trousers. He pulled it out and examined it. The copper penny gleamed; and as it caught the sun's last rays slanting through the window, Fred thought it was almost beautiful.

CHAPTER 4

FRED HAD NEVER SPENT much time alone with his father; but after losing Will, Walter began to take more of an interest in his remaining son. Walter shared his love of crossword puzzles with Fred; and in the evenings and on weekends, he made a point of seeking him out alone to ask him about his art lessons and classes at school. On one such chilly afternoon that promised winter, Fred and his father sat on the front porch of their small but immaculate row house that was wide enough only for two ladder-back chairs. Autumn leaves from the almost bare trees skittered across the wooden planks, and the blind eye of the living room window that fronted Loney Street was already closed against the cold. His father had a fountain pen poised in his hand and the real estate section of the Sunday *Philadelphia Inquirer* spread open on his lap, dated November 27, 1931. Only the scratch of his father's pen broke the silence as he circled foreclosures.

Walter Green had emigrated from Latvia when the twentieth century was new and had worked for the Metropolitan Life Insurance Company for more than a decade. The older of two brothers, he was a proud man who held his head high when he spoke of his lifelong career selling insurance. Like thousands of immigrants who had flooded America's shores in search of a dream, he believed that Lady Liberty's torch was raised aloft for him. Now, in Depression-era America, the dream of gold in the streets had been reduced to cobbles of fear.

Walter was a handsome man with silver in his full, thick hair and steely-blue eyes that expressed a mien of perpetual gravity. He seemed taller than he was, a man for whom levity was an effort, but he was not unkind.

"They've foreclosed on the corner of Sixteenth and Chestnut," he said without raising his eyes from the page. The bank's notice of auction was now ringed in funereal black. "That's prime property right there. There'll be a high rise building on it one day. You mark my words."

Fred opened his mouth to speak, but slouched in his chair instead, extending his long legs in front of him. He was already taller than his father, his late growth spurt contributing to his lanky frame. They shared the same blue eyes, but Fred's had not hardened. He had heard his father say similar things many times before. Routinely since Black Tuesday, his father talked of the opportunities available to anyone, especially those who still had what he euphemistically called "a few dollars," to purchase some of the real estate that now crowded the list of foreclosures published in the newspaper every week. He assiduously studied the descriptions and labeled those that he believed would make the best investments, but he made no inquiries, only to resume his fruitless game the following Sunday. It was a monotonous, never-ending game of solitaire with only fifty-one cards, an impossible challenge that no one could win.

'Mark my words,' Fred repeated to himself. *That's literally all you ever do. Mark the ads; talk about life's chances; do nothing.* He cut his eyes sideways at

his father, feeling a mixture of frustration and empathy. He knew that his father would never invest his "few dollars" because risk was anathema to him.

Fred hugged himself with the sleeves of his plaid coat and secured the top button against the chill of evening. His father allowed the paper to rest on the porch railing in front of him. Walter blew warm breath into his cupped hands as he shifted in his seat to look at his son. "The only thing you can count on in this world is yourself, Frederick. Your place in it will be determined by what you can make with your own two hands or conceive by your wits and cleverness. Some will try to keep you down while others will try to use you for their own gain; but in the end, there will be no one for you but you." His father reached across as if to bridge the short distance between them, but then retracted his hand. Fred was cold, not just from the weather, but from a kind of icy dread that comes from within. *You mark my words,* reverberated in his head. His father's warning was as indelibly etched in his soul as the black rings that encircled the newspaper notices.

"OK, Pop," he said, picking up another discarded section of the newspaper. He smoothed the wrinkled pages containing the crossword puzzle, word games, and other brainteasers and swiveled in the uncomfortable chair to face his father. Walter had introduced him to a daily regimen of working the various puzzles to build his vocabulary and improve his speech. Some of his friends in the neighborhood had begun calling him the "Walking Dictionary;" and although he felt a growing separation from his peers, he was secretly proud of the differentiation. *If you are ever going to be somebody*, he thought, *you have to start by speaking like a somebody.*

Skimming the columns of clues, his eyes fixed upon one of them. "Hey, Pop, what's a six letter word for 'drool?'" Before Walter could hazard a guess, Fred inked in his answer. "D-R-I-V-E-L," he exclaimed emphatically. "Did you know that it also means nonsense?" Walter stared at his son unblinking.

"As in, 'What you just said is drivel,'" he continued. Fred grinned at the double entendre. He wondered whether his father accepted what he had just said on its face as merely an apparent show of intelligence or recognized the essential nuance of this verbal coincidence? Fred also questioned his own motive in selecting this particular question, twenty-seven across, to divert attention from his father's exposition on his philosophy of life. He could have chosen any of the many challenging clues to both impress his father and bring the course of their conversation back to the word puzzle, something they could enjoy together and in which they could share success, but he had deliberately settled upon "drivel." His grin soon faded due to his father's prolonged silence. "Never mind, Pop," he said, returning his eyes to the page, "I guess it's just drivel." They both laughed uneasily. "Let's see," Fred said engagingly, as he moved the newspaper closer to his father and covered the foreclosure section. He ran his long finger down the list of clues. "Fifty-three down, the longest river in South America. Come on, Pop, we can finish it together."

CHAPTER 5

I N THE YEARS SINCE Will's death, Lorraine had been rudderless.

She still played the piano, supporting herself by playing at small restaurants and social gatherings, but no longer practiced seriously. Will had helped her to realize her musical talent; but without him, she had lost her passion for it. Now, at twenty-seven, she just used it as another way to attract attention.

Younger than most of his classmates, Fred had always been shy around girls; and in his mid-teens, he had little understanding of the undercurrent of disapproval that ran beneath the growing estrangement between Lorraine and their parents. Watching Lorraine return home with one of her many suitors, Fred sensed only that her laugh was a little too loud, her lipstick a shade too bright, the sparkle in her eyes preternatural. Still, to him, these men were cats looking at a queen.

Their parents would part the curtain in the front window and shake their heads in dismay. As soon as they heard her key slide noisily into the lock, the onslaught would begin. "I see you've been out with another dandy," their father would say in disgust. "What kind of standards do you have, Lorraine? Is your head so easily turned by pretty words and a cheap suit?"

Eventually, one of the suitors stuck. No one knew much about Danny Loeb. Lorraine had met him at a small hotel bar where she sometimes played the piano on Saturday nights. He always seemed to have money but evaded questions about his job or family. His banter was usually slightly off-color, as was his taste in neckties.

"He's unrefined," Fred's mother said, compressing her lips into a straight line of censure.

"Danny's a nice guy, Mom," Lorraine replied, coyly removing her gloves and dropping into a chair. She crossed her legs, revealing a slim turn of ankle. "Besides, he makes me laugh," she added with a wink at Fred.

"What happened to that Phillip who used to come around?" their mother asked encouragingly. "He had that good job at the bank and seemed very reliable."

Lorraine made circles out of her thumbs and forefingers and raised them to her eyes to mock thick glasses. Then, she pulled the corners of her Cupid's bow mouth down in an exaggerated frown and replied in a false baritone, "Phillip's a bore, Mother. Good, steady, reliable Phillip wouldn't know how to have fun if it came up and bit him." She could barely suppress a giggle.

"Fun and good looks are not what make a good man. Your brother would turn over in his grave if he could see the little bums you've taken up with," their father decried. Lorraine stopped smiling and sprang angrily to her feet.

"Well, he's not here, is he?" she snapped back. "He's gone, and I'm here, and I'm tired of hurting. I'm going to do what makes me feel good. I want to live. Is that so awful?" She glared at her father defiantly.

A few weeks later, Danny presented Lorraine with a large diamond ring. Lorraine waggled her long, artistic finger under Fred's nose, and the stone flashed in his eyes like the sun's refection off white ice.

"I suppose you didn't ask him where he got the money for such a ring," their father scoffed when he saw it. "A diamond like that costs a fortune. Oh, I know. He picked it up after it fell off the back of a truck. I'm telling you, Lorraine, that guy runs with a bad crowd, and he's going to bring you nothing but trouble. I forbid you to marry him. Do you hear me? I forbid it!"

Heat seemed to radiate from Lorraine's skin. Her eyes blazed, and her mirthless laugh was filled with derision. "You forbid it? You can't stop me. I'm going to marry Danny and get out of here. This isn't even a home since Will died. It's a morgue!" Lorraine locked eyes with her father, and he was the first to blink.

"You're right. I can't stop you," he muttered. He stood with his head bent and his arms slack at his sides. With a last burst of authority, he clenched his fists and spat, "Don't come crying to me when you've ruined your life! If you leave this house to marry that bum, you're on your own."

Lorraine married Danny Loeb on a hot summer day just two weeks later. They had a brief ceremony at City Hall because Lorraine insisted that being married by a judge was modern, and Danny was not religious. Fred knew that Lorraine had not set foot in a synagogue since Will died. He didn't blame her. Walter and Ruth did. They were so mired in their own grief that they did little to prevent her from drifting away, and Danny was their reward.

The newlyweds set up house in a small but comfortable apartment in the Northeast section of Philadelphia. After the wedding, the family saw little of her. "Can't you come home for dinner one night this week? We haven't seen you in months," Ruth begged her on the phone. But Lorraine never did.

Danny had a group of childhood friends whom he called "the boys." Together, they had graduated from being teenagers hanging out on the street corner to night prowlers at The Shamrock, the local bar. They were on a first name basis with the bartender, and they could be found there most nights after work, if they were employed, all day when they were out of work, which was most of the time. Somehow, they always had money to blow. Danny stopped going to The Shamrock for a short time after they were married, but soon he resumed his nightly meetings with the boys for what he referred to as "just a pop" on his way home. At first, he was late for dinner. Then he wasn't home for dinner at all.

Lorraine tried sweet-talking him, massaging his neck before he left in the morning. "The boys can do without you tonight, honey. What do you say to an evening of just the two of us? I'll fix your favorite, and we can listen to the radio together."

"I didn't get married to be told what to do," he snapped. He shrugged her hands off his shoulders, and the chair clattered to the floor as he wheeled to face her. "I'll come home when I'm good and ready. I get enough bossing from the foreman at the factory, so just shut up about it." His handsome features contorted in anger. He shoved her aside, making for the door. Danny did not come home at all that night.

About a week later, Lorraine tried again. "Danny, I'm worried about you. You've missed dinner four times this week, and I don't think you're getting enough sleep. I was hoping…."

Before she could finish, Danny was out of his seat and caught her by the wrist. His breath was warm and reeked of bourbon, and she could see the web of red capillaries snaking at either side of his nose as he leaned his face just inches from hers. "Do you think you're my mother? Is that it, Lorraine? Well, let me tell you something; you're not; and I don't have to account to you or anyone else for where I go or who I'm with. I told you to butt out before, and I'm telling you again." When he released Lorraine's arm, the white imprint of his fingers formed an ugly bracelet. With his hand now free, he batted the dinner plates from the table. Lorraine knelt amid the broken china and sobbed. Minutes later, the slam of the door reverberated in her head.

It wasn't long before Lorraine stopped cooking or expecting him home. Night after night, she sat in the dark, a glass of bourbon by her side, watching the headlights below marching into the night and drinking herself into oblivion.

One particularly cold and dark Thursday night, Lorraine sat in a chair in her empty apartment cuddling an afghan around her knees. She stared at the opposite wall where she had hung the drawing Fred made when he was ten of her and Will playing their instruments to a large audience. She had taken this drawing from Will's room after he died, a cherished reminder of the past joy they had shared through music and of his promised success that was never to be. She had been drinking and listening to the ticking of the clock since dusk. The mantle clock struck nine. She rose and went to the hall closet for her coat. Checking her hair in the foyer mirror, she smoothed on her gloves and tightened the scarf at her throat. She locked the door carefully behind her and walked the short distance from her apartment building to The Shamrock.

It was dark inside the bar, and it took a moment for her eyes to adjust, as she panned the bar and the scattered tables. At first, she didn't see him. Then, in a rear booth, there he was, the sheen of his immaculately slicked back hair reflecting the pale overhead light. Getting closer, she saw his friends, too, each laughing with a woman seated beside him. The surface of the table was littered with empty glasses, and one of the boys was replenishing Danny's drink from a nearly empty bottle of amber whiskey. She froze at the open end of the booth when she saw Danny's face buried in the brassy blonde hair of another woman, his hand on her thigh. It wasn't until the others at the table fell silent that he turned his head.

He looked at her menacingly and growled softly. "Go home, Lorraine."

For a moment, it was silent, and then his friends started to laugh. She opened her mouth to speak, but the laughter was too much to bear. It seemed to push her out the door and follow her home. She drank well into the night, trying to obliterate the memory; but Danny's derisive, furious face mocked her from the bottom of the glass. She finally stumbled to bed and feigned sleep.

Hours later, a key sounded in the door. She could hear Danny making himself another drink in the kitchen, the rattling of the cabinet doors and the clink of the ice in the glass. She clutched the sheet tightly around her neck, curling into a fetal position under the blankets. She squeezed her eyes shut when the door rocked back against the wall. Danny ripped the bedding away and pinned her to the mattress, pressing his arms across her chest and wedging her thighs apart with his knees. She screamed, and he clapped one hand over her mouth and grabbed a fistful of her hair with the other, yanking her head back.

"Don't you say a word, Bitch! You're nothing but a worthless piece of shit drunk, and you disgust me," he yelled. "How dare you embarrass me in front of my friends! I'm going to show you who's boss once and for all."

She tried to scream again, but he slapped her hard across the face. The metal edge of his wedding band caught the corner of her eye. Blood, mingled with the tears that tracked down her face, leaked into the corner of her open mouth, and she could taste it, briny on her tongue. After a while, her cries remained strangled in her throat.

The pain between her legs was searing as he thrust himself into her again and again. Each penetration punctuated his hateful words. "Bitch…Whore… Piece of shit…" he screamed. Lightning bolts of lurid colors flashed behind her eyelids: red, white, purple. Then, she felt nothing.

CHAPTER 6

IN THE SPRING OF 1932, Fred would be graduating from high school at sixteen, having skipped two grade levels. Younger and less socially adept than most of his classmates, Fred garnered attention by excelling academically, and sometimes, by being the kid who laughed too loudly or gyrated too wildly on the dance floor. While he would likely be accepted to the college of his choice, he had his sights set on the University of Pennsylvania, but he would be unable to attend any college without a scholarship.

Now, in the spring of his senior year, the announcement of the Jeffers Scholarships was imminent. Harland Jeffers was a legendary Philadelphia businessman and philanthropist who made a fortune in shipping and established one of the city's most prominent banks. At the time of his death, he set up a perpetual endowment that would grant full academic scholarships to the two most deserving high school graduates in the city each year. One student would attend the University of Pennsylvania, the Ivy League college founded by Benjamin Franklin and the jewel in the academic crown of Philadelphia's many institutions of higher learning. The other would matriculate at Temple University, a fine school but lacking in the cachet of its renowned neighbor. Each high school principal could recommend one senior based on his scholastic average, and the candidate submitted a research paper on a topic of his choice. The applications were judged by a five-member panel composed of three Harland Jeffers heirs, one rotating professor from Penn, and another from Temple. While the competition was ostensibly open to all students, no recipient of the Jeffers Scholarship had ever been female nor had the winner ever been a Jew.

Fred had been nominated but knew only a little bit about his competition. His high school principal told his English teacher that the front-runner supposedly was a boy from South Philadelphia with an almost perfect academic record and a flawlessly written essay on the American labor movement. His science teacher had heard about another top-ranked senior from North Philadelphia who submitted an essay detailing the geological factors contributing to the San Francisco earthquake of 1906.

Fred's own application was a philosophical analysis comparing the works of Plato and Descartes. He had spent hours in the library and in conversation with his teachers trying to unlock the ideological mysteries of these great thinkers. He was satisfied with his submission, but doubt gnawed at his stomach nonetheless.

While walking the halls after his last class, Mr. Eastman, the principal, stopped him. "How is our scholar today?" he said, placing a large hand on Fred's shoulder.

"I'm fine, sir. I don't suppose you've heard anything from the scholarship committee?" Fred asked eagerly.

"Not yet, son, but it's never good to get your hopes up." Mr. Eastman patted Fred's shoulder as if the rhythmic movements were punctuation to his advice. "Better not to be disappointed and best yet to be pleasantly surprised." The principal looked around in all directions as if he were about to impart to Fred the secret of the universe. Satisfied that they were alone, he leaned in toward Fred's ear and whispered, "Besides, you need to be exploring other options. I know you have your heart set on winning the Jeffers, and I know that you are dreaming of becoming a Penn man, but let's face it, the Jeffers isn't going to a Jew. You're a smart young man, Fred, and I'm sure you already know that."

Fred felt the weight of Mr. Eastman's clear, steady gaze and looked away. His stomach twisted, and he thought momentarily that he might be sick. He had the urge to run down the hall and out the door that seemed to move further away mocking the idea of his escape. His feet were leaden. Small, cold beads of sweat broke out along his hairline; and his hands, which he flexed at his sides, were clammy. He raised his eyes to Mr. Eastman's face and was surprised at the icy clarity of his own voice, "No, I did not know that. I thought that the Jeffers Scholarships were awarded to the two most deserving high school seniors. I guess we'll just have to see which one of us is right."

Mr. Eastman's hand fell from Fred's shoulder. He ran it over his balding pate and shook his head, looking like a Good Samaritan misdirected to the wrong victim. "Well, then. I only meant to caution you against the agonies and frustrations of false hope. I mean, history speaks for itself and all that. One can't ignore the past, after all." He opened both of his arms and shrugged in a plaintive gesture.

"Maybe not," Fred demurred, "but perhaps the Jeffers Committee won't be able to ignore all of my hard work and achievement either." He thought of his father, sitting at Uncle Julius' dinner table, convinced that there was no way that Fred could fail. There, too, was Ruth sitting in the back seat of Uncle Julius's car, her arms wrapped around her tall, statuesque frame in a solitary self-embrace. *"Fred will win that scholarship…"* *"Ruthie, don't you just feel like a queen?"*

Hope hung like a soap bubble between them, fragile and perfect, borne by the warm wind of youth and possibility. "Anyway, we won't have long to find out," Fred offered generously. "They will announce the winners tomorrow."

Mr. Eastman resumed a cheerful, paternal tone as he squeezed Fred's shoulder in a final pat. "Good luck, son. You're a fine young man, indeed." The sound of their footsteps resounded in opposite directions down the empty hall.

Fred opened the heavy door and exited into the humid heat that rose from the sidewalk in the late spring afternoon; and suddenly, he wished that he could stop time. At that moment, he could still win. For himself, for his parents. At that moment, there was hope.

CHAPTER 7

THE NEXT DAY DAWNED hot and hazy. Fred dressed carefully and gave himself a final review in the bathroom mirror. He checked the part in his freshly washed, wavy brown hair. His mother had meticulously pressed his starched white shirt, and the crease in his blue gabardine trousers was perfect. He met his own gaze and practiced looking confident although, even to himself, his eyes appeared more anxious than self-assured. He busied himself in his room arranging and rearranging the books and papers on his desk in order to delay going downstairs where he could hear muffled conversation between his parents and the customary morning sounds of breakfast. Snippets of their words floated under the crack beneath his closed door. "What's he doing up there?" his father demanded. "It won't do for him to be late."

"I'm sure he's just dressing carefully," his mother said reassuringly. "Fred is never late, and he most certainly wouldn't be late today."

"Well, I'm just going to call him," his father announced. "Fred! Are you coming down? Your mother has breakfast ready, and everything is getting cold."

Fred was imagining the auditorium one last time, envisioning what was about to happen. The many rows of seats were filled with students, faculty, family and contenders who came to hear the representative of the Jeffers Foundation announce the recipients of this year's awards. He could hear the silence as the man approached the microphone. He could feel the anticipation, as if everyone in the room had taken and held a collective breath. *"This year's distinguished winner of the Jeffers Scholarship to the University of Pennsylvania is...."*

Fred stirred from his reverie finally and headed downstairs, launching his lanky frame into his seat at the kitchen table. "I was just getting ready," he said, trying to assume a guise of normalcy. He began eating his breakfast, but his stomach lurched at the two eggs, rye toast and tea, so lovingly prepared by his mother. He tried to move the contents of his plate around with the side of his fork to make it appear as though he had eaten, and then pushed the plate aside. Although he had brushed his teeth and gargled with warm water and baking soda, Fred's mouth tasted at once sour and dry.

His parents were dressed for the occasion as well. His father wore his best grey gabardine suit and navy blue silk tie. His mother's hair was carefully coifed in waves around her face, and pearls studded her ears and ringed the neckline of her simple but elegantly tailored blue wool chemise over which she had tied her cooking apron.

Walter rose from the table. "We'd better be going. We can't be late." He pushed back his chair, neatly folded his napkin, and turned toward the door. Ruth cleared the dishes from in front of Fred and shook out her starched cotton apron before replacing it on the hook behind the pantry door. She smoothed the folds of her dress and patted her hair. She turned from the sink and placed both arms around Fred's neck, as he remained rooted to his kitchen chair. He could feel her presence behind him. *Always behind me,* he thought, *supporting and believing in me.* He covered both of her hands with his. They exchanged no words.

Then they were all outside, walking in a horizontal line across the sidewalk toward the school. Fred and his father were shoulder to shoulder with his mother, who occupied the middle of this trio of tall, erect gladiators, armed not with swords with which to fight in this world but rather, as his father always told him, only with their own wits.

When they reached the auditorium, many of the seats already were occupied, each nominee surrounded by a cadre of supporters including members of the administration and faculty from their respective high schools, classmates, family members, and friends. Fred spotted Uncle Julius and Aunt Pauline and led his parents to three vacant chairs next to them near the middle of the room with a good view of the stage. He offered his father the aisle, but his father motioned for him to sit there. Fred, having recently morphed into a gangly sixteen year old, wondered if this concession was for the comfort of his long legs or was a subliminal suggestion that sitting on the aisle would provide more convenient access for him to reach the stage. Panning the now crowded assemblage, Fred saw Lorraine slip through the side door to the auditorium and join a group of latecomers lined up against the rear wall. Fred took his seat and waited for the principal to arrive at the podium to address the assembly. The room fell silent as Mr. Eastman surveyed the audience with a beatific smile.

"Good morning fellow faculty members, students, parents, and most especially, Mr. Hewing, the distinguished representative of the Jeffers Foundation. This is, indeed, a special occasion as we gather together to recognize the recipients of the 1932 Jeffers Scholarships. As you may know, Harland Jeffers established at the time of his death a foundation for charitable works. Among the many philanthropic purposes to which the Jeffers Foundation generously offers its financial support are annual full academic scholarships to two of our city's renowned institutions of higher learning, the University of Pennsylvania and Temple University. Today's two honorees have been selected as the best and the brightest among an outstanding field of applicants throughout our great city. They have been chosen after careful review of their exceptional academic credentials representing four years of perseverance, dedication, and exemplary results, as well as additional consideration of their applications and essays. It is our high school's distinct honor to host this awards ceremony this year. I would now like to introduce, Mr. Wallace Hewing, Chairman of the Board of the Jeffers Foundation and a grandson of Harland Jeffers. Mr. Hewing will present the awards."

Wallace Hewing was a patrician gentleman dressed in a gray three-piece pinstriped suit and a black and silver regimental striped tie. He was not tall, but he carried himself with the elegant bearing of an aristocrat. His silver hair was the same color as the frames of his spectacles. He looked out over the hushed throng and intoned, "The winners of the Jeffers Scholarships share a heritage of excellence. They carry the banner of those who came before them into an infinite future of possibility marked by accomplishment, invention, and discovery. This year, as in past years, our decision was a difficult one. Among the applicants for the Jeffers were many qualified and worthy individuals, yet we were charged with the Herculean task of selecting only two winners. The Jeffers Foundation would like to congratulate all of the candidates for their stellar academic performance, and we would like each of you to know that by virtue of having been recommended for consideration for the Jeffers by your respective high schools, you are all winners. Now, without further delay, I take great pride in announcing the Jeffers Foundation Fellows for the year 1932."

Wallace Hewing paused and looked up from the podium surveying the hushed assembly. Fred could hear only the sound of his own breathing. He sat motionless in his chair, his eyes fixed on a peeling spot on the wall behind Wallace Hewing's immaculate, gray head. His collar suddenly felt too tight, and he did not know what to do with his hands so he gripped his knees until his knuckles showed white and tense.

Wallace Hewing cleared his throat and pronounced, "The winner of this year's Jeffers Foundation Scholarship to the University of Pennsylvania, a senior from The Boys High School of Philadelphia, is James Harrison Davis." Thunderous applause erupted in the auditorium. A blonde, bespectacled boy stood in the far corner of the room and made his way to the center aisle amid shouts and embraces of congratulations. He passed so near to Fred's chair that Fred could have reached out and touched him, and many did just that as if they were momentarily fingering the robe of the Pope or Jesus Christ himself. *And why not?* Fred thought. For that instant, James Harrison Davis had ascended to being a god. He willed his hands to come together in the repetitive monotony of clapping. Out of the corner of his eye, he could see both of his parents applauding mechanically, too. Their faces in profile were marked by the identical rictus, their eyes gaping first at the man on stage who had articulated their loss and then at the boy wonder who mounted the stairs to join him at the podium - the young man who should have been their son.

The room was suddenly still once again. James Davis stepped to the side of the lectern, and Wallace Hewing lowered his hands, having raised them in request for quiet. "The recipient of the second Jeffers Foundation Scholarship will attend Temple University," he continued. Mired in his disappointment, Fred momentarily forgot that the awards presentation had not concluded.

Hewing's ongoing drone became a static din in his ears that seemed to grow in amplitude. *The Jeffers isn't going to a Jew.* "The winner is…."

Fred was stunned. The entire auditorium exploded in a cacophony of deafening applause. Having home field advantage, Fred became the momentary hero of his school. He felt many hands pushing him out of his seat and into the aisle. Scattered throughout the assembly, some well-wishers were standing as the ovation continued. At the back of the room, he saw Lorraine's tall, slim figure. In blatant disregard of all decorum, she was grabbing the stranger standing next to her. Arms entwined, they were jumping up and down, their legs like the uncoiled spring of a Jack in the Box, as Lorraine screamed his name. Then, he was at the steps, surmounting the stage. Mr. Eastman pumped his hand and cradled his elbow as he guided him to the podium. Wallace Hewing was so close that the rich fabric of his coat brushed against Fred's arm. The leather-bound certificate was in his hands, his name embossed in letters of gold on the burgundy cover. Fred stood among the anointed and beheld the crowd. The rest of the audience was a colorless blur as his eyes fixed on his parents who seemed to stand out in brilliant relief. His father gave an almost imperceptible nod, his blue eyes twinkling. His mother was ramrod straight, the picture of pride. Beside them, he could just make out Uncle Julius and Aunt Pauline. There was no mistaking it; they, too, were standing.

CHAPTER 8

A FTER REGISTERING FOR CLASSES at Temple University, Fred attended the freshman orientation the following week that included presentations in the gymnasium from fraternities, sports, clubs, and other organizations or activities represented on campus. Fred witnessed fellow entering students congregating around tables that lined the walls with large identifying banners hanging above them. He enthusiastically scanned the banners, dismissing the fraternities, which he knew he could not afford. His attention was drawn to a table of eager young men surrounding an athlet-ic-looking older man who stood under a banner that read "CLUB BOXING." He approached the group, stopping at the fringe, where he heard him say, "Club boxing builds confidence, and it teaches you how to defend yourself." This spurred him to move closer because, always the youngest student in his class and painfully thin, he was frequently bullied and quickly learned that confrontation was often the only way to expose the cowardice that underlies most assaults. Fred cringed at the memory of one fight he had been in during high school when a short, muscular Italian kid had called him a kike. His parents were livid when he came home with a broken nose; but Lorraine had defended him, ignoring their parents' anger and handing Fred an icepack. "Way to go, Freddy," she said. "You don't have to take crap from anybody. You just have to hit 'em back."

Fred waited his turn while the older man finished answering the questions of another freshman with fiery red hair and an expression to match. The man extended his hand and said, "Hi. I'm Coach MacFarland. Can I answer any questions?"

"Yes," Fred replied, "Do you have to be an experienced boxer to be considered?"

"Absolutely not. This is a club activity, which is open to all who are interested in learning to box. We have intra-club matches at Temple open to all; and for those who excel at Temple, inter-club matches with other schools that have club boxing. Of course, there are weight divisions in all matches."

"Where do I sign up?" Fred asked without hesitation, having received all the information he needed. Coach MacFarland handed Fred a pen and pointed to the sign-up sheet that lay on the table.

Over the course of his undergraduate years, he became a favorite of the coach because he spent so much time at the gym building his strength and learning the tactics, feints, aggressive moves, and defenses, so that he could best his fellow assailants in the boxing ring. As Fred matured and gained muscle mass through frequent workouts, he became a middleweight.

Despite Fred's intense interest and repeated assertion that his participation in boxing caused him to gain self-confidence and engendered competitiveness, Fred's parents frowned on boxing, insisting that any type of fisticuffs was not a sport. They feared for Fred's safety and worried constantly about injury, especially as he was now their only remaining son. His parents' disapproval didn't thwart Fred; rather, his desire for athletic prowess became further inspiration. He had always excelled academically and artistically and now wanted to prove himself athletically as well.

In his junior year, as he walked to the gymnasium with his athletic bag slung over his shoulder, he felt the pinpricks of anticipation tingling in both of his palms. Today was the final round of inter-club matches for each weight class at the Philadelphia area championships at which Fred would represent Temple. Fred had defeated his opponents in the opening and second tier middleweight matches with relative ease, but his adversary in the semi-final, compact, quick, and solidly built, was a formidable opponent. Fred, too, was fast. Moreover, it became apparent that Fred was in better shape when, as the match progressed, his opponent slowed; but Fred's quickness remained. He avoided a vicious left hook and counterpunched with a devastating right cross that sent the other fighter reeling into the ropes and to his knees for a technical knockout, sending Fred to the finals.

When Fred arrived at the athletic arena, the spectator stands already were full. He surveyed the reserved section looking for his mother and father but didn't see them in the crowd. He wasn't terribly surprised; they had refused to attend any of his matches and barely even acknowledged his victories.

He tried again that morning to persuade them to attend the final match of the tournament. "This is important to me," he explained, cutting to the heart of the matter. "Why do you support me only in things that matter to you?"

His father kept his eyes fixed on the newspaper in his lap. His mother, her pretty face looking tired and haggard, wiped her hands on her apron and crossed her arms across her chest.

"What is there to support about two young men beating each other until one is either too injured to continue or is rendered unconscious?" she asked.

"Does it take any brains to hit someone or to endure being hit?" She pushed a stray lock of hair off her forehead with the back of her hand and shook her head at the barbaric image that boxing summoned in her mind.

"People who resort to fighting with their fists do so because they are devoid of any other means with which to defend themselves or prevail," Walter confirmed with disdain. "You're better than that, Freddy. Words are more powerful than fists."

Fred self-consciously fingered the bump on his nose, the souvenir of his high school fight, remembering his parents' distraught reaction. Fred had been proud that he had defended himself, but his parents were even more upset when the break was not set properly, and Fred's formerly straight nose was rendered permanently aquiline. The bumpy nose was even more fodder for some neighborhood boys, who continued to call him "kike" and "Jew-boy." He burned at the memory, but once under the tutelage of his college coach, he tried to channel his anger into the ring. He didn't want to fight on the streets anymore. *I'm a boxing champion*, he thought. *My reputation will precede me and pave the way to respect. I won't have to brawl anymore.*

"Boxing is a sport no different than football or tennis," Fred said defensively, though he could hear the defeat in his own voice. "The fights are conducted in accordance with collegiate athletic association rules; and despite what you say, there is a lot of strategy and athleticism involved. I have worked hard the last three years honing my skills by investing my free time in working with Coach MacFarland. He has taken a special interest in me outside of team practices and says I can win the championship. Besides, I didn't ask what you thought about boxing. I asked why you won't support me by coming to the match."

His parents were silent.

"Never mind," he sighed. "Think it over, and surprise me for once."

Fred's opponent in the final match was a blond student with rippled muscles named Mickey Gordon from Villanova. He had a reputation as an in-fighter, a boxer who closes in on an opponent, overwhelming him with bruising power and a willingness to receive punishing blows in his pursuit of a victory. Mickey's lumbering technique had earned him the snide moniker, "Flash Gordon," after the newly popular comic hero. Flash appeared confident as he did deep knee bends in his corner and rotated his head on his thick, corded neck.

Coach MacFarland, a former boxing champion from Penn, massaged Fred's shoulders and encouraged him to use his speed and dexterity. "Use your footwork, Fred," MacFarland instructed. "You have to use your agility to evade him. He's a slower fighter. You got lucky in the last bout because you landed a blow that knocked your opponent off his feet. This time, you need to land more point-scoring blows. Get out there and throw more clean punches."

His words were obfuscated by Fred's anxiety. The bell signaling the opening round stirred him from his reverie; and in one fluid motion, he snapped the chinstrap of his protective leather head gear and was on his feet, moving to the center of the ring. The two adversaries touched gloves, and the referee signaled the beginning of the bout.

Flash was aggressive and started with a series of missed uppercuts, then landed a mean left hook above Fred's right eye. A swollen bruise flowered around the point of impact, and his eye closed within it. Fred was momentarily dazed, but he managed to bob and avoid the next punch. He knew he was on the defensive and was grateful to hear the bell sounding the return to corners.

"What's the matter?" Coach MacFarland asked urgently, as he tended to Fred's eye. "You're letting him control. Use your jabs and straights to keep him at range; use your long arms to maintain the gap between you with faster, longer-range punches. When you get back out there, take charge. I want to see the quickness and strategy that got you this far! He's got a good chin, Fred. He can take your jabs while maneuvering inside where an in-fighter like him is more effective. But this guy clearly is weak on the left side; so when he drops his left, that's when you score with your right. You're also faster, and you need to use that to dance away from him when he's on the offensive. You can win on points by landing more solid blows from a safer distance." Fred nodded silently, his ears still ringing from the crushing impact of his adversary's fist.

Fred could hear the crowd from Villanova chanting, "Kill him." Flash already was skipping around the ring with his gloved hands raised high above his head, urging on the crowd confidently. Fred felt a surge of anger. When the bell sounded the second round, Fred came out swinging and met his opponent's smug, unguarded stance with an unexpected flurry of blows to his head and body. As he staggered to regain his balance and protect himself from further contact, Flash momentarily dropped his left, offering Fred the opportunity to inflict an unanticipated, wicked blow. Fred's fist quickly curled into a tight, hard orb inside his boxing glove. He coiled his arm and unleashed a devastating roundhouse right that landed squarely on the side of his opponent's head, which snapped around and seemed to collapse against his right shoulder. As if in slow motion, sweat sprayed from his hair, and his legs buckled under him. He managed to regain his footing enough to swing at Fred, but he flailed at the air as Fred danced out of reach. Flash lost his balance and crumpled to the mat. The referee's count reached four just as the bell sounded the end of the round.

Back in his corner, Fred felt relief as his coach squeezed a sponge above his head, and the water trickled down his bruised face. He gratefully sucked on ice chips as his coach cheered him on, "That's more like it! He's got nothing left. Stay out of his reach; and when you see opportunity, pour it on."

The bell rang again. As he rose from his stool, Fred could almost feel the loyalty of the crowd shift, as more and more spectators took up the chant, "Fred-dy, Fred-dy!"

Flash was clearly dazed as he returned to the ring. His movements were leaden, and his self-assurance was gone. He seemed oblivious to the instructions shouted by his own coach, and the referee, repeatedly forced to separate the two boxers, reprimanded Flash twice for holding Fred. Flash's punches were weak and random, and his footwork was awkward and slow. When Fred saw his chance, he delivered a left jab immediately followed by a right uppercut.

The bell sounded the end of the third and final round, and Fred returned to his corner, flushed with relief and elation, as the referee awaited the results from the judges. The referee called the two fighters back to the center of the ring and, gripping their wrists, raised Fred's arm straight above his head and declared him the Philadelphia Intercollegiate Boxing Club middleweight champion. Except for the deflated Villanova loyalists who silently exited while Fred was declared victor, the crowd exploded in applause and shouting. The chairman of the Philadelphia Intercollegiate Boxing Club approached with a gold medallion in his hand. Fred lowered his head as the official slipped a red, white, and blue ribbon around his neck and shook his hand. He smiled and waved to the crowd, and suddenly saw Lorraine coming toward him from the stands. He was thrilled at the sight of his smiling sister with whom he could truly share his victory. The medal gleamed on his chest, yet it would not truly shine until he could see it reflected in the approving expressions of his parents.

Fred dressed hurriedly in the locker room. The team trainer had applied a salve to his eye and told him to keep ice on it for twenty-minute intervals throughout the rest of the day. He surveyed himself in the mirror. The bruise around his eye had erupted into a rainbow of magentas and blacks. The aperture of the eye was reduced to a slit, and any light that entered through it produced a stab of pain. He grinned wryly at the thought that his nose had been spared, but his smile looked incongruous on his bludgeoned face. Clutching his medal proudly with his free hand, he had little doubt about which new acquisition would be the object of his parents' attention.

When he and Lorraine walked into the house he still shared with his parents, he could hear them talking softly in the living room. He centered the medal on his chest and tried to banish his fears. He positioned a smile on his face and entered the room. "Mom and Dad, I won!" he called excitedly as he thrust out his chest. "Look at my gold medal!"

His father took one look at his battered face, shook his head in disgust, and rose to leave. He pushed past Fred where he stood without even glancing at the medal. Fred's mother's eyes spit fury. "You actually think you have anything to be proud of?" she fumed. "You look like a common street punk! They give you a piece of tin to wear around your neck, and you think that changes you from a thug into an athlete?" All the time that she was shouting, she was moving closer to where Fred stood frozen to the floor. Now, she was inches from him, and he could feel her hot breath as she tilted her face upward to meet his stare. "Give me that!" she shrieked. She grabbed hold of the ribbon around Fred's neck and yanked it hard. Fred's neck chafed and his ears stung as she jerked it over his head. Medal in hand, she shoved him aside and stamped past an open-mouthed Lorraine to the front door. The door careened on its hinges as she slammed it against the foyer wall in a mad effort toward the street. Fred rushed out behind her. She threw the medallion with adrenal strength, and it hurtled in a long arc bouncing across the pavement. When it came to rest near the far curb, the waning rays of the sun glinted off the medallion's surface. Fred's face froze; his glittering eyes filled with unshed tears. He could not rip his gaze away from his mother's face, red with exertion, her chest rising and falling rapidly as her breath came in short, sharp gasps. "If you are going to behave like you belong in the streets, then your medal can join you there," she hollered. She drew her arm across her perspiring brow and wiped her damp palms on her skirt. Drawing herself up to her full, statuesque height, she had the air of a warrior righteous in her defense of the sacred. She strode back up the walkway to the house, leaving Fred on the sidewalk. The door closed with a bang punctuating her departure.

A long shadow fell over the medal where it lay. Its shiny patina was marred by dust and gravel pits. It looked like what it had become, a cheap, gaudy emblem of coveted success. Fred felt vulgar for ever having desired it. Yet, he longed for it still.

CHAPTER 9

W HEN WORD OF THE boxing championship spread on campus, Fred, who already was recognized as a superior student and talented artist, ran for the Student Council and was elected as a senior class representative. Since he was spending less time at the gym, he began reading about the possibility of war in Europe, and he became particularly distraught over the articles in the Jewish Press about the Nazis' ascension to power in Germany and their flagrantly aggressive anti-Semitism.

When Fred smoothed out the newspaper and spread the front page, the headlines of the September 15, 1935, *Philadelphia Inquirer* blared, "Nuremberg Laws Deprive German Jews of Citizenship and Civil Rights". Walter and Ruth looked up from where they sat huddled around the radio to see their son's face clouded in anger. Fred started to speak, but he was drowned out by the grating voice of Gertrude Berg on the radio, familiar and beloved star of "Rise of the Goldbergs".

"Shhhh, Freddy," Ruth called, putting a finger to her lips, "it's about to start."

"Yoo-hoo! Mrs. Bloom…," she yodeled, leaning into the airshaft of her Bronx, New York tenement. *There she is, folks,* announced her husband, Jake, *Molly Goldberg, a woman with a place in every heart and a finger in every pie.*

Fred's family, like millions of other Americans, were loyal listeners of the weekly program, which chronicled the continuing daily saga of Molly, Jake, their children, Rosalie and Samuel, and her Uncle David as they explored the theme of family, neighborhood, and the intricate interplay between old world values and new world assimilation.

But that day, Fred could not listen in silence.

"Did you hear that?" he demanded. "Molly's not scared to talk about what's going on! She just mentioned receiving a letter from relatives in the old country asking for help to leave Germany. She knows what's happening, and she's not afraid to say so!" As the episode concluded with Molly's hawking of Ecko stainless steel kitchen tools, Fred snatched up the newspaper again and continued to boil. "Hitler's leading Germany straight to Hell, and the United States government sits on its hands. Gerald Nye and his damn Committee have convinced the Senate, and most of America for that matter, that the munitions industry's financial stake with the Brits caused it to succeed in lobbying our way into the Great War. These businesses made huge profits during the war, and the Nye Committee's findings are fueling the non-interventionist movement as we speak!"

"Yes," Walter agreed. "Two weeks ago, FDR signed the Neutrality Act. Now, we've got a general embargo preventing us from aiding anyone threatened by Hitler. I didn't think Roosevelt would stand for that. Apparently, so many people are in an isolationist mood today, FDR felt he had no choice."

Walter shook his head in dismay, and Ruth twisted her handkerchief into a worried knot as she looked from her husband to her son.

Fred sighed deeply, searching for a way to become involved. He had found a niche in student government because he was willing to work tirelessly. His success was based on dedication rather than on his short-lived popularity, and he was painfully aware of it. Nevertheless, he eagerly anticipated that his crowning achievement would be to represent Temple at The National Congress of Collegiate Governments in Chicago. Among the topics to be discussed was a student platform containing a plank declaring their position on American isolationism.

"I've made up my mind," he said as much to himself as to his parents. "I am going to speak to the student government conference. I have to try to open some eyes to what's going on in Germany." He tossed the newspaper aside, wiping his sweating palms on his pants legs in a gesture of good riddance. His parents admired his receding form, rigid and determined, as he strode from the room. The newspaper sat on his empty chair, the black print detailing the prohibitions of the Nuremberg Laws spread out like an ugly stain.

Fred had never traveled outside of Philadelphia, and couldn't help but feeling excited as he boarded the train to Chicago at Broad Street Station, which together with City Hall were two of the architectural jewels of Philadelphia. He took a window seat, and was hypnotized by the ever–changing scenery that whizzed by. The train click-clacked its way along the winding tracks amid the beautiful, forested hills and cultivated fields of Pennsylvania, Ohio, Indiana, and Illinois, until darkness shrouded his interest; and Fred fell asleep in his seat.

Finally, the train clamored into the terminal at Chicago's Central Station at Roosevelt and Michigan Avenues. Fred became part of the teeming passengers who disembarked and melded into the throng of people already on the platform. The wind lifted his hair and raked his face when he stepped out into the gusty afternoon, as he hurriedly turned up the collar of his coat. Turning back to look at Central Station, he admired the imposing, Romanesque edifice. The soaring arches of the nine-story structure were heightened by the thirteen-story clock tower, its spire blanketed in an ethereal cover of clouds. Fred curled his long, lean body into a question mark and butted his head into the opposing gale. The sidewalk was artificially darkened by the shadowy silhouettes of skyscrapers on both sides of the street.

Fred had never seen a skyscraper before and was awed by their impressive dominance. In Philadelphia, a historic municipal ordinance prohibited any building from exceeding the height of the statue of William Penn atop City Hall, stunting the growth of the skyline. Next to the brick and glass monoliths of Chicago, his hometown buildings felt like endearing urban dwarves.

He found his way to Berghof's for lunch before the Congress convened at the Drake Hotel. Aunt Pauline was the only member of the family who had been to Chicago, and she recommended the restaurant. Ever mindful that she was an Ashkenazi, descended from the Jews of central and Eastern Europe, she had the hauteur of her German-Jewish birth to reinforce her overblown self-worth. Naturally, she had gravitated to Berghof's. *Frederick, you must eat at Berghof's. You have never tasted dark rye bread like theirs in your life. I'm telling you; tam-ganeydn! It tastes like heaven!*

The waiter placed a basket of dark rye bread, still hot and moist with freshness, on the table and said that he would return after bringing Fred's drink order. Thinking that water was free, Fred asked for ice water. After placing his order for sausages and sauerkraut, Fred, noting to himself that Aunt

Pauline was correct about the rye bread, inquired whether the waiter might bring more bread and butter.

As the waiter walked away, Fred was distracted by a loud conversation taking place at a nearby table. One gaunt young man with an ardent expression and humorless bearing was arguing with a large group of students about America's need to maintain neutrality in the incipient conflicts in Europe and Asia. "These are not our fights," the young man shouted, punctuating his words by slamming his clenched fist against his open palm. "Our entanglement in foreign conflicts has always carried the hefty price tag of too many lives and too much money. Have we learned nothing from the debacle of the first Great War?" His passion silenced the others who nodded their assent. Fred wondered, as he hurriedly finished his lunch, whether they also were delegates to the Congress.

The Drake Hotel on Michigan Avenue, overlooking the great lake and a small park, was a progeny of the Roaring Twenties, with grand Italianate architecture. Fred walked through the Palm Court, impressed by the lush indoor garden filled with potted palms, a handsome central fountain, and magnificent mirrored ceiling. In the gargantuan lobby, a large sign advertised that Benny Goodman, a hometown music hero, would be styling his jazz clarinet that evening in the Gold Coast Room. A smartly attired man behind the reception desk directed him to the meeting room reserved for the National Congress of Collegiate Governments.

The convention registration area was manned by a dapper young delegate whose badge read Carlton College. He was wearing a Harris Tweed sport coat and a subtle, matching silk tie. Fred hastily buttoned his worn blue blazer to cover the hula dancer on his tie.

"Nice tie," the Carlton delegate smirked. Fred's cheeks reddened, but he assumed a serious expression that belied his favorite, playful tie.

"Hi, I'm Frederick Green from Temple University in Philadelphia. May I have a copy of the program?" he asked. "I want to see the order of issues to be taken up by the Congress. I would like to reserve some time to speak about the agenda item pertaining to non-interventionism."

The registrar handed Fred his badge and a copy of the day's events. Fred perused the page. "Is there an opening on Proposition Ten?"

The Carlton student didn't look up but began filling in a line on a schedule. "Three twenty-five," he confirmed. "That's your timeslot. You have five minutes."

After opening the large entry door, Fred stepped into a cavernous space that already was crowded and noisy. He made his way through the long rows of alphabetized seats and found his chair, trying to distinguish snippets of conversation among the other representatives. One group was particularly animated, led by a powerfully built, immaculately groomed student with red hair and expressive eyes who stood beside the Princeton placard, flailing the air with his arms to emphasize his point.

"Hitler is a hero," he insisted. "He is bringing hope to an economically and socially destitute German people."

"What about the Jews?" came a tentative query from the group surrounding him.

"German Jews are not our problem," the redhead fired back. "Certainly not a justification for our involvement. Besides, rabid journalists have blown that completely out of proportion."

Fred kept his council, although he feared that many delegates' minds already were made up. He took his place and listened distractedly throughout the day as the others concluded the more mundane business of the convocation. Fred had thought long and hard about what to say and had engaged himself in heated debate about the nature of his job as Temple's student government delegate. *I did not come here to represent the vast majority of Temple students who could not care less about Hitler, the fate of Europe, the Nazis' wholesale violations of human rights, or any other matter of wider concern than the quality of food in the dining halls. I am here to lead. This issue is too important to ignore.*

Finally, the moderator brought his gavel to rest with a loud call to order. "The next matter for our consideration on this year's platform is Proposition Ten, whether the United States should become more deeply involved in the turmoil in Europe. I call upon Leland Hawthorne, our colleague from Princeton." The redheaded student rose from his seat and made his way to the microphone.

"I believe I speak not only for the students of Princeton," he began, "but also for the consensus of this Congress and college students nationwide when I say that the political upheaval in Europe, particularly the rise of the National Socialists in Germany, is not the problem of the United States. Wilson convinced many that we were making the world safe for democracy when we fought the Great War, but who are we to tell Germany or any other country what kind of government they must have? We need to stay on this side of the Atlantic Ocean that blessedly protects us from Europe's strife." Other delegates, catching the contagion of enthusiasm he expressed, stamped their feet and hollered their agreement. "After holding over ninety-three hearings and questioning more than two hundred witnesses, the Nye Committee's findings make clear that the United States was duped into the Great War by the munitions industry. The Committee reported that the United States loaned Germany only twenty-seven million dollars between 1915 and 1917. Throughout the same period, the United States loaned the United Kingdom and its allies the gargantuan sum of 2.3 billion dollars, a staggering eighty-five times as much. There is no doubt in the face of this mass of evidence that we went to war to protect our commercial interests. The avarice of American banks and arms businesses was the impetus to our entering the war on the side of the United Kingdom. The Treaty of Versailles was a punishing blow to Germany intended to cripple her in perpetuity. Hitler does not want a war. He wants only to return to the German people what was stripped from them."

Fred did not know if the reaction of his fellow students was spontaneous, but loud cries of affirmation and deafening cheers seemed orchestrated to follow each of the impassioned speaker's sentences. Fueled by his reception, Hawthorne continued.

"Adolf Hitler has risen to the helm of Germany to restore his country's position as a world power. He has recognized a Jewish conspiracy to destroy Germany both economically and socially. Jews represent less than one percent of the German population, and it is Germany's problem to control this troublesome minority. We must not allow ourselves to be carried away by paranoia. Just as Hitler puts Germany first, we must put America first.

"We have the wide, blue oceans to protect us. Let not one additional drop of American blood be shed on foreign soil. The delegates assembled here must stand at the forefront of college students whom we represent across this great country and vote no to Proposition Ten. We must articulate in a loud and clear voice, *Never again!*" The tall redhead cast his icy blue gaze over the tumultuous gathering. He gripped both sides of the podium, and his mouth was a resolute line.

The moderator banged his gavel in a vain attempt to bring order to the obstreperous group. Following three other unimpressive presenters in favor of isolation, the moderator called out, "Frederick Green, the delegate from Temple University, will now have five minutes."

Fred stood at his seat; and as he began to make his way to the stage, few delegates seemed to notice him, in contrast to the thunderous applause Leland Hawthorne had received. Fred battled a momentary rush of fear. He straightened his tie, swallowed the walnut-sized lump obstructing his throat, and gravely began to address the Congress.

"When human rights are trampled," he began, his voice cracking, "we are all at risk. It is everyone's problem." He heard murmurs of assent but no outcry of support. Fred breathed deeply, forcing himself to focus on the importance of his statement, and persevered in earnest.

"Human rights should be a concern for all. Speaking out and speaking up against violations is in the best interest of society and is the moral thing to do. Adolf Hitler is a menace." The undercurrent of protest was becoming increasingly audible. "In his megalomaniacal quest for power, he has preyed upon the economic depression of his own people. He has used their despair to fuel hatred within his own boundaries and seeks to spread it throughout Europe. He has deprived the Jewish population within Germany of their basic human rights. Hitler unlawfully seized power on January 30, 1933, but anti-Semitism has been a major theme of his rhetoric for almost fifteen years. He and his Nazi party began a systematic program to disenfranchise the Jews starting with the boycott of Jewish businesses on April 1, 1933. Since then, Jews have no longer been able to vote or hold public office, and they are barred from employment as lawyers, doctors, journalists, or civil servants. They are prohibited from using state hospitals and cannot be educated by the State past the age of fourteen. Jewish names must be expunged from war memorials, despite their heroic service to Germany throughout its history and as recently as the Great War. In May of this year, Jews were forbidden to serve in the Wehrmacht, the German armed forces. So widespread is this oppression that even the lottery cannot award winnings to a Jew. Only weeks before this convocation, at a Nazi party rally in Nuremberg, two new laws were passed, the Law for Protection of German Blood and German Honor, which prohibits marriage or sexual relations between a German and a Jew, and the Reich Citizenship Law, which deprives Jews of their German citizenship.

"At the same time, the United States, largely in response to the Nye Committee report mentioned by the esteemed delegate from Princeton, enacted the Neutrality Act on August 31 of this year. Despite the fact that Roosevelt and Secretary of State Cordell Hull lobbied for embargo provisions that would allow the President to impose international sanctions selectively, Congress rejected the administration's position and instead imposed a general embargo on trading in arms and war materials with what they termed 'all belligerents,' making no distinction between aggressor and victim. When Italy invaded Ethiopia in October, Roosevelt invoked the Neutrality Act to prevent all arms and ammunition shipments to both countries, while simultaneously declaring a 'moral embargo' against belligerents, covering trade not encompassed by the Neutrality Act.

"No one wants to shed American blood or waste American dollars, but the cause of human rights is never unjust, and the integrity of international borders is critical to maintaining peace. Our fellow delegate from Princeton is correct that we must make our voices heard, but we must acknowledge the plight of German Jewry, and we must recognize true belligerents wherever and whenever we find them. We must vote 'Yes' to Proposition Ten and support those who stand for these principles."

"Shut up, Jew-lover," someone heckled from the audience.

"Yeah," screamed someone else, "I'm not going to die for a bunch of German Hymies."

Chants of "America first!" began to build throughout the auditorium.

Fred drew in his breath and lifted his chin. With the moderator's gavel crashing again and again, he heard the echo of his wasted words, as if he were listening from outside himself. He descended the steps from the stage and made his way back to his seat, willing his posture to remain tall and proud.

In an effort to restore order, the moderator announced, "We will now take a ten minute recess, after which I will call for a vote."

Fred was surrounded by a small group of supporters, when he saw a young man elbowing his way toward him. He felt a flash of recognition: it was the same student he had seen lunching at Berghof's.

"You don't know what you're talking about," the enraged student ranted. "If America follows your philosophy, we're going to have Jews flooding in here from every corner of Europe, taking our jobs, ruining our cities, the same way the niggers have!" Fred could feel the hot words in his face as the outraged protester punctuated them with a hard shove to Fred's left shoulder.

Fred angled ominously toward the heckler. "Well," he rejoined, his voice at once pedantic and disdainful, "it's clear that you don't subscribe to the immortal words of Emma Lazarus." Several other students in the gathering crowd snickered or nodded approvingly in recognition of Fred's intellectual counterpunch.

"Who the hell is that?" his perplexed adversary asked, his complexion apoplectic.

"Only our great American poetess! I guess you've never heard her words, 'Give me your tired, your poor, your huddled masses yearning to breathe free.' If you ever get to New York, you'll find that we Americans have so revered and embraced this guiding principle that we immortalized it on the base of our nation's universal beacon of welcome, the Statue of Liberty."

Fred saw the blur of the arm arcing, the hand balled into a fist. Clearly, the outraged student had no idea that Fred was also a middleweight boxing champion. Instinctively, Fred blocked the punch with a parry of his left arm and immediately followed with a crushing right cross to his assailant's face. Blood spurted from the other boy's nose after an audible crunch of broken bone and cartilage, his bigoted face transformed into a cubistic distortion. He hit the floor and began rocking back and forth in a fetal embrace. Two muscular young men raced to grab Fred's arms, but he had no intention of hitting his crumple foe again. Fred shook his head in revulsion at the scene. He hadn't come here for a fistfight.

"I'm sorry," Fred stammered, as the chairman of the conference stood before him. "He was coming at *me*. I had no choice!"

The other delegates continued to hold him loosely by each arm. "Our charter provides for automatic expulsion from the conference for engaging in any physical violence," the chairman said, piously. "You two must relinquish your seats immediately."

"But I…. He…." Fred saw that he already was talking to the chairman's back, as bodyguards escorted him from the meeting room.

He was permitted to pick up his briefcase and coat before beginning the slow march to the exit. As the heavy, wooden door whooshed closed, he heard the call for the vote on Proposition Ten and the sonorous voices of the delegates responding, in turn, to the moderator's demand, "How say you?"

Despite his ignominious return to Philadelphia and the failure of Proposition Ten, Fred rationalized that perhaps he had made an impact on a small cadre of supporters through the force of his argument. Recognizing that he could apply his talent for oratory as a lawyer, he concentrated even more zealously on his studies, hoping to finally fulfill his dream of a Penn degree, this time from the law school.

CHAPTER 10

DENIED ONCE, THIS TIME the University of Pennsylvania did not elude him. Fred was admitted to the school of law on a full academic scholarship. The first day of class was a new world for Fred. Walking on the campus of the storied university among the subdued coat and tie clad young men, he felt flushed, despite the cool autumn temperature. He quickened his pace after looking at his watch and was glad when the law school loomed in front of him. He found room 104 and slipped into an aisle seat midway among the rows of chairs. Almost immediately, an arm extended from the immaculately tailored tweed jacket next to him. "Chapman Stirling," said the handsome young man. Fred smiled as he pumped the other student's hand. "They say the first day is the hardest," Chapman commiserated. "All that about being told to look to the right and left of you because one of you won't be here by the end of the year, or at least that's what my father says he was told on his first day at Penn Law. My bet is we'll both be here," he concluded confidently.

Fred liked Chapman immediately. A prep school graduate and scion of the socially and economically anointed, Chapman hailed from a small town in central Pennsylvania where his grandfather was mayor, and his father had been appointed a federal judge. He had attended Andover and Harvard, yet he had the easy smile and understated speech of one who was born comfortable in his skin. Like Fred, he was tall and lean, but his impeccable clothes and ingrained manners bespoke an effortless confidence foreign to Fred. They shared a love of books, sports, and a quick-witted sense of humor. Certain of his identity and equally sure of his charismatic impact on others, Chapman lived in a world where it was natural that he decide whom to admit into his orbit. He chose Fred.

As had become their wont, the two met after class for coffee and to mull over the day's notes. The intellectual exchange was the great equalizer between them. Chapman's immaculate ebony tresses would almost touch Fred's chestnut locks as they sat side by side bent over their books, putting to trial the facts of a case. Their faces were animated by the nuances of the law, and a bystander would not have been able to discern the chasm of wealth and social class that separated the two young men attired in their tweed sport coats and obligatory neckties, for Fred had been a quick study in the trappings of the privileged. Gone was the flamboyant tie and threadbare blue blazer. Steam rose from their cups and twisted in an intricate helix, scant protection from a world on the brink of war and an American society in which a Jew from the Frankford section of Philadelphia and a Protestant who could trace his family's ancestry back to William Penn rarely broke the fertile ground of friendship.

Chapman closed his book with a thud of satisfaction. "That's it for today, Fred. We have emerged from the annals of common law, and we shall live to fight another day," he said with a grin as he cupped Fred's shoulder in a comradely grasp. He drained his cup and casually threw his scarf over his shoulder, gathering his books and papers in a neat pile to insert into his leather briefcase. "By the way," he continued amiably, "my parents are having a small dinner party next weekend at the Bellevue. Just a few family friends. I was hoping you'd come as my guest."

Fred looked up from his book. While he had come to regard Chapman as a brother over the course of the past months, he had yet to meet his parents. Fred instantly felt the jitterbugging of his heart. He ran his fingers through his hair and fastened an eager smile on his face. He looked down at his schoolwork determined to organize his swirling thoughts while he arranged his belongings. "That would be swell, Chapman. Thanks for asking me," Fred enthused.

"All right, then," Chapman replied. "I'll expect you at the Bellevue on Saturday night at seven. Mother and Dad will be delighted." *So, that was it, then,* Fred thought. *No turning back now.*

"Right, Saturday at seven," he said, rising from his seat. "I'll walk you to the corner." Both young men left the coffee shop and strode in amiable silence, parting ways at the intersection where Fred turned toward the elevated train and Chapman caught a cab heading uptown.

Saturday night arrived with a warm wind and a star-studded sky. Fred had dressed carefully. From the perfect part in his freshly cut hair to the mirrored shine on his polished shoes, he paid attention to every detail. Evaluating his reflection, he smoothed the gabardine of his navy blue chalk striped suit and wished that it were of better quality. *Still,* he thought as he adjusted the Windsor knot of his best silk tie, *I'm presentable, most presentable.*

He arrived at the Bellevue at exactly seven o'clock. Punctuality was a virtue he had cultivated long ago, believing that it epitomized good manners and breeding.

The lobby of the grand hotel was alight with crystal chandeliers and Aubusson rugs demarcating luxurious seating areas furnished with the finest antiques. Fred stifled the urge to touch the elegant upholstery and scanned the room for a bellboy who might know the location of the dinner. He approached a uniformed man near the elevator and inquired, "Excuse me. Do you know where the Stirling dinner party is taking place in the hotel tonight?"

The bellboy, snapping to attention and consulting a calendar of the day's events, replied smartly, "Yes, sir. It is in the Parisian Room on the ballroom level. You can take this elevator to the first floor." He stepped aside to allow Fred to pass into the elevator, and then assumed the controls.

"Thank you," Fred said. The bellboy nodded his head and faced forward. The elevator doors opened, and he gestured to his right, indicating the direction of the private dining room. Fred quickly estimated thirty guests, and he could see ladies resplendent in flowing silk and dazzling jewels gliding on the arms of immaculately groomed gentlemen in precisely cut dark suits. The melodious strains of a string quartet wafted from the room where silver gleamed on white linen, and crystal refracted the light from long tapers surrounding the artistically arranged blood red rose centerpieces.

Fred searched the faces for Chapman. He could hear the throb of his heartbeat in his ears, and his stiffly starched white collar seemed suddenly too tight. He ran his finger around his collar. *Hadn't Chapman said 'a small dinner party for a few family friends,'* he thought? Perhaps the bellboy had misdirected him. He turned back toward the door when a firm hand gripped his elbow.

"Glad you made it, Fred," Chapman said in his slow, easy manner. "Come with me. There are some people I'd like you to meet."

He guided Fred to a small group of people standing together in a convivial knot. A tall, silver-haired woman with regal bearing held a champagne flute in her gloved hand. She spoke softly to a stately man in an elegant suit who looked like an older version of Chapman. Clearly, these were Chapman's parents.

The couple was conversing comfortably with three others: an older gentleman with the thick, gray mantle and clever features of a fox; his wife, who stood subtly apart, surveying the room over the rim of her wineglass, more interested in whom she saw than in what was being said; and a young, beautiful woman. As Chapman and Fred approached, she broke ranks with the others and met them halfway. She was truly lovely, with raven hair and ebony eyes. She approached them with arms extended and a warm smile on her delicate features.

"Chapman," she said taking his hand in both of hers, "who is your handsome friend?"

Kissing her hand with a dramatic flourish and grinning broadly, Chapman turned to Fred. "Deborah, I'd like you to meet Frederick Green, my close friend and comrade in arms at Penn Law School. Fred, allow me to introduce Deborah Klein. Her father, Nathan Klein, serves on the hospital board with my father; and of course, these are my parents, Colin and Marilyn Stirling."

Fred shook hands with each of them, but his attention returned immediately to Deborah who had linked arms with him and Chapman.

"We've all heard so much about you, Frederick," Deborah said. "Chapman says that you are, without question, the smartest student in his class." Fred felt heat rise to his cheeks. "He has made all of us feel as though we already know you," she continued, squeezing his arm. Deborah wore a sophisticated dress of sapphire blue brocade. Diamonds adorned her ears and wrist, and she smelled like camellias, an exotic, heady fragrance. The air in the spacious room suddenly felt close and overheated.

"Smoke and mirrors," he scoffed humbly. "The trick is to find the best study partner, and then you both appear to be brilliant." He glanced at Deborah to judge her reaction and was satisfied that he had struck the proper balance between humility and self-confidence.

"You and Deborah will be dinner partners, Fred," Chapman interjected as he motioned them to a nearby table. Fred assisted Deborah with her chair, and Chapman offered him a conspiratorial wink as he assumed his place at the head table.

The rest of the night passed in a haze of exquisite gourmet food, ripe vintage wines, stimulating conversation, and dance after dance with Deborah. Fred had the gift of grace; and when he was on the dance floor, all of his apprehension about the evening seemed to fade away. Whether the band played a waltz, a Lindy, or a Charleston, he lost himself in the music; and with Deborah in his arms, he felt like Fred Astaire. They danced so often and so naturally that people began to notice. "You two were made for each other!" gushed one onlooker. "A perfect pair," agreed another. And Fred couldn't have agreed more. He didn't want the night to end.

Soon enough, though, the music slowed; and guests began to pay their respects to the hosts. Fred lingered over his coffee, nervous that Deborah's parents would reclaim her before he mustered the courage to ask if he could see her again.

"I'm very glad I came tonight," he began tentatively.

"That makes two of us," she replied warmly. "I hope to see you again." She opened her beaded evening purse, removed a silver pen, and wrote her phone number on a small calling card embossed with her name. She slid the card across the table until the edge slipped under Fred's fingertips where they rested on the linen cloth. Their fingers touched. Her eyes never left his.

Relief flooded Fred's mind. "I will call you this week," he managed to utter before Nathan Klein loomed proprietarily behind Deborah's chair. Fred hopped up from his seat and pumped her father's hand. "It was awfully nice meeting you, sir," he said.

"Good to meet you, too, young man. The Stirlings seem to agree that you're going places. We'll look forward to seeing you around." Nathan Klein wrapped Deborah's silk stole around her shoulders and pulled back her chair as she rose to depart.

"Goodnight, Frederick," Deborah smiled.

"Goodnight," he exhaled, realizing that he had been holding his breath.

CHAPTER 11

BUSY WITH LAW SCHOOL and trying to see Deborah whenever he could, Fred nevertheless missed Lorraine, who since her marriage rarely came to their parents' home. She had been the one to teach Fred to dance, when he was so small that he had to stand on her feet. She took him to his first movie and bought him his first pair of long pants. As he got older, she became his confidante. The chasm of years between them meant that they could never have the kind of relationship that she had with Will; but since Will's death, Fred and Lorraine had come to openly depend on each other.

Fred had seen Lorraine's apartment only once. One Friday evening, he decided to skip dinner at Uncle Julius's and take the bus to surprise her with a visit; but when he got to the door, it was quiet. Several minutes elapsed, and he knocked again. "Hey, Lorraine," he yelled. "It's me. Open up."

"Freddy, is that you?" she asked apprehensively through the closed door.

"Yeah. I figured if you wouldn't come to us, I'd come to you. Aren't you going to let me in?" Fred was beginning to worry. "Is something wrong, Lorraine? Why won't you open the door?"

The lock clicked, and the door creaked open to reveal a slice of light behind it. Lorraine was outlined against the light, and Fred did not notice at first that her usually impeccable appearance was disheveled and her hair matted. "Where's Danny?" he asked as he crossed the threshold. "What's going…?" Turning to look at his sister, he stopped in mid-sentence.

Lorraine was feebly attempting to smooth her hair and straighten her wrinkled skirt. Makeup could not conceal the welt by her left eye or the concentric arcs of black and blue that encircled it. Forcing a smile, she said in a falsely lilting tone, "Danny's out with some friends. He likes to stop off at The Shamrock after work."

"Stop off? You mean he hits the bars?" Fred looked around the apartment. There were no signs of dinner, and he could see the unmade bed through the bedroom door. Next to the armchair in the living room, a solitary highball glass sat on the floor, the dark remnants of what looked like whiskey still in the bottom. "Looks like you drink your dinner too. Does he even bother to come home? How often does this happen?"

Lorraine looked at the floor. Raising her eyes to Fred's, she managed for a moment to look like his sister again. Then, her expression crackled like a worn piece of pottery.

"I don't know," she began tentatively. "At first, it was just every once in a while. Then, it got to the point that he was out every night, but he usually came home… until he didn't even do that. I don't know where he is."

"Why didn't you tell Mom and Pop? Or me, for that matter?" Fred implored.

Lorraine's mouth twisted in a wry smile. "What for? So they could say, 'I told you so.' And you, what could you have done? Challenge him to a boxing match or a war of words, little brother?" Fred had never seen his sister's lovely features distorted by such dripping sarcasm.

"Leave him, Lorraine. Why don't you just pack up and come home? Come on, I'll help you. Mom and Pop will understand." Fred found a battered valise under the bed and began to stuff it with Lorraine's clothes and shoes, anything he could find. He felt her hand on his arm.

"You don't know anything yet, do you kiddo? Can you even begin to imagine what Mom and Pop would say if I told them I wanted a divorce? Nice girls don't get divorced, Freddy. Nice girls marry nice guys; or if they don't, they pretend they did. Otherwise, they bring disgrace on themselves and their families. That's the only understanding Mom and Pop would have. I know you're trying to help, but you don't understand." She reached up and cupped his face in her hands. She pulled him close and kissed his forehead. "Go on home, Freddy. Back to your university and your books. Make us all proud." Lorraine's shoulders slumped and her willowy figure, so like their mother's, was bent in resignation. She took the clothing from his hands, and they both sank to the edge of the bed. Fred reached for her hand, and she squeezed his. "Go on, Freddy. Go on."

CHAPTER 12

L ORRAINE CONTINUED TO KEEP her distance, but now Fred stopped by her apartment to check on her as often as he could. He could tell she appreciated his visits, but as soon as the topic of Danny came up, she shut down. Instead, Fred did most of the talking, regaling her with stories from law school and, lately, about his budding relationship with Deborah Klein.

"I saw Deborah again last night," he began one Sunday afternoon, peering at her over his coffee cup at the table in her tiny dining room. "We had dinner with her parents at their country club."

The Kleins were longstanding members of Philmont, the prestigious Jewish country club located in Huntingdon Valley outside of Philadelphia. The exclusive club, founded in 1906 by Ellis Gimbel, who headed the eponymous department store chain for several years, and a consortium of Philadelphia's captains of commerce and industry, described its membership as "the leading Hebrews of the city." By 1907, it boasted five hundred members, two golf courses, twelve tennis courts, a baseball field, a swimming pool, and a sprawling clubhouse. Its golf professional was none other than John Reid, Jr., son of the "father" of American golf.

"Tell me everything," Lorraine demanded. Lorraine's eyes glistened as she fixed them on a far off spot on the wall, imagining the opulence of Philmont. "What was the club like? How was the food?" she asked hungrily, peppering him with questions.

"Lorraine," he glowed, "it was first class from start to finish. We rode to Philmont in Mr. Klein's Cadillac. And when we got there, we didn't even park our own car; a uniformed valet parked it for us. He even called Mr. Klein by name. Then, the doorman helped Mrs. Klein and Deborah out of the car and called them by name too. And the clubhouse, Lorraine, you should see that place. The dining room looks like one of those pictures that you see in *Life* magazine of a royal banquet hall inside a European castle. Silk on the walls, handmade plaster appliqués on the ceiling, antique furniture and chandeliers, and crystal and china on the tables."

Lorraine hung on Fred's every word, picturing the scenes in her mind and then playing them back as a movie reel inside her head. "What about your dinner? What did you have to eat?"

"There were at least four forks at my place, and as many courses," Fred rewarded her. "Deborah insisted that I have an artichoke to start with. I've never had one before, have you?" he asked without waiting for an answer, his unabated enthusiasm causing the words to continue to tumble from his mouth. "The artichoke looked like a giant green flower. It was served warm and accompanied by two different dipping sauces, drawn butter and one called hollandaise made from egg yolks, butter, lemon juice, and seasonings. I didn't have the faintest idea how to eat it, but I watched Deborah and copied her every move. You pull off each outer leaf, dip it in the sauce, and then eat the meat by pulling the leaf through your clenched teeth. When you've finished that part, you reach the center that looks like a big hairy bug! That section is called the choke, for obvious reasons. You could actually choke if you tried to eat that. So, you scrape off the choke with the edge of your fork to get to the heart, which actually is the best part. It's meaty and delicious, and you cut it up and dip it in the sauce as well. The whole thing is considered a delicacy, and you eat the leaves with your fingers! Can you believe it? You would absolutely love it, Lorraine. Someday, I'm going to take you to a restaurant that serves them."

"What else, Freddy? What did you have for a main course?" Lorraine prodded.

"We had steaks, each the size of a small state. The club flies them in daily from the Kansas City stockyards," Fred continued. "And Mr. Klein ordered a red wine called Chateau Neuf de Pape from the south of France along the Rhone River. He said it was a special vintage called *premier cru*; in other words, the best of the best." Fred's smile strained the limits of his thin face.

"What does Mr. Klein do for a living?" Lorraine asked. "Whatever it is, he must be awfully successful. I saw his picture in the *Inquirer* a couple of times, once in the business section and once on the social page. The mayor and some judge were with him."

"He calls himself a businessman," Fred replied. "He operates several businesses under the umbrella of Nathan Klein Industries; but whenever I try to get specific, he just laughs and says his primary business is giving people what they want. He says that's a service that has always enabled him to make money; so everybody's happy, and there can't be anything wrong with that."

"Tell me about Deborah. Are you seeing her steady, Freddy?"

Fred hesitated before answering. He didn't know what to make of Deborah. She always seemed happy to hear from him, but she often said she was busy when he asked her out on a date. When they were together, he felt like he had her rapt attention; but other times, he wasn't sure that he meant anything at all to her.

Recently, after meeting Chapman for lunch on Chestnut Street, Fred saw Deborah at a distance on the arm of another young man, her head thrown back in laughter. She didn't even seem to notice him when she walked past or acknowledge him when he called her name. He had seen the other man before; in fact, he had been seated at a nearby table at the Stirlings' dinner party where Fred and Deborah had first met. He was dapper and arrogant and had a swagger Fred didn't care to master. When he asked Deborah about him, she was dismissive, saying only that he worked for her father.

"I like her a lot," Fred confessed, "but I'm not sure I'm the only guy she's seeing."

"Well, a girl should keep playing the field until she has a commitment," Lorraine said thoughtfully. "She has no reason to give up other opportunities if you haven't declared yourself. It doesn't mean she doesn't care for you, but how's a girl to know?"

Fred pictured Deborah's face as Lorraine talked. She always looked him directly in the eye when he was speaking, and sometimes her fingers would touch his sleeve proprietarily. "I suppose you're right, Lorraine. I haven't told her how I feel about her. For all she knows, I'm just out for a good time and nothing more."

The doubts he had about her sincerity since seeing her with someone else now seemed unjustified. After all, Lorraine had a point. What right had he to expect her to see him exclusively when he had been playing his cards so close to the vest? More and more, with his law school graduation approaching, he had been thinking about his future. If that future were to include Deborah, he would have to speak his mind.

"Tell her what's on your mind, Freddy, if you don't want to lose her. By the way, when is that big graduation day of yours?" Lorraine asked with a smile as she elbowed him playfully in the ribs. "Mom and Pop told me that you have to reserve seats for us, and you know I wouldn't miss it!"

Fred knew that, unlike his boxing championship, every member of his family would be clamoring to come to this milestone event. They all were proud of his becoming a lawyer, a professional man.

"It's at the end of May," Fred replied. "By the way, tickets are limited, but I managed to get four seats. I remembered you said Danny works on Saturdays so you don't think he'll mind not coming, do you?" Fred hadn't seen Danny in months, but he and Lorraine had made an unspoken pact to give the nod to normalcy whenever possible.

"Oh, no, not at all. He'll understand," Lorraine replied, well-practiced in excusing the absence of her husband. She fingered a small scar by her left eye, a permanent reminder of the abuse that she endured silently.

"So, there'll be one for you, two for Mom and Pop, and one for Deborah," he said averting his eyes shyly. "I asked her if she'd like to come, and she said she would."

"So, your whole family, or should I say future family, will be there," Lorraine said teasingly. Fred blushed but did not reply. Instead, he rose to go. "Don't be so shy, Freddy," Lorraine counseled. "If Deborah's world is what you want, reach out and grab it." She stood and brushed a lock of hair across his forehead. As he stepped across the threshold into the hallway, he felt her hand on his shoulder. "She may have the money now, little brother, but you've got the brains and talent of a moneymaker."

It was the first time that she had given voice to his anxiety that he might not be good enough for Deborah. She, with her country club, fine clothes and luxurious house, seemed to inhabit a different planet. Fred's eyes met Lorraine's, and he could see that she was in earnest.

"You can live in that world through your own devices, if you want to. Just you remember that."

He smiled and kissed her cheek.

"Just you remember that."

Later that evening, Fred telephoned Deborah. Her father answered the phone, and Fred identified himself and asked whether Deborah was home.

"Sure, Fred, she's here; but before I call her to the phone, tell me how you've been. Deborah tells me that your graduation is coming up."

"Yes, sir. Just a few weeks from now in May. In fact, I've invited Deborah to be there."

"Well, we're all very proud of you, son. Have you given any thought to what you'll do afterwards? There must be lots of opportunities out there for a bright young lawyer with your talent and personality."

Fred warmed to the praise and thought about the various job interviews he had recently. He was torn between the prestige of a large Philadelphia law firm and the lure of building his own practice. His parents advocated the security of an established firm, but Fred wondered if Nate Klein, a self-described capitalist, might have a better understanding of the independence that comes from striking out on one's own, despite the obvious risk.

"Well, Mr. Klein, I've been fortunate to have been invited to interview at several of the big firms in the city. Still, to be perfectly honest, I have mixed feelings. Just yesterday at an interview with Dechert Price and Rhodes, I had an interesting talk with one of the senior partners, John Hampton Barnes. He said that my grades and law review work at Penn made me a candidate for serious consideration by the firm; but he went on to say that, after meeting me, he was impressed with my drive and individuality and asked if I'd considered starting up on my own. I found it strange that he urged me to go into practice for myself. He said he was convinced that with the country on the brink of war, this might be the last time in our history when a guy could hang out his shingle and actually build his own practice. Since you brought it up, sir, and because I really respect you and your business accomplishments, I would be grateful for your advice." Fred waited expectantly, and he could hear Nate Klein breathing on the other end of the line.

"There are some pretty attractive perks that go along with climbing the ladder at one of the big firms," Nate said at last. "Club memberships, golf, holiday parties, expense accounts, not to mention hobnobbing with Philadelphia society's high-toned Jacks and Jills. Still, all that comes with a price, Frederick. The firm will call the shots, and those shots include when you work, what kind of work you'll do, and for what clients. It's not a bad deal for someone who doesn't mind or even enjoys being a bird in a gilded cage. You know, son, life's like business. It's all a matter of cutting deals. The deals we make, and the deals we break. Tradeoffs and compromises, but I can see that other fellow's point that some trades just might not be for guys like us."

Fred tried to digest what Nate Klein was saying. *Guys like us.* He had never thought of himself and Nate as similar. He imagined Nate's perfectly pressed suits, his starched white shirts with the large gold links studding the French cuffs, the Countess Mara ties in their immaculate Windsor knots, and the Italian wingtips that shined like mirrors. He detected something grim in

Nate's tone, and it confused him. Nate seemed so at ease in his world, yet his reference to Philadelphia society was damning.

A deep, throaty laugh came over the telephone wire. The hard edge was gone from Nate's voice when he continued, "Nice problem to have, kid. With Hitler denying our people their rights and threatening their very way of life, it's good to see a smart, Jewish boy from the Frankford section make good. Listen, before you decide what you're going to do, I've been meaning to talk to you anyway. I want you to come down and see my operation. Who knows, if you do decide to go out on your own, maybe I could throw a little business your way, bright guy like you. You know, the way the government is always trying to stick its fat hand in the pocket of hardworking Americans who are trying to make a buck, I'm always in need of a lawyer. Who knows? Maybe we could help each other. What do you say? How about dropping by on Monday?"

"Sure, sir. I would love to come by your office. Monday would be fine." *Guys like us.* Fred was intoxicated by the very prospect of it.

"Well, then, Monday it is!" Nate confirmed enthusiastically. "Now, let me get that daughter of mine." There was static on the line and then a lilting, feminine voice.

"Frederick, is that you? It's swell to hear from you." She sounded eager, which encouraged Fred.

"Hello, Deborah. I was hoping that you were free for dinner this Saturday. I know how much you like lobster, and I thought we could go to Bookbinder's. You know, down on Walnut Street near the waterfront where they have that big tank with all the live lobsters in it. They say they bring them in daily from Maine." Fred had never been to Bookbinder's, although its seafood had become legendary since its opening in 1865. He was planning to splurge on this dinner, paying for it with the small stipend he had saved from working in the dining hall during his undergraduate years at Temple. His parents knew that outside of their home he did not adhere to the kosher laws prohibiting Jews from eating shellfish, but he wondered how they would feel about his courting Deborah at a restaurant famous for *treif*, forbidden food, not to mention its price tag. He pushed these thoughts out of his mind and waited for her answer.

"Bookbinders would be lovely, Frederick, it's one of my favorite restaurants," she gushed, "I'll look forward to it."

"Great. I'll call for you at seven on Saturday," Fred replied, relieved that he had picked the right restaurant. He replaced the telephone receiver on its cradle and sat back in his chair. *Deborah must care for me,* he reassured himself, *and her father seems to like and respect me too. What had Lorraine said about their world? Grab it! That was it. She said that if I want it, I must reach out and grab it.*

CHAPTER 13

FOR FREDERICK, TIME SEEMED to crawl until Saturday finally came.

Finally, after being shown to their table, he sat across from Deborah in a high-backed leather booth in the corner of the noisy Bookbinder's dining room. They studied the menu and ordered lobster. The starched waiter then escorted them to the large lobster tank near the restaurant's entrance to select the live crustaceans that would be specially prepared as their entrees. Fred took the waiter's suggestion on the wine, a French Sauvignon Blanc, and he was enjoying the mellow haze that accompanied the two glasses he consumed along with his shrimp cocktail. Deborah leaned forward and gazed at him over her wine glass.

"My father says that you are meeting him for a tour of his office on Monday. He thinks a lot of you, Frederick. He says you're a bright, ambitious man." Deborah's fingertips grazed his hand. "He's convinced that you're going places."

Fred felt the heat in his face and was not sure whether the wine or her words caused it. He sat straighter in his chair and concentrated on breathing deeply.

"Yes, I was telling him the other day when he answered the phone that I am torn between joining a firm or striking out on my own after graduation." Fred hoped that he sounded casual and relaxed. "He was kind enough to invite me to see his office. I must say that I am very excited. Your father has a reputation throughout the city as a very successful businessman. Funny thing is, though, no one who talks about him seems exactly sure what he does." He laughed nervously. "I know he's involved in a variety of service industries, but could you tell me a little more about his core businesses?"

Deborah sat back and sighed. She seemed to be considering her reply as she rearranged her silverware and carefully spread her napkin on her lap. When she looked up, her open, familiar expression had changed as if a door had imperceptibly closed. She was still smiling, but Fred thought he saw her eyes darken. "I don't really know much about my father's business. He has never brought much of his work home with him. All I know is that I am very proud of him. He started out with nothing and has been very successful, as I am sure you know. Why don't you save your questions for him on Monday?" She patted her lips daintily with her napkin and clasped her hands together in front of her on the edge of the linen-covered table. Her eyes narrowed slightly. "Let's not spoil this beautiful dinner with talk of business," she continued. "Did I tell you about the gorgeous dress I bought to wear to your graduation? It's a pink organza, and I even found a hat to match!"

As she prattled on about her new ensemble, she seemed to recapture the lighthearted mood of the evening. Fred was relieved that the cloud had passed, but he was discomfited by Deborah's unwillingness to discuss her father. He had read a newspaper article recently describing certain military tactics that the Germans were employing in the war in Europe. One phrase had stuck in his head: "the closing of ranks." It referred to a situation in which military forces would mount a defense by attempting to form an impenetrable line around the protected target. *That's what the Kleins do every time I broach the subject of Nate's business dealings, he thought; they close ranks.*

He fixed a smile on his face and said, "I'm sure you'll look beautiful, Deborah. You always do."

Deborah's face spread into a confident smile and the evening was redeemed. *They might know how to close ranks,* he thought to himself, *but I am an expert at another military tactic: the salvage operation.*

Fred dressed nattily for his meeting with Nate Klein. He eschewed his lingering penchant for what Lorraine laughingly called flashy ties and selected instead a subdued regimental stripe to compliment his gray flannel suit, a style of which he knew Chapman would approve. He pulled the cuffs of his shirt the requisite inch below his jacket sleeve to expose his one indulgence, a pair of gleaming gold cufflinks, a gift upon his admission to Penn Law School to which all of his family members had contributed. His shoes shone in the sunlight, and his freshly cut hair was swept back from his wide, unlined forehead. He caught a glimpse of his reflection in the glass door to the office building at Sixteenth and Walnut Streets where Nate Klein had his corporate headquarters, and hardly recognized the professional young man looking back at him. As he pulled the door open, he smoothed his hair and walked purposefully toward the elevator.

The elevator doors opened soundlessly on the twenty-seventh floor to reveal a wood paneled reception area. An attractive blonde sat behind the walnut desk manning the switchboard and greeting visitors. Behind her, in impressive brass letters was the name of the company: Nathan Klein Industries. Fred waited impatiently for the receptionist to notice him. His hands, dangling at his sides, suddenly seemed large and out of place, so he stuffed them in his pockets. Finally, the young woman looked up and, after surveying him from head to toe, inquired, "May I help you?"

"Yes. Good morning. Would you please tell Mr. Klein that Frederick Green is here to see him?" She scanned him again, and her hooded eyes looked bored.

"Do you have an appointment?" she asked disinterestedly. "What is this in reference to?" Fred was beginning to feel the flush of annoyance rise above his collar.

"Yes. Mr. Klein is expecting me. If you would just tell him that I'm here, I'm sure…." Just then, Fred heard Nathan Klein's deep, raspy baritone among a group of voices emanating from the hallway to his left. He turned in that direction, and Mr. Klein saw him immediately.

"Frederick," he exclaimed, terminating his conversation with the other men. "I was just on my way up here to see if you'd arrived." Checking his watch, he smiled. "Right on time. I like that." He approached Fred with his arm extended for a welcoming handshake. "Frederick Green, I'd like you to meet three of my best men. Michael Maraschino, Abe Fine, and Bruce Miller."

Fred shook hands with each man, and when he got to the third, he realized that Bruce Miller was the same young man who he had seen squiring Deborah on Chestnut Street. Bruce Miller kept hold of Fred's hand and sized him up unabashedly, taking in everything from his wardrobe to his words.

Fred smiled diffidently, also attempting to take his rival's measure. Fred returned his attention to Mr. Klein.

"Frederick is about to graduate from Penn Law School," Mr. Klein informed them. "He and Deborah are quite good friends." Placing a welcoming hand on Fred's shoulder, he added, "I'm happy you could break away to see our little outfit."

The three other men sniggered as if privy to an inside joke.

"Glad to be here, sir. I have a great deal of curiosity about your operations."

Nate clapped him on the shoulder and separated himself from the other three men. "Well, gentlemen, I'm going to give Frederick here the five dollar tour. We'll continue our discussion at another time."

The three men nodded affably and retreated to the inner sanctum of the offices. Nate steered Fred through the long corridors, gesturing broadly and describing the activities of what seemed like hundreds of employees occupying pools of desks in large, open office space. "We have what you might call diverse business interests," he began. "Mikey, that's Michael Maraschino, whom you just met, he and I go way back to grammar school in the old neighborhood. He heads up our supermarket division." They walked on, and Nate pointed out an equally large area to the right. "Now, Abe, he's in charge of our dairy sector." Fred tried to interject questions to determine the specifics of the various enterprises; but each time he did, Nate either would evade the question or answer in such broad terms that Fred felt like he had gained no greater insight. "You know Penn Fruit?" Nate asked, a curl of disparagement on his lips. "They are our primary competition. They are really nothing more than the glorified fruit stand they started out with, but Morris and Isaac Kaplan and Sam Cook are growing that fruit stand into a regional chain. Why, they've got six produce stores already. Well, they'd better watch their back because Klein's, our answer to Penn Fruit's expanded store, has just been renamed Klein's Super, and we consider it the backbone of Klein Industries that now includes the supermarkets, dairy, tire business, and construction. We intend to give Penn Fruit, A&P, and Acme all a run for the money!" Before long, Fred realized that they had wended their way back to the reception area.

Still smiling, Nate extended his hand again, this time as a clear indication that their meeting was over. "Well, Frederick, it certainly was nice of you to come down to see our setup. I really think we could do great things for each other after you graduate. I hope you'll give some serious thought to joining our family. I mean, that's what we consider ourselves at Klein Industries, a family." He pumped Fred's hand as he spoke.

"Thank you, sir," Fred replied. "Oh, by the way," he said assuming an offhanded tone, "you said that the third fellow I met, Bruce Miller I think his name was, was also one of your best men. What does he do?"

Nate reached into his pocket for one of his favorite Partagas. He adeptly trimmed the end with his double blade guillotine, and Fred saw the flash of flame from Nate's silver lighter. Nate guided him to the door, blowing cigar smoke as he answered. "I just promoted Bruce to lead our small but growing tire division. Had to fire his predecessor. He was always bucking me and didn't like playing on my team. Bruce's best asset to the company is that he knows how to carry out an order. He's young and doesn't have a lot of formal education, but he's got a lot of common sense, and he's willing to do what it takes. He's always there when the company needs him, and I'm teaching him how to do things my way. I think we have real opportunity in the tire business with Bruce heading it up." It was obvious that Nate Klein did not inspire loyalty; he required it.

As Fred stepped out of the elevator and through the glass doors of the lobby into the street, the spring breeze was fresh on his face, a herald of a new beginning. The clean scent could not fully disguise the musky odor of Nate's cigar smoke that clung to Fred's jacket. Smiling to himself, Fred thought, *That must be the smell of success.*

CHAPTER 14

EVENTUALLY, FRED COULDN'T DELAY his career decision any longer.

A choice was put in front of him, in the form of an ecru-colored business envelope embossed with the name of the firm, Dechert Price and Rhodes, which stood out among the advertisements and bills as Fred checked the family mail.

Fred ran his fingers over the raised printing and carefully pried the flap open. The letterhead boldly repeated the founding partners' names, and below their appellations, in alphabetical order, taking up almost a third of the page, were the names of all the other partners and associates.

Dear Mr. Green, it began. *On behalf of our firm, it gives me great pleasure....*

There it was: "The Hobson's choice." Fred could accept this offer from one of the premier law firms in Philadelphia along with everything it embodied, prestige and payment, parameters and parasites; or he could politely decline and start out with nothing. Nothing, except being his own man. He folded the single thick sheet of ivory stationery and slid it back into the envelope. He slipped it inside his coat pocket and thought of Lorraine. She said that he should grab the life he wanted. As he walked toward the el to catch the train to meet her, his fingers curled around the envelope concealed in his pocket. He had no idea what to do.

When he reached the platform, the train was just pulling into the station. He hopped onboard and grabbed a rail between two other men. After a brief ride, the train lurched to a stop; and Fred pushed his way out the door, looking up and down the platform for Lorraine. In the distance, he could see her willowy figure in silhouette; and they could have been bookends, each with one arm raised in greeting after their moment of recognition.

They linked arms and exited onto the street, their feet marching in unison, to the Automat that had become their weekly rendezvous. Horn and Hardart's had opened the first Automat in Philadelphia in 1902, a direct descendant and crowning achievement of the Industrial Revolution, at which the freshly prepared food behind each glass door was available for a nickel a serving and a turn of the wrist. Everyone seemed to love the Automat. For the growing class of urban office workers, it was a quick, hot lunch break. For the great mass of unemployed still suffering from the pummeling of the Depression, the Automat provided a warm haven where they could buy a single cup of coffee and nurse it all morning long until it became too cold to drink. Those who were even less fortunate would sometimes concoct a drink from hot water and the ketchup and Tabasco that sat on each shiny, lacquered table in the large rectangular hall.

"My treat," Fred said to Lorraine, "but I need some change." He approached the row of "nickel throwers", women who wore rubber tips on their fingers and sat in glass booths dispensing the five-cent pieces required to operate the food machines. Fred and Lorraine eyed the day's selections hungrily. Still young and slim, they were blessed with the luxury of being able to eat anything they wanted without fear of a weight penalty; and they both studied the desserts first. Simultaneously, they reached out a slender hand to turn the same chrome-plated knob, corresponding to a generous portion of coconut layer cake.

"Oh, no, you don't," Fred chided her. "I saw it first." He assumed a look of feigned indignation and reached forward to turn the handle.

"Not so fast, little brother. How does that saying go? 'Age and beauty before....' Well, it's something like that, and I'm way ahead of you on both, so that coconut cake is mine." She playfully slapped his hand away from the knob, ever the big sister.

"Ok, ok, you can have it," Fred conceded. "Never let it be said that I'm not a gentleman." He grinned broadly and placed another nickel in the slot of an adjoining compartment, which revolved to reveal a piece of chocolate cream pie. "Not only that," he continued, "but just to show that I have no hard feelings, the coffee's also on me." He placed two steaming cups together with their sweets on a tray, and Lorraine followed him to a table.

They passed the first few minutes in companionable silence eating their food and warming up from the coffee. Lorraine pushed her chair back slightly from the table and wiped coconut icing from her delicate mouth. "Did it come?" she asked finally.

Fred felt the envelope like a weight in his pocket. He pulled it out and set it on the table between them. Neither one of them seemed to want to touch it, but they both stared at it the way two comrades would gape at the discovery of a live landmine. At last, he pushed it toward her gingerly, and she opened the letter, skimming its contents.

"This is just so typical of you, Freddy. You get precisely what you want, but now you're not sure you want it after all, isn't that right? You're like the kid on the carousel who is dying to grab the brass ring; but when he does, he's disappointed because he thought it was gold. Well, the thing is, it never is. What you've got to decide is which ring is shinier than the other, that's all. I don't need to tell you that there's a lot of glitter associated with this offer from such a well known, prestigious law firm, but only you can say if it's for you, kiddo." She covered his hand with hers and squeezed it with encouragement.

"Did I tell you that Nate Klein invited me to his office to tour his operation? He as much as made me an offer to work for him after graduation. He kept telling me that he thought I have a head for business and that I could make a great contribution." Fred searched her face for a reaction.

"I saw Nate Klein's picture in the paper again last week," Lorraine said. "He was with a judge, and they were both cutting the ribbon on a new community center in South Philadelphia." Fred searched her face for a reaction, but she continued, stone-faced. "Anything new with you and Deborah?"

"Yes. She's excited about coming to my graduation next month."

Lorraine stirred her coffee absently and replied, "I'll be there with bells on," she said squaring her shoulders and beaming at him. She looked at her watch, and a look of dismay replaced her smile. "Hey, I didn't realize what time it is. I've got to go. Danny will be expecting me." She picked up the paper bag filled with macaroni and cheese, baked beans, and creamed spinach that she had purchased to take home. "Less work for Mother," she said sheepishly, referring to Horn and Hardart's slogan popularized to promote their new foray into takeout food. She stood up and rummaged in her purse for carfare. Fred knew that she would be returning to a dark and empty apartment to eat alone. He started to speak, once again tempted by the urge to tell her to leave him, but was reminded of what she said the last time, "I made my bed."

"Same time, same place next week?" he inquired instead, trying to inject the words with reassurance and enthusiasm.

"Same time, same place; but next time, I get the chocolate cream pie," she said over her shoulder with a wink. As the door swung shut behind her and she disappeared into the crowded street, Fred shook his head. He gathered up his letter and refolded it neatly into the envelope.

The remainder of the school year rushed by in a haze of exams and preparations for the bar exam, which would take place in July. He still tried to make time for Lorraine, but it was she who kept canceling. At their last meeting, she had complained of a sore throat and a nagging cold that she said she was unable to shake. Her eyes were feverish, and her complexion was pasty. Fred implored her to see a doctor.

She shrugged off his concern and insisted, "It's just the change of seasons. All of these beautiful flowers and new leaves on the trees really aggravate my allergies. I'll be fine." She swiped at her nose with her handkerchief and attempted a smile. But she begged off their next two weekly dates as well, all the while claiming that she was getting better and would surely meet him the following week.

The next week, she didn't even call. Fred waited at the Automat for over an hour, until he finally went home, not sure whether to be annoyed or worried. As he placed his key in the lock, he heard the telephone ring. Stepping across the threshold, he dropped his briefcase on the floor and grabbed for the phone on the small table at the foot of the stairs. His mother also heard it ringing, and he could see her coming down the hall from the kitchen, wiping her hands on her apron. He reached the telephone first and, in his haste, knocked the receiver off the cradle. Fumbling with the earpiece, he answered "Hello?"

There was static on the line, but he could hear breathing on the other end, so he asked again, this time exasperated, "Hello? Is there anybody there?" His mother gave him a questioning look and stepped closer.

"Fred, this is Danny," came the reply, followed by another silence. The fine hairs on the back of Fred's neck prickled. He could not remember the last time Lorraine's husband had called the house. Certainly, it had been while they were still dating; and as Lorraine had caustically described it, the bloom was still on the rose. Why would he be calling now? Fred cast a furtive glance at his mother, knowing that she was wondering why he stood gawking at the telephone. "Yeah, hi. What's going on?" he asked, trying to sound as though he were talking to a classmate or a friend.

More static crackled across the telephone wire in another awkward silence until Fred heard Danny breathe in sharply, then exhale. "It's Lorraine," he said finally. "Fred, she's gone."

Fred bit his lip so hard that he thought he would draw blood. His mother touched his arm, but he wheeled around to face the wall, knowing there was no escape from Danny's words or his mother's hovering presence. Dropping any pretense of normality, Fred spat, "What the hell do you mean, 'She's gone?' Are you saying that for once you bothered to come home, and she's not there? Maybe, she finally wised up and decided to leave you. You must have more nerve than brains to call here and expect me to help you find her. Do you think I don't know what kind of a son of a bitch you've been to my sister? You're nothing but a...."

"Fred, Lorraine's dead." Danny interrupted, his words tightening like a vise around Fred's heart. "She was sick, but God, I didn't think she was that sick. When I got home, she was passed out on the floor. I called the doctor as soon as I could. I swear I did, but he said it was too late. Something called mastoiditis caused by a middle ear infection. Christ, I had no idea; you've gotta believe me!"

The room seemed to suddenly close in on him. All he could hear was breathing, Danny's, his mother's; but suddenly, he had to remind himself to do it, to breathe in and breathe back out, because he knew that if he stopped thinking about it, he would stop doing it, just as surely as first Will and now Lorraine had.

Danny's voice came again over the line. "They took her, Fred. I mean, I didn't know what else to do. Should I make some kind of arrangements? We don't have a plot or anything. God, she was only thirty-six years old. Should I have a plot? I don't think I should be expected to have a plot."

Danny's defensiveness bit at him. "This isn't about you, Danny," Fred spat through clenched teeth, uncomfortably aware of his mother. She touched his arm again, looking at him quizzically. "But if it makes you feel any better, nobody expects any more of you now than the stellar behavior you've always demonstrated. In fact, nobody expects anything more from you, ever." His head ached, and his arms were heavy, as if the weight of this new grief were palpable. He commanded his hand to replace the receiver on the cradle. He turned to face his mother, steadying himself, one hand on her elbow, and the other braced on the table. *Breathe in, breathe out*, he repeated to himself.

"Mom, remember I told you Lorraine was sick?" His words echoed inanely in his throbbing head. *How do you introduce death by talking about a head cold? How do you tell your mother that her beautiful, talented daughter, the one member of the family who seemed the most alive, is gone?* Images of Lorraine flashed in his brain like a slide show: Lorraine playing jazz piano, her hands flying across the keys; Lorraine leading him through the Charleston and the

Lindy, her eyes alight with pleasure; Lorraine laughing at her own jokes even before she could deliver the punch line; Lorraine.... He could see the look of expectancy in Ruth's eyes. He opened his mouth to speak again, but he felt the track of a tear that had escaped his downcast eyes. He swiped at it angrily, and as he looked at his mother, he felt her grip on his elbow loosen. Her legs collapsed under her; and both hands flew to cover her mouth, failing to stifle the guttural wail that filled the space between them and seeped into every corner and crevice of their small house.

"I swear I didn't know, Mom. I mean I had no idea it was anything serious. Maybe I should have taken her to the doctor myself. She said it was just a cold. You know Lorraine, Mom. Nobody could make her do anything she didn't want to. Maybe I should've gone by her house when she cancelled our last meeting. I don't know, Mom. I'm so sorry." Fred crouched on the floor next to his mother, reaching his long arms out protectively, as she rocked back and forth with her eyes closed, embracing herself in a straitjacket of anguish.

Eventually, he heard the sound of the key in the front door lock. He had no idea how long they had been in the foyer, his mother sobbing softly and he wallowing silently in his own misery made of guilt and loss. He turned his head toward the door and watched it slowly open, his father's perfectly polished shoes now visible on the threshold. Neither Fred nor his mother made an effort to stand.

Walter's briefcase made a thud as it hit the wood floor. He searched their faces. "What's wrong? Ruth, did you fall down?" he asked as he approached his wife and son. "For heaven's sake, Frederick, what are the two of you doing on the floor?" He encircled Ruth's waist and tried to get her to stand, but she crumpled into a formless heap at his feet. "What's wrong?" he repeated, this time with noticeable fear in his voice. "Frederick, what's going on here?"

"Lorraine's dead," he blurted. "She was sick, and now she's dead." The space between Fred and his father ripped with the ugly sound of his words in the same way that the earth rends when two plates move against each other, an irrevocable seismic shift.

"What happened?" Walter demanded, shaking Fred's shoulder. "Where is she?"

"I don't know," Fred managed, his chest tight and his breath coming in short rasps. "Danny said she developed a bad middle ear infection, something called a mastoid, and there was nothing anyone could do."

Fred stood and faced his father, suddenly noticing details he never had before. The lines at the corners of his father's penetrating, blue eyes were deep crevasses. His skin was creped, and his hair and moustache were virtually white. His mouth pulled down at the corners extending the diagonal furrows that flared from each nostril. *He looks…old*, Fred thought. Why hadn't he ever seen that before? He looked at his mother, noticing the silver in her hair, the prominent cheekbones visible through her translucent skin, the slope of her shoulders. *When had they become so old*, he wondered silently?

Walter was breathing hard. He looked back and forth from Fred to Ruth, wordlessly begging for it not to be true. "We have to go to her," he said finally, grabbing his hat and buttoning his coat. When neither Fred nor Ruth moved, he repeated more insistently, "We have to go to her!"

Walter's sharp words broke their fragile bubble. Fred helped his mother to stand and held her coat for her, guiding her arms into the sleeves. She robotically lifted her purse and gloves from the small demi-lune table under the mirror in the foyer. She patted her hair in place and tied a scarf around her head. Fred shrugged into his topcoat and angled his fedora over one eye. Glancing at himself in the mirror, he wondered why he was taking such care with his appearance. He saw Lorraine's approving face when he looked at his reflection. *Because she would have noticed*, he thought. *She was the one that taught me to have style*. He guided his mother through the door with a steadying hand at the small of her back and pulled the door closed behind him.

Halfway to the curb, Walter realized that he didn't know where they were going. When he turned inquiringly to Fred, his son anticipated his question. "Danny says they took her to the funeral home. I assume that means Joseph Levine & Sons, since Lorraine probably told him that's who handled Will's arrangements, Dad. God, I never even asked." He hung his head in shame.

"We'll go there," Walter said flatly. As they walked to the el three abreast, Fred remembered another time, so long ago it now seemed, when they had walked the same way. When they had gone together to the Jeffers scholarship announcement, Fred's family had seemed to him like an impenetrable wall. But even this wall could not hold death at bay. Death had robbed them of Lorraine; and while they still stood, their wall now felt bowed and vulnerable.

As they neared the mortuary, Fred wondered whether Danny would be there. Fred knew he had sounded angry over the phone and had stopped just short of telling Danny not to come. Still, he was her husband. Maybe he would try to be heroic in the face of death. "You know," he began tentatively as he held the door of Levine's for his parents, "Danny might be here. He might have to fill out some forms or sign some papers as next of kin. I wouldn't be surprised if...."

Walter wheeled and put the flat of his hand on Fred's chest.

Fred froze.

"Don't you ever mention the name of that schmuck to me again. He was a terrible husband, and he kept Lorraine away from us. Now, my daughter is gone, and that bastard is dead to me." Walter punctuated each word by jabbing his index finger just above the top button of Fred's overcoat. Walter's eyes burned with rage and anguish. Never having been a profane man, his words were at once incongruous and menacing. "I will sit shiva for seven days for my daughter, but I will not spend one second on that bum she married. He isn't worth the dirt under her shoes, Frederick." Walter's arm dropped to his side and, for a moment, his chin rested on his chest. Then, he rasped an uneven breath, squared his shoulders, and led the remains of his small family into the funeral home.

CHAPTER 15

D ANNY CAME TO THE HOUSE late on the evening of Lorraine's death.

He stood on the stoop, eyes cast down, clutching the brim of the hat that he had hurriedly scraped from his head when Walter answered the door. He tried to fill the unbridgeable gap between them with words. "Mr. Green, I came about Lorraine. I guess Freddy told you that I don't have a plot. I don't have much money either, but I could come up with something. I don't know how much a plot and a decent casket and a headstone cost, but I could pay over time...." His words trailed off and seemed to melt in the molten glare of Walter's silent wrath. Danny waited, continuing to rotate the hat through his fingers in an endless circle. He could not meet Walter's gaze.

Walter's anger bored into the top of Danny's bowed head like a laser. When he finally replied, his voice was a low, malignant whisper. "My daughter needed you in life, not in death. Do not insult her memory or her family with your feeble offer of money or your spineless and belated attempt to shoulder any responsibility where she is concerned. She is dead, and you are dead to me." He closed the door, and the audible sound of the lock placed a final, unassailable period on his sentence.

So, it was Fred and his father who attended to the painful business of Lorraine's funeral arrangements. They stood like two pillars of salt in Levine's Funeral Home as the obsequious mortician wrung his hands and clucked his tongue over Lorraine's youth and the fleeting passage of life.

Only once, when they were invited to examine the wide array of caskets that Levine's offered, did Walter's veneer crack.

"Might I recommend this handsome walnut casket?" the mortician offered. He looked over their wool topcoats and suits with a practiced eye toward determining what arrangements they could afford. "Notice the lovely satin lining." He gestured to the inside of the polished wooden box and seemed to encourage them to touch the padded interior walls. Walter pointedly ignored him and turned to his son.

"Frederick, that is the right one over there. The mahogany casket with the silk lining." Walter walked with deliberate steps to the platform where the much more expensive casket was displayed and gently touched the surface of the pillow. "Yes," he continued as if he were talking to himself, "this is the right one, and her headstone must be the finest granite."

Having decided on all the accoutrements, they returned to the mortician's office to sign the necessary documents. As they filled in the details of the various forms, the mortician asked about the inscription. "And how would you like the wording on Mrs. Loeb's headstone to read?"

Fred saw his father drop his pen and open his mouth to speak. He put a cautionary hand on his father's arm and leaned across the desk.

"Mr. Levine, we would like the headstone to be inscribed 'Lorraine Esther Green,' and we would like it to read, 'Beloved daughter and sister.'" He sat back in his chair still applying gentle pressure to his father's forearm.

A small group gathered the next day for the graveside service. Several neighbors, some childhood friends, and even two of Lorraine's piano teachers who had read the small death notice in the *Philadelphia Inquirer* made the effort to bid her farewell in person. Fred and Walter stood on either side of Ruth, not so much a wall this time as a protective shield. Uncle Julius and Aunt Pauline, a pair of deflated windbags, slouched behind Walter. Deborah, ever lovely even when attired in sober black from head to toe, stood respectfully to the side among the other mourners, her arm linked through Chapman Stirling's.

As the rabbi began to recite the Kaddish, the Jewish prayer for the dead, the Hebrew sounded alien to Fred, despite his years of study. Everything about the ritual seemed strangely inappropriate, wrong for his vivacious sister. He had read once that in New Orleans, the Creoles honor their dead with a Dixieland band. *That would have been more like it.* He looked up and saw Lorraine's face in the clouds, pictured her lithesome body swaying, her beautiful head thrown back with her hair a corona, as her elegant fingers plied the keyboard. He closed his eyes and his lips moved noiselessly in what looked like a prayer. *There should have been music,* he told himself, as tears leaked from his eyes.

Lorraine's casket was lowered into the eternal abyss next to Will's immaculate grave. First, William dead at twenty-five; now, Lorraine at thirty-six. Fred took no comfort in seeing his brother's and sister's resting places side-by-side, together for all time.

As he watched her casket, Fred spotted a furtive figure in the middle distance moving uneasily amid the trees and mausoleums. He followed the man with his eyes for a few seconds, realizing with a start that it was Danny. He wore an ill-fitting black suit and a hat pulled low across his eyes. The wind had begun to pick up, and Danny held tightly to a bouquet of yellow tulips, Lorraine's favorite flower. He never approached.

The rabbi asked each family member to come forward to throw a clod of earth on the grave. Fred supported his mother's left elbow as she stood, and Walter linked his left arm through her right elbow. Even so, she faltered as she approached the deep hole. Her hand shook as she released the handful of granular dirt, and it made a dull thud as it hit the coffin's lid. Walter took his turn, followed by Fred. Still, Danny lurked in the background.

When the funeral was over, the rabbi shook their hands, and the others kept a respectful distance until it was time for them to murmur their condolences. A rented limousine hugged the curb nearby, waiting to take them home. Fred had arranged this small luxury for his parents out of savings from part-time jobs, but Walter and Ruth regarded it sightlessly, just another incongruity in this most incongruous of days. As the driver slowly pulled away, Fred looked back out of the rear windshield toward the grave. Bright yellow petals danced in the wind for Lorraine.

All of the mirrors in the house on Charles Street were draped in black crepe in accordance with the Jewish mandate for the first week of shiva, the mourning period. Sitting on low stools with his family in the front room where a steady stream of neighbors and friends came to pay their respects, Fred questioned this custom. The rabbi told him that it originated from the belief that man was created in God's image. With a single death, he explained, the very image of God is diminished, and a reflection of the Divine Image is eclipsed. To symbolize this eclipse, the mirrors in a house of mourning are covered. *Hokum*, Fred scoffed, his agile mind forming its own questions. *Were the mirrors covered because even a clandestine glimpse of oneself was considered a frivolous vanity on the part of the grief-stricken? Or was there some primal fear that one would somehow see the Angel of Death peering back from the reflection? Maybe it was something much more obvious. After all, he wondered, who would want to see themselves in heartbreak's embrace? The empty eyes, the swollen face, the blotched complexion-all part of misery's sick makeover. Maybe we cover our mirrors for the same reason that we are required to tear our clothes, he concluded. We wear our grief as a rip on the outside so that others can see our desolation.*

CHAPTER 16

T HE EARTH CONTINUED ITS magnetic tango with the sun, spin-
ning and circumnavigating, blatantly challenging Fred to rejoin the
inexorable forward motion of life. He had chosen to think of the process as
recovery, rather than mourning. As if it were a plane crash or a war, he was a
survivor of Lorraine's death. He would heal; but like a lesion that leaves a scar,
his heartbreak would mend leaving him different than he had been before.

For him, that scar seemed to manifest itself in an increased anxiety about
his own future. Lorraine had been so adamant that he make the right decision,
that he take ownership of the life on which he was about to embark. And the
timing couldn't have been more prescient. Just two weeks after her funeral, he
was set to graduate from the University of Pennsylvania Law School.

He had promised to call for Deborah at nine o'clock in the morning. She
and her parents had been sympathetic and supportive since Lorraine's death,
calling often but also giving him the space that he needed. Now, as promised,
she would join his parents in the reserved section of the seating area.

Fred had anticipated this day for so long that he could hardly believe it finally had arrived. He was nervous and excited as he walked up the serpentine path leading to the Kleins' front door. But something didn't feel quite right. Here he was on the brink of achieving his dream of becoming a lawyer, yet neither Will nor Lorraine would be there to see it. Was joy always tempered with loss? As he pressed the doorbell, he squared his shoulders and affixed a smile to his face. Life had robbed him of so much happiness; but on this halcyon day, he had to remember what he still had.

Deborah answered the door so quickly that Fred wondered if she had been watching his approach through the foyer window. Her pretty face was flushed with excitement as she swung the door wide in welcome. "Frederick, I'm so happy for you. I've been up since early this morning because I couldn't sleep. I kept thinking about the commencement exercises and how proud we all are of you. I've been ready for hours." Deborah blushed the same shade of lipstick pink as her summer dress. She picked up her purse and beamed at Fred: "Let's go, counselor."

Fred held the door open and followed her into the sunshine.

Walter and Ruth already were seated when Fred installed Deborah in one of two empty chairs next to them; the remaining chair had been reserved for Lorraine. He kissed each of his parents and took his mother's hands in both of his. Ruth cupped her hands around his face and managed a rare smile.

Because he was graduating with honors, Fred was seated in a special section of the class. He tried to concentrate on the words of the dean and the various commencement speakers as they addressed the graduates and audience. Despite his efforts, his eyes kept wandering back to look at his parents and Deborah. His father sat erect and looked distinguished in his best summer suit, the same steel gray as his hair. His mother looked gaunt but refined, her head held high and her eyes focused forward toward the stage. Deborah looked like the proverbial petunia in the onion patch that Fred had heard about in nursery stories of his childhood. She was a burst of vibrant spring color amid a sea of dismal and somber grays and blues. Her eyes glinted with an air of unadulterated optimism. Then, his gaze fell upon the vacant chair next to his mother. For an instant, he saw Lorraine. He blinked hard, and the chair was empty again, a symbolic void marring the commencement of his career. Since Lorraine's death, Fred had given little thought to his two offers of employment. At that moment, unable to refrain from staring at the chair that had been meant for Lorraine, Fred made up his mind.

He was startled at the sound of his own name as the dean read the list of graduates alphabetically. "Frederick Maier Green, magna cum laude." He rose from his seat, mounted the steps to the stage, and strode toward the dean to meet his outstretched hand. Having received his degree, Fred moved the tassel on his mortarboard from the right side to the left, just as the students had practiced. He panned the audience one last time and saw his parents smiling politely while Deborah, heedless of the earlier admonition to hold all applause, stood at her place reddening the palms of her hands with relentless clapping. He wanted to laugh at the inappropriate behavior of this perfect girl but couldn't stop looking at the silent, empty chair.

Fred had kept himself busy in the week since his graduation and had not seen Deborah since then, so he looked forward to their date the following Saturday night as a possible panacea for his lingering grief. They were having dinner at a small Italian restaurant where the homemade pasta and regional wines were as authentic as the immigrant family who ran the place.

At the end of the meal, Deborah finally broached the topic that had been at the forefront of Fred's mind for weeks. "So," she began, taking a delicate sip from her coffee cup. "Have you come to any conclusions about which job offer you are going to accept?" Her tone was offhand and conversational, but Fred wondered if she already had reached her own decision about which career route he should pursue. Her expression revealed nothing.

Fred cleared his throat and said, "Actually, I have. It's funny how you think you know what you want; and then when it's offered to you, you somehow realize that it's not what you really want after all. I thought for so long that I wanted the prestige and reputation of a big name law firm. Then, when that partner interviewed me and told me how both personally and professionally constraining that kind of law practice can be and said that he thought I could make it on my own, I started to see things differently. I think when Lorraine died, I knew then what I was going to do. I want to go out on my own, Deborah. I know it'll be a hard scrabble life at the beginning, but hopefully not always…." He realized that he had covered her hand with his; and listening to himself, he sounded as if he were pleading his first case in front of her. The words tumbled out of his mouth, "What do you think, Deborah? I want to start my own law practice, and I want you there beside me. Will you marry me?"

"What about my father's offer of a job?" Deborah asked. She sounded hurt, and for a moment Fred failed to realize that she had answered his proposal with a question of her own.

"Well, uh, like I said, while I appreciate the wonderful offers that I have from the law firm and from your father, I've decided that being a solo practitioner is what's right for me."

"Are you saying that working for my father would somehow hem you in?" Deborah asked. "I know my father gives people tremendous freedom and rewards initiative." She raised her chin and sniffed, her mouth a pouty frown.

"I'm sure he does," Fred soothed, "but I think a man like your father who built such a successful business on his own would be the first to understand why I want to try to do the same thing. Besides, I know I would always regret it if I didn't try to establish my own law practice." He sat back in his chair having presented the best evidence to support his case.

The clouds over Deborah's eyes passed, and her radiant gaze broke through. She paused. "It seems to me you asked me something else far more interesting before I so rudely changed the subject. What was it?"

Fred leaned toward her again and asked with more urgency this time, "Will you marry me, Deborah?"

"Yes, Frederick," she replied, "I most certainly will."

CHAPTER 17

FRED AND DEBORAH WERE married the next winter at the Bellevue Hotel where they had first met at Chapman's family dinner party. What he remembered most about that glittering evening was the moment he stepped on the delicate crystal glass, shattering it into infinitesimal shards. This Jewish custom, he knew, had been assigned a range of meanings, from commemorating the destruction of the Temple in Jerusalem to the one he preferred, that the love between the husband and wife would last as long as the glass remained broken; forever. It was at the moment when the heel of his patent leather evening shoe made contact with the fragile glass that Fred felt unequivocally that the next happy chapter of his life had begun.

Fred was able to afford a small office in the Pennsylvania Savings Fund Society building that boasted an impressive address on Chestnut Street. He put in long hours trying to establish his law practice by taking a mélange of cases ranging from divorce and criminal matters to contracts and admiralty. His clients were working class people and small businessmen, referrals from friends and neighbors, and longshoremen from the Philadelphia waterfront. If his clients could not come to his office because of work, Fred went to see them after hours or on weekends to offer them legal representation. He became familiar with the blue-collar areas of the city and its environs; places like Marcus Hook, Media, and Camden became his frequent haunts. His reputation spread by word of mouth as an honest and accessible attorney who was a friend to his clients and whose persuasiveness would bring plaintiffs large awards from juries in injury cases.

He and Deborah lived on a quiet street of row houses that Fred loved, especially when the deciduous trees would leaf out in spring creating a canopy of shade along the sidewalks and in their fenced backyard that, one day, would be ideal for children at play. Fred hoped that it would not be long before he and Deborah had a baby who would grow up there.

Deborah quickly made friends in the neighborhood. She liked the other young wives and mothers and filled her time with a bridge club, gardening, and weekly visits to her parents' home on the Main Line. She and her mother often lunched and shopped together, and she arrived home brimming with conversation about the latest restaurant and packages filled with expensive clothing and objects for their home. At first, Fred was happy that Deborah had found ways to occupy herself, but the bills began to mount. Fred could not hide his concern. "I know that it is hard for you to resist some of the beautiful things you see in the stores," he said one day as she modeled some of her new acquisitions, "but we are just starting out; and some of these things are just more than we can afford right now."

Deborah's expression deflated like a pin-struck balloon. She ripped the new cashmere sweater from her shoulders and stuffed it back into the bag from John Wanamaker's. She gathered up the other shopping bags and hugged them to her chest exclaiming, "Well, Frederick, if you're not interested in my looking nice or in my trying to decorate our home, I just won't bother to show you what I've bought. Besides, if all you're going to talk about is money, I'll just tell my father that we're having trouble making ends meet; and I know he'll be glad to help us. He wants me to be happy."

Fred felt the heat of shame and anger. "I didn't say I wasn't interested, and I didn't say we were having trouble making ends meet. I merely meant to suggest that you don't have to buy everything in sight." He regretted the words as soon as he had uttered them. Deborah's eyes narrowed, and her mouth dropped open in a perfect "O."

"I'm sorry," he conceded. "We're doing fine. We don't need any help from your father. I guess I'm not used to having a pretty wife who needs pretty things," he continued, forcing a smile. "Buy whatever you like."

Deborah carried the bags toward the door of their small bedroom. She turned to Fred and said over her shoulder, "I'm used to having certain things, Frederick. I know you wouldn't want me to have to change who I am." She grinned and kicked the door closed behind her with the stiletto heel of her new red patent leather shoe.

Fred returned his concentration to the stack of unpaid bills on the desktop. He breathed deeply as he opened the checkbook ledger in front of him. He did all of his own personal and professional accounting and kept meticulous records of his finances. Each month, he reconciled his books and made sure that every credit or debit coincided exactly with an entry made to his account that he then filed away for future reference. He maintained these files so that he could calculate his income tax each spring, as well as account for his expenses. He neatly printed out each check, signed it, and stamped the envelopes. When he was finished, he ruefully regarded the stack waiting to be mailed, noting that the vast majority of checks had been written to department stores and specialty shops. Fred laced his fingers and stretched his arms over his head. He revolved his head in slow circles while he massaged the tight muscles in the back of his neck. He could hear Deborah humming softly along with the radio behind the bedroom door, oblivious to his concern. He stacked the envelopes neatly and rose from his chair. He reminded himself that he recently had signed several promising cases and had been referred to other prospective clients. *Deborah's right*, he chided himself. *I'm a worrier. Things are going really well for us, and I need to smell the roses a little. What's the point of making money if not to spend some of it?*

"I'm going to the post office," he said as he walked toward the door. "Put on something pretty, and we'll take a walk after dinner." He liked the carefree tone of his voice and applauded himself for holding the specter of self-doubt at bay.

On his way to the post office, Fred's thoughts turned, as they often did, to Deborah's father, Nate Klein. In the six months since they had been married, Fred had learned little more about the business dealings of his father-in-law. Any questions he asked were met with either good-humored evasion or stony silence and a change of subject. Regularly, Nate Klein's picture would appear on the social or business pages of the *Philadelphia Inquirer* with an important jurist, government official, or fellow business leader. His sphere of influence cast a wide net, encompassing notables from every powerful arena in the city.

Only last week, Fred had bumped into Nate, as he was finishing lunch at a restaurant on Walnut Street. Fred had met Chapman for a rare, midweek break, and both young men had approached Nate's table in greeting.

"Hi, Mr. Klein," Fred had said pausing by his chair. Fred had yet to become accustomed to calling Nate by his first name. The formality of his upbringing simply wouldn't allow it. Nate called him to task about it every time.

"Fred," Nate replied warmly, rising from his seat, "if you can't bring yourself to call me Dad, I won't settle for anything less than 'Nate.'" Turning to Chapman, he clasped his hand and clapped him on the shoulder warmly. "Good to see you too, Chapman. I'm especially glad to see that you've rescued this hardworking son-in-law of mine from the paper chase."

Fred looked expectantly at the familiar face of the gentleman who accompanied Nate at his table and who now stood at his place. Nate followed his eyes to his companion and made the introduction. "Judge Woodward, I would like you to meet my son-in-law, Frederick Green, and our mutual friend, Chapman Stirling, both young lions at the gates of your courthouse." Fred recognized the name immediately. The Honorable William Mackenzie Woodward was the Chief Judge of the Eastern District Court of Pennsylvania. His incisive legal mind and his stiff sentencing practices were legend. Both Fred and Chapman shook the judge's hand, a bit awed by the experience.

"It is a pleasure to meet both of you," Judge Woodward said. "Nate has spoken highly of your legal abilities and his belief that both of you will become men of influence. I hope to see you again soon, gentlemen, even if it's only in my courtroom." The judge took his seat and Nate followed suit, signaling that their encounter was over.

"Enjoy your lunch, *Nate*," Fred said, emphasizing his name. "Sir," he continued addressing the judge, "it has been an honor to make your acquaintance." Chapman smiled and nodded, and the two friends made their way out of the restaurant.

"He makes me nervous," Fred confided to Chapman once they were alone.

"Who? Nate or his honor the judge?" Chapman asked with his easy laugh.

"You know who I'm talking about," Fred answered, "Nate, of course. Even after all this time, I can't figure him out. He's always been friendly enough, but it all seems to be on the surface. All I've ever been able to know for sure is that he's connected, very well connected. Other than that, he's an enigma to me."

"He's in the power business, buddy. That's all there is to know. You can bet your last dollar that whether it's lunch, the opera or a round of golf, Nate Klein will not be there unless there's something in it for him. I'm not saying I don't like the man; but you've heard the expression, 'He doesn't suffer fools gladly?' Well, old Nate doesn't suffer anyone unless he's already calculated long beforehand that he's going to come out on the plus side of the ledger." Chapman stuffed his hands deep into his pockets and shrugged his shoulders in a silent, "That's that."

There was something unsavory about what Chapman said about Nate that caused Fred to have an uneasy feeling of something unknown and sinister crawling along the back of his neck.

Returning from the post office, Fred called out through the entry hall. "Deborah, are you ready for that walk?"

His young wife came towards him from the kitchen brushing her hair from her forehead with the back of her hand and untying her apron. "I've put a stew on to simmer," she said. "It should be just about ready when we get back." Lately, Deborah had developed a new interest in cooking, and Fred took this announcement as a flag of truce after their earlier disagreement.

"Sounds great. Let's go," he said making a grand gesture to the open door.

As Deborah walked out ahead of him, he could not help but notice that her previously trim silhouette had thickened somewhat around the middle, perhaps a result of her new domestic interest. He fitted his hand around her waist, and they began walking down the shaded street.

"Frederick, I'm sorry we quarreled earlier," she smiled up at him. "I've just felt a little moody lately." She turned to face him and took both of his hands. "I'm afraid you're going to have to put up with that and my gaining weight for the next several months." She looked down seeming unusually awkward and embarrassed.

"Oh, I haven't even noticed." Fred fibbed gallantly. "All couples have small disagreements from time to time, and you look as lovely as ever to me."

Deborah squeezed his hands and raised her face to look at him. "Frederick, I don't think you understand what I am trying to tell you. I am going to have a baby. You are going to be a father."

There are moments that last longer than others, indelible moments that are life altering and seem to cheat time of its transit. This was one of them. Fred couldn't remember ever being so happy. He lifted Deborah off her feet in wordless joy.

"If it's a girl, I'd like to name her after my sister, Lorraine," Fred smiled. "You know how much she meant to me."

Protectively placing a gentle hand on her still flat belly, Deborah agreed. "That would be lovely, Frederick, and so in keeping with the beautiful tradition of our Jewish people to name a new life after a departed loved one." She placed Fred's hand on top of hers. "I believe we're going to have a daughter."

CHAPTER 18

F REDERICK GREEN'S DAUGHTER, LYDIA, was born on a beautiful autumn day. The sky was clear and cloudless, and the trees formed a canopy of russet, burnt umber, and gold, their leaves just beginning to fall and swirl in the eddy of the crisp breeze. Somehow, he had known the baby would be a girl, or perhaps he had wished it would be so, a daughter who would fill the void left by Lorraine. As agreed, he and Deborah named their daughter for his beloved sister. Keeping her first and middle initials, they chose Lydia Elaine. To Fred, the name was like music; and he was charmed from the moment the nurse placed the tiny, perfect bundle in his arms. She even looked like Lorraine, with the same long, aristocratic fingers and thick, auburn hair. Her alert brown eyes danced with the promise of the same mischief, and she looked up at her father with understanding, as if they already shared a secret.

Walter and Ruth came to the hospital, and Fred identified their new granddaughter through the nursery window as she slept in a bassinette. For the first time since Lorraine's death, they seemed alive again. Ruth kissed Fred on both cheeks, and Walter pumped his son's hand, all the while exclaiming over the baby's beauty.

Soon, they heard Nate Klein's booming voice announcing his arrival from a distance down the hall: "So, Frederick, Mazel Tov! I understand that my daughter has given me a grandchild. Sight unseen, I can tell you that she is the most beautiful and the brightest baby in this city, if not the world! Walter, Ruth, congratulations to us all."

Nate thrust flowers and cigars into Fred's arms and inserted himself in front of the glass partition. "No, don't tell me," he said. "I can pick her out. I would know my flesh and blood anywhere."

Fred shot an apologetic glance at his parents who had been politely but firmly elbowed out of the way and now found themselves blocked by Nate Klein's massive frame. "There she is right there," Nate stated authoritatively pointing at Lydia. "Just look at her, the spitting image of her mother."

Walter opened his mouth to speak but thought better of it. Fred was shocked to hear his mother's voice, strong and permitting no contradiction. "Actually, Nate, our granddaughter looks very much like Frederick's sister, Lorraine. Little Lydia is her namesake, you know. I don't think you ever met her, but she had the same artistic hands, long, delicate fingers, and the identical hair color. She was a pianist. Perhaps Lydia will share that talent with her too some day. Now, if you'll excuse me, I'd like another look at her." Ruth sidestepped around Nate, squeezed past, and tapping on the glass, cooed at the sleeping baby.

"Yes, well, I think we'll look in on Deborah," Nate said, taking his wife's arm and relieving Fred of the flowers. "Cigars all around, Fred. This is a great day." He walked off in the direction of Deborah's hospital room, passing out cigars to doctors and orderlies as he went.

CHAPTER 19

A S FRED'S FAMILY GREW and flourished in Philadelphia, the war in Europe raged. American attitude toward the war and involvement of the United States continued to waver.

Everything changed on December 7, 1941. It was a Sunday, and the house was quiet. Fred was at home enjoying the leisurely morning. Deborah was indulging in what Fred called her "day off", sleeping deeply in the adjoining room. As had become his weekend habit in his three months of fatherhood, Fred bathed and fed Lydia; and she now watched him from her playpen while he performed another, much longer-established rite, working the Sunday *New York Times* crossword puzzle. He had never lost his affinity for word games, and he had become so proficient at such brainteasers that he used a fountain pen instead of pencil to increase the challenge.

Finishing the puzzle and the weekly cryptogram, he turned on the radio. A few notes of music were abruptly curtailed by the interruption of an authoritative newscaster's voice, "We interrupt this program to bring you a special news bulletin. The Japanese have attacked Pearl Harbor, Hawaii by air. Three of the eight battleships have been sunk, and the others have been severely damaged. A total of nineteen ships have been sunk or disabled. The Japanese also have destroyed approximately 250 airplanes, and more than 2400 American military personnel and civilians are dead."

The firm voice continued, but Fred couldn't bear to hear any more. He lifted Lydia into his arms and held her protectively to his chest as he crossed to the bedroom door in a few quick, long strides. He sat down on the edge of the bed, still clutching Lydia. She continued to grasp the buttons on his shirt, and Fred patted her back distractedly.

He looked down at Deborah's sleeping form. The world had stopped turning, yet she slept, and Lydia fussed good-naturedly as though nothing had happened. He shook Deborah's shoulder lightly but insistently. She rolled over onto her back and stretched before opening her eyes.

"The Japanese have attacked the U.S. fleet at Pearl Harbor," he said without introduction. "There can be no neutrality now, Deborah. Those sons-of-bitches don't know what they've done. America won't take this lying down. It will mean world war."

Deborah pushed herself up against the headboard and rubbed the sleep out of her eyes. "What will you do, Fred?" she asked, instantly alert. Fred's face was grim. He handed Lydia to her mother and paced the floor.

"Join up, I guess. That's what every able-bodied American man will do now that we've been attacked. I've got a lot of skills the war effort will be able to use. I was a champion middleweight boxer in college, you know. Besides that, I've got my law degree; and I might even be able to help out with cryptography. You know, put all these years of solving word puzzles to good use by inventing secret codes for us or breaking the ciphers of the Gerries or the Japs." The more Fred ranted, the more agitated he became.

Deborah looked horrified. "Frederick Green, I'll tell you a couple of things that you've got that you seem to have forgotten about. You've got a wife and a child, for God's sake. You're also not exactly the typical age for the cannon fodder that joins the army."

"What are you saying, Deborah? Are you saying I shouldn't even try to enlist? What kind of a man wouldn't join up to defend his family, if not his country? What kind of life would any of us have if we fail to defend ourselves?" Lydia, far too young to understand the substance of her parents' argument, still sensed their anger and began to cry, burying her face in her mother's neck.

"Now see what you've done?" Deborah asked. "I can't stop you, especially if you think you have some responsibility greater than the one you owe us."

Deborah threw back the bedcovers and carried Lydia from the room as the radio blared further details of the attack on Pearl Harbor and Roosevelt's declaration of war on Japan. There was no doubt that Japan would reciprocate and that the Axis Powers, Germany and Italy, would follow suit. He could hear her on the telephone complaining to her father. She rushed to him, as she always did in any perceived crisis, and was asking Nate to intervene with Fred to prevent him from volunteering.

Despite Deborah's feelings, Fred went the next day to Philadelphia's Army Recruiting center. He had waited in line for two hours with what seemed like every male in the city who was or could pass for seventeen or older.

Finally, Fred stood in front of the desk and looked the sergeant in the eye. "I'm twenty-five years old. I have a wife and a baby daughter. I am a graduate of the University of Pennsylvania law school, and I was an inter-collegiate boxing champion in college. I also..." He hesitated before continuing. "I also have been solving word puzzles all of my life, and I think I might be able to, as you say, 'contribute to the war effort' by joining up and working in cryptography."

The sergeant looked up from his stack of paperwork and asked, "Crypto what?"

"The breaking of codes," Fred explained evenly. "Don't you have a test for something like that?"

"Look, your local draft board has made it clear that, for now, you're exempt from military service. Married, a father, and, it says here on your form, the only living son of your parents." He looked around Fred's stiff and unyielding body at the ever-lengthening queue. "Listen, if you've really got the skills you say with the code breaking, there is a test; but it's a civilian test. You'll have to come back on Friday for that. The army will be testing for special skills civilian personnel at 09:00. Hey, don't take it so hard. If you help the army out like that, you're still doing your bit." He leaned around Fred again and waved the next boy, a shaggy-haired teenager with pimples on his face, over to his desk. The interview was over.

"Thank you, sergeant. I'll be back on Friday."

Fred left the recruitment office and headed toward his office on foot. He was tired to the bone. He knew that Deborah, and his parents for that matter, would be relieved that he couldn't enlist, and he supposed a part of him felt that way too, but there was another part that felt rejected and emasculated at this crucial time in history when the whole world seemed to teeter on the edge of a black abyss. He reached his office and unlocked the door. He sat down behind his desk and stretched his long legs out in front of him. Maybe the sergeant was right. Of course, he was. There was more than one way to do his bit. He would go back on Friday and take that special skills civilian test. He might never hold a weapon, but he could help break the backs of the Germans and Japanese in his own way.

He picked up the newspaper that he bought from the stand on the corner of Fourteenth and Walnut Street. The headlines screamed about the German advances in Europe. He thumbed the pages in frustration until his eyes came to rest on a small article buried deep in the news section. The small title read, "Germans Rounding up the Jews." The article was based on the account of a young man who had escaped from the Germans by crouching for eleven hours in a makeshift space behind the radiator grill of a lorry driven across the border by a sympathetic German cabinetmaker. The journalist reiterated the spreading belief that the Jews of Europe were being taken to forced labor camps, but the young man insisted that they were the victims of a planned and systematic mass genocide by the Third Reich. The thought of contributing to the defeat of the Nazis with only his pen made the bitter taste of gall rise in the back of his throat.

When Fred arrived back at the recruitment center on Friday morning, he was surprised at the number of other applicants who had come to take the test. Many, like him, appeared to be educated professionals. Others were older than the typical G.I. but perhaps possessed some necessary trade skills or other special abilities. As he waited, Fred was reminded of an old lawyer joke that his father told him and found exceptionally funny. "A lawyer calls a plumber to his office to unclog a drain in his bathroom sink," Walter said, barely able to contain his laughter. "The plumber spends about five minutes in the lawyer's bathroom; and when he comes out, he says to the lawyer, 'The drain is unclogged, and that will be fifty dollars for my time.' 'Fifty dollars,' the lawyer yells. 'I'm a lawyer, and I don't even get fifty dollars for five minutes of my time.' 'I know,' agrees the plumber, 'neither did I when I was a lawyer!'"

Fred looked around at the eclectic group of men waiting with him and smiled as he recalled his father's glee. *The world's at war, and I'm in line with lawyers and plumbers,* he thought wryly. *And they probably need the plumbers a whole lot more than they need the lawyers.*

Fred sat for the written test and was told a week later that he qualified for a special civilian group that would assist the army in decoding and cryptography. He was satisfied that he could do work of value, and he knew that Deborah would be happy that he would not be on active military duty. As he made his way home, Fred took small satisfaction in the fact that his wife's and his father-in-law's repeated attempts to persuade him not to serve had amounted to a colossal waste of their time and effort. Once again in his life, he had been excluded by circumstance. This time, it had not been because of his religion, his finances, or his social standing. This time, he was just too damn old.

Over the next several months, the war ground on. Fred was busier than ever trying to maintain his law practice and fulfill his duties as a civilian employee of the army. The ironic repercussion of his having been rejected for military service was that he seemed to be one of the few younger lawyers still practicing in Philadelphia, which meant that Fred now had a plethora of clients requesting his representation, and his law practice thrived.

Amid the grim resolution that marked the faces of most Americans as they went about their daily lives collecting tin cans, growing "victory gardens," buying war bonds, and generally tightening their belts in support of the war effort, Lydia provided Fred with a sense of normalcy. He could forget his fatigue at the end of each long day when he saw her outstretched arms and smile of recognition. He could shut the door on the ever-increasing galaxy of yellow stars in the neighborhood's front windows connoting that the family had a serviceman abroad and, in a world gone mad, retreat into his daughter's innocence. Behind his closed door, Lydia helped him create a microcosm of sanity. Her wavy auburn hair and bittersweet chocolate eyes reminded him of Lorraine. Yet, Lydia seemed to have been born with a heady self-confidence that would immunize her against Lorraine's virulent need for the approval of others. Fred had read that what we love most in our children is the reflection of ourselves, but what he cherished above all in his infant daughter was that quality of self-possession and gregarious ease that he most lacked.

Lydia saw none of his sores. With her, he was never awkward or shy. He did not misstep or misspeak. He did not fail. To her, he was *Daddy*, a word synonymous with perfection to the laughing toddler; and by the time she became old enough to realize that her father was human, with frailties just like everyone else, it would not matter to her. He would always be *Daddy*; and that would always be more than enough.

On one such blustery spring day in 1942, Fred turned his key in the lock and pushed against his front door. The door would not give way, and he saw that there was a large cardboard carton obstructing it. He pushed harder until he had made a space large enough to slip through and then locked the door behind him. He could hear Deborah preparing dinner in the kitchen. After hanging up his coat and stowing his hat and briefcase in the foyer closet, he turned his attention to the carton. It was filled with an assortment of French wine and the twelve year old scotch that Nate Klein favored. "Deborah, I'm home," he called. "What's all this wine and liquor?"

Deborah appeared from the kitchen at the back of the house preceded by Lydia, who moved with short, unsteady steps toward her father's voice. Fred scooped her up in his arms and kissed her plump cheek. "Someone who works for my father dropped that off this afternoon," she said casually. "I left it there because I thought you'd want to put it away in the liquor cabinet. I know how you like to keep things organized."

Fred twisted a bottle so that he could read the label more easily. "Macallan twelve-year-old scotch was expensive before the war, Deborah. I can't imagine what it must cost now or how difficult it is to come by. Where does your father get this stuff?"

"Honestly, Frederick," Deborah sighed. "What difference does that make? My father does a nice thing, and all you can do is make something negative out of it. Just get the bottles out of the foyer before Lydia trips on them, and come to dinner." Watching her return to the kitchen, Fred noticed that she was wearing another new pair of shoes. Rationing and price controls had been imposed on many things—including shoes; but the Kleins, and through them their daughter, still seemed to have unbridled access to anything they wanted. Food and wine flowed, but not so information. Fred had all but given up on asking Nate about his work because his queries were invariably met with a benign smile, evasive humor, or a change of subject. Asking Deborah was worse, because she became tightlipped and sullen or flamed in angry defense of her father and his shrouded business dealings. Fred's suspicions hung between them, an invisible curtain that divided his family.

CHAPTER 20

BRUCE MILLER ALWAYS ENJOYED the private refuge of Nate Klein's office. With dark, walnut paneling and overstuffed furniture, the room almost felt like a gentleman's club. There was a bottomless decanter of twelve-year-old, rare scotch and the finest cut crystal glasses on the mahogany credenza behind Nate's massive partner's desk. The vegetable dyes of the antique Persian rug had faded to warm, earthy tones. Bruce stretched his legs out and sank back against the sofa cushions. He laced his fingers behind his head and closed his eyes, imagining that it was all his, then heard the doorknob turn and instantly straightened his posture as Nate rounded the door.

"Hello, Nate. I got here a little early. I hope you don't mind me waiting in here." Bruce smiled ingratiatingly.

Nate's eyes skimmed over the room as if he were checking that everything was just as he left it. Noting no disturbance, he smiled back at Bruce and headed to his desk. "Would you like a drink?" he asked, pouring himself a generous shot of his favorite scotch. "I know we don't usually indulge during business hours, but this deal that I have to tell you about is too sweet not to toast." Without waiting for Bruce to answer, Nate poured him a drink and thrust the glass into Bruce's hand. "Here's to the infinite wisdom of the United States government and specifically to the convoluted rules of the Office of Price Administration. Thanks to them and their interference in the marketplace, we have a great opportunity." Bruce raised his glass, paying tribute to Nate, waiting for him to explain how the OPA, part of the alphabet soup of federal government agencies that had sprung up during the war, figured in Nate's latest scheme. Nate took a seat in one of his leather club chairs and inhaled a long pull of his cocktail.

"Brucie, we're about to get even richer in the rubber tire business. As you know, in order to divert tire production to the war effort, the OPA has rationed the sale of rubber tires or tubes to the public and requires a buyer to produce a coupon or permit from their local rationing board establishing that the use of the vehicle is essential to the greater good of the war effort. There's a big market for tires right now, and people are willing to pay almost anything to get them. But the problem is they can't get the required coupons from the rationing board. The regulations require that for every sale you must maintain on file a rationing coupon or show a bill of sale to another tire dealer. That's our opportunity. All we have to do is show a bogus sale to a dealer in another state. Any auditor looking at our records will think that we have complied and most likely won't follow up to verify receipt since the other tire dealership is in another jurisdiction. And here's the thing. If we're unlucky enough to get audited by a real hard nose, I have assurances that my connection at OPA will give it a pass. Then, of course, we sell the tires at a markup the customers are willing to pay. The customers get the goods they need, and we get rich." Nate sat back in his chair and took another swig of scotch.

Bruce thought for a minute and sipped his drink, then sat up straight in his chair. "I can make this happen, Nate. I have a driver named Eddie Lomax who I trust completely, and he can help us. I've already got several customers willing to pay double to get tires for their personal requirements, but they can't get the rationing certificates. I'll collect the money from them to buy the tires, and we'll give Eddie explicit instructions on making the transfer. He'll make his runs at night and shift the tires from his truck to the customer's truck that will be waiting to take them away. We'll bill the tires out to a dealer in another state, say the one in Camden, New Jersey. It's foolproof."

"I knew you were the man for the job," Nate affirmed, grinning like a fox.

Bruce set his glass down on the table and extended his hand in a gesture of solidarity. His brow was smooth, but his heart beat faster from anticipation. "I'm your man, Nate," Bruce assured him. "Consider this little project done."

CHAPTER 21

IN THE EARLY SUMMER of 1943, some fourteen months since the government imposed rationing affecting tires, Nate Klein's secretary buzzed the intercom from her desk just outside his spacious office. "Yes, Emily?" Nate asked.

"Mr. Klein, there is a gentleman here from the OPA to see you. He says he is with the Philadelphia office. His name is Otis Jenkins."

Nate stiffened. He straightened his tie and rose from the high-backed leather chair behind his desk, affixing on his face as pleasant a smile as he could muster. "Send him in, Emily." As the door opened, Nate extended his hand.

Otis Jenkins looked to be no match for Nate Klein. His bland gray suit was rumpled, his tie nondescript, and his black leather briefcase was battered and worn. But behind his horn-rimmed glasses, his sharp eyes burned like small coals behind his thick lenses, making a quick, thorough survey of Nate's office. He met Nate's extended hand with a perfunctory handshake. "Thank you for seeing me, Mr. Klein. I know you're a busy man."

Nate gestured to the chair in front of his desk. "We're all busy these days, Mr. Jenkins. Have a seat. Can I have Emily get you any coffee, a soda perhaps?" Nate remained standing.

"No, thank you, Mr. Klein. I won't trouble you for too much of your time." He unsnapped his briefcase and removed a thick manila folder that he placed on Nate's desk. "The reason I am here, sir, is that your business has been under investigation by the U.S. government for some time. We have reason to believe that one of your subsidiaries, the Quality Tire Company, has been in serious violation of the rationing program." He held Nate's eyes in his beady lock, daring him to blink. Nate did not.

"Mr. Jenkins, I am sure you are mistaken. I am a law-abiding, patriotic American, and I have only those who are likewise disposed working for me. I have lawyers on my payroll as well as outside legal counsel whose responsibility it is to keep abreast of all of the government laws and regulations that pertain to our diversified businesses and see to it that we are one hundred percent in compliance. One hundred percent, Mr. Jenkins," Nate said, enunciating each syllable. He spread his bejeweled fingers across the surface of the manila folder but did not pick it up, as if to imply that its contents were irrelevant.

Otis Jenkins was unimpressed. His words remained measured and his voice even. He pushed the manila folder closer to Nate. "The purpose of my coming here today is to inform you that your office will be subject to a federal government audit beginning a week from Monday. In this file, you will find requests for a variety of records that you are required to make available to our auditors, including tire rationing coupons, one to substantiate the sale of each tire, or verifiable records that you've sold them to another dealer, dating from the inception of our program."

Nate suppressed the urge to squash Otis Jenkins like a bug. He maintained his well-practiced smile and came around his desk. "Like I've been saying, Mr. Jenkins, we're in complete compliance. I feel certain that your auditors will find everything in order."

"Very well." Otis Jenkins stated matter-of-factly, as he snapped his briefcase shut and made for the door. He still had his hand on the doorknob when he turned to Nate and said, "Then, you have nothing to worry about. My team and I will be back at 9am one week from this coming Monday morning." He stepped through the open door and headed for the elevator.

Emily O'Hara followed him with her eyes as they passed her desk. "What are you staring at?" Nate barked, framed in his doorway. She lowered her eyes to her typewriter.

"Nothing, sir."

Nate glared at her, and his door made an uncharacteristic, audible bang as it slammed behind him. He grabbed the telephone almost knocking the cradle to the floor and dialed Leonard Carmichael, his contact at the Philadelphia regional office of the OPA. "Leonard," he yelled, "what the hell is going on? Some self-righteous little shit named Otis Jenkins from your office just left here threatening me over some alleged violation of the tire rationing program. He says we've been under investigation for quite some time, and he's demanding all kinds of records for an audit starting on Monday. Why the hell didn't you give me a heads up about this? I thought we had a deal." Nate's breath continued to come in hot gusts as he awaited a reply.

"Sorry, Nate," Leonard wheezed. "Two months ago, I was transferred to the gasoline division. I don't know anything about this."

"What?" Nate fumed. "Your mother has continued to live in one of my apartment houses at a reduced rent, hasn't she? How come you didn't let me know about your transfer?"

"Well, I thought I still could be of use to you, Nate," Leonard demurred. "What I can tell you is that Jenkins is a bulldog, and he won't back down. Once he gets a hold of your pants leg, you won't easily shake him off. I guess I should've...."

"Shut up, Leonard, you useless dumbass!" Nate slammed the receiver down so hard that the cradle jumped off the shiny surface of the desk.

Moments later, his voice boomed over the intercom. "Get me Bruce Miller right away."

Chapter 22

BRUCE MILLER NEARLY WORE a hole in the Persian carpet as he paced back and forth in front of Nate's desk listening to him recount his meeting with Otis Jenkins. "The little worm was cool, I'll give him that," Nate stormed. "He obviously thinks he's got something on us. Says he'll be back a week from Monday with some other bean counters, and he left this file listing what they want to see." He flicked the folder sardonically with the back of his hand as he spoke.

"So, what does it mean, Mr. Klein? Do we have to let 'em in? Do they need a court order? Can they get one? I mean, we can be burned as much by what they don't find as by what they do! What do we do?"

Nate was frustrated by Bruce's barrage of questions and his lack of answers. He had promoted him over and over again because he was the kind of worker that never had questions. Nate wanted a solution. "I'm not looking for questions, Bruce," Nate snapped. "I'm looking for answers. That's why I called you in here. The way I see it, we have only two options. We either can find someone with the clout to take the heat off of us, or we can come up with some way to cooperate with the Feds without giving them what they want."

Bruce stopped pacing and looked at his boss in confusion. "Why would someone...? How can we cooperate?"

"I'll tell you what, Bruce. Let's both just think about it for a while. In the meantime, don't answer any calls from the government." Nate steered Bruce toward the door. "I think I'll call Frederick and see what he has to say. Put that brain of his to work for us! He's a rising star, that one, a real thinker! He's always been creative in drafting contracts in our favor or in negotiating dispute resolution. We're lucky we can keep this in the family and have someone we can trust to figure a way out of this mess. After all, he'll recognize that we're hardly the only corporate citizen in America who thinks the government should keep its nose out of our business. We made a deal among gentlemen for the purchase and sale of those tires, and no government lackey should have the right to tell us what's fair. Frederick will understand that. He'll come up with some way to send that Jenkins fellow packing."

"I'm sure I can come up with something, Mr. Klein," Bruce said, attempting to regain his boss's confidence and inwardly seething at the mention of Fred. "Just let me know if there's anything you want me to do, boss."

"I'll let you know what Fred comes up with. Emily, get me a cup of coffee. Two sugars. And get me Frederick Green on the line." Once again, the door to his office slammed shut.

Nate sat in the Corinthian leather chair behind his desk and drummed his fingers on the arm impatiently. He stood and walked to the window, surveying the bustling scene on Walnut Street fourteen stories below. "Damn people look like an ant colony," he muttered to himself. "Emily, what's taking so long?" he shouted through the closed door, his words seeming to ricochet back at him and bounce off the paneled walls. He took a rattling, deep breath through his nose and finger combed his thick grey hair with both of his meaty hands. "Fred will know how we should play this," he said, trying to calm himself. "He doesn't have any love for the government or going down the trodden path either. He could've taken the offer from that fancy law firm or come to work for me, for that matter, but he didn't. He understands about wanting to be your own man. Hell, that's what we have in common! We're both salmon swimming upstream." The bleating of the intercom buzzer on his desk interrupted his mumbling.

"Mr. Green is on the line," Emily said. "Should I put him through?"

"Yes," Nate shouted.

Then, picking up the receiver, he said without preamble, "I've got a problem."

CHAPTER 23

BRUCE MILLER WAS BACK in his office. Shouting to his secretary to hold his calls, he opened the bottom drawer of his desk and removed the flask that he kept there for times such as this, times when the weight of the masquerade he was performing became almost unbearable. He took a drink, and the heat of the bourbon seared his stomach. He wiped his mouth with the back of his hand and took another swig, letting his thoughts take over. *How much longer will I have to play the role of simpleton? For years now, I've done Nate's bidding, convincing him that my loyalty was what made me his most valuable asset. I've stood by while that Ivy League pussy, Freddy Green, stole Deborah and, with his worthless degrees and book smarts, established himself as Nate's favorite. .*

Who does he think has really built Quality Tire Company, the biggest moneymaker at Klein Industries? I have, that's who! All the time that he's been off gallivanting with the big wigs, having his smug puss photographed for the papers, I've been working every day to grow this business.

And now that Nate's coupon scheme is about to blow up in his face, who do you think is going to take the fall? Not Nate! He's successfully insulated himself from the tire business with his holding company, and he'll create as much distance between him and me as he can. And clean hands Freddy will receive Nate's admiration for doing his lawyer dance. By rights, when the old man is gone, this business should be mine. But it won't be, the way things stand now. That schmuck, Freddy, thinks he's played things just right. Marries the boss's daughter and then says he doesn't want to come into the business. Says he's going to make it on his own as a highfalutin lawyer. And Nate saying he respects that, always talking about what a good head Fred has and what an independent thinker he is, when it's so obvious that Freddy is just waiting in line to take the rest of what's mine. Now, just because there's a wrinkle with the government, Nate thinks that wuss, Freddy, will know how to handle it instead of turning to me. Well, you don't solve many real problems with what they teach you in books, and this is a real big problem. You solve it with what you learn on the streets from the hoi polloi where it's down and dirty. They make me sick, the pair of them. His highness and his heir. Uncle Sam shows up, and Nate struts and preens as if that's going to make him go away. When that doesn't work, he calls Freddy. Does he actually think I don't see the contempt behind that practiced smile when he talks to me? That smile that never reaches his eyes?

Bruce's heart was racing, and his breath was coming fast. *Think,* he demanded of himself, *think!* He sat down behind his desk and tried to slow his breathing. He closed his eyes and rubbed his face with the palms of his hands. He massaged his temples.

Bruce knew all too well what would come next. Nate would send for him to sit in on the meeting with Fred, but he wouldn't be a full participant. Nate and Fred would engage in a dialogue that both believed was over his head.

They would not ask his opinion, but at the end, they would give him instructions to carry out. *Like a well trained dog.*

His intercom buzzer sounded. "Mr. Miller, Mr. Klein has asked that you join him in his office right away." Bruce smirked. *Bingo,* he thought to himself. He stood and smoothed back his hair, then walked to Nate's office and knocked on the door.

"Bruce, come in. Frederick has just arrived. I've been filling him in on our little predicament. Have a seat." Fred stood, and the two young men shook hands. Bruce took the empty chair in the pair that faced Nate's desk. He observed that Fred had made a few notes on a yellow legal pad. The word *"COUPONS"* was written in large, capital letters and underlined several times.

"Why don't you fill Bruce in on where we are, Fred?" Nate asked.

"Well, the main thing that we've established is that we've got a problem with the coupons. The way the tire rationing program is supposed to work is that no sale of tires can take place unless a coupon is exchanged for the product at the time of payment. So, the problem is not with the sales that any division of Klein Industries may have made, but rather with the fact that it did not accept coupons equaling the total number of tires sold. In other words, when the government auditors arrive here a week from Monday, they are going to begin what is called Discovery. That means that they have subpoenaed records pertaining to each sale of tires since the inception of tire rationing early in the war; and if Klein Industries can't produce such records, including the coupons, they could be deemed in violation of the rationing program, which includes fines and even potential criminal charges if they deem the offenses egregious. It all comes down to how to explain the missing coupons." Fred paused and looked at Nate and Bruce. Bruce's face was impassive; Nate's looked like an overripe plum. Nate sputtered in reply.

"Goddamned government has gotten too big, I tell you. I remember a time when business was conducted on a handshake. Now, you could die in the avalanche of paper the government puts out; and everyone, starting with FDR on down, thinks they know better than I do how to run my affairs. Who are they to say who can sell what to whom and at what price? Rationing, price controls …bullshit! Some four-eyed little shit working in some Washington cubbyhole has the bright idea that laws and rules that force people to do things their narrow minded way are better than a free market. The war? It's just an excuse for those power mongers to order all the rest of us who work for a living to kowtow to them so they can get reelected. I haven't done a fucking thing wrong. The only thing I did was take care of my customers, but we could go down just the same. Fred, I'm counting on you to come up with something to get us out of this jam. Sons of bitches…!" Nate wiped the perspiration from his furrowed brow and, deflated, collapsed into his desk chair.

Fred hadn't seen this side of Nate before. He squirmed uncomfortably in his seat and rifled through the papers in the file that Nate had provided containing the government's subpoenas.

"Maybe I can request some extra time before the commencement of the audit to go over the records myself. At least then I could see the extent of the alleged violation. It would almost be better if you had no records," he mused aloud. "After all, their only proof of a violation of any magnitude is the absence of those coupons. Without establishing what records you *don't* have, they really haven't got a thing. Oh, well, not much help there." Fred managed a hollow laugh. "Don't worry, Nate. I'll contact the government's lawyer and try to get a continuance. In the meantime, I'm sure that I can find a legal basis to challenge their case."

Fred began stuffing the files in his briefcase. In the room that just moments ago had reverberated with the angry tones of Nate's diatribe, there was now a heavy silence. Nate stood by the window, turned his back on his son-in-law and Bruce, and watched the traffic on the street below. Bruce rose, sensing that the meeting was over.

"We're all counting on you, Fred. If there's a way out of this, we both know you'll find it." Bruce clapped Fred on the back and ushered him to the elevator.

When the doors closed on Bruce's supercilious smile, Fred rotated his shoulders in a quick, self-conscious movement to throw off the revolting sensation that Bruce's hand was still there. But he couldn't shake Nate's words: *I haven't done a fucking thing wrong.* It was clear that Nate's heated outburst was as much a self-justification as a barebones statement of his business philosophy. Fred's years of unanswered or avoided questions devolved into a morass of certainty that Nate was on the wrong side of the law. *Nate expects me to misrepresent the facts,* he thought. *I don't know if I'm willing to do that. Where do I go from here?*

Bruce turned away from the elevator and began to walk toward his office when he stopped to pick up a shiny object that caught his attention on the carpet. He immediately recognized it as one of the gold cufflinks that Fred had been wearing. He pocketed it and continued down the hall, worry about the audit and his future creasing his face.

Unable to concentrate, Bruce left the building and walked to the Horn and Hardart Automat. He sat alone, his coffee going cold on the table in front of him, thinking about the problem until a solution began to germinate. He reached into his pocket and began feeling among the change absently until his fingers closed around the cool metal of a small, round object. He withdrew the cufflink from the depths of his pocket and brought it up in front of his face for closer examination. The scales of justice were deeply etched into the cufflink's gleaming surface. Bruce flipped it over in his hand, and his eyes widened as they came to rest on the engraving, *FMG*. A smile slowly spread across his face. He carefully placed it back into the secure depth of his pocket and thought, *Let's see you talk your way out of this one, college boy.*

He pushed his chair back from the table, having made up his mind. The cold air on his face felt bracing as he stepped out the door of Horn and Hardart's. He felt a surge of energy and a growing sense of confidence as he hastened toward Quality Tire Company.

CHAPTER 24

NATE KLEIN WAS JARRED awake by the insistent ringing of his telephone. He had fallen asleep in his favorite chair with the newspaper spread across his lap. The base fell from the side table as he fumbled for the receiver. "What?" he yelled into the darkness. "Oh, hell! I'll be right there." He hurriedly threw on the trousers and shirt that hung on his valet from the previous day, grabbed his keys, wallet, and watch from the top of his bureau, and rushed to his car. As he approached the central office of Quality Tire Company, he could see hideous red tongues of flame licking the windows from a block away. A crowd had gathered on the sidewalk, and three fire engines blocked the street.

Nate abandoned his car among the tangle of vehicles in front of the building and began to elbow his way toward the front of the gathering throng. A cordon of police officers and firemen were stationed at the front entrance keeping the spectators at bay. *Damned curiosity seekers,* he thought as he pushed ahead.

"Excuse me," he yelled to no one in particular. "This is my building. What's going on?" He saw a fireman, who seemed to be in charge, screaming into a walkie-talkie. He had a gold shield on his hat and a fancier uniform with gold braided epaulettes and brass buttons. With one more strategically placed elbow, Nate was standing in front of him on the opposite side of a yellow police tape barrier. "My name's Nathan Klein, chairman of the board of Nathan Klein Industries," he shouted over the crowd noise. "This building is the central office of Quality Tire Company, one of our divisions. What happened here?"

The fireman barked something to one of his subordinates who was running inside the building and cast an annoyed glance at Nate. "You need to step back, sir. This fire has not been contained." He started to turn away, but Nate persevered.

"I'm not trying to interfere," he insisted. "I just need to know whether my building is in jeopardy. Do you have any idea what caused the fire? I have a duty to…."

"That's up to the investigators to determine. It looks like it started in the electrical room. You'd better get back, sir," the fireman urged.

Suddenly, there was an explosion from one of the upper stories, and glass shards rained down on the onlookers below. There was a collective gasp as part of the roof caved in. The policemen raised their billy clubs to waist height and began pushing the crowd back and dispersing the bystanders for their own safety. Nate found himself pressed into the mass of human flesh once again.

Over the din, a familiar voice shouted at him. "Mr. Klein, over here." It was Bruce Miller. He signaled to Nate that he would meet him across the street and out of harm's way. Nate kept his eye on Bruce and forced his way back through the crowd that now surged away from the fire. When the two men were reunited, both were breathing heavily and wore a sweaty sheen on their faces.

"This is some kind of shit," Bruce said, trying to smooth the wrinkles out of his suit and digging in his pocket for a handkerchief with which to cover his nose and mouth. "I came as fast as I could after you called, but I never expected anything like this. They'll be lucky at this point if they're able to prevent the fire from spreading to the adjoining buildings and the rest of the block. It looks like the gates of hell over there." Bruce shielded his eyes and craned his neck in the direction of the building. He shook his head hopelessly.

"What the hell could have happened?" Nate asked bleakly. "The whole thing's spread so fast that the building's going to be nothing but a pile of rubble. All the inventory, the sales records, and the coupons…." He gripped Bruce's arm, and their eyes locked in a moment of realization.

"You know," Nate said with a thinly veiled smile, "that fire chief was right. This isn't a safe place for us to be. Whole thing could come down any minute. Damn shame, a goddamn shame, but you call Worldwide Insurance first thing in the morning to make a claim; and hopefully, we can document enough of the inventory to collect in full. As to OPA, Fred was right when he said they wouldn't have a case if the coupons were legitimately missing."

He cuffed Bruce on the back of the neck, and they headed their separate ways away from the scene of their destruction and redemption.

CHAPTER 25

CAPTAIN MICHAEL TIMOTHY DOYLE of the Philadelphia Fire Department was chosen to lead the investigation because of his reputation as an insightful and analytical investigator. He had twenty years of experience, and both his father and older brother had been firemen with the force. He worked his way up through the ranks and developed a specialty in arson investigation.

Mike also had grown up with Nate Klein in South Philadelphia, and neither friend had forgotten the other along their respective paths to success. Over the years, Mike had connected Nate with an official at City Hall who turned a blind eye to construction code irregularities or expedited forms that hastened the permitting process on one of Nate's development ventures. Each time he did, Nate rewarded Mike handsomely. Mike had paid for both of his daughters' weddings and nice cars for all three of his boys out of what Nate called "tips." He also was able to fulfill his wife Maeve's lifelong dream of touring Ireland and finding her ancestral home as a gift for their silver wedding anniversary. When Maeve died three years ago, Nate and his family came to the funeral in force. His eyes were wet when he hugged Mike at the wake, and he promised him that he would continue to take care of him. Nate had been true to his word, and now it was Mike's turn to repay him.

Only a day after the fire, the two old friends embraced in a brotherly hug. "How're you doin', buddy?" Mike asked. "That fire left a whole lot a nothin' at your place," he added shaking his head. "I gotta tell you 'cause you're my friend. It looks like arson. You know anyone who'd want to burn down your warehouse?"

"I've made enemies over the years, Mike, but I can't think of anyone who hates me enough to burn down my warehouse. I'll have to think about it. As for anyone who works for me, I've got a lot of money tied up in those tires, and until the insurance company makes us whole, Quality Tire is in trouble. Rationing has limited our sales anyway, and losing our inventory could put us under or certainly put the people who work for the tire division in jeopardy, so they certainly don't have a motive. I know you think it's arson, but I have a hard time believing it.

"Well, you know I'll keep you in the loop," Mike assured him. "My guys are searching for trace evidence, anything that will show how the fire started and who started it."

"Isn't this some shit?" Nate asked. "I remember when our biggest problems were football, girls, and getting drunk." Mike looked at him, an expression of sadness creasing his ruddy face. "Hey, what is it, man? You know you can tell me."

"It's Maureen," Mike said almost as an exhalation. "You always called my little girl 'Bonnie Maureen,' remember? Doc says she needs an operation for a congenital heart defect, but there's a doctor in Boston, name of Robert Gross, who's pioneering a technique to fix it." Wringing his hands, he added, shame in his voice, "I don't have the money, Nate."

"Hey, you're like a brother to me, Mike, and Bonnie Maureen is like my daughter. Say no more. You start making arrangements for that operation and consider all the expenses taken care of. Got something in your eye?" Nate asked, as Mike rubbed his eyes with the heel of his hand.

"Nah, I'm all right, but I owe you one." Mike smiled, regaining his composure. "I gotta go, but thanks, and I'll keep you up to date about Maureen and… that fire." The two men hugged again and walked in opposite directions down the sidewalk.

CHAPTER 26

T HE FOLLOWING MONDAY, when Otis Jenkins and his team of OPA auditors appeared at the headquarters of Nathan Klein industries, they were escorted into Nate's office. "We're here to commence the audit," Mr. Jenkins said without preamble.

"I'm sorry, Mr. Jenkins," Nate said, rising from his desk chair. "You haven't heard? There was a terrible fire at the central office of Quality Tire last Wednesday night, and it destroyed everything. I mean everything, right down to the last tire. There is no tire office, nothing. It's all gone"

Otis Jenkins blanched. "You don't have any records or files anywhere else?"

"We keep our financial records such as our balance sheet, income statement and banking records here at Klein Industries headquarters. But nothing else. It all went up in flames." he replied.

"That's mighty convenient and certainly suspicious. I'll have to report the matter to OPA to see where we go from here. I'm sure there will be an investigation."

After a month, Worldwide Insurance Company was questioning whether the fire was an act of arson. The case was still under investigation by both the Philadelphia Police and Fire Departments, and OPA was awaiting the results. The preliminary findings of the investigators had determined that the fire had started near the electrical panel, but there were several other places where they found slight remnants of combustible materials, indicating the possibility of arson. In fact, the intense heat generated by the burning rubber tires had destroyed almost everything that was combustible. Nevertheless, neither investigation at this point had ruled out the possibility of arson. Until the case was closed, Nate would not see a penny of the $1,250,000 policy that he carried on the central office of Quality Tire Company and its considerable inventory.

In the meantime, at least, Otis Jenkins and his OPA cohorts had backed off since all of the coupons and files were gone. Despite this favorable development, Nate was never going to be happy. As he sat across from Fred in the bar of the Philmont Country Club, he couldn't help but think that he had gotten a raw deal. After all, Fred would surely have found a legal defense to the charges of violating the rationing program, and now he would be denied the opportunity to exonerate himself and show the government once and for all that they could not put a strangle hold on American business. Moreover, if the insurance company did not pay off, he would have to absorb all of the losses incurred in the fire personally.

Nate drained the last of his martini and pulled the olive off the end of the toothpick between his clenched teeth, tossing the pick onto the table distractedly. "Hell of a mess, Fred. Seems we've just traded one set of g-men for another. The fire has caused Otis Jenkins and Company to back off, but the cops and firemen have been sniffing around the rubble trying to see if they can throw a charge of arson against the wall and make it stick. The minute they found out about the tire rationing investigation, they puffed up like bantam roosters and started strutting their stuff making all kinds of insinuations about what they call the 'convenience' of the fire and squawking about our having something to hide! Damn little peckers! They make me sick."

Fred knew that the investigation was still open because he was present in his capacity as Nate's attorney when the police and fire department detectives assigned to the case questioned Nate about his alibi for the night of the fire. Fred was more concerned with the fact that they had come to his office to interview him after Bruce Miller pointedly told them that he had met with Fred and Nate earlier that day about the federal government's allegations. While Fred's rendition of his activities lined up with theirs to a point, he recognized uneasily that he had no verifiable alibi for his movements for the rest of the day and evening. He had taken a long walk after leaving the meeting in order to assess Nate's legal position. Afterwards, he went home, but the house was empty because Deborah was at a meeting of a community action committee that collected scrap metal for the war effort. He was deeply involved in reading case law involving denial of government discovery efforts and successful defenses by those accused of rationing violations when he received a telephone call around 9pm notifying him that the central office of Quality Tire had gone up in flames.

Disconcertingly, Fred also was aware that Deborah provided the basis of Bruce Miller's alibi because the two served on the same community action committee. Deborah spoke to Bruce at the meeting and told police that they were together at the estimated time that the fire started. It irked Fred that his wife had provided staunch support for his earlier rival's alibi while neither she nor anyone else could corroborate that he had been home.

Fred wrapped his long fingers around the base of his glass to steady his hands. He was nervous under Nate's gaze, even though he had done nothing wrong. He knew all too well that circumstantial evidence could bury an innocent man, particularly in instances where he had motive, opportunity, and means to commit the crime. As the son-in-law of the Chief Executive Officer of Nathan Klein Industries, who had full knowledge that Quality Tire was the subject of a federal criminal investigation, he certainly had the motive to torch the evidence. Without any witnesses as to his whereabouts on the night of the fire, he could not substantiate that he had been home at the time of the blaze.

"You met with the fire department detectives, didn't you, Fred?" Nate leaned forward, both hands spread on the table. "What did they ask you, and what did you tell them? I want details." Fred racked his brain about his most recent interrogation.

"Mostly, they wanted to know about our meeting earlier on the day of the fire," he said. "You know, who was there and what they said. I told them that Bruce, you, and I were present at the meeting and that we were discussing the OPA's request for records pertaining to Quality Tire. I said we had every intention of cooperating. But when they began to question the content of our conversation, I invoked the attorney/client privilege, and I could tell the investigator didn't like it."

"Yeah, Bruce said they asked him the same questions, but he didn't know he could invoke attorney/client privilege or take the fifth, so he told them a whole lot more."

Fred winced and hoped that Nate didn't notice. He did remember more. Every detail. He thought about the chief investigator from the fire department, Mike Doyle, his paunch hanging over his belt so that it strained the buttons on his uniform and his beefy fingers flipping through his file as he tried to locate the transcript of Bruce Miller's statement. "We have questioned Mr. Miller about his recollection of his activities on the day in question," he had said, without looking up from his papers. "He is firm in his recall that you made the following statements to him and Mr. Klein at that meeting. 'It would almost be better if you had no records…. Their only proof of a violation of any magnitude is the absence of those coupons. Without establishing what records you don't have, they really haven't got a thing.' Is that correct, Mr. Green? Is that what you said?"

Fred took a deep, calming breath. There still had been no formal accusations, no charges brought. After all, except for the suspicion engendered by the coincidence of the timing of the OPA investigation and the fire, there was nothing to substantiate that the fire was an act of arson. Without evidence tying someone to the means by which the fire had been set, they really had nothing at all.

"You need to calm down, Nate," Fred said finally. "In the case of a fire of this magnitude, a thorough investigation is routine. The authorities are going to talk to everybody with any potential involvement, probably more than once; and they are going to comb through every cinder and ash that are left at the scene until they are satisfied about the cause of the fire. Your becoming apoplectic over this isn't helping the situation. Let's allow everyone to do their jobs, and I'm sure that they will find no credible evidence of wrongdoing. Then, we can devote our energies to the constructive process of locating new space for Quality Tire and resuming business."

Fred sat back in his chair and took a sip of his drink, projecting an aura of composure. Nate, too, appeared more relaxed as he nodded his head in agreement. In truth, Fred was all too aware that he did not have a firm alibi for the night of the fire, and despite the palliative effect that his few well-chosen words had on Nate, Fred could not rid himself of the niggling feeling of unease in his gut.

CHAPTER 27

T HE NEXT MONTH WHILE Nate and Fred were having drinks, Bruce again found himself at the monthly meeting of the Community Action Committee. He was watching Deborah as she prepared to leave. The waning late afternoon sunlight caught the auburn highlights in her hair. Even after childbirth, her waist remained small, and there was still something girl-ish in her laughter. *Damn, she's beautiful.*

As Deborah gathered her purse and shouldered her coat, Bruce fell in beside her. He held the door open, and she ducked under his arm. "Thanks," she said, buttoning her collar against the wind. "I was glad to be here tonight. I feel good about doing my bit for the war effort, even if it means giving up my evening. Besides, it took my mind off those detectives who keep coming by the house to speak to Frederick. He says they've been by his office too. What about you, Bruce? Have they been harassing you, too?"

"Yeah, they're talking to everybody. 'Course, the innocent have noth-ing to worry about, do they? You tell them where you were that night, and somebody backs you up. That's all there is to it. Like me, for example. I was here, with you, at this same monthly meeting, remember? I'm sure Freddy has told them where he was, too. He's the kind of guy who would know exactly where he was. Organized, you know what I mean?" Bruce smiled benignly at Deborah.

Deborah hugged her purse to her chest and shivered in the autumn chill. "We all know Frederick was nowhere near that building when the fire broke out," she affirmed defensively. "But the problem is, he's kind of a loner. He always says that he gets some of his best work done on long walks analyzing the facts of a case. Apparently, that's what he was doing after he met with you and my father that day. Then, he got home after I'd already left for this committee meeting. So, the thing is, nobody saw him."

Looks like old Freddy's between the proverbial rock and a hard place, Bruce thought to himself.

"Oh, that's rough, " he said, feigning sympathy, "Let me know if there's anything I can do. You know I'm always here for you." He stuffed his hands in his pockets and looked down at his shoes, afraid that his show of concern for Deborah might reveal the feelings he still had for her. He smiled at her sheepishly.

"I'm sure the whole thing will blow over," Deborah replied. "Frederick assures me that the entire investigation is standard procedure. I appreciate your support, Bruce." Deborah squeezed his arm with her gloved hand.

"Like I said, I'm here for you." Bruce's skin tingled at the spot where she had lightly touched him.

"Well, I've got to be going. Frederick and I are attending a Philadelphia Bar Association dinner tonight," she said proudly. "I can't be late. I'll see you next month," she added as she hailed a cab.

"Sure, Deborah, I'll be here," Bruce said, with an unexpected deep inhaling and exhaling of his breath before slamming the door of the taxi firmly behind Deborah.

"That damn Fred! She should have been mine," he muttered to himself as he headed home alone.

When Deborah entered the house, she heard Fred in the bedroom and the sound of drawers opening and closing repeatedly.

"Lose something?" she asked, removing her gloves and tossing them onto the bed with her handbag.

Fred was dressed for dinner in a gray suit and starched white shirt. His Countess Mara tie had a regimental stripe in the red and blue colors of the University of Pennsylvania. Deborah surveyed his sartorial splendor admiringly until she noticed that one of the French cuffs of his shirt hung open at the wrist.

"Missing a cufflink?" she asked. Fred was fastidious in his attire, and his personal fetish was a collection of unique cufflinks. "Which one? Can I help you look? You're making us late." She moved toward his dresser where his black leather jewelry case lay open, the contents already in uncharacteristic disarray. "Just hurry up. I don't want to miss the cocktail hour."

"I can't seem to find the mate to this scales of justice cufflink," Fred replied in dismay. He pulled his other cuff to an inch below the sleeve of his suit coat exposing the cufflink, a gold circle with a raised relief bearing the symbol of the legal profession. "I thought they'd be appropriate for the Bar Association dinner, but there was only one in my jewelry case."

He overturned the jewelry case, and the contents clattered across the top of the dresser. He began rummaging through the jewelry.

Deborah glowered. "We don't have time for this. Put on another pair." Fred continued to search, making pairs of the cufflinks and separating the tie clips. He began to restore order to his collection by aligning the matching sets in neat rows on the velvet tray.

Fred shook his head. He withdrew another pair of cufflinks, simple gold buttons, from the now meticulously reorganized jewelry case and shut the lid. Bowing to her demands, he grumbled, "Let's go. With all that's been going on lately, it's no wonder that I didn't notice that the cufflink was missing when I put the other one away. My mind must have been on something else."

Deborah smiled encouragingly. "Let's go and have a good time. We could both use the distraction of a relaxing night out." She ran a comb through her luxurious hair, picked up her purse and gloves, and they headed for the door, the lone symbol of justice forgotten behind them.

CHAPTER 28

T HE FIRE DEPARTMENT'S INVESTIGATION of the blaze had been ongoing for a month, and although there were some signs pointing to arson as the cause, Mike Doyle was frustrated by the lack of trace evidence pointing to anyone as the torch. The weather was turning, and Doyle was concerned that the possible onset of rain or snow would eradicate forever any evidence at the scene that might determine once and for all whether the fire that had destroyed the building had been set and who had set it.

He ducked under the yellow caution tape that ringed the scorched and twisted skeletal structure of what had been the Quality Tire Company's central office and warehouse. Tangled ashen piles were scattered about where noncombustible material not subsumed by the blaze remained. He made his way toward the remains of the electrical utility room where his investigators had placed several evidence flags marking places where they had found faulty wiring. A habitual gum chewer, Mike spat out a wad of chewing gum onto the blackened ground. Replacing the flavorless gum with a new handful of

Chiclets, he turned to go into another part of the wreckage when his eyes lighted upon a small object that winked in the waning afternoon sun among the debris surrounding the basement electrical box that his team already determined had been tampered with. "What's this?" he muttered. "Looks like a cufflink." Doyle turned over the cufflink to reveal an engraved monogram, *FMG. Well, I'll be damned,* his recognition instantaneous. *None other than the honorable Frederick Maier Green, counselor at law.* "Shit," Doyle exhaled through clenched teeth.

He pocketed the cufflink as a light drizzle began to fall. He half-jogged to his fire engine red Chevrolet; on its door, the gold insignia of the Philadelphia Fire Department caught the late autumn light. He drove straight to the nearest phone booth.

"Nate," he said without introduction, "we gotta meet."

CHAPTER 29

DOYLE WAITED IN A dark booth at the rear of the bar where his father had taken him and Nate for their first beer. The joint had not changed in three decades. The cracked leather seats were the same, as were the smell of stale beer and the dim lighting. He took a sip of his draft and kept his eyes fixed on the door. After a few minutes, Nate entered and made his way to the back. He wore an old leather jacket and an Irish tweed brimmed hat pulled low across his eyes. He slid into the booth opposite Doyle, took a long pull of the beer that awaited him, and banged the glass down on the table.

"What do you know?" he asked his friend.

"Well, first of all, it looks like your building was torched. My team has discovered remnants of some electrical wiring in the basement that we believe was the source of the fire. It's clear to me that it was no accident." Nate splayed the fingers of both hands on the table and leaned forward.

"Yeah," Mike continued, his voice barely above a whisper. "We found a gas can among the wreckage in what used to be a utility room."

Nate composed himself and sat back in his seat. "Why would someone want to do that to me?" He asked forlornly. "Now, I'll never collect on the insurance." He stopped talking abruptly when he recognized the grim set of Doyle's mouth. "Hey," he said, "there's something else, isn't there? I assume that's not the end of my troubles."

"Take this as a heads up," Doyle whispered. "The cops and the feds are about to rain down some heavy shit on someone you know, and it could implicate you. I wanted you to hear it first." He moved his hand from where it rested across the table toward Nate and turned his palm upward to reveal a lone cufflink.

Nate picked it up and rotated it. His gaze rested on the engraving on the backside, and though he was silent, his eyes turned cold with anger.

"You're a good friend, Mikey," Nate said, as he quickly put the cufflink in his jacket pocket. He proceeded to tell Doyle about the meeting with Fred and Bruce at which Fred had said they would be better off without the coupons. "That's as much as stating his motive," he concluded. "Damn fool is an academic, I'll give him that, but he apparently has no common sense. If this gets out, I'll be more than screwed financially because the insurance company won't pay; I'll be ruined socially because that idiot's my son-in-law! I've got to protect my daughter and granddaughter and my family's reputation."

"Of course. I remember Deborah's wedding. You spent a mint on that evening. That's why I came to you," Mike explained. "How 'bout I say in my report that there is no conclusive evidence of arson?"

"You do that, and I can handle the rest," Nate said, smiling for the first time during their meeting. He stood and extended his hand to Doyle who rose as he shook it. "And Mikey, I'm glad Bonnie Maureen is recovering so well from that surgery. Consider that one you owed me paid in full."

CHAPTER 30

THAT NIGHT, NATE KLEIN paced the floor of his den for so long he felt like he had walked miles over the antique Persian carpet. The ice cubes in his crystal highball clinked dully as they melted, but the scotch had been drained long before that. It hadn't succeeded in calming him.

"Stupid prick," he raged to himself. "Doesn't he know that this isn't how the game is played? All that goddamned education, and instead of using it to figure a way out of that rationing mess, he decides to set a match to the place. Now, all hell is going to break loose; and we're in worse shape than before, all the attention focused right on our family with a high probability that there will be criminal charges." Eventually he sat down behind his English walnut desk, placed his hand on the telephone receiver, and dialed.

"Hello." Bruce Miller answered on the third ring.

"I've got a problem," Nate said without introduction. "I'll be waiting for you in my den as soon as you can get to my house."

"On my way," Bruce replied to a line that already hummed with a dial tone.

Bruce couldn't help smiling as he drove to the Kleins' tony Main Line neighborhood, and had to remind himself to put on his poker face as he reached the door. When the housekeeper answered the doorbell, he brushed by her. "Mr. Klein is expecting me," he stated. She rushed to catch up to him as he walked purposefully down the wide, center hall. When they reached the den, the dark-stained double doors were closed, so she stepped in front of Bruce and knocked firmly. "Mr. Miller to see you, sir," she said.

"Come in," Nate barked. Bruce turned the doorknob and entered the room, closing the door behind him. He strode confidently across the floor and sat facing Nate on the opposite side of the desk. The room smelled of furniture polish and cigarettes, and the smooth, dark green leather inlay in the desktop reminded Bruce of a golf green at dusk. Bruce waited for Nate to speak, his stomach knotting.

"I've got a problem," Nate reiterated, "And this time, it's on the inside." For a fleeting moment, Bruce felt a sense of cold dread creep up his spine. He willed himself to remain silent until Nate elaborated. He veiled his face in a look of interest and concern.

"It seems that the authorities have confirmed evidence of arson at Quality Tire Company," Nate continued. "They also appear to have concrete proof of who did it. The thing of it is, they're going to figure that if we torched our own place, our only motive has to have been that we had something to hide. And we're talking about a felony here. This is no parking ticket to fix. This is going to mean calling in a very big marker." Nate still had not explained what he knew or how he knew it.

Bruce cleared his throat and asked, "What are we talking about?"

Nate began to pace behind the desk again impatiently. Without another word, he reached into the pocket of his trousers and tossed a small object toward Bruce. Bruce palmed it and then slowly opened his hand. His eyes moved from Nate's face to the small gold cufflink.

"That cufflink was found at the scene near some faulty electrical wiring that had been tampered with," Nate said wearily.

"Yeah, so?" Bruce said. "I bet there are a million of these zodiac sign cufflinks around. How's this gonna pin the fire on anyone?"

Nate stopped in his tracks. Never one to suffer fools gladly, he reached across the space between them and snatched the cufflink from Bruce's hand. "That's no zodiac sign, you goddamn idiot. That's the fuckin' scales of justice." When Bruce registered no sign of recognition, Nate spewed even more angrily, "The emblem of the honorable legal profession, and what's more, look at the back." He shoved the cufflink so close to Bruce's eyes that they seemed to cross in his effort to read the inscription with which he was already familiar. "That's the monogram of my brilliant son-in-law, you asshole." Nate threw the cufflink onto the desk with such force that it bounced off the leather and landed at Bruce's feet.

Bruce had never heard Nate so angry. "What can I do, Nate? I know this puts you in a jam. What needs to be done?"

Nate heaved himself back into his chair, deflated but alert. "Damage control, Bruce, damage control. Here's how it's got to go down. I don't care what Fred's intentions were; I've got no choice. He can't take the heat; I've got to make this go away. If he's accused of arson, my family will be in disgrace personally; and even if we try to distance ourselves from him, there's the distinct possibility that some of us would face additional criminal charges if they float a conspiracy theory, or I could be deemed a principle if our buddy caves and says I instructed him to set that fire. Damn fool has a lot of book smarts but no common sense. He can't be trusted, and that's all there is to it. I'll figure out how to handle Fred. You need to make sure everyone even remotely associated with this mess keeps his mouth shut."

"Sure, Mr. Klein. Whatever you say, but what do you mean, 'He's got to go?'" Bruce suddenly considered that Nate might go even farther than he had anticipated.

"Never mind that," Nate snapped. "Just get out of here, and do what I pay you to do, follow orders." Nate reached down and pocketed the cufflink. Without another word, he put on his glasses and began to read one of the reports on his desk dismissively.

Bruce left quietly, the slow smile spreading on his face again.

Nate rapped three times on the door and waited impatiently for Deborah to let him in.

"What are you doing here, Daddy?" she asked, stepping aside so that he could cross the threshold.

"We need to talk," he replied as he strode down the hall into the living room and seated himself in Fred's reading chair. Deborah dutifully sat down opposite him in the corner of the sofa. Without preamble, Nate launched his attack. "The fire at Quality Tire Company was not an accident. It was set deliberately. Fred is the one who did it." Nate's staccato delivery landed on Deborah's ears like the rat-a-tat-tat of a submachine gun.

"That's impossible," Deborah mustered. "Frederick would never...." Her meager defense fizzled as her eyes came to rest on the glinting but battered surface of the cufflink that Nate placed in front of her on the coffee table.

"*That,*" he spat, his lip curled in disgust and his finger pointing accusatorily at the cufflink, "was found in the debris of the basement of the building near the electrical panel that clearly had been tampered with. I'm sure you recognize it as one of a unique pair belonging to Fred; and in case you don't, his ownership is confirmed by the monogram on the reverse side."

Deborah reached toward the cufflink but retracted her hand. Instead, she placed both of her hands in her lap and bowed her head, a posture she always assumed whenever her father was disappointed in her.

"Deborah, this is the last straw. You've been whining that Fred works too hard and hasn't been spending enough time with you and Lydia. I've been slipping you money on the side so you can live in the style to which you're accustomed, but you're still not happy because you say Fred's not the social guy you thought he was. You know better than I that his big personality is all on the surface. I've defended him, but now I'm tired of propping him up.

"Frederick Green is a fool, and we should distance ourselves from him as fully and as quickly as possible. I forgive you your mistake, Deborah, and I always will take care of you and my granddaughter, but I am certain that you agree that Frederick has not turned out to be what either of us expected. Now, it is up to you to do what is necessary."

"Daddy, are you talking about divorce? No one in our family has ever gotten a divorce!" Deborah's eyes widened in shock.

Nate reached across the small space between them and raised his daughter's chin. "You're a resourceful girl, Deborah. It's like I've always told you. There are opportunities all around you. I am sure that you will make the most of them. Don't be glum. Now, he won't be holding you back any longer. Isn't that right? Of course, your Daddy is right!"

"But, Daddy…." Deborah tried again.

"Look, baby. If you don't do the right thing for our family, I'm stopping the money I've been giving you and Fred, and you can try going it alone."

Deborah toyed with the gold bracelet she had bought only last week. Nate followed the sound of the tinkling charms and said, "I knew you would see my point."

"Whatever you say, Daddy," Deborah conceded.

Nate got to his feet after planting a kiss on his daughter's perfectly rouged cheek. "Oh, and your mother and I will expect you for dinner at Philmont on Friday night, as usual. Come alone."

"Yes, Daddy," Deborah said to the broad side of his already departing form.

CHAPTER 31

NATE KLEIN WAS A man of action. Only twenty-four hours had elapsed since his meeting with Deborah, and he already had summoned Fred to his home. As Fred crossed the threshold and followed Nate to his den, Nate's greeting was perfunctory; he motioned Fred to the chair across from his desk and began. "You've caused me a big problem, Frederick. The Fire Department is about to conclude that the fire at Quality Tire Company was arson. Not only that, they believe that the probable motive behind the fire was the destruction of evidence related to the rationing case. I know you thought you got rid of the paper trail with the strike of a match, but if that's how the final report ends, I won't collect on my lost inventory claim with Worldwide Insurance. I'll be out a million dollars. I don't have to tell you that you'd be looking at a potential felony rap."

Nate stopped talking momentarily, annoyed that Fred was wearing what he thought of as his lawyer's face, a dispassionate expression reserved for assessing impersonal facts. Nate dropped his masquerade of calm.

"What the hell's wrong with you?" he asked. "Did you think that when I asked for your help with the rationing mess that I would be happy if you torched the place? I wanted something done about the feds, sure, but I thought that you'd come up with something clean. Now, if you cooperate, I can keep this quiet. If you don't, things will blow all to hell."

Fred looked baffled.

Nate's anger rose. "Don't just sit there like you don't get it," he raged.

He unlocked his center desk drawer and fumbled inside for a few seconds before closing his fist around a small object. He smashed his hand down on the desktop and leaned in close enough to Fred that small droplets of spittle landed on Fred's face as Nate spat out his accusation. "I guess I'll have to spell it out for you, counselor. It is only because certain officials in this city owe me that you aren't already under arrest. They know you set that fire, and this is how they know it."

He shoved the cufflink inches from Fred's eyes.

Fred was on his feet. "I don't know where they found that cufflink, how it got there, or why you have it now, but I did not set that fire." Even as he spoke, a part of his mind ached with the realization that he had no alibi for the night of the blaze. He looked earnestly into Nate's cold, unreceptive eyes.

"Fred, I wasn't born yesterday. They know it's arson. They found your cufflink near an electrical panel that showed signs of tampering. Don't you get it? There's no denying it. Game over. You not only committed a crime, but you acted in a stupid way by putting me at risk of losing everything. Worst of all, you did it without consulting me and without my approval. Did it ever occur to you that I'm smarter than you? Just look at the wealth that I've been able to accumulate. With your impulsive behavior, you have proven to me that you're incapable of ever becoming successful. You'll never have two quarters to rub together. I asked you to help me with a minor legal problem posed by an OPA audit pertaining to the tire rationing program, but you created a far bigger problem. It's like trying to remove one rotten seedling by setting the entire forest on fire. Wake up, Fred. I own the forest." Nate spoke callously, his eyes on the cufflink that rested innocuously on the leather desktop. "I also know from my daughter that you work all the time, yet you can't afford the things she wants. In fact, I've been supplementing the meager pin money you give Deborah. I know that you hardly see my granddaughter, except for telling her an occasional bedtime story, because you're rarely home before she goes to bed. I know that life is about choices, Frederick, and you made a bad one when you set that fire. Let me tell you what little is left for you in the way of choices now."

A chilled and calculated calm replaced Nate's belligerent tone. "You can fight the arson charge, in which case you'll be fighting it alone, and you stand to risk everything you've worked for all these years. If you lose, and you've got to admit, things don't look so good, you can probably figure on disbarment and some jail time. Even if you win, the matter will have cast some serious aspersions on your reputation that will undoubtedly affect your ability to practice law. Or, I can call in some chits and fix this. If I do, that comes at a big price."

Nate laced his fingers together meditatively. His eyes made a visual tour of the framed photographs and newspaper articles that lined his walls. Represented were leading figures in city government, the judiciary and the upper strata of Philadelphia society, all captured in amiable consort with Nate Klein. He returned his gaze to Frederick. "As I said, it will be no small feat, but I can bury this thing. There will be no arrest, no formal charges, no trial, hell, there won't even be any negative publicity. But, if it goes away, so do you. You will have to give Deborah a divorce on her terms."

Fred's vision blurred, and an image of Lydia formed in front of his face. He could hear her trilling laughter and see her widespread arms as she ran down the path to greet him. He thought of Deborah, her slim elegance and the confident upturn of her chin. Then, he conceded the many nights that he returned home from the office long after Lydia was asleep. He saw Deborah's face, contorted in anger or wreathed in disappointment, the many times they argued over her spending. Lately, all they seemed to do was argue: he spent too much time working; she spent too much money. He thought of his career, of the sacrifices that he had made to go to law school, to succeed as a sole practitioner, and how it could all vanish. He was experiencing firsthand how it felt to be falsely accused of a crime. How could this be?

"But if the investigators determine that the fire was deliberately set, you won't be able to collect the insurance money. You said so yourself," Fred said, a last glimmer of hope lighting his face.

"Oh, come on, Fred," Nate retorted dismissively. An act of arson voids my policy only if I, as the insured, or someone as my agent, set that fire in order to collect the money. If you're charged, I will distance myself from you faster than Jesse Owens can run!

"Put plain and simple, I have to be able to trust those around me, especially those close to my family, and you have proven yourself to be untrustworthy. I suppose I should thank you for the fact that the feds aren't going to be able to make any of their alleged rationing violations stick without any records to back up their claims; but you were overzealous and sloppy. I can't have that. So, you're going to have to decide. You can risk it all, everything you've worked for, or you can fade away with your law practice intact. In short, my fee, counselor, is that you agree to be removed from this family like the cancerous cyst that you have become."

"Does Deborah know about this?" Fred managed to ask. But he knew she did. *Deborah has always been a Daddy's Girl. She most certainly has confided our problems to him, and Nate already will have spoken to her and condemned this as the last straw. He'll have dangled that cufflink in front of her as if he saw me light that match, and she'll believe him.*

"Of course she does," Nate said, "And she'll do what is expected of her. She is a Klein after all. The Kleins and shame are not comfortable bedfellows."

"I'm telling you I didn't do it," Fred insisted. "You may not think I've been the best husband and father, but that's only because I've been working hard to make a name for myself so that I will be able to give Deborah and Lydia the best. You can reproach me for that, but that doesn't make me an arsonist."

Nate smoothed his tie and tugged at the cuffs of his suit coat. He flicked a crumb from the perfectly creased leg of his trousers. "Look," he said finally. "We're not all that different, you and I, so I understand you. You've spent your life courting and cultivating a certain image. That's what you're all about. Don't tell me you don't know that sometimes even the appearance of impropriety is enough to be your undoing." He dropped the cufflink back into the drawer and locked it. He waved Fred away with the same distasteful flick of his fingers that he used to rid himself of any other detritus. "Now get out."

"Deborah, where are you?" Fred called even before he was across the threshold. He could hear her footsteps coming from the kitchen in the rear of the house.

"We need to talk," she said without preamble, as she took a seat in the wingchair beside the small fireplace. "I know what you did, Frederick. My father...."

"I don't care what your father told you," Fred interrupted, his voice already rising. "I did not set that fire."

"Then, how do you explain your cufflink at the scene?" Deborah asked. "Daddy says the investigators found it near the electrical panel in the basement and that the wiring had been tampered with. How could you, Frederick? Daddy says...."

Fred was on his feet. "'Daddy says.... Daddy says....'" His tone was at once mocking and accusatory. "Can't you think for yourself for once? Why don't you believe me?"

Deborah's gold charm bracelet tinkled as she, too, stood up. "I *can't* believe you in the face of irrefutable evidence, Frederick. I also cannot stand by while you bring shame on my family and on Lydia and me. I want a divorce."

The word hung between them like a curtain that had come down marking the end of a scene.

"I thought Lydia and I were your family," Fred snapped, "but I guess you never stopped being a Klein. I had hoped you had more of a fighter in you and would stand up to your father, but I guess I was wrong about that too."

"Don't try to make this about me," Deborah said, "And don't you dare even imply that my father has ever done anything besides try to help both of us. You'll never see the day that you're half the man my father is," she shouted as she swept from the room. "We're done here."

CHAPTER 32

BRUCE STRAIGHTENED THE KNOT of his tie and adjusted his lapels before entering the coffee shop. Deborah had called Bruce only a couple of days after she had demanded a divorce from Fred and asked him to meet her as soon as he could. Scanning the restaurant, Bruce saw her already seated in a booth toward the rear. She looked pale and drummed her fingers distractedly on the tabletop, a steaming cup of coffee cooling in front of her. He slid onto the vinyl banquette opposite her and waited for her to speak.

"Thank you for coming, Bruce," she said. "You've always been such a good friend, and I sure could use one now." The word *friend* stung, but Bruce motioned to the waitress to bring him some coffee and fixed a reassuring smile on his face. He was determined not to squander this opportunity, not now when he was so close to achieving his recently resurrected goal. He had seized his chance to eliminate Fred as a business rival, and now he was ready to take over his personal life too.

Deborah looked around the nearly empty café and leaned forward with a whisper. "I know my father told you what's happened," she began. "I still can't believe it. I suppose Fred thought that what he was doing would help my family, but it was a stupid, stupid act."

She wrung her napkin until it was a shredded twist of paper and continued. "Well, I suppose it's like my father says - I have to think about my daughter and myself now. I've been up for the last two nights thinking about it, and I've decided to leave Frederick. Whatever embarrassment divorce will bring upon my family and me doesn't compare to what my life would be like if Frederick is disbarred or, worse, imprisoned. I'm sorry to be laying all of this at your feet, Bruce, but I had to tell someone." Deborah set her cup in its saucer and looked down into the dregs as if they held the answer to some important, unarticulated question. She reached across the table tentatively and touched Bruce's arm.

"Nobody could blame you, Deborah. You and Lydia are innocent bystanders who shouldn't get caught in the crossfire. Whatever happens now, Fred brought it all on himself." Bruce looked across at Deborah, hoping he had appeared sufficiently sympathetic; and then went on. "We all need to focus on the future now. What's done is done, and nothing will be served by looking back. I guess it's like my grandfather used to say, 'Man plans, and God laughs.' I know you can't find anything to laugh about right now because none of us ever dreamed that this would happen, but you've got a great support system in your family, and, if I'm not being too presumptuous, in me."

He slid his free hand slowly to cover hers. His touch was deliberate, designed to remind her of their past and to suggest their future. She did not withdraw. He could feel his heart pounding. "Look, Deborah, let me see you home. You shouldn't be alone right now."

"Ok," she said, gathering her purse and gloves. "Frederick's working late again, and Lydia's with my parents. I really wasn't relishing the prospect of an empty house."

They drove in charged silence the short distance from the coffee shop. Bruce parked in the narrow driveway and handed Deborah out of the car. He stood in the shadow of the overhead light that illuminated the front door, one foot on the raised threshold, the other on the path.

Deborah met his eye, and said: "Come in."

Fred sat alone on the edge of the bed in the spare bedroom. In the few days since Nate had pointed his gnarled finger of accusation in Fred's direction, Deborah had insisted that he move out of the room they had shared for the four years of their marriage. She was convinced of his guilt and demonstrated no inclination to be disabused of her father's sordid rendition of his role in the fire.

Only Lydia, too young to understand the fundamental shift that had occurred in her paradigm of the world, continued to treat him lovingly. He tried to make a game for her out of their new living arrangements. Each night after tucking her in, he reminded her, "I'll see you when you wake up in the morning, Sweetie. We'll play before I have to go to work." Then, barely having slept all night, he would await the glimpse of her dark curls and her chubby fingers grasping her stuffed clown that she had named Bobo after the main character in his creative repertoire of characters that came alive through his nightly storytelling. Each morning, her sleeping form was all knees, elbows and giggles as he tickled her belly. It was the highlight of his day.

Fred knew that there was no hope for Deborah and him. He had been attracted by the glitter of her orbit, but he had not seen how easily she would jettison anything she felt no longer fit in it. Fred rose wearily and forced his leaden legs toward the bathroom. He splashed his face with cold water, trying to rid his head of the cobwebs of sleeplessness. As he lathered his face to shave, he searched his reflection in the mirror. He had gone over his conversation with Nate Klein innumerable times, but the red-rimmed eyes that stared back at him from the glass still offered no answer.

He thought he had learned something about loss when he was a child, but the prospects that faced him now were beyond anything he could have imagined. Like a mirage, he saw Will's face in the mirror, then Lorraine's, then finally Lydia's. He instinctively reached out to touch her cheek, but she vanished in the steam that clouded the room. Fred covered his face with his hands and his shoulders heaved as he sobbed.

Over the rush of the faucet, Fred could hear Lydia padding down the hall. He hastily finished shaving and threw open the bathroom door. He knelt in the corridor and opened his arms wide. "How's my girl?" he asked, enveloping her small frame in his long arms. He breathed deeply of the fresh, floral scent of her hair.

"Daddy can't play with you this morning, honey, but I will see you later, ok baby? Right now, I have an important phone call to make." He picked up her clown that had fallen to the floor and restored it to her arms. Lydia snuggled her clown into the crook of her elbow and toddled back down the hall to her room. "I promise to be home in time to tell you another Bobo story tonight, and I will definitely have time to play with you before work tomorrow morning."

"Ok, Daddy," she smiled. "Bobo and I will be waiting."

Chapman Stirling picked up the phone on the second ring. "Chapman, it's Freddy. I need to talk to you right away." Fred was frightened by the panic that he heard echoing in his voice. His façade of calm resolve cracked as he spoke to his best friend. "Can you meet me at the Rittenhouse Hotel in half an hour?"

"I'll be there."

Chapman was already waiting in the dining room of the Rittenhouse when Fred arrived. The table was laden with a carafe of freshly squeezed orange juice, a silver coffee pot, and a basket of breakfast pastries and brioche. Fred sat down across from his old friend without touching the food. He bit his lip so hard that he thought he would draw blood, suddenly afraid to start speaking because he thought he might never be able to staunch the flow of words. Chapman reached over and squeezed his shoulder. "I'm here to listen and to help if I can. Take your time."

An hour later, Fred sat back against his chair, having laid out everything to his friend. He was empty, unburdened. It seemed that the beautifully set table was now littered with the debris of his life: Nate Klein, Deborah, the fire, the incriminating cufflink. The only possibilities for salvage were his career and his daughter.

Had it only been a few days ago that he had believed that the law, his chosen, hard won profession, was not only the guardian of the truth but also its champion? Now, with its dying gasp, truth mocked him. He had nothing to do with the fire at Quality Tire Company, but that didn't matter at all.

Suddenly, truth was no longer drawn in stark shades of black and white. It had been blurred into hideous grays by people in a position to change his life unalterably. He had put so much faith in blind Themis and her scales of justice, but that was a fantasy. In reality, justice was not blind to power or prejudice; and Nate Klein, who had spent a lifetime cultivating connections and currying favor, would now bring their full force to bear against him; and the truth be damned.

Chapman pressed his linen napkin to his lips and looked at his friend for what seemed like a long time before he spoke. "First, I need to tell you that I believe you. I could never be convinced that you had anything to do with setting that fire; but I can't tell you what to do, of course," he began. "Second, based on what you've told me, I can tell you that Nate Klein will bring you down in every way possible, both personally and professionally, if he believes that you've acted against the best interests of his family. I know it must hurt like hell that Deborah is cut from the same cloth, but that seems to be the case. The Kleins don't like mess, Freddy; and this is one big, ugly mess. I'm afraid that one thing Nate said was right. He'll either use his influence to help you, or he'll use it to ruin you. He's left the Faustian decision up to you." Fred's eyes searched Chapman's as he continued. "The thing is this. He's going to make you pay, and your decision will determine how much. Deborah wants a divorce, and Nate will retain the best lawyer to see to it that she takes you for most of whatever you're worth right now. The bright light at the end of that tunnel is that she can't touch your sharp mind and fine education that will eventually resurrect your success. You're smart and you're motivated, maybe now more than ever, so you can make back whatever she gets and then some. Don't you worry about that. But the only way that's going to happen is if your reputation as a lawyer remains intact. That's where Nate holds the cards. If you fight this thing, you and I both know that you might even beat it; but if you do, there is no way to measure the impact that such public accusations of criminal conduct could have on you. That's the best-case scenario. If you are convicted, everything for which you've worked so hard all these years will be erased by that verdict. The impact of that will be felt not only by you, but also by Lydia. Look, I know I can't be telling you anything you haven't already thought of, but we both also know that sometimes truth is trumped by treachery. When it is, it's sometimes best to just cut your losses and move on." A hardness had crept into Chapman's eyes that Fred could not remember ever having seen before.

When Fred returned to his house that no longer felt like home, parked in the driveway was a familiar black Chrysler, hulking in a strange, new context. It belonged to Bruce Miller. When Fred entered the house, he startled Bruce and Deborah, who disengaged from an embrace; but Bruce's arm remained proprietarily around Deborah's shoulders. She made no move to separate from him.

Emboldened by Bruce's presence, Deborah glared at Fred and said, "I've decided that you should move out. I saw a divorce attorney today, and you will be receiving papers. Don't bother to say anything. I refuse to spend another night under the same roof with you."

As Fred opened his mouth to speak, Lydia bounded down the stairs, and Bruce removed his arm from around Deborah. Lydia threw her arms around Fred's legs. Instinctively, Fred cupped her head in his hand and drew her close to his side.

"Say goodnight to Daddy, Lydia," Deborah said evenly, never taking her eyes from Fred's. "He will be going away on a trip for a while. Isn't that right, Frederick?"

Fred's chest heaved with his ragged breath. Lydia's grip tightened, and her anguished voice pierced the silence. "Don't go, Daddy," she cried.

"Daddy must go," Deborah answered for him. "You can give him a kiss goodbye."

"Take me with you," Lydia wailed.

Fred knelt beside her and smoothed the hair out of her eyes. "I can't, honey, but Daddy will see you soon. You know Daddy loves you more than anything else in the world."

He pried her small arms from around his neck and lifted her into Deborah's arms. The sight of the three of them, Bruce, Deborah, and Lydia, like some perfectly cast theatrical family, tore the fabric of his life. The husband and father was his role, and Bruce performed like an understudy who was happy to finally take center stage.

Lydia continued to sob, her face buried in Deborah's neck. Bruce moved his free hand to pat Lydia's back so that he now enclosed her and Deborah in a protective circle. Fred looked at the wall of his broad back and picked up his briefcase. Already, he felt like a voyeur observing a former life now lost to him. He walked toward the door.

CHAPTER 33

FRED MOVED BACK TO his parents' house. Explaining the divorce to Walter and Ruth was hard, but he even managed to concoct a story that vaguely resembled the truth. "Deborah's father wanted me to do something that was unethical and potentially illegal to help his business. I refused," he said, "and Deborah sided with her family. She wanted me to risk my professional reputation and violate my value system in order to comply with her father's wishes. I couldn't do that."

"What about Lydia?" Ruth asked immediately. "Will we be able to see her?" Tears welled in her eyes at the thought of losing her only grandchild.

"Lydia will live with her mother," Fred conceded. "It won't be as easy to see her, but I'll insist on liberal visitation rights for all of us as part of the divorce settlement."

Walter paced the room, and Ruth began to cry in earnest. Fred had his fill of tears lately and slumped dry-eyed in his chair. "I'm sorry," he said, for what felt like the hundredth time that week, even though he didn't feel like he had anything to be sorry for.

A week passed; and sitting alone in his office, Fred's hand shook as he lifted the telephone receiver and dialed Nate Klein's private number. Nate answered on the second ring. "Hello."

"Nate, this is Frederick Green. I have decided to accept your offer of assistance."

"That's a smart decision," Nate replied curtly. "I will set the wheels in motion, and you won't have anything further to concern yourself about, provided you keep your end of our little agreement. Come to my office at 9am tomorrow."

Fred walked the short distance to Nate's office and soon found himself seated across from his father-in-law. He extended his hand to Nate, but instead of a handshake, he found himself clasping a sheaf of neatly typed paper.

"What's this?" Fred asked as he began to read the first page.

"I had my lawyer draw up the terms of our agreement, Fred," Nate stated perfunctorily. "Basically, it states that you will sign over the house, its contents, and sole custody of Lydia to Deborah; and in exchange, you get the family car, your personal belongings, and fifty percent of your cash assets. I think that's quite generous under the circumstances." Nate leaned across his massive desk, poising a pen over the signature line on the last page of the document, as if it were an explanation point.

Fred continued to read to the end of the document. "I'll sign, Nate," Fred began, drawing himself up to his full height, "but I want you to know that I maintain my innocence, and the only thing that matters to me now is my daughter. Deborah can take everything for all I care, but no matter what this piece of paper says about legal custody, I will never stop being Lydia's father, and I intend to spend a lot of time with her."

Nate sneered. "Just sign and get out."

Fred scrawled his name across the bottom of the page. He looked at the small, framed picture of Lydia sitting on Nate's desk. "I won't be troubling you any further," he said.

CHAPTER 34

I T SEEMED TO FRED that every time he went to visit Lydia, Bruce
Miller's car was in the driveway. It almost felt surreal. His street, as he
turned on to it, was familiar, and so was his house. Even Lydia's pink tricycle
and inflatable wading pool littering the front yard were the same ones Fred
had bought her at Ponnock's Toy Store on Chestnut Street just months ago.
The curtains blowing in the upstairs window were the same ones that he had
looked at every morning when he woke up. But now, there was another man's
car in his driveway. Another man answering his door. Another man playing
with his daughter.

Deborah only spoke to him when it was absolutely necessary, coldly ironing out the details of his visits. But today, when she opened the door to
admit him, she seemed edgy, like she had an itch she could not reach. Fred
noticed that she worked her mouth twice in an effort to begin, but both starts
proved false. Finally, as he was mounting the stairs to announce his arrival to

Lydia, Deborah pulled on his sleeve and blurted to his back, "We're moving to Florida."

Fred was about to call Lydia's name, but his breath caught in his throat. He didn't turn around. "Who's moving to Florida?" he asked when he had managed to refill his lungs.

"Bruce and I," Deborah said, "and, of course, Lydia."

Fred closed his eyes and gripped the banister. He could see little pin-pricks of light as he squeezed his lids shut tightly and tried to wait until the first wave of nausea passed. Slowly, he turned to look at his wife. "Bruce and you and Lydia are moving to Florida," he repeated, as if it would make him understand. "Why?"

"My father has offered Bruce a business opportunity down there; and frankly, I think that after everything that's happened, we need a fresh start. We'll be getting married soon after the divorce is final." Deborah's speech seemed rehearsed, but she gathered steam as she continued. "This is for the best, Frederick. Besides," she added, "my attorney says there is nothing you can do to stop us."

Fred's thoughts reeled as he tried to formulate a response; but just as he was about to protest, Lydia bounded down the steps. "Daddy, Daddy!" she shrieked. "I'm all ready to go." She raised her arms toward her father, and Fred enfolded her into his embrace.

Father and daughter skirted past Deborah and out the door. The crisp autumn wind slapped their faces. Lydia scrambled onto the car seat next to him, pressing her small body against his side. As he pulled away from the curb, Fred took a last look through his rear view mirror at the shards of what had been his life. Fighting another surge of nausea, he tried to identify the emotion that engulfed him. Then, he recognized it for the debilitating disease it was: fear.

CHAPTER 35

A WEEK AFTER RECEIVING the news that Deborah and Bruce were moving to Florida and taking Lydia with them, Fred turned the oversized brass knob on the mahogany door with the gleaming block letters, Isaacson Roberts and Berger, Attorneys at Law. He had a ten o'clock appointment with Ralph Berger, a partner in the premier family law firm in the city. Fred introduced himself to the receptionist and sat down to wait. He flipped blindly through a magazine, stealing glances at the other people seated nearby. *This is like waiting in an oncologist's office*, he thought glumly. *Annulment, separation, divorce, custody, support…Everyone here is afflicted with some kind of malignancy of the family, yet they're sitting in this room trying to feign normalcy.* Like some of those who receive a diagnosis of cancer, Fred felt ready to fight.

Ralph Berger was a handsome man with a leonine mane of hair. When it came to advocating for his clients, he had a reputation for looking like Gorgeous George, the famous wrestler, and like him, for always winning.

After shaking his fleshy hand, Fred got right to the point. "Mr. Berger, I'm here about my daughter, Lydia. My wife has filed for divorce, and I have not contested it. I also gave her custody of Lydia in the divorce settlement, but now she has announced plans to move to Florida and take Lydia with her. I want to know if there is anything within the bounds of the law that I can do to prevent that." Berger's eyes narrowed as he assessed Fred from the generous breadth of his high-backed leather chair.

"You're a lawyer, yourself, aren't you, Frederick?" he asked, while continuing unabated. "I'm sure you know it's the rare instance that a judge rules against the natural mother in a custody case, particularly since you signed the agreement giving her full custody." Berger sifted through his file on Fred's case and brandished the document as he spoke. "Moreover, courts are reluctant to inhibit an individual's freedom of movement. Why does she want to go to Florida? Is there another man in the picture? Do you have any evidence of your wife's unfitness? Does she drink?"

Fred watched Berger remove the top of his black Waterman fountain pen and hold it poised over his yellow legal pad, ready to take notes. Fred self-consciously wiped his sweaty palms on his trousers and swallowed hard. "She's getting remarried, and her new husband will be taking a job in Miami," he answered uncomfortably. "I want to know if there's anything I can do without dragging the mother of my child through the mud."

"Your desire to protect your estranged wife's reputation is high-minded and, I might say, unusual, but leaves us very little to work with," Berger said, capping his fountain pen. "I will be happy to file a suit asking the court to reopen the custody issue, but the existing agreement to which you were a willing party and your reticence give us very little chance of success. Where the courts have no evidence that retaining custody with the biological mother would not be in the best interest of the child and, particularly in cases such as this, where you have no new evidence to present, the only remaining issue is visitation. Look, son, you might make out better by talking things over with your wife. Sometimes in these cases, once the emotional pain of the decision to separate has dissipated, the parties are apt to be more reasonable where the children are concerned. I'm sure you both love your daughter and want what's best for her; so at this stage, talking this out is the best advice I can give you. If you decide that you want to go forward with a court action, I will do my utmost to help you." He stood and extended his hand to Fred.

"Thank you, sir," Fred said. "I'll be back in touch." *He knows*, Fred thought with irritation, as he dragged his feet along the pavement. *He knows there's more to the story, and he knows I'm holding back. He just doesn't know why.*

Fred despised the simple act of ringing the doorbell of the house on Loney St. that he no longer owned, so he pushed the button only once and stood impatiently listening to the staccato beat of Deborah's heels, louder as she approached. "We have to talk," he said, as he paced the living room.

"I think we've said everything there is to say to each other," Deborah replied frostily.

"I'm not here about us," Fred said. "I realize I can't change what you think about me. I've already tried many times. I'm here about Lydia. I want to ask you to reconsider taking her to Florida, Deborah. She's our child, for God's sake! She is just a little girl who needs both of her parents."

Deborah was unmoved. "My mind is made up, Frederick. Children are resilient, and you'll just have to deal with it."

Fred's voice rose, even though he tried to control it. "But it's so far! I won't be able to see her more than a few times a year! No matter what you think I've done, you can't possibly believe that I'm not a father who adores his daughter. Please, Deborah, don't do this."

"I really don't have time for this, Frederick," Deborah said, rising from her chair and smoothing her skirt. "I have a lot of packing to do. The movers come tomorrow, and we're leaving in the morning. Don't bother me about this again; and if you do, I will be forced to tell my father whom I'm sure will feel that you have breached your agreement and have no choice but to take what he knows and what he has to the authorities."

"Can I take Lydia for ice cream so I at least have the chance to say good-bye?" Fred asked, defeated.

"Yes, but keep it short because I don't want you upsetting her," Deborah admonished.

Soon, Fred sat across from Lydia, separated by a banana split that was so big it hid her face, as she kneeled on her chair in an effort to reach it. Fred's spoon remained unused, his throat closed in anguish. "Daddy loves you so much," he managed.

"I know," she replied, the stem of a cherry protruding from her lips that looked like a kiss, as she pulled the fruit free. "I love you too, Daddy."

"And I will come to Florida to see you as soon and as often as I can," he reassured her. "I'll call you on the phone in the meantime, and you can tell me everything just like you always have, ok honey?"

"I don't want to go, Daddy," Lydia cried, quickly losing interest in the mountain of ice cream.

"I don't want you to go either," Fred said, "but for now, just remember that I love you," he repeated.

Lydia nodded her head in silence, her lips quivering and her small chin dropping to her chest. They left the ice cream parlor hand in hand. When Fred returned Lydia to her mother, he kneeled before her so that they could embrace; and she squeezed him tightly around the neck.

"I love you, Daddy," she said again.

"And I love you," he whispered.

With the departure of Lydia for Florida, Walter and Ruth mourned their loss as if there had been another death in the family. Their daughter-in-law was an absent target for blame, and they were frustrated by Fred's inexplicable inertia, so they cast an accusing eye on their remaining son. They padded heavily through the halls of their small house in silent reproof or reproached him openly with questions he could not answer.

Fred's heart was already breaking without his daughter, and his parents' added anguish eventually became too much to bear. The days, inseparable in their excruciating sameness, dragged on; and when three months passed, Fred could stand it no longer and decided to talk to his father.

"Dad," Fred began, "I don't know what I'm going to do. I miss Lydia so much; but with her living in Miami now, I don't know how I'll be able to see her more than once a year." He looked away from his father's face, away from the sadness that seemed to abide there since Lydia was taken from him.

"What do you mean, Frederick?" Walter demanded, his voice accusatory. "Lydia is so young. She'll forget all about you if you don't make frequent visits to see her."

Fred continued to hang his head. "I know, Dad. But it's at least a twenty-four hour train ride sitting up the whole way or several days on a two-lane highway. Flying is just too dangerous and expensive. Anyway, I can't take that kind of time away from my law practice more than once a year, or I'll never get it off the ground. You've got to believe me, Dad; I had no idea Deborah was going to leave Philadelphia let alone move our child to Miami. It's another world down there; and as far as I'm concerned, with the arduous trip getting there, it might as well be another planet."

Walter's tone softened, as he registered Fred's genuine misery. "Look, Freddy," he said, laying his hand on his son's hunched shoulder. "What you need to do is go see your little girl as soon as you can! Your mother and I will go with you on the train. Once we see Lydia, we'll figure out the rest; and everything will be all right." Walter hugged his son and then released him quickly. Swiping at his eyes, he added, "Let's go tell your mother. She'll be so happy!"

The following Friday, the train hurtled southward, and Fred stared out the window as the scenery rushed by, hardly able to contain his excitement about seeing his daughter. He had found out the name of Lydia's elementary school in a rare conversation with Deborah and decided that he and his parents would go directly there and ask to see her. He hoped that his plan would spare Lydia disruption from her new routine, and Fred was not eager to see Deborah and Bruce. Deborah's life and his continued to intersect at only one point, the daughter they shared. He had no desire to witness more of the painful transformations that time, or Nate Klein, had wrought.

When the train finally lumbered into the station, Fred wrestled both his bag and his parents' small valise from the overhead rack. After a short walk through the crowded terminal, they exited into the humid Miami heat. Fred felt the crispness of his seersucker suit wilt as the perspiration trickled between his shoulder blades. Walter wiped sweat from his forehead and flicked it from his fingers absently, running his finger around the circumference of his collar in a vain attempt to loosen it.

Fred hailed a cab, gave the school's address to the driver, and he and his parents rode in silence toward their destination. When the driver deposited them at the curb, Fred felt his earlier anticipation recede as it was replaced by a stolid determination. With Fred in the lead, accompanied closely by Walter and Ruth, they walked up the sidewalk to the low, brick building and entered the large, glass-paned door. They followed a sign near the entrance to the principal's office and waited as a small, birdlike woman hunched over a typewriter in the reception room.

Finally looking up from her work, she asked perfunctorily, "May I help you?"

"Good afternoon," Fred began. "My name is Frederick Green, and these are my parents, Ruth and Walter Green. We are here to see my daughter, Lydia. I believe she is enrolled here in the kindergarten." Fred smiled expectantly.

The woman eyed the threesome like a hawk; then her features pinched together as she swiveled her chair around toward the filing cabinet behind her. "Just one moment, please," she said, pursing her lips and opening a file drawer marked G-I. She extracted a folder from the G's and licked her finger as she opened it. Her arthritic finger flicked the corners of the pages until she came to a handwritten letter. Fred recognized the handwriting as Deborah's, and the incipience of the knowledge that he had brought his parents all of this way only to be met by failure crept down his spine along with a cold bead of sweat. He watched the woman's eyes scan the neatly written page. Finally, she closed the folder and clasped her hands on top of it.

"I am afraid that will not be possible, Mr. Green. We have received written instructions from Lydia's mother that she is not to be released to anyone's care except Mr. or Mrs. Miller or her maternal grandparents, Nathan and Florence Klein." She patted her hair and turned back to her typewriter, indicating that her audience with them was over.

Fred leaned toward the desk and placed his hand on the folder. "Surely, that letter is intended for my daughter's safety, but it is not meant to exclude me or my parents from seeing her. We have come all the way from Philadelphia."

He could hear the desperation in his own voice and could feel the weight of his parents' presence just behind his right shoulder. He could not bear to turn around and face them.

"There must be some mistake," he mumbled, more to himself than to the secretary.

The woman slipped the file from beneath her hands and replaced it in the cabinet. "Mr. Green, I will be happy to call Mrs. Miller, and if she confirms that there has been a mistake, I will gladly escort you to Lydia's classroom." She reached for the phone with one hand and efficiently flipped through the school directory with the other. Using her pencil to dial the phone, she nodded toward Fred, as Deborah answered on the third ring. "Mrs. Miller, this is Peggy Blaustein at Maplewood Elementary School. Mr. Frederick Green and his parents are here to see Lydia. Yes, yes. I informed them about the letter on file, but Mr. Green seems to think there has been a mistake. Oh?" she asked. "You say that the letter is correctly written? Well, I'm sorry to have troubled you, Mrs. Miller. I will convey your message to the Greens." She replaced the receiver in the cradle and looked up empathetically at Fred. "Mrs. Miller says that she does not want Lydia to be disturbed, Mr. Green. I'm sorry. There is nothing more that I can do," she said as she resumed her typing.

Walter gripped Fred's elbow and steered him out into the hall and then through the door into the muggy, oppressive heat. The pain of his father's grip was Fred's only link to reality as he stumbled away from the school building. Lydia was right there, in that very building, and he couldn't see her.

He lurched out into the bright sunshine and turned to face his parents. Fred opened his mouth to speak, but the words constricted his throat, and he thought he would choke on the truth that assailed him. Nate's voice resonated in his head: *"Remove yourself from this family like the cancerous cyst you have become."* He had known that Nate would see to it that his marriage was over, but he didn't know he meant to take away his daughter. Standing with his parents outside the school in which Lydia was learning and laughing so close by, he suddenly understood that he had made a choice without understanding the stakes of the game. Never a gambler, he failed to realize that, in the end, the house always wins.

Walter shook his arm, and Fred forced himself to focus on his father's words. "Deborah can't do this, can she, Frederick? You are Lydia's father, and we are her grandparents. Surely, we have rights," he demanded.

"Yes, Dad, we have legal rights," Fred managed, as a sudden, deep fatigue overtook him. "But my only realistic chance of getting to see Lydia from now on lies in trying to convince Deborah."

Fred shook his head in a futile effort to clear it. This time, it was he who took Walter's arm and led him to a taxi waiting at the curb.

"I'm not willing to subject Lydia to a custodial tug of war between her parents. Let's face it, Dad. Deborah's married to Bruce Miller now. Her lawyer will say that the marriage moots any infidelity; and that she and Bruce, not I, can provide Lydia with a stable, two-parent environment. What do I as a single, working father have to offer? A nanny whom Lydia won't even know? Later, when she's older, turning her into a latchkey kid? I don't know, Dad, I just don't know. Right now, all I do know is that I've got to confront Deborah."

Fred gave the taxi driver her address, and they drove in silence to her house just a few blocks away.

"You wait here, Mom and Dad," Fred said, shutting the cab door as he left to ring the bell.

Deborah's mouth narrowed into a thin, derisive line. "What are you doing here?" she asked.

"You know very well that I came to see Lydia. I stopped by her school, but they wouldn't allow me to see her. What's going on, Deborah? I agreed to divorce you, not my daughter."

"Apparently, you didn't recognize the full extent of that agreement, Frederick," Deborah replied disdainfully. "When I said that I was moving here to start a new life, I meant a new life, and that is not to include you in any way. You got your law practice and your precious reputation; I get Lydia. I can't believe I have to remind you of what is at stake for you here."

"You can't do this!" Fred yelled, all semblance of reason gone from his voice.

"Oh, but I can," Deborah retorted dismissively, the door now inches from Fred's face. "Get out!"

The door slammed in Fred's face, and he stood staring at it for a few minutes, in pure disbelief. Deborah had known him, had loved him, had married him. She had to know in her heart that Fred would have done anything for her and Lydia.

But now, it was really over. He would never see his precious daughter again.

Slowly, he turned and walked back to the cab, a lone tear falling down his cheek.

"What did she say?" Ruth asked anxiously, as Fred climbed into the seat next to her.

"She won't let me see her, Mom," Fred said, numbly.

"But she's your child, and you love her," Walter whispered, his voice as weak as his argument.

"Yes, Dad, I love her," Fred affirmed, turning his head away. He felt a door close in his heart, and locked inside, too fragile to touch, were his feelings for Lydia.

Chapter 36

F RED SAT BEFORE HIS easel, brush in hand, poised in front of the canvas. He stared at the spare, charcoal outline of a little girl, which was all that prevented the sensation of snow blindness. *Lydia*, he thought in anguish. *My God, I'm beginning to forget your face!* He set the brush aside and screwed the heels of his hands into his bleary eyes. He went into his bedroom and lifted the small silver frame from the nightstand. The smiling face of his five-year-old daughter looked back at him.

"What's the use," he said to the image. "I'm sure you've changed so much already." He replaced the photograph and left the room in despair.

A year had passed in tortured, snail-paced sameness since he returned from Florida. For each of those fifty-two weeks, he had written his daughter a letter, increasingly convinced that she did not see them, that they were not read to her, that they were most likely consigned to the trash unopened. Deborah was unyielding in her refusal to allow him to see Lydia, and she no longer took his calls. Now, his only communication with Deborah was through her attorney. Fred's own lawyer, Ralph Berger, had grown increasingly frustrated with his client's resignation at this point saying only, "If you won't give me anything with which to fight, you can give up on what you're fighting for."

The once front-page investigation of the arson at the central office of Nate Klein's tire division made the newspapers only infrequently and was relegated to a minor mention buried in the back of the news section. Eventually, Fred heard that the fire was ruled accidental and that construction had begun on a new building for Quality Tire Company paid for with the insurance proceeds.

Since his personal life was in shambles, work became Fred's obsession. With nothing and no one to come home to, Fred spent much of his time cultivating relationships among the longshoremen of the Philadelphia waterfront and the blue-collar workers in his old neighborhood of Frankford and similar working class areas. He called on many of his clients at their homes, saving them the time they would otherwise have to take off from work to come to his center city office. Through such personal attention, he earned their trust. Word of mouth spread among them that he was the people's lawyer, and his professional reputation as a tenacious and eloquent plaintiff's advocate rose like a phoenix from the ashes of his brush with ignominy. As Chapman Stirling predicted, he steadily began to recoup the financial losses he sustained in the divorce settlement.

In November 1950, he moved his law offices from the bank building where he had shared space with several other young sole practitioners to a newer, more spacious suite of his own on Walnut Street. He brought his father into Center City to see it. When they stepped off the elevator onto the fourteenth floor, Fred proudly drew Walter's attention to the gleaming brass lettering on the entry door to his office: "Frederick Maier Green, Attorney at Law." Walter stood for a moment, fixed on his son's name adorning the heavy oak door. He touched the letters admiringly as Fred opened it. Walter passed through the entrance in silence and surveyed the waiting room. Floor to ceiling mahogany bookcases lined the walls on both sides. Always a lover of books, Fred had purchased his law library secondhand from a retiring lawyer; and it provided his office with the studied look of legal scholarship. Seating areas with richly upholstered chairs and tables stacked neatly with magazines lined the perimeter of the room. A secretary's desk faced the door. A modern Smith Corona typewriter, a telephone, and an intercom dominated the surface. Stenopads, typing and carbon paper were stacked neatly on a credenza behind it.

Fred ushered his father into his private office. Fred's taste in furnishings leaned toward the new, contemporary style. His massive desk was a combination of dark walnut wood and tubular steel. A high-backed, tufted brown leather chair on a circular swivel base made of chrome stood behind the desk and was faced by two matching clients' chairs. A sleek leather sofa extended most of the length of the opposing wall, and the clean lines of a glass-topped coffee table complimented it. The walls were filled with portraits Fred had painted of the Nine Old Men, the most famous justices of the United States Supreme Court. Associate Justices Willis Van Devanter, James C. McReynolds, George Sutherland, Pierce Butler, Louis D. Brandeis, Benjamin N. Cardozo, Harlan F. Stone, Owen J. Roberts, and Chief Justice Charles Evans Hughes presided over the office, much as they had over the high court. There was even a photograph of Fred presenting a portrait to Louis Brandeis framed with a letter of thanks from the venerable associate justice. Fred's diplomas and degrees as well as various court admissions certificates and citations of his professional achievements faced the clients' chairs forming the backdrop to his desk.

"Frederick, you could have a million dollars and not have a nicer office than this," Walter enthused, running his hand over the grain of the fine mahogany desk.

"Thanks, Dad." Fred looked out the window at the bustling street below. He felt a sudden infusion of the warm glow of pride that had become a distant memory over the last arduous year. The country was moving forward in the post-war spirit of optimism, and Fred wanted to believe that if this wrecked world could reinvent itself, then so could he.

"Hey, Dad," he asked with a grin, "are you hungry?"

Without awaiting his father's answer and his coat and hat still on, Fred headed back toward the door. "I bet you've never been to the Automat," he said as he depressed the elevator button. "You're in for a treat."

Fred's obvious pleasure was infectious, and Walter smiled his assent. Once seated with their identical slices of coconut crème pie and steaming cups of hot tea, the two men sat companionably in silence enjoying their late afternoon indulgence. Relaxed and satiated, Fred leaned back in his chair.

"You know," he began, "I've been thinking about taking a little vacation. I haven't been away in a long time, and I heard about a resort in the Catskills that is very nice at this time of year. It's also not supposed to be too crowded before the holidays. I could drive up there and spend a few days and just come back to myself. Know what I mean?" The more he talked about it, the more wonderful the idea sounded.

"You should do that, son. You've been a hard worker all of your life. It would do you good." Walter looked across the small table and thought he saw a glimmer of the light that had gone out in Fred's eyes on that terrible day when they were turned away from Lydia's elementary school on their ill-fated trip to Florida.

"Really," Walter continued encouragingly, "it's amazing how invigorating a long weekend in the country can be. Besides, a young man like you should have some fun every once in a while." At thirty-one, Fred smiled at the appellation of youth; but he appreciated his father's support.

"The name of the place is Scaroon Manor. I think it's an Indian name. Supposedly, a lot of young men and women, either individually or in groups of friends, come there from cities all along the Eastern seaboard. Mostly from New York and Philadelphia, but some from as far away as Boston or Baltimore and Washington to the south."

Catching his father's smile, Fred looked away in momentary embarrassment because he realized that his father had picked up on his inference that the resort's clientele was famously single. "I just need a few days of rest and relaxation."

Walter dabbed at his mouth with his napkin, obscuring his pleased expression. "Well, your mother and I will be happily awaiting your return and will want to hear all about it," he said behind the curtain of white linen. "I suppose we should be heading home now. Your mother will be wondering what delayed us. Let's just keep that delicious cake our little secret, shall we? We wouldn't want to be accused of having spoiled our dinner."

Fred left the following Friday in his new Cadillac, a present he'd bought himself when his law practice took off. It took him several hours to drive from Philadelphia to Scaroon Manor, which was nestled in the Catskill Mountains. The resort was about four hours north of New York, located on Schroon Lake, a popular retreat along US 9, the major highway between Albany and

Montreal. The trees were mostly bare, and the November air was brisk and clean. Turning into the long driveway from the winding, two-lane road, Fred saw a rambling building made of cedar shake shingles with its imposing barn style roof and wrap-around porches. Guests sat in rocking chairs with fluffy afghans tucked under their legs. Others, bundled up in autumn jackets and hiking boots, were starting out on the trails leading into the forested hills surrounding the hotel.

Fred parked his car in the lot and strode up the wide stone steps and through the door to the lobby. A fire crackled in the grate of the immense stone fireplace, sending a fresh pine scent all the way to the beamed rafters. There were several games of cards and backgammon, and some guests simply read by the fireside or sipped hot beverages as they made friendly conversation.

Fred checked in and followed the bellboy to his room, a lovely spot in the main building that overlooked the swimming pool. When the bellboy left, Fred changed from his sport coat into a crisp cotton shirt and poplin pants. He looked out of his window to the pool below and the sprawling expanse of lawn beyond. In the distance, he could see a small lake dotted with boats and several tennis courts at the edge of the property. He hadn't taken many trips—the one to Chicago as a college student, two to Washington for business, his honeymoon to Niagara Falls, and of course, the ill-fated trip to Florida, which had ruined his once fond memories of the ocean. He was far from there now, in a lovely place full of crisp mountain air, on his first vacation alone; and he was determined to make the best of it.

He put on his white tennis sweater, the V-neck trimmed in a wide band of navy blue with a red accent stripe, the colors of his beloved University of Pennsylvania, and walked briskly out of the lodge's entrance, deciding to explore the resort before dinner. The air was cool and fragrant with the leaves and harvest of autumn. There was a row of cottages along the path, and Fred could hear the lilting laughter of several young women emanating from one of them as he rounded the bend.

Fred turned his head away from the laughter and almost bumped into a group of four young women, who were walking towards him on the same path. He stepped aside to let them pass, and they all smiled back at him. He turned to look as they walked away. They were all very pretty and well-dressed, but one in particular stood out to him. She was a brunette, with short dark hair that framed her face and a white angora sweater that complimented her shapely figure. He noticed that she had popped the collar of her navy blue boiled wool jacket and was wearing red shoes. She turned and looked back at him over her shoulder for a brief moment, and he knew what had attracted him. Her eyes. So dark and intelligent with a hint of both mischief and pain. Those eyes so like Lorraine's. Fred stuffed his hands deeper into his coat pockets and hurried along the trail.

CHAPTER 37

L EONORA PEARL HAD RECEIVED an invitation from her friend Carolyn to join her for the weekend at Scaroon Manor. Leonora was the younger of two children, her parents' firstborn having been her much-adored brother, Aaron. Undoubtedly ambitious, she came of age at a time when education was believed to be the ticket out of poverty, but in most poor families, that was meant only for the boys. Leonora eschewed Jefferson High School in her Brooklyn neighborhood, even though Aaron and most of her friends had chosen to attend. Instead, she insisted on making the long subway ride to the Bedford-Stuyvesant neighborhood early each morning to matriculate at the academically selective Girls' High School, where she hoped to enjoy the advantages of an advanced education and be prepared for college.

When Aaron, in whom the family had invested all of their aspirations for success, was stricken with spinal meningitis and left blind at the age of eighteen, Leonora knew that her plans to attend college would not come to fruition. The family spent its meager savings on his care, rehabilitation, and a series of experimental cures that came to nothing.

Leonora was struck particularly hard by Aaron's disability. It was Aaron who first introduced her to the wonders of the public library. It was in him that she had confided her dreams of education and her desire to lift herself out of Brooklyn's version of the Jewish shtetl. In the wake of Aaron's blindness, Leonora willingly agreed to subjugate her desires to his. She became the eyes that had deserted him. She read his textbooks and newspapers to him aloud and accompanied him to buy his clothes. She experienced the vicarious joy of his graduation from St. John's University and was thrilled three years later when he was awarded a degree from its law school. Leonora accompanied him to his New York bar examination where the state provided a separate room in which he took the grueling test, Leonora reading the questions to him and transcribing his answers by hand.

After Leonora graduated from high school, she took a job working for the Voice of America and later became a civilian employee of the Army on Governor's Island. The war was raging on, so most of the eligible young men were in uniform, and the vast majority of these were overseas. She dated a few officers who remained stateside; but the pages of the calendar turned; and at the end of the war, Leonora found herself nearing thirty still looking for the right match which, to her, meant educated, motivated, someone on his way up.

Her father, who cherished his only daughter, couldn't understand why this special woman remained unattached. Shaking his head, he would tell her, "You're certainly pretty, but you need to be more relaxed around boys and let your great personality shine through." Although she had grown up with an older brother and a houseful of his friends, Leonora remained reserved around men and did not believe that dinner or a movie entitled her date to paw her as a matter of right. Although a few of her girlfriends confided that they were more popular because they were willing to use the "tricks of the trade," if encouraging or engaging in casual sex constituted the tricks of the trade, then, she supposed, she didn't want to know them.

When her adored father developed cancer at the age of only fifty-four, Leonora feared that he would never see her happily married. Her family was devastated by her father's diagnosis, especially in the wake of Aaron losing his sight. The heaviest burden fell on her mother, Netania, who bore it with stoic perseverance. Leonora, not only because she was the only other female in the household but also because of her deep affection for her father, did as much as she could to help her mother through the difficult time. She came home most nights straight after work and listened longingly when the other office girls recounted their weekend getaways to the Catskill or Adirondack Mountains, but she never went herself. Much as she wanted to accept her friend Carolyn's invitation to Scaroon Manor, both to briefly escape the atmosphere of impending death that had overtaken her home and to experience firsthand this mountain retreat that was known to be a magnet for unmarried young adults, she couldn't bear the thought of leaving her declining father and her devoted, weary mother.

Trying to convince Leonora to come away with her as she read from the resort's brochure, Carolyn wheedled, "Oh, come on, Leonora. How can you resist a weekend at a place that got its name from an Indian word meaning large lake; or better yet, from French soldiers who named it in honor of the Widow Scarron, bereaved former wife of the noted French author and playwright Paul Scarron? Personally, I much prefer the latter explanation. It's much more romantic!"

"Oh, French, is it? *C'est une chose tellement ridicule*," Leonora replied airily, attempting sophistication with one of the only phrases she retained from her high school French. She lowered her voice to a whisper, cupping the mouthpiece of the telephone receiver to muffle her voice, "No, I can't get away this weekend. I know, I know, but my father is really sick, and I can't leave him right now."

Leonora's mother closed the door to the bedroom noiselessly just as she was speaking. She feigned straightening a picture on the hallway wall so that she could linger within earshot of the conversation.

"I know it's just a weekend," Leonora continued, "but it's just not a good time. Mom needs me. You go on and have a great time. You can tell me all about it at work next week."

Leonora felt her mother's presence and then a gentle hand on her arm. "Hold on a minute, OK Carolyn?" she asked, dropping the phone receiver to her side. "What is it, Mom? Do you need some help? Does Pop need anything?"

"No, honey, your father is sleeping. I couldn't help but overhear a little of your conversation just now, though." Her mother made a show of wiping her hands on her apron so that she did not have to look her daughter in the eye. "Leonora, I want you to go with Carolyn. You deserve a break from…."

Her voice trailed off, and her small hand fanned the air in an all-encompassing gesture. She sighed heavily, conveying more of the despair that permeated the atmosphere than any words she could have said. Then, she found the words that she knew her daughter could not ignore. "Your father wants you to go."

Squeezing Leonora's hand, she smiled and walked down the hall toward the kitchen. Leonora took a deep breath and opened her mouth to protest, but she raised the phone to her mouth instead.

"Carolyn, are you still there? I just talked with my mother, and I think I'll be able to go after all."

The two women planned the details excitedly for the next several minutes, and the sound of Leonora's enthusiastic laughter, so recently absent from her home, drifted down the hall to the kitchen. Netania brushed the hair from her brow with the back of her hand and smiled to herself. She sprinkled flour on the yeasty surface of the dough ball in front of her. After kneading it and punching it down, she picked up her rolling pin and attacked it with renewed vigor, seized by a lightheartedness that had become unfamiliar.

Leonora commuted to her office on Governor's Island by ferry. As it was unofficially frowned upon for coworkers on the Island to fraternize, young men and women who formed inevitable social liaisons endemic to the workplace deliberately left work separately taking different ferries back to the city only to rendezvous later at predetermined destinations.

Tonight, Leonora had just such a dinner date. She had met Bert Adler several weeks earlier when one of her friends organized a birthday party for one of the girls in his department, and they had been casually seeing each other since then. Bert was a nice enough guy, Leonora thought, but she knew almost immediately that he was not "the one." He had gone to college and done his bit during the war, for which she gave him credit, and he was handsome and always impeccably dressed, traits that were important to her, but he was singularly lacking in ambition and talked frequently about his expectation that he would work for the government in his low level managerial position until his retirement. Still, he liked to have fun, and a girl was entitled to some of that, even if she were still looking for Mr. Right.

Leonora was set to depart for Scaroon Manor the next Friday, and standing at the rail on the ferry with the autumn breeze in her face, she couldn't help but feel more excited about that than her impending dinner date. Nonetheless, when the ferry docked, she hurried off in the direction of the small Italian restaurant where she had agreed to meet Bert for dinner. The sun had set, and the seasonal chill of evening penetrated her thin coat. She spotted the awning marking the restaurant's entrance and gratefully expressed her thanks to the elderly man who held the door for her. Peeling the black leather gloves from her hands, she scanned the tables and spotted Bert waving from a dimly lit table in the rear. He rose to help her off with her coat when she approached.

"You made good time," he said, hanging her coat on a nearby brass coat rack.

He held the chair for her, and she sat down. "What's your poison? Some nice Italian wine or your usual Manhattan?" Leonora had adopted the bourbon concoction as her signature drink after seeing Audrey Hepburn order one in a movie that was otherwise forgettable. To her, a Manhattan was synonymous with sophistication, even if a girl did limit herself to one.

"I think I'll stick with a Manhattan," she said in her most erudite voice.

Leonora opened her small, leather handbag and withdrew her other favorite accessories, a red and white box of Marlboro filtered cigarettes, and a matchbook from 21 Club, the famously exclusive restaurant and bar where she had stopped for a drink with Carolyn after work the previous week. It was one of her favorite hobbies—she could never afford a meal at any of the famous Manhattan restaurants, but she and one of her friends often stopped at one of these New York legends for a drink after work. The following day, Leonora would leave a matchbook or business card in a conspicuous place on her desk, hoping to intrigue her coworkers who noticed it. Now, Bert eyed the matchbook from 21, obviously impressed, and then signaled the waiter to the table. Soon they were drinking companionably while munching on grissini, the thin, crisp Italian breadsticks that Leonora loved.

"Guess what?" Leonora asked after a few minutes. "Carolyn and I have made plans to go to Scaroon Manor this weekend." She knew that Bert, like most of the other singles on the Island, had heard that the mountain resort was all the rage.

"Really? How'd you like some company? I've been meaning to check out that place myself, and I don't have any plans this weekend." He smiled, covering Leonora's hand with one of his as he raised his glass with the other. "We could have a fantastic time up there."

Leonora felt uncomfortable with his innuendo and wished now that she had not mentioned her trip. After all, she had heard that besides being a great place for unattached young men and women to meet each other, Scaroon Manor also was a popular rendezvous for those who felt free to do in the country what they would never dream of doing in the city under the watchful eye of friends and family.

Her mind was racing, trying to formulate an appropriate response that would still sound friendly while excising Bert's sudden urge to accompany her. "Yeah, I've heard it's great, and it would be swell to see you and all, but Carolyn's kind of between boyfriends right now, so I wouldn't want her to feel like a third wheel. I mean, she's put together a group of girls, and this whole trip was her idea in the first place. You do see what I mean, don't you?" She assumed her most engaging smile and took another sip of her cocktail.

"Sure, kid, I see what you mean," Bert said, his enthusiasm still peaked. "How about this? You go on with Carolyn, and I'll just ride up there on my own. You girls can have your fun; and who knows, I might even turn out to be Carolyn's hero by introducing her to some fine fellow I meet." Bert patted her hand and opened his menu.

Rats! Her plan foiled, Leonora nodded and mustered a smile before she raised her own menu. She hoped her weekend wouldn't be ruined by this unintended twist.

Like most people, Leonora could not figure out why time was such an imprecise measure of life's pace. It would be neither hurried nor slowed, yet there were some days that passed in an instant while others could decelerate to a freeze frame. The rest of the week before her departure, Leonora's days dragged on as if a mighty giant had set his massive weight against the hands of the clock, inhibiting their forward progress.

Two days before her departure, she packed her clothes carefully. Although she could not afford an extensive wardrobe, Leonora's grandfather was a talented tailor who, each season, made her several skirts and blouses in basic colors and classic designs. To these, Leonora added her personal touches. A stylish belt, a scarf, or silk flower tucked into her waistband changed an ordinary ensemble into a fashion statement, and only a very discerning eye would have recognized that these outfits that appeared so unique were actually composed of seemingly endless combinations of the same few pieces.

One of her most versatile garments, and therefore her favorite, was a perfectly tailored white cotton blouse. She laid this shirt on her bed and smoothed it with her hand. Leonora augmented the appearance of her clothing by taking meticulous care of them. She had elevated ironing to an art form, and she smiled with satisfaction as she regarded the crisp, perfectly pressed fabric that still looked like new.

Her brows knit together in concentration as she planned her outfit for each day. The furrow became deeper as she thought of Bert and his insistence on coming to Scaroon Manor. Somehow, despite Bert's obvious intentions, she would have to make it clear to him and everyone she met that they were not, in fact, together. She shook her head in an effort to rid her mind of him, as she neatly folded her clothes into the suitcase, vowing to keep a positive outlook on the weekend.

On Friday afternoon after work, she waited for Carolyn outside the Empire State Building. Carolyn was late, but nothing could spoil Leonora's happy anticipation. She amused herself by fantasizing about the type of eligible men she would meet at Scaroon Manor in only a few hours. She noticed an immaculately coifed dark-haired man in a finely tailored suit, starched white shirt, and silk paisley tie who also stood by the curb. His shoes were polished to a mirror shine. He was classically handsome, and his hands, she always noticed a man's hands, were not calloused, the nails smooth and even. *A professional*, she thought admiringly. When Carolyn appeared at her elbow, Leonora whispered to her friend, "Now, that's what a gentleman looks like! I hope we meet some high class men like that at Scaroon."

Just as Carolyn followed her gaze, the man reached into his briefcase and withdrew a sign that he then displayed prominently in the direction of the exit doors of the Empire State Building. It read, "Mr. Lawson Brinkley". Carolyn could barely contain her laughter as she cupped her hand over Leonora's ear, "For God's sake, Leonora, he's a chauffeur!"

"Well, he still looks like a gentleman," Leonora sputtered between clenched teeth. She picked up the handle of her valise and strode quickly down the sidewalk toward the subway, trying to distance herself from her embarrassment. Carolyn had to walk double time to catch up.

Once on the train, Leonora got her first good look at her friend. She noticed immediately that Carolyn's hair was freshly cut, and her slim, knee length pencil skirt and mohair sweater were new. They hugged her slender, curvaceous body like a second layer of skin. The pink cotton candy color of her manicured fingernails matched her sweater exactly, as did the shade of her lipstick. If the state of a soldier's uniform and military accoutrements indicates the level of his preparedness for battle, then Carolyn had declared all out, take no prisoners, war.

Dressed in a simple but well-cut navy blue sheath, Leonora felt out-classed by her stylish friend. Nervously, she pinched the bangs and sideburns of her pixie hairstyle into perfect little points, a self-conscious gesture that she repeated often throughout the day.

"Well, Carolyn," she trilled, trying to subdue her envy, "I'm ready to go. Let's get this show on the road."

Carolyn placed her suitcase at her feet and smoothed her skirt over her knees. "Look out, Scaroon Manor," she exclaimed. "Those boys aren't going to know what hit 'em!" She winked at Leonora, as the train headed for Grand Central Station.

Once they had checked into Scaroon and unpacked, it was Carolyn's idea to ask the other two girls, Evelyn and Phyllis, with whom they were sharing a cottage for the weekend, to go for a walk right after they unpacked. "You've gotta see and be seen, girly girls. No one's gonna discover us hidden away here in our room."

Leonora noticed that the other girls' casual attire also was studied down to their matching hats and scarves. It had taken them longer to dress for the walk than the amount of time they intended to absorb the great outdoors.

"Heck," Carolyn laughed when they finally pulled the door shut behind them, "any of you girls who thinks this is actually about walking better stop me at the first sign of sweat! I'd say I'm more on the hunt, and what I'm hunting definitely does not like even a hint of unladylike perspiration."

"Yeah, you're right," Evelyn confirmed with a sly grin that belied her French school girl bob and pedal pushers, "but I wouldn't mind getting sweated up later."

Leonora laughed uneasily along with the others, but as she turned up the collar of her boiled wool jacket and stuffed her gloveless hands deep into her pockets, she realized that Carolyn and her new roommates meant business. *Did they really think they would find the love of their life just by happenstance, out on an evening walk?* She scoffed to herself, determined not to get too caught up in their charades.

But just minutes later, she found herself wondering if she had spoken—even just to herself—too soon, when they encountered a tall, attractive man on the path. He sidestepped their group in order to let them pass, and his smile seemed genuine rather than lascivious. He didn't speak to them, but Leonora was as much impressed by what he didn't say - no glib comments, no slick sexual innuendo veiled as flattery. Just in his silence, he seemed different.

"Well, there's one I wouldn't kick out of bed!" Phyllis cried. The other two girls giggled and nodded appreciatively, while the heat rose to Leonora's face.

Carolyn added, "Even if he doesn't know it yet, I think Tall-and-Handsome just made a date with me for dancing after dinner tonight." She picked up her pace slightly and swung her arms energetically as she led the group down the path, the not at all subtle flip of her hair and sashaying hips marking her territory as she surveyed other prospects.

Leonora looked back over her shoulder; and as she did, she caught the stranger's eyes. They locked for an instant, and she thought she saw him smile at her before he turned and continued on his way.

Leonora looked at her reflection with annoyance as she put the finishing touches on her outfit for the evening. When she had purchased the sleek black crepe de Chine halter dress, she had felt pretty and chic. Now, as she pivoted in front of the mirror to view herself from all angles, she worried that the soft, thin fabric looked more like an invitation than the message of understated elegance she first imagined. At least the strappy black stiletto-heeled sandals added three inches to her height. Catching herself pinching her bangs together again, she concentrated on her reflection as she recognized the real source of her anxiety. Bert would be arriving tonight.

Leonora picked up her purse and sweater from where they lay on the bed and headed for the door. Lifting her chin ever so slightly, she strode from the cottage down the path to the dining room. When Bert arrived, she would give him her best smile; but she would also have a good look around at the other eligible young men. *After all*, she thought, *a girl pushing thirty only gets so many chances.*

CHAPTER 38

GUESTS AT SCAROON MANOR were assigned tables at which to dine for the duration of their stay, and Fred's table was made up of eight men who had escaped from various metropolises to the country for a few days. They were all amiable sorts, white-collar types who were not shy about expressing their hope that they might connect, if even for just a weekend, with one of the attractive, single women seated at the adjoining tables.

Fred surveyed the spacious dining room trying to spot the group of girls he had passed on his earlier walk, hoping to see the dark-eyed brunette, and was pleased when he recognized her seated only three tables to his right. She was wearing a black halter dress that showed off the shapely line of her shoulders and the suggestion of her full breasts. Her dangling black and white earrings sparkled when she threw her head back to laugh. She was beautiful.

Fred tried to observe her unobtrusively, but he caught himself staring as another man approached her from behind and leaned over her chair to whisper in her ear. She seemed to know him and introduced him to her friends and tablemates as the band began to play. The new arrival slid her chair out, offering his hand to lead her to the dance floor. They joined several other couples that already were gliding along, and Fred felt his face burn with envy. He didn't know this girl, not even her name, yet something about her made him feel possessive. He turned back to his dinner partners and tried to engage in the conversation, but she kept drawing his attention back to the dance floor. He was pleased when the music stopped, and the dancers returned to their seats.

A spectacled, balding, jovial man to Fred's left, who had introduced himself as Paul DiMotto, followed Fred's eyes to her table. "Do you know her?" he asked Fred. "I couldn't help but notice that you've been watching her all night."

"No, I…."

Suddenly, Fred didn't know how to explain his behavior toward this total stranger. He inadvertently glanced back in her direction and saw that her dancing partner had pulled a chair up from the adjoining table of men so that he was now sitting directly beside her. He turned the chair around backwards and straddled it with his arms resting on the back. His hands gestured casually as he spoke to her, and she and her friends laughed periodically.

Looking back at his neighbor, Fred tried again. "You said you've been here for a few days. Do you know her? You wouldn't happen to know if that guy who's talking to her is her boyfriend, would you?"

Fred didn't feel like himself. Never assertive with women, he couldn't believe that he was making personal inquiries about one from a man he had only just met.

Before he answered, Fred's newfound friend removed his glasses, blew on them, wiped them with a corner of his handkerchief, and replaced them on the bridge of his broad nose. He smiled at Fred, pushed back his chair and, without a word, gave Fred's shoulder a confident squeeze. The band began to play again, and Fred watched with wonder as the man walked over to the woman and asked her to dance. Several minutes and one waltz later, he escorted her back to her table and resumed his seat next to Fred.

Paul used the same handkerchief to mop the perspiration from his ample brow. Smiling at Fred, he whispered, "Well, let's see. Her name is Leonora Pearl, and she's here with a girlfriend from New York. She's twenty-seven and works in the City, but she lives with her family in Brooklyn. Oh, and the guy? He came up here from New York to see her, but she made no bones about the fact that he's not her boyfriend."

Paul sat back in his chair looking self-satisfied and sipped from his scotch on the rocks. "See how easy that was? Are you going to just sit there, or do I have to bring her over to introduce you? If I do, I'm going to have to start charging you for my services," he chortled.

Fred smiled as the music began again, and he saw that Leonora, who now had a name to go along with those incredible eyes, was once again dancing with her erstwhile suitor. The autumn wind began to rise, and Fred noticed a chill creeping into the air. When he saw her back, exposed by the halter style of her dress, swirl by him, he rose and went over to pick up her wrap, which was draped on the back of her chair. Emboldened by Paul's good-natured kidding, he strode to the pair on the dance floor and handed her the sweater. "Excuse me, but you'll be needing this. The temperature has really dropped, and the wind has made it quite cold."

Leonora was taken aback, but then she looked into Fred's smiling face and her surprise was replaced by recognition. "You're the fellow from the walking path this afternoon, aren't you?"

She turned to her companion who stood, angry and motionless among the other dancers and explained, "Bert, this is…. Oh, I'm sorry, I didn't get your name," she said turning back toward Fred.

"Fred, Fred Green, and I'm sorry for interrupting your dance." Fred started back to his table, but he felt her warm hand on his arm.

"Well, thanks, Fred. That was swell of you. Maybe I'll see you around," Leonora said, extending her hand. "My name is…."

"Oh, I know who you are, Leonora Pearl," Fred said with growing confidence. "You're twenty-seven years old, and you work in the city, but you live with your family in Brooklyn."

"But how did you…?" Leonora asked.

"I have my ways when I want to know something," Fred said over his shoulder, smiling as he walked back to his table.

Bert encircled her waist in a feeble attempt to appear and led her back to the center of the dance floor.

As dessert was served, Fred caught Leonora's eye and impulsively crooked his finger in her direction, gesturing for her to come join him at his table. The band had just announced its last set; and when she appeared by his chair, Fred immediately rose; and as he'd been wanting to for the whole night, finally asked her to dance.

He put his hand lightly on the small of her back, directing her to a small clearing in front of the bandstand. Fred was a natural dancer; and as soon as the music started, his social unease and inhibitions melted away in graceful, rhythmic movements. Leonora, by contrast, usually felt stiff and self-conscious and had only ever felt comfortable dancing with her brother Aaron. But as Fred adeptly glided her around the other couples, singing the words softly in her ear, she relaxed and enjoyed herself. With the last strains of the music fading, Fred returned her to her seat next to her glowering companion.

"I'll see you around," Fred said, as he handed her into her chair. Making his way back to his table a short distance away, Fred saw Paul DiMotto wink as he took another long, satisfied pull on his scotch.

For the remainder of the weekend at Scaroon Manor, Leonora had twin shadows in the persons of Carolyn and Bert, although the only person she really wanted to see was Fred. When Fred asked her to accompany him on a boat ride around the lake, Carolyn insinuated herself into the conversation until there was no choice but to ask her to join them. Although not a tennis player herself, Leonora agreed to meet Fred by the courts for a lesson. There was Bert, waiting in his tennis whites with his sweater tied jauntily around his shoulders, offering pointers every time she missed a shot.

"I never thought I'd find myself trapped inside a Shakespearean comedy," Fred laughed when they finally had a few minutes alone over a cold drink. "We've got our very own version of *A Midsummer Night's Dream* going on here."

Leonora sipped her iced coffee and looked out across the lake toward the mountains. She wasn't sure what Fred meant, but she certainly didn't want to appear ignorant in front of this obviously intelligent and educated man. Finally, she opted for an ambiguous reply. "What makes you say that?" she asked.

"Well, perhaps you are Helena and Bert and I are Lysander and Demetrius, both in love with you. Or Carolyn may be fair Hermia, confused because she seems to have lost the affection of both suitors." Fred smiled broadly at his literary analogy, and Leonora stifled a giggle with her hand.

"Look, while we have a few minutes, I was wondering if I could have your phone number. I get into New York fairly often on business, and I would like to look you up when I'm there. We could meet for dinner," he added hopefully.

When Leonora looked up, she already could see Bert and Carolyn making their way down the cobbled path toward the gazebo where they were seated. She quickly removed a pen from her purse and scribbled her number on a paper napkin. She pushed it across the table toward Fred who secreted it in the inside pocket of his sport coat.

"I'll call you," he managed to say just before Bert and Carolyn spotted them. "Hermia, wasn't it?" he asked Carolyn cryptically as he stood to offer her a chair, and Bert slid another one close to Leonora's. Bert and Carolyn exchanged a confused glance, but Leonora laughed out loud.

All the way back to the city, Carolyn talked about Fred. "I was certain that he was going to ask for my number before he left this morning," she said disappointedly. "I can usually read guys like a book, but obviously not that one. Maybe if ol' Bert hadn't been sticking to me like leaves to a blanket. I mean, really, Leonora, the guy comes up there to see you, and I wind up not being able to get rid of him!"

Carolyn turned her face toward the train window and huffed, her breath making a moist circle of fog on the glass. Leonora watched her out of the corner of her eye and flipped the pages of her magazine absently.

"Well, it was fun anyway," she offered. "I thought the resort was beautiful, and there were lots of nice guys and girls there. I'm really glad we went. Guys are just hard to figure, that's all. Don't worry about it." Carolyn continued to stare sullenly out the window, so Leonora returned her attention to her magazine, grateful for the distraction.

A week passed before Fred telephoned Leonora. He said he had business in the city in late November and asked if she would like to meet him for dinner. Leonora had tried to minimize the impact that meeting Fred had on her, but she was undeniably intrigued by this intelligent, amusing man who also had a noticeable air of vulnerability behind all of his bravado. She tried to dampen her hopes; in the post-war years, the distance between New York and Philadelphia was unlikely to be easily bridged by romance. Most of the girls and boys with whom she had grown up in Brooklyn would have considered it radical to move to another borough, let alone to another state where they had no family and knew no friends. She was getting ahead of herself, she knew; but she couldn't stop herself from imagining the repercussions of a future with Fred in it, even if their immediate reality included only dinner.

Her mother paused in the doorway of her bedroom just as Leonora draped an elegant, black linen coat over her shoulders. "That's a pretty coat, honey," she admonished, "but it's much too light weight for that chilly wind out there. You'd better bundle up more if you're going out."

Leonora pirouetted in front of the mirror and smiled at the effect of her well-tailored coat. She had splurged on it after she saw it in the window of Saks Fifth Avenue the previous week, having preferred to devote her lunch hour to window shopping rather than eating. Always rushing the season, Saks had devoted all of its new displays to spring fashions, enticing passersby to believe that warm weather, sun, and blooming flowers were just around the corner. The coat was clearly not intended for the icy winter temperatures that had begun to blanket New York, but Leonora didn't care. She liked the way it looked and felt; she hoped Fred would feel the same way.

"I'll be fine, Mom," she told her mother. "I only have to dash from the subway to the restaurant."

Her mother opened her mouth to protest but decided against it. Leonora could be strong headed; and there was no doubt that in matters of fashion, she believed that style took precedence over good sense.

Her mother conceded the point with a smile and said instead, "You look lovely, dear. I hope you have a wonderful time."

She reached out to smooth a wrinkle from the linen coat, her small hand brushing Leonora's sleeve in a delicately disguised caress. Leonora raised the collar to frame her face like an Elizabethan cloak and hurried out of the apartment.

When she exited the subway near the Russian Tea Room on Fifty-Seventh Street, Leonora could already see Fred's tall, lean frame silhouetted under a nearby lamppost. A cold gust lifted her hair and the hem of her coat, but she modulated her step so that she appeared eager but not anxious to bridge the distance between them. She silently chided herself for the vanity of that ridiculously spring-like coat and cursed the wind both for its chill and the havoc it had wreaked upon her hair. She fought the urge to pinch her bangs into place yet again, acknowledging the futility of the effort even as another blast of air laid waste to her tresses. Then, she was beside him, and he smiled down at her and gently steered her through the doorway of the restaurant into its dim, warm interior.

"Hello," he said cheerfully. "I'm glad you were free this evening. This looks like a nice place. Thanks for suggesting it."

He slipped her coat from her shoulders and accepted a claim check from the cloakroom attendant. A hostess showed them to a table in the ornately decorated dining room, and Fred assisted her with her chair before seating himself.

Leonora would be eating at the acclaimed restaurant for the first time, but she looked around with a familiar expression as she spoke to Fred. "The Russian Tea Room is a landmark restaurant in New York," she explained, assuming a tone of both knowledge and experience. "The food and service are excellent, and the atmosphere is unique and beautiful."

She took a matchbook from the table and surreptitiously slipped it into her purse to add to her collection. *This time*, she realized, *when I strategically place it beside my typewriter, it will have earned full rights to be there!*

A mildly obsequious waiter approached them, and Fred ordered Leonora a Manhattan and himself a Beefeater gin martini with a twist of lemon.

"I didn't expect you to know what kind of cocktail I prefer," Leonora noted with surprise. At Scaroon Manor, they had not had drinks together.

Fred's face reddened slightly. He realized that by presumptively ordering Leonora a Manhattan, he might have revealed that he had tried to memorize every detail of their brief encounter at Scaroon Manor. He had noticed her ordering the cocktail the first night at dinner, before he'd even spoken to her.

"I had an inspiration," he said sheepishly. "Maybe I should have been more of a proper gentleman and asked you what you'd like to have this evening. Would you like me to get the waiter's attention to change your order?"

"No, a Manhattan is fine. It's actually my favorite cocktail," Leonora affirmed. She was pleased to see the tension recede from Fred's face as the waiter set a chilled martini in front of him and a highball glass before her.

Smiling, Fred lifted his drink and toasted, "Here's to things to come."

Then, he set his glass down before him. "I got a very interesting case today," he ventured. "It involves misfeasance by a funeral home."

Although Leonora did not particularly want to discuss death or funeral rites over dinner, there was something about the small smile that played at the corners of Fred's lips that peaked her interest. Besides, here she was with an attorney who used the word misfeasance in ordinary conversation the way most people would talk about the weather. Leonora flushed at her attraction to his intellect. It was difficult to explain the chemistry she felt for this man's agile mind when her friends only seemed to care about a man's physical attributes.

"Really?" she asked aloud. "Tell me about it." Her curiosity was genuine, as the law had interested her ever since she helped her brother, Aaron, with his legal studies.

Fred exhaled comfortably and began to regale her with the facts of the case, ever the master of detailed and punctilious descriptions. "This brother and sister called me last week to set up an appointment for today. They said that their father recently passed away, and they had a legal matter pertaining to him that they wished to discuss with me. I assumed the issue was something to do with his estate, either pertaining to the disposition of his assets, as set forth in his will, or some potential conflict among his heirs. The funny thing was that when I spoke to them over the phone, they sounded like working class people who typically don't have complex estate issues.

"Anyway, they came in this morning bright and early at nine o'clock. The man was a big, burly sort; the kind you'd never think would have a sensitive side. His sister was the complete opposite. She was small and almost waiflike. She kept knotting her handkerchief in her lap and had large, watery eyes that looked like they would spill over every time she blinked, which was too often. It would be impossible to pinpoint their ages. They each could be anywhere from forty to sixty, judging from the one fraternal characteristic they shared, a tired, beaten look around the eyes. The man did most of the talking, with his sister punctuating his story with sporadically placed sighs or honks into her handkerchief. This is what he told me. Their father passed away suddenly some weeks ago after a seemingly minor bout with the flu. He was a robust man whose demise was not in the offing. As he was not a religious man, his two shocked and grieving offspring approached a neighborhood mortuary to conduct a viewing and a graveside burial service. On the day of the funeral, family and friends gathered at the funeral home to bid farewell to their loved one. Both the brother and the sister say they noticed that even their father's closest friends and relatives seemed to spend an inordinately brief time bidding goodbye to the dearly departed. Some even burst into tears the minute they looked down into the casket and beat a hasty retreat up the aisle. Nevertheless, the brother insisted that he attributed this strange behavior to the varied and inexplicable ways in which different individuals deal with grief. When it seemed that everyone else had paid his respects, the brother says that he took his sister by the arm and led her to the side of the coffin where they could commune with their father, seeing him as he had been in life for the last time. They both looked down lovingly at the body laid out in the satin-lined mahogany final resting place. They turned instinctively toward each other, and the brother exclaimed to his sister, 'It sure don't look like Pop.' At this point in his monologue, his sister loosed the floodgates accompanied by a piercing wail. It seems that the emaciated, disease- ravaged corpse that presented itself as their father was not, in fact, Pop. Their father already occupied a newly dug grave in someone else's plot, the mortuary having mixed up the two bodies whose funerals were to take place on the morning and afternoon of the same day. Because the other funeral had a closed casket, no one at that service knew they were burying someone else's beloved Pop. Not so fortunate were these bereaved who sat opposite me. They are confronted with the exhumation of one body representing the mortal remains of their beloved father and the indelible memory of having been forced through the funeral home's incontestable negligence to bid farewell to someone else's anonymous Pop."

Fred balled up his napkin, tossed it on the table, and sat back in his chair as if to indicate that he had finished his summation to the jury. Leonora clasped both hands over her mouth to stifle her laughter. She could understand implicitly why Fred already was a successful trial lawyer representing a variety of plaintiffs. He was a master storyteller who wove a tale that was at once compelling and spellbinding. He could expertly walk the fine line between tragedy and its inextricable Siamese twin, comedy, to make her see the humor in the situation, but she was equally certain that the jury would find in favor of these two beleaguered siblings because Fred would play to each juror's sense of tragedy until they felt the full impact of his clients' trauma and grief. Leonora clapped her hands quietly in admiring applause.

"That's quite a story," she managed to say, as a giggle fought to emerge from her throat. "And I can see that they came to the right lawyer."

The conversation continued unabated for the remainder of the dinner. Leonora described her job in employee relations for the Army. She spoke about her family and the toll that her brother's blindness and her father's illness had taken on them. She established common ground with Fred as she explained with pride her brother's achievement of a law degree from St. John's University and extolled his passing the New York bar exam. For his part, Fred spoke lovingly of his parents and thoughtfully about the loss of his brother and sister. Both of them made the first tentative steps toward crossing the abyss that separates strangers, hoping through such revelations to begin the journey toward intimacy that defines friends and lovers.

Finally, when only the dregs remained in their coffee cups, Fred pressed his napkin to his lips and contorted his features in an expression that was, at once, serious and pained. "There is something else that I want to tell you before you decide if you want to see me again," he began. "I was married, and I have a six year old daughter, Lydia. Her mother moved to Florida and took Lydia with her. She remarried and has prevented my parents and me from seeing my little girl, even though we traveled all the way to Florida to do so. I love my daughter very much, and I struggle every day with not being part of her life. As a lawyer, I can tell you that short of proving the mother unfit, the father doesn't have many rights that are acknowledged in a court of law. And the last thing I wanted was to drag my child through an ugly battle between her two parents. I thought you should know about my marriage and my child. I will understand if you don't want to pursue a relationship with me." He paused and looked dejectedly at Leonora. A war of emotions battled across his face, leaving defeat in its wake. "I just thought you should know," he repeated vulnerably.

Almost immediately, it felt like Leonora's whole being had entered a heated argument. Her head advised her to bail out before she committed anything more than a dinner to this complicated man from Philadelphia. But her heart wouldn't let her. *Everyone accumulates baggage of one sort or another,* she reminded herself, *and I have to give him credit for being honest. He was clearly determined to tell me about his past at the inception of our relationship rather than much later, when I might already have invested much more and had something to lose.* And then there was the look on his face when he had spoken of his little girl. His love for her was obvious. His pain at their separation was equally apparent. This was a good man.

Almost with a will of its own, her hand moved across the table and covered his fingers where they rested in front of him. "I'm sorry," she said; and for a moment, she could tell from his expression that he assumed that she did not want to see him again. "I'm sorry that you are in such pain. I'm sure you are a good father, and I can't imagine what you must feel not being able to see your child. I appreciate your honesty in sharing this with me. I'd like to see you again. I hope that you will be coming into the city again soon and that when you do, you will call me."

She gave his fingers a small, encouraging squeeze before withdrawing her hand. Relief softened his face as Fred stood to pull out her chair, assuring her that he would, of course, contact her again soon.

Leonora thought about how her mother would react. Could she handle the revelation of Fred's previous marriage? She wasn't exactly modern in her thinking, but she was a kind and understanding woman. *I'll explain Fred's marriage as a youthful mistake. We're all entitled to those,* she told herself, as her heels clicked down the subway steps. Although, she also knew then that there was no way her mother would be ready to hear about the child.

CHAPTER 39

MORE THAN A YEAR passed, and Fred and Leonora had become a serious couple. Though the distance was always a challenge, seeing each other had become increasingly difficult as Leonora's father's condition was steadily worsening, and Leonora felt the strong pull of home. Aaron, now a young lawyer turned businessman, had taken over the duties as the head of the family, although beloved Zaydeh, their maternal grandfather, remained as the titular patriarch. Zaydeh was a man of few, but well-chosen words.

One day, he approached Leonora as she readied herself for work. "So, Leah," he said, referring to her by her Hebrew name. "This young man you have been seeing, do you like him?"

Leonora blushed at his directness, but she saw the twinkle in his eye and forgave him instantly.

"Yes, Zaydeh," she replied. "I like him. He's a good man."

She returned to brushing her hair, hoping that this uncomfortable interview was at an end.

"No, *shefele*, little lamb," her grandfather prodded. "I mean, do you really like him?"

He crossed his arms over his narrow chest and waited for her response.

"I know what you mean," Leonora said. She stood almost eye-to-eye with this small, gentle man who had been a bulwark of the family for as long as she could remember. She kissed his cheek and smiled. "I really like him Zaydeh. So, are you satisfied, and can I go to work now?"

"Well, you must invite him to dinner. Your mother will make a wonderful meal. We should all meet this *mensch*, this good man of yours, and he should come to our home." Then, reverting to his native, precise German to which he always resorted to make an important point, he took her by the hands and stated, "Leah, *ich hoffe er wird dich auf seinen Händen tragen.* I hope he will carry you in his hands. You are precious."

"OK, Zaydeh, I will ask him to dinner," Leonora conceded, not missing the certitude in her grandfather's statements. Her grandfather stepped aside to let her pass. Pulling on her gloves and cocking her hat at a jaunty angle, Leonora grinned at the satisfied look on his face.

The date was set soon enough; and although her mother said little when Leonora told her that Fred would be coming to dinner, the importance she attached to the occasion was evident in everything from the meal she began to prepare the day before to the glitter of her best crystal and silver flatware as they caught the early evening light.

When the doorbell rang promptly at six-thirty, Netania whisked the apron from around her waist and smoothed her skirt with one hand and her silver hair with the other. Aaron and Zaydeh, also hearing the bell, quickly joined Netania in the small front hall to greet their guest.

"Welcome, welcome," Netania said warmly, accepting the bouquet of spring flowers that Fred placed in her outstretched arms. "Please, let me take your coat."

As always, Fred was dressed immaculately. His hair was neatly combed, and a regimental striped tie peaked out of the vest of his pinstriped suit. His shoes reflected the glow of the candles already burning on the table. Leonora stepped forward and made the necessary introductions. Fred shook hands firmly with her brother and her grandfather, and Zaydeh returned his genial smile.

The family soon sat down to the table, and Leonora watched Fred tuck into the meal, which she knew would please her mother. Netania was known for her kreplach, airy pasta pillows filled with a mixture of meat and spices, which floated weightlessly in the golden chicken soup. The main course, a crisply roasted chicken stuffed with a dressing flavored with chestnuts and chicken livers, was really just a backdrop for Netania's other culinary masterpiece, the knishes. While many knishes were doughy and heavy, Netania's pastry was delicate; and the filling of whipped potatoes, sautéed onions, and secret seasonings was creamy and flavorful. Fred took a second knish, and told Netania that he could happily make a meal of them alone. There was a leafy salad with ripe tomatoes harvested just that morning from the vegetable garden in the small plot behind her Brooklyn brownstone. Leonora knew that her mother did not pride herself on her baking, and couldn't help but suppress a smile when she saw Netania bring in a lovely porcelain plate laden with homemade baklava, which must have taken all morning to prepare. She communicated a silent thank you with her eyes to her mother for having gone to so much trouble in recognition that, to her daughter, this was no ordinary guest.

During the meal, the conversation was light-hearted and frivolous, but as Leonora helped her mother clear the table and serve the coffee, she noticed her grandfather's demeanor change. He sat very straight in his chair at the head of the table, leaned forward toward Fred at the opposite end, and cleared his throat, garnering the attention of everyone seated around him.

"So, Frederick," he began, "you like the food, and you like my grand-daughter. But do you want to marry her?"

Leonora, Netania, and Aaron gasped simultaneously, nearly depleting the room of oxygen with their deep breaths; and all three heads swiveled in Fred's direction as the color drained from their faces. Only Zaydeh was unfazed by the torpor that now hung over the previously animated group as he awaited Fred's response.

Fred patted his lips with his napkin and sat back in his chair.

"Mrs. Pearl," he said, directing his remarks to Netania as if Zaydeh's unanswered question were not hovering over the table like a nuclear cloud. "I want you to know how much I appreciate this wonderful meal. As thin as I have always been, I may have to loosen my belt a notch on my way home."

He rested his long fingers gracefully across his trim midsection with satisfaction and smiled. Netania's face flushed with pleasure.

"Don't tell my mother," he continued in a conspiratorial whisper, "but I think your kreplach and knishes have just replaced hers as the reigning champions, and she was previously unassailable as the world record holder."

Leonora and Aaron exchanged uneasy glances as Zaydeh cleared his throat again. Fred looked calmly down the length of the table.

"And you are right, Zaydeh," he said, the smile never leaving his face. "I do like your granddaughter very much. As to marriage, when there is something to tell, you'll be the first to know."

Zaydeh let out a hearty chuckle, and Leonora felt the world lurch, as if it had just resumed its turning after a momentary but terrifying halt.

CHAPTER 40

AS IT TURNED OUT, Zaydeh did not have to wait long for an answer, as Leonora and Fred were married within the year. They wore matching suits at Fred's suggestion, and Leonora wondered silently whether this idea came from the fact that he had already had a white wedding. No matter, she reassured herself. She would not allow anything to mar this day of days, not even her incurable regret that Fred had not met her father, who had remained in his sickbed, too ill to join them for dinner when Fred had first visited her family home. Her father had found peace and blessed release from his pain only a month later, but he would never know that she had found happiness.

And find it she did. Only weeks after returning from their honeymoon, Leonora discovered that she was pregnant. Both she and Fred wanted children right away. After all, in 1949, a twenty-nine- year-old woman and a thirty-three-year-old man were considered unconventionally late to be starting a family. Besides, Leonora hoped that a child of their own would scab the wound of grief that Fred bore so stoically from his loss of Lydia. He did not speak of his daughter, but Leonora saw the child's photograph in his top dresser drawer when she was putting away his clean laundry. Its jagged edges were well loved from the many times her husband must have cradled it in his hand. She had picked it up and examined it guiltily, looking for any resemblance to her husband, any clues to the bond that she knew still existed between them, at least in Frederick's heart and mind. When Fred had first described her, he said that she greatly resembled his sister, Lorraine. Her hair was dark and wavy, her eyes a matching brown. She had a lovely olive complexion and a delicate nose and mouth. She looked more intelligent than beautiful, but one could never tell about the woman she would become. Mostly, Leonora was struck by how happy the child looked, even in a photograph. Tucking the picture back beneath a pile of immaculately pressed undershirts, Leonora wondered if the child's uprooting from her home and sudden removal from any contact with her father and grandparents, whom she certainly had loved, had shaken the foundation of that happiness. Were her eyes still dancing as they were in that photograph?

Leonora collected the mail from the curbside box as she did every afternoon. Sorting the bills, periodicals, and letters, she noticed the return address of a Florida law firm on the heavy white stock of one of the envelopes. The correspondence was addressed to Fred, so despite her heightened curiosity, she placed it unopened with his other mail on the table in the foyer where he would see it upon returning from work. But as she moved through the house, it was as if the cold, white envelope beckoned to her. She continued to perform her routine cleaning and cooking chores, but the presence of the legal documents that could only be from attorneys representing Frederick's ex-wife were an unwelcome intruder in their home.

Leonora had never asked Frederick to explain the details of the demise of his first marriage. She was satisfied with what little he had told her, that the relationship had foundered after Deborah's father had tried to involve Frederick in some illicit business dealings. Fred related this information to her almost matter-of-factly; but when he described how he and his parents subsequently were prevented from seeing his daughter, his eyes welled up; and his face crumpled like a used tissue.

Trailing her fingers across the envelope and instinctively wrapping her other hand around her unborn child, Leonora grew increasingly anxious. Would Frederick, like many misguided mariners, be lured to destruction by the intoxicating cry of his daughter, a siren of his own flesh? Would the prospect of having her once again be a part of his life draw him back toward his past and away from the future he was building with Leonora? Wasn't there an inherent inconsistency in her fervent belief that Frederick Green would be a wonderful father to their unborn child and the possibility that he could sever ties completely with his daughter? If these papers were some sort of invitation back into Lydia's life, would Leonora and her child have to share him with this daughter whom he obviously adored? Could she or should she influence him against such reinvolvement; and if she did, would he come to despise her for such selfishness? Would she come to despise herself? Leonora clamped her hands over her ears in a futile attempt to drown out the cacophony that roared inside her head.

She heard the key turn in the lock of the front door. Instinctively, she backed away from the foyer table where the letter lay, like a thief caught in the act tries to distance himself from the stolen goods. Fred seemed surprised to be facing her in the foyer when he stepped across the threshold.

"Hi, honey," he said, removing his hat and coat and handing them to his wife. "Something smells good. What's for dinner?"

Leonora placed his hat on the closet shelf and hung up his coat. Turning back to face him, she stepped forward and kissed his cheek.

"Beef stew," she smiled up at him.

Fred moved toward the table and picked up the stack of mail. He carried it into the living room and laid it on the top of the liquor cabinet. Beginning to fix himself a dry, Beefeater Gin martini, he made his only concession to informal attire by removing his suit coat and placing it carefully on the back of a nearby chair.

"Now, here's another reason I'll be glad when your pregnancy is over," he said, as he placed a twist of lemon in his cocktail. "I'm not one to drink alone. Here's to the three of us."

He patted Leonora's expanding middle, collected the mail again, and carried it over to his favorite chair. Leonora perched on the arm of the sofa next to him as he began rifling through the envelopes. He hurried through the junk mail, and finally his eyes met the stark black print of the law firm's name on the envelope he held in his hand. He put his drink on the table and gripped the sides of the envelope with both hands. His knuckles whitened, and his nostrils flared slightly like an animal that smells danger.

Leonora willed herself to stay quiet. Fred did not look up as he slit the envelope open with his monogrammed silver letter opener, a gift from Leonora for his last birthday. She watched as his eyes scanned the typewritten pages. He refolded them neatly along the same creases some lawyer's secretary had made before inserting them back into the envelope, then placed it on the table in front of him and laid both of his hands, palms down, fingers splayed, on top of it. He breathed deeply and closed his eyes. Just as quickly, he opened them and reached for his martini. Leonora could see his Adam's apple working as he took a calming sip. Still, she remained silent, expectant.

Turning his head slowly in her direction, Frederick's words were labored, and his voice was small. "They're adoption papers," he barely managed. He looked away again and took another swallow of his drink.

"What do you mean, 'adoption papers'?" Leonora was confused.

"Deborah has retained a lawyer to draw up the necessary papers that would allow her husband, Bruce Miller, to legally adopt Lydia."

Frederick's flat tone made him sound like a recording of a lesson for laymen on the legal requirements for adoption as he methodically explained that his signature on the papers would clear the way for Bruce Miller to become Lydia's legal father while simultaneously extinguishing all of Fred's parental rights to the child. He continued on at some length while Leonora listened in stunned silence. Finally, Fred uttered the question that Leonora had dreaded.

"What should I do, Leonora?"

Leonora had turned this same question over and over in her mind throughout the day, although she never anticipated that the papers pertained to adoption. Her worries had been limited to what role, if any, Frederick would play in his daughter's life and the concomitant impact of that participation on her own life and that of her unborn child. It was the finality of the adoption decision that ambushed them. She supposed that even if things continued on as they had been since Fred had been barred from seeing Lydia, he secretly harbored the dream that this imposed estrangement would someday be lifted. Agreeing to the adoption would mean more than giving up his paternal rights and obligations. It would mean exchanging the pain of separation for the permanence of irrevocable partition, snuffing out hope forever.

She stood and placed her hand on his shoulder. "You know I can't tell you that," she said softly. "You have to do what you think is right. I wish I could help you, but I can't influence a decision that is only yours to make."

Her hand trailed across his back as she made her way to the kitchen. She began to bring their dinner to the table; and each time she stepped through the swinging door that separated the kitchen from the dining area, she glimpsed Fred still seated in the living room, his drink abandoned on the table, the papers once again in his hand. They ate in silence, lost in their own thoughts; and when they finished, Leonora was glad for the opportunity to retreat once again into the safety of her kitchen.

She could hear Fred walking through the house restively, pausing now and then but soon resuming his agitated pacing. Finally, she heard his footsteps on the stairs and the creak of the door to their room as it opened and closed. She busied herself with cleaning up after the evening meal and invented other tasks to distract herself and fill the time, but eventually she had to join him in the bedroom. As she entered, she saw Frederick already in bed, his shoulders hunched and his face turned toward the wall. She could not tell for sure whether he was sleeping as she watched the blanket move rhythmically in time with his even breathing, but she went quietly into the bathroom and closed the door behind her.

Several days passed, and they tiptoed through the minefield that had become their lives since the arrival of the adoption papers. On the third night, Fred came home, went straight to the small den that served as his home office, and closed the door. Casting a guilty glance over his shoulder, he removed the deckle edged photo from the breast pocket of his suit coat where he had hidden it the morning after the adoption papers arrived. He held it gingerly in cupped hands like an offering and pressed it to his chest, closing his eyes and emitting a troubled, ragged sigh. *Lydia, what can I do? Do you even begin to know that my heart is breaking? Or have they turned you against me? Or have you, in your young life, forgotten me? My hope of seeing you again, of being a father to you again, is gone.*

Fred stared into the picture held just below his heart and whispered to it. *You are to have a sister, Lydia. Yes, I know in my soul that my next child will be a girl. I have been given a chance to start over, my darling daughter. I made choices, God help me, but I swear I will do it right this time! Forgive me!*

He unlocked the drawer of his writing desk and carefully pushed the photo to the back. He closed the drawer, and turned the key in the lock. It clicked with a sound of finality.

The next day, Fred arrived home from work and moved from the foyer to the living room, performing his evening routine as if it were ceremonial ablutions. He hung his overcoat neatly in the closet and placed his hat on the shelf directly above it. He went into the powder room off the living room and washed his face and hands. After carefully hanging his suit jacket on the customary chair, he mixed himself a cocktail.

"How are you feeling?" he asked Leonora who had joined him from the kitchen. "How was your day?"

Leonora affixed a smile on her face, hoping that it camouflaged the look of expectancy. "I'm fine. I had a nice day. I tried to organize some of the baby's things in the nursery."

Her voice trailed off as she found herself talking to her husband's back. Eventually, he turned toward her and sat down with his martini.

"I made a decision and signed the papers," he said brusquely.

"But I…you…"Leonora suddenly could not think how she had meant to end her sentence.

"I sent them back by return registered mail this afternoon, Leonora. It's over." Fred's voice was firm, but he spilled his drink on the walnut coffee table as he reached for it with an unsteady hand.

"God damn it!" he exclaimed as he looked around for something to mop up the puddle of gin before it seeped into the surface of the beautiful wood.

Leonora looked away. She had seldom heard him curse before. She rushed forward and soaked up the damaging liquid with the corner of her apron, grateful that she could busy herself.

"Never mind, honey," she said consolingly. "It won't leave a mark."

She squeezed his hand and tried to smile; but when she looked in her husband's eyes, she thought she could see through to his heart. In that momentary glimpse, she saw that a mark was already there.

CHAPTER 41

SAMANTHA ELYSE WAS BORN during a snowstorm in early March. When the nurse placed her new daughter in her arms, Leonora held her gently and gratefully counted her ten tiny fingers and toes. "You have a matching set," she cooed gently to the baby. "Yes, you do, little Sam."

She was named to honor two beloved relatives: Samantha was for Leonora's father, Samuel, and Elyse was a derivative of Lorraine's Hebrew name, Esther. This time, there was no mistaking that the infant had culled the best from her father's gene pool. She had large, luminous blue eyes, and dimples on either side of her perfect mouth that, with time, would undoubtedly curve into a beautiful smile. Her full head of hair was the color of dark cinnamon, and her complexion was flawless peach tinged with honey.

Leonora smiled up at Fred who stood close by her bedside. "Here, Fred, you hold her," she said supporting the baby's head and back, as the maternity nurse had instructed her. Fred mimicked her hand positions and cradled his newborn against his chest. Samantha opened her eyes and seemed to look right back at her father.

"I think she knows you," Leonora observed. "Look at the way she's looking at you."

Fred had tears in his eyes and bowed his head to whisper quietly to his daughter. The lines that had deepened across his forehead and around his eyes seemed fainter; the sharp grooves from his nose to the corners of his mouth softened in a smile of pure joy.

"She looks just like you, Fred." Leonora wanted the unexpected bonus of his being able to see himself so clearly in his child to bond them closely together. She thought guiltily again about the tattered photograph of Lydia, the dark hair and eyes so unlike Fred's.

"It doesn't matter which one of us she looks like," Fred responded without ever taking his eyes off the child. "She's absolutely gorgeous, and you can see how alert she is. She's already following the light with her eyes and trying to grasp my finger. She's smart, Leonora. Our little girl can grow up to be whatever she wants to be in this world."

Fred's devotion to Samantha never waned; but as steadfastly as he loved her, he guarded his secrets just as tenaciously. And Leonora was a full participant in this conspiracy of silence. Although she knew that it was impossible for Fred to forget, no matter how much time passed, Leonora was convinced that Samantha would enable him to carry his burden more lightly and that there was no reason why their daughter ever had to know.

With each developmental milestone that Samantha passed, sitting, crawling, standing, walking, speaking, Fred's heart swelled with pride overlaid by the ache of memory and longing. Yet, silent he remained, for what daughter could love a father who had left his other daughter behind?

Samantha grew to watch her father as if he were the magnetic axis around which her world revolved. At six years old, her eager eyes followed his sure hand as he worked the *New York Times* crossword puzzle, in ink, with only a rare mistake or correction. Caught in the thrall of his love affair with words, Sam sat beside him, trying to decipher his methodology, and noticed that her father held his pen in a peculiar way. Instead of resting it on his middle finger, his thumb and index finger encircling it to hold it in place, Fred bent his thumb completely around the pen, his index finger arching over the knuckle like a caterpillar in motion.

"Daddy," she exclaimed. "Did you know that I hold my pen exactly the same way that you do? I have never seen anyone else do that. Not at school or anywhere. See?" Sam picked up a pen from the table and demonstrated her grip for her father, who was smiling broadly.

"That's called a 'cuneal' thumb, Sammie," he said. "'Cuneal' means wedge-like. See how our thumbs form a wedge-like shape when the knuckle bends around the pen and slides under the pointer finger? I used to get wrapped on the knuckles with a metal-edged ruler by my teachers who were trying to break me of holding my pencil that way. Of course, they never did break me of it. Now, I know why. It's genetic."

He moved his large hand, pen in grasp, next to his daughter's small one, still holding her pen; and they both laughed. "Besides," he continued, "if you don't take your own path along the way, you may never learn such terrific crossword puzzle words as 'cuneal,' c-u-n-e-a-l. Now, you know what it means and how to spell it."

"I'm glad I'm like you, Daddy," Sam beamed.

"Me, too, Sammie," Fred agreed, kissing the top of her head.

By the time Samantha was in the fourth grade at Highland Elementary School, she learned something else-- the sting of her father's disappointment. Her school had initiated a new, supposedly more enlightened grading system: A student would receive two grades for each subject based on a scale of High, Medium or Low. The first grade was determined by the teacher's view of how the student's work compared to the rest of the class; the second grade reflected the teacher's measurement of the student's work as it related to her actual ability. Although she had received all H's as compared to the rest of the class, Miss Peterson, her teacher, intending to send a strong message that Sam actually was capable of doing even better work, gave Samantha six M's in the second column.

Stopping by Samantha's desk at the end of the day as she passed out the report card envelopes, Miss Peterson said, "Samantha, I know you are not going to be happy with your marks, but it isn't enough to best your classmates. You have great potential, and you need to tap into that if you are going to succeed in the wider world."

Sam felt the cold fingers of failure for the first time as she took the manila envelope from her teacher's hand. Her mother made her sit at the top of the stairs with her report card in her hand where she would have a clear view of the front door. When her father crossed the threshold, she was to hand it to him and await his judgment. Samantha felt the sweaty palms and dry mouth that accompanied that simple transfer of paper to her father's hand; and forever after she could summon the gray ghost of his disappointment in the disembodied words that hovered between them.

"Well, Sammie, you and I both know that you can do a lot better than this."

He pressed the report card back into her hand so quickly and without even reading the teacher's laudatory comments that it was as if he were seeking to rid himself of something so dreadful that it should have been deposited in the garbage long before it touched his hand. She barely remembered her two perfect report cards for the remainder of that year, all H's in both columns.

Eventually, Sam was old enough, even without knowing it, to ask her father the difficult questions. When she was in the sixth grade, she announced, "We're studying World War II, Daddy." Fred had just come home from work; and she met him at the door, flinging it open before he reached the threshold. Feeling herself an important participant in her father's evening ritual, Sam took his briefcase and placed it in the foyer closet. Taking his hand and leading him to the living room, she continued. "Lots of the other kids said that their daddies were in the war. Were you in the war, Daddy? Sally said her Daddy was a submarine captain in the Atlantic. My teacher said that after the bombing of Pearl Harbor, practically every able-bodied American man lined up to volunteer. What's 'able-bodied,' Daddy? Were you able-bodied?" Questions always poured out of Samantha like water over a dam after a springtime flood.

"Slow down, Sam. One question at a time," Fred said. Caught off guard and anxious to avoid discussing this period in his life, Fred desperately tried to buy time to gather his thoughts into a plausible story to tell his daughter. He took a seat on the sofa and patted the cushion next to him. Sam sat down and waited expectantly. "'Able-bodied' means healthy, fit to serve. Your teacher is absolutely right, Sam. When Japan struck the United States and we entered the war against Hirohito and the Axis powers led by Nazi Germany's Adolph Hitler, I was among the many young men eager to enlist to defend our country because we had been attacked. I wanted to join the Navy. At my physical, the doctor reported that I had a 'chicken breast;' and this kept me out of the Navy."

He laughed, pointing at his sternum, which did resemble a wishbone. Sam giggled. "I went down the street and immediately joined the Army. I was part of the OSS, the Office of Strategic Services. I parachuted behind enemy lines into Czechoslovakia. I finished the war as a Lieutenant Colonel."

The lie lay upon Fred's tongue like the sour taste of gall. He tried to push away the realization that he had lied so easily to his daughter. "I really don't like to talk about it, honey," he said, hoping that he could now change the subject.

Mistaking the cause of the uncomfortable look on her father's face, Sam said, "Oh, I totally understand, Daddy. My teacher says that lots of soldiers returned from the war and didn't want to talk about their experiences. He says, 'War is hell.'" She assumed a look of gravity and sagacity beyond her years and seemed lost in thought. "But you know, Daddy," she mused. "I just figured out that you were almost twenty-six years old when the Japanese bombed Pearl Harbor. My teacher told us that the average age of an American soldier serving in World War II was twenty-one. How come you were so much older?"

Fred sighed heavily. "Well, honey, I already had been to a year of graduate school in philosophy and then law school at the University of Pennsylvania. That's why they made me an officer." *That's at least a half-truth*, he said to himself, now measuring the weight of his dishonesty. *The other half is that I was a too-old, married father!*

"Oh, I get it," Sam acknowledged.

"Dinner's ready," Leonora called from the kitchen.

"C'mon, Daddy," Sam said, pulling her father to his feet. "Mommy doesn't like it when we let our dinner get cold."

Fred followed her to the table, watching her shiny hair swing at her shoulders. He noticed that her childish shape was beginning to metamorphose into a lovely female form. He had a chance to tell her tonight. He chose not to. There would be other opportunities; of this he was sure. He, who claimed to venerate honesty like a religion, could not say if he would make the same choice again. Over and over again in her short life he had assured her, "Daddy is honest as the day is long. Daddy never lies." The thought of this mantra made his tongue feel thick, and the empty words seemed to stick to the roof of his mouth like a spoonful of peanut butter with nothing to wash it down.

As her elementary school years gave way to junior high, there were other threads of similarity that bound Fred and Samantha together. Father and daughter whiled away hours with modeling clay, pipe cleaners, cardboard, and glue transforming autumn leaves into thatched houses and plastic witches' heads that once adorned the icing of Halloween cupcakes into colonial farmers or soldiers.

"Look, Daddy," Sam exclaimed holding up a green clay leaf that she molded. "I've used this toothpick to mark the veins that always appear on each tobacco leaf."

Fred inspected his daughter's work and prompted her to even greater accuracy. "Don't forget, Sammie, the tobacco plants would have been planted in very even rows. You can use this dime store mirror to simulate a water source on the plantation because all good farming occurs near a river, lake, or stream, a water source for irrigation or farm animals."

Sam carried these dioramas of a Virginia tobacco plantation or the Texas Alamo into her classrooms as if she were presenting precious works of art, for indeed they were. Miniature historical replicas born of her and her father's ingenuity, imagination and talent, they were a testament to the patience and love that flowed through the fingers of their creators.

Throughout her school years, Fred was unquestionably generous with his time when it came to his daughter. He went to work early or on weekends in order to be home faithfully at 5:30 to have dinner with his family. Afterwards, as Leonora worked at the kitchen sink, Fred took his seat in his favorite chair in the living room where he was always available to help Sam with her school projects or quiz her in preparation for a test the following day. No subject was too dry or uninteresting. Fred's love of learning allowed him to make a game of even the most brute memorization.

"I need to learn all of the prepositions in Latin," Sam frowned one day while still in junior high. "I hate when teachers force you to learn lists of words just to prove you can." She hung her head and crossed her arms over her thin chest in a deep pout.

"See that round cocktail table over there?" Fred asked with a twinkling eye. "How about if I quiz you on the vocabulary, and for every one you get right, you get to take another skip or dance step around the table? I bet you'll be all the way around in no time!"

Sam opened her mouth to protest; but Fred held up his hand like a track flagman, dropped it, and shouted, "Go."

"Ab, cum, de," Sam began reluctantly.

"Ok," Fred encouraged enthusiastically. "That's three steps of your choice around the table."

Sam hopped, skipped, and jumped a quarter of the way around the circumference. "Let's go, let's go," Fred rooted. "I want to see some fancy footwork after you give me three more prepositions.

"Ex, in, pro." Sam rolled the Latin words off her tongue with greater conviction as she pirouetted, cha cha-ed, and performed a perfect cartwheel. Fred suppressed a laugh because he knew that there was no stopping her now. Her competitive spirit had taken over, and the memorization was no longer drudgery.

"Prae, sine, and sub," Sam concluded with aplomb. She executed a handstand, a back somersault, and ended where she had begun with a split. Her smile of satisfaction reflected her father's.

Always the teacher, Fred handed the list of Latin prepositions back to her and began to talk. "All romance languages are a branch of the Indo-European family of languages that descend from Latin, the language of ancient Rome. There are twenty-five surviving romance languages, and the six most spoken are Spanish, Portuguese, French, Italian, Romanian, and Catalan. Master the language of the ancient Romans, and you will be able to dissect and discern the meaning of most of the more complex and compound words in any romance language. To get there, you will undoubtedly have to apply yourself to all kinds of assignments that do not seem stimulating or even necessary, but you will never be sorry. Education is the antithesis of ignorance and the key to success." Sam knew intuitively that her father had set a course for her; and she followed, drawn in the same way that a moth flutters toward the light.

CHAPTER 42

JUST AS ASSUREDLY AS Fred influenced every aspect of Samantha's academic and artistic development, he also tried to extend his reach to his daughter's personal life, beginning with the usually inconsequential dating choices of high school. It was nineteen sixty-five. Ted Mervin was a senior in high school; Samantha was in the tenth grade. The table was set for dinner in the dining room, a rare occurrence in Samantha's household, where her mother loved to cook but behaved as if having even a couple of guests required putting on a state dinner. Fred walked into the kitchen where Leonora had been preparing all day and snatched a piece of Italian bread from the basket just as Leonora brushed his hand away. "Oh, why do you have to get so uptight over a snot-nosed kid coming to dinner? Just because Sammie invited him doesn't make him the Prince of Wales. His father is in the textile business, for God's sake, and he's just a regular kid. Can't you just relax?"

Before Leonora could reply, the doorbell rang. Samantha swung it open, and Ted sauntered into the foyer, shopping bag in hand. He shook hands with her father peremptorily and strode past Samantha. She rushed to keep up with him as he entered the living room. Ted's eyes made the rounds of the room, and he slowed down to pick up a crystal bowl from the sideboard. Samantha's jaw dropped in shock that Ted would pick up a piece from her father's beloved and valuable crystal collection. "Lalique, isn't it?" he asked no one in particular.

"Actually, it's Baccarat," Fred snapped, as he pointedly relieved Ted of the bowl and cast a disappointed look in Samantha's direction. Ted was what her father always referred to as "cocksure". He was of average height, medium build, and adequate looks; in fact, everything about him seemed ordinary, except his obviously too high opinion of himself.

"Let's all go into the dining room," Leonora said, with a pleading look at her husband. Samantha, Ted, and her parents took their seats at the round table. Samantha sat between Ted and her father, stealing surreptitious sidelong glances at them. Leonora had made her homemade spaghetti sauce that her family loved. There was crusty Italian bread, English peas, and a mixed green salad that Samantha had contributed.

Over salad, Fred turned to Ted and asked, "What are your plans for college?"

Ted patted the corners of his mouth with his napkin and smiled. "Well, Mr. Green, I want only the best. I'm planning to go to Princeton, and I'm very excited about it, but my counselor made me apply to Penn as a fallback. Of course, no one wants to be stuck going to their safety school."

Fred's face reddened at Ted's dismissive attitude toward the very university that had been his boyhood dream. "Really, Ted," he said, biting off each word. "I wouldn't be so sure. What's that saying, 'Life is what happens when you're busy making other plans?' Things don't always go according to Hoyle."

Leonora excused herself from the table. "Time for the main course, spaghetti Bolognese," she said in what she hoped would pass for an Italian accent.

As soon as he was served, Ted pretentiously twirled a forkful of pasta on his spoon and closed his lips appraisingly around the sauce-laden noodles. Samantha nudged her father's knee under the table when she saw his eyes roll to the ceiling. Fred responded by making an exaggerated show of lifting his fork to his mouth without the aid of his spoon.

Seeming not to notice Fred and turning to Samantha's mother as if he were a judge in the Betty Crocker cook-off, Ted pronounced, "Particularly fine use of the green pepper." Leonora smiled broadly. "And might I say," Ted continued, "while your daughter certainly has great potential, it is obvious, Mrs. Green, that you already have arrived!"

Leonora preened visibly, basking in the afterglow of Ted's endorsement. "Why, thank you, Ted," she sputtered. "Please have some more." She ladled another heaping portion of spaghetti and meat sauce onto his plate.

Fred's lip curled, and he cleared his throat audibly. "Personally, I think that people are far too uptight in situations like this," he lectured a little too loudly. "The hostess worries too much about the meal, and the guest feels compelled to offer some inane compliment just to alleviate the stress of being the beneficiary of all the work that has been expended on his behalf. I don't see why something as simple as eating together shouldn't be an opportunity for everyone to relax and be themselves."

Samantha had no idea where this monologue was leading, but she knew it was nowhere good. Before she could think of something to say, her father leaned across her and spoke directly to Ted.

"For example, just to make a point, let's say that I felt like putting these peas in my hair." He scooped up a generous portion of his peas, making sure to use his spoon that had up to that moment rested innocently beside his plate, and held them in suspended animation before him. "Well, if that's what I felt like doing, why should I have to adopt some false, arbitrary rules of etiquette just because we have company?" He deposited the spoonful of peas onto the crown of his silver mane with one hand and massaged them in place with the other until the top of his head looked like it had been the victim of a passing bird in flight. Three pairs of astonished eyes fixed in horror on the mess, but he went on undeterred. "Don't you think that would be preferable to the play-acting that usually goes on?"

Leonora reached for a clean napkin from the sideboard and offered it to her husband, the edges of her too tight smile straining into a grimace against her rouged cheeks. Fred ignored her, his unblinking, challenging stare fixed on Ted, who seemed momentarily struck dumb. Leonora, with the pristine napkin still in her extended hand, dropped back heavily into her chair.

"Come on, Dad," Samantha urged, her eyes begging him to permit a change of subject.

Her father returned his concentration to his plate, as if there were nothing unseemly about having mashed peas in his hair. Gloating like a playground hero who has momentarily captured the flag, he finally accepted the proffered napkin and finished wiping the peas from his hair that now lay matted against his scalp.

Recovering quickly, Ted was not to be outdone. He pushed his chair back from the table and lifted a shopping bag onto his lap from where it sat on the floor. Directing his attention to the contents of his bag, he held up what looked to be an ordinary men's rain hat. "This," he said proudly, "is my father's invention. It is the wave of the future." He slowly pivoted the hat 360 degrees as if he were demonstrating a moon rock.

Looks of confusion passed among Samantha and her parents; but again, her father was the first to speak. "It looks like a rain hat to me. What's so special about it?"

"It's made out of a new miracle fabric that my father developed," Ted enthused. "It's called Permanent Press because, no matter what you do to it, it never wrinkles." Samantha caught the mischievous gleam in her father's eye and wondered what disaster could eclipse the pea routine.

"May I see that?" her father asked, reaching for the hat. Crushing it between his large palms and kneading it with his long fingers, he never broke eye contact with Ted. "So, you're saying that no matter what you do to this, what did you call it, Permanent Press, it will return to its original shape none the worse for wear?"

He dropped the unrecognizable ball of grey material onto the carpet as he spoke and ground it beneath his heel. Finally having mercy on his dinner companions, if not on the remnants of the hat, he picked it up and handed what was left of the wrinkled fabric back to Ted. His expression was the picture of innocence.

Ted's face was the green of the English peas. He dropped the ruins of the hat into his bag and stood. "I'm sorry, I'm really not feeling well," he said. "I think I'd better be going. Thank you for the dinner," he managed.

"Oh, that's too bad," Samantha's father said, offering his hand. "You'll miss dessert. We certainly hope you'll be feeling better soon."

"Let me see you to the door," Samantha said, directing a narrow-eyed look of annoyance at her father's placid face. Ted left without another word, and Samantha returned to the dinner table where her father was eating with gusto.

"I think you can do a lot better, Sammie," he said, looking up at her. "If there's one thing I can't stand, it's a guy who's full of himself, and you shouldn't fall for it."

He spread a fresh napkin on his lap and attacked his spaghetti with renewed vigor. Samantha's plate grew cold.

Two years later, when she was selected to deliver Springside School's senior class valedictory address, she could still feel in the pit of her stomach the dread that something about her achievement would not quite meet her father's standards. She labored long and hard on her speech, practicing it until practically committing it to memory.

As graduation day drew closer and the maintenance men began to set up the neat rows of white wooden chairs and the speakers' podium in the grove of leafy oak trees that had been the site of commencement exercises since the school's founding in 1845, she thought she would remember every studied detail of that day forever. When the headmaster introduced her, she stood at her place, first in the front row of seats facing the audience behind the lectern. She turned to her right and left her bouquet of red and white roses in her chair. As the headmaster resumed his seat to her left, she mounted the podium where her neatly printed note cards already were in place. She breathed deeply, looked out over the assemblage of families, friends, and school personnel, and began to deliver her thoughtfully crafted remarks.

She spotted her parents in the audience. Her mother sat on the edge of her seat on that balmy spring day in May 1967; the only part of her that moved was her hair as the wind gently lifted it. Her father, too, sat ramrod erect, fingers laced in his lap, never taking his eyes off of her, and listened intently to every word. The other faces faded, and Samantha spoke directly to him. Her knee shook involuntarily with nerves, and she could feel the flapping of her white graduation robe with each movement of her leg. She hoped that the audience, and particularly her father, could not detect in her voice the same nervousness. She lifted her chin higher and projected her voice more strongly with each barely perceptible nod of his head or affirming forward lean of his long body demonstrating his rapt attention.

Her parents joined in the applause and smiled as they accepted the kind remarks of the other parents and friends seated around them. At the end of the commencement exercises, Samantha joined them; and her mother grabbed her and kissed her cheek so many times that she wondered if the lipstick would ever come off.

But Samantha didn't feel relieved until her father finally spoke: "Sam, your voice was strong and clear. You did a wonderful job."

Later that day, and for the rest of her life, Sam could not remember a word of that speech for which she had been the meticulous architect. The only word that became synonymous with that rarefied event was approval, and the only praise she remembered was her father's.

When time and distance had staunched her anger, Samantha could laugh at her father's feigned innocence and his reaction to Ted Mervin's outsized teenaged air of superiority; yet over the next few years, Ted was not the only boyfriend of Samantha's whom Fred impacted. Samantha met Mitchell Baleman, who was her friend, Cindy's cousin, during the summer after

Samantha graduated from Springside. Mitchell had just finished his second year at Dartmouth and was visiting Philadelphia for a family wedding. He had hair like a Brillo pad and black plastic-framed glasses with lenses thick as the bottoms of Coke bottles; but he had the sensitive heart of a poet and the incisive mind of a Renaissance thinker. They discussed books and films, foreign and independent ones unlike the big Hollywood blockbusters her classmates favored. When he spoke, Samantha forgot about his looks because he challenged her and respected her ideas.

They became pen pals, writing each other long, thought-provoking letters filled with youthful, idealistic opinions that are the hallmark of liberal arts scholars who, for the only time in their lives, have four years to devote to the luxury of erudition. Never considering that Mitchell harbored a secret longing that their friendship would blossom into romance, she agreed that he would spend a weekend in late July at her home in Philadelphia the following summer.

A year and innumerable letters after they had met, he arrived on a sizzling summer day. The insufferable humidity curled his hair even more tightly to his head; and when he stepped from the sanctuary of the air-conditioned airport, the thick air immediately fogged his glasses so that he looked bug-eyed like the insect from Samantha's childhood game, Cootie. He carried a suitcase in one hand and a cardboard box tied with string in the other. His smile overshadowed the sheen of sweat that swathed his features as he hefted his belongings into Samantha's trunk.

"Hey," she said warmly.

"Hi, yourself," he replied. When he bent to kiss her, Samantha instinctively turned to offer her cheek. In the momentary awkwardness of his embrace, Samantha realized for the first time that Mitchell was hoping that this visit would provide the opportunity to alter the platonic foundation of their relationship.

"How 'bout this heat?" she exclaimed, as she slid into the cool safety of the driver's seat. "It's been over ninety every day this week. I feel like shedding my own skin." Mitchell seemed to accept the heat as explanation for her aloofness, and beamed at her from the passenger seat.

"What's in the box?" Samantha asked as they joined the flow of traffic on the Schuylkill Expressway headed north out of the city. "The way you were carrying it, it must be fragile."

"It's a significant portion of my record collection, including every album that *Chicago* has ever released, and I am making a belated present of it to you for your birthday." He leaned happily against the passenger door of the car to face her.

"That's amazing, Mitchell," Samantha blurted, "but you don't actually have to give them to me. I don't think I can accept such a gift, especially knowing how much music means to you. We can just listen to them while you're here, and then you can take them home."

"No, I've thought about it, and it's because this music is such a part of who I am that I want you to have it." He looked like someone who would gladly donate a kidney for someone he loved.

Samantha's palms perspired against the steering wheel, and she could feel her pulse throbbing at her temples. This was not what she wanted from her long-distance friendship with Mitchell. She was angry at her own naivety and acutely aware that it had brought her to this awkward impasse. She smiled weakly and quickly changed the subject, rambling awkwardly as she always did when she was ill at ease. Mitchell actually seemed to enjoy it as she flitted like a hummingbird from one topic to the next all the way home. It was with a modicum of relief that she pulled into the driveway and parked the car.

"Can I carry anything?" she asked, coming around to the passenger side. Mitchell already had hefted his suitcase in one hand and his precious records in the other.

"No, I got it," he assured her over the edge of the cardboard box.

Samantha walked ahead to open the door, and yelled, "We're here," as it swung open. Judging from the nanosecond that it took her parents to appear in the foyer, they must have been watching for them through the window. They both smiled broadly as Mitchell deposited his belongings on the floor.

Her father extended his hand and said, "Fred Green, Mitchell, and this is my wife, Leonora. Welcome to our home. How was your trip?"

Mitchell shook his hand warmly. "Fine, fine, sir," he replied. "I'm just glad to be here." He beamed a wide, toothy smile at Samantha that her parents could not help but notice.

"Come in and make yourself at home, Mitchell," Leonora offered, gesturing toward the living room. Samantha could see a spread of cakes and coffee on the table. Her mother led the way, and everyone followed suit. *Food, Mom's solution to every awkward situation,* Samantha mused, as she helped herself to a lemon square. It seemed to have worked this time; and in what passed as only moments, the four of them were talking companionably.

"Well, I hate to put an end to the party," her father said, rising and stretching his arms in a yawn, "but I have a big day tomorrow, and you kids can sleep in, so I'm going to call it a night. It was very nice to meet you, Mitchell."

He patted Mitchell on the shoulder and kissed the top of Samantha's head as he made his way to the stairs. Samantha and Mitchell helped her mother clear the dishes and the remnants of dessert.

"Samantha will show you to the guestroom," Leonora said as she tied her apron around her waist and squirted dishwashing liquid into the sink. "Have a good rest. I know that Sammie has plans for you to go downtown to see the sights tomorrow, so you'll be doing lots of walking."

"Thanks for dessert, Mrs. Green," Mitchell said. "See you in the morning."

Samantha kissed her mother's cheek and led Mitchell away.

Mitchell retrieved his suitcase and parcel from the foot of the stairs where he had left them and followed Samantha to the guest room. Surmounting the last step, Samantha opened the door to her room and joked, "Well, this is where I get off. Your room is next door." It was not lost on Mitchell that his room was flanked on one side by Samantha's and on the other by her parents'.

"Goodnight, then," she said, slipping into her room.

"Goodnight," Mitchell said. She could hear his footsteps receding down the hall; and she expelled a generous sigh of relief as she heard her door latch, the full weight of her back against it.

The following day, amid a profusion of smiles and well wishes from her parents, Samantha and Mitchell set off to explore the historical sights of colonial Philadelphia. She supposed that it was in part because central Philadelphia was considered dangerous and had not yet rescued itself from the grip of urban decay that she had never seen such hallmarks of American revolutionary history as Independence Hall, the Liberty Bell, or Betsy Ross's House until she brought her college roommate to visit the previous November during her freshman year. It seemed obligatory to take a non-Philadelphian to gape at these relics of our national past; and here she was again, with Mitchell in tow, describing the hallowed ground of our Founding Fathers. Majoring in American History, Samantha was in her element, and Mitchell contentedly listened and followed her from one tourist attraction to the next. It was another sweltering day, so Samantha had an excuse to keep her distance, although Mitchell tried several times to hold her hand as they walked. Samantha kept talking, hoping her nervousness didn't show; and she busied her hands with a map and tour guide. Hot and satiated on history after a long afternoon, they turned the air-conditioning and music up full blast for the ride home.

After dinner, Mitchell excused himself and returned to the living room with his cardboard box. Using his penknife to cut the string, he spoke lovingly as he turned back the flaps to reveal a cache of record albums.

"Now, don't try to stop me," he said, lifting them out and spreading the album jackets across the coffee table for Samantha to review. "I told you already that I want you to have these."

He carefully released one of the LPs from its protective cover and walked over to the stereo. In seconds, *Does Anybody Really Know What Time it is?* blared through the speakers. Mitchell rocked back on his heels and smiled.

Samantha smiled back at him and tapped her foot to the beat. "I love *Chicago*," she confirmed. "I can't believe you would give me such a gift, but I really thank you."

She leaned over and hugged him, but the moment quickly became uncomfortable because he clung to her conspicuously longer than she to him. When he finally let go, Samantha pretended not to have noticed and sat back against the sofa. She wondered how someone as smart as he was could be oblivious to the strain between them. After what she hoped was a protracted enough show of enthusiasm over the music, she told him that she was exhausted from the day's activities and excused herself to bed.

But when she got to her room, and heard the door to the guestroom shut down the hall, she couldn't make her eyes close. She turned her face to the window and tried to distract herself with her childhood game of finding faces among the leafy branches of the crabapple tree that grew outside. She truly valued Mitchell's friendship; but despite her father's lifelong admonitions that she should value character and intelligence over physical and ephemeral beauty, she could not make herself regard his sensitivity and intelligence outside of that context. She could not make herself desire him; she could not make herself love him. She finally fell into a restless sleep, and the morning came too soon.

When the sunlight streamed through the diaphanous curtains, Samantha squinted against the glare and rolled away from the window. She could hear the muffled sounds of her mother preparing breakfast amid muted conversation. She showered and dressed quickly, feeling somehow that she had abandoned Mitchell to an uncomfortable conversation with her parents. She chastised herself for worrying that any of the three could not handle themselves without somehow doing or saying something awkward. Her reflection in the bathroom mirror looked guilty. She silently prayed that the towel with which she dried her face could wipe away the self-loathing she knew came from her real worry, that her father, who undoubtedly would recognize Mitchell's kindness and intelligence, would fall in love with him when she could not.

She descended the stairs and walked through the living room toward the swinging door that separated the dining area from the kitchen but could hear her father talking to Mitchell before she could enter the room. Their voices curled under the door like smoke, wreathing her head in a dizzying miasma.

"There are certain things you can do to improve yourself," she heard her father advise him. "I mean, man to man, you and I both know that there is no denying the role attraction plays in a relationship. If you want Samantha to respond to you in a physical way, then you are going to have to make certain changes to appeal to her as a man. I think you know what I'm trying to say to you, Mitchell."

"I'm not sure, sir," Mitchell replied wanly.

Samantha, imploring again her inner God, prayed that her father, in an epiphany of grace, would change the subject.

"Well, for starters," her father's critique continued unabated, "you need to do something about that hair."

Through the crack in the door between the jam and the hinges, Samantha could see Mitchell's hand instinctively jerk upwards toward his unruly curls.

"Don't they have a straightener for that kind of frizz these days? Then, of course, you should cut it so it looks less like a white man's excuse for an Afro."

Samantha thought about pushing the door open before the silence evaporated, but her leaden legs seemed glued to the spot. Mitchell's arm dropped back to his side, and his unblinking eyes registered shock through the thick lenses of his glasses. Her father was undeterred by Mitchell's silence. As if she had sent a telepathic message to her father, she saw his head pivot slowly toward the door, but then he spoke again.

"And another thing, those glasses. No one with any style wears those thick plastic frames anymore. Wire rims are in now. Even I have them." To prove his point, he reached into his breast pocket and extracted a pair of aviator-style gold-rimmed glasses and placed them on his face. "Perhaps, you've considered contact lenses. A young man like you could learn to wear them in no time."

Mitchell removed his glasses with one hand and began to wipe them unceremoniously with a copious white handkerchief that he extracted from his pants pocket. Before replacing them, he used the handkerchief to mop up the sweat that had beaded across his forehead and the bridge of his nose. "Sir, I don't…." he began hesitantly.

"You don't have to thank me. I can see how you feel about my daughter, and I think you are a fine young man. You just need a little help in certain areas," he said, reaching over and patting Mitchell's arm that still lay listlessly at his side. "If you don't mind a little advice, you can really improve your chances with her, is all. You're very bright; and from what I've observed, you're a kind fellow; but you just need to work on your chemistry. A boy and girl have to have good chemistry. That much has never changed. Never will." He sat back in his chair looking satisfied.

Samantha made a noisy entrance into the kitchen. The swinging door slapped against the wall and swung back and forth several times on its creaking hinges before finally coming to rest. The humiliated look on Mitchell's face was crowned by both of his hands as he made a futile, self-conscious attempt to trap his hair that, despite his efforts, looked like Medusa's snakes escaping between his fingers. Still perspiring profusely, his glasses had slid to the tip of his nose. Behind them, her mother was busy preparing breakfast for everyone. Her father beamed at her from his place at the head of the table.

"Look who's finally awake," he grinned. "Mitchell and I were just having a nice conversation. You're just in time for one of your mother's special Sunday breakfasts."

He took his napkin and spread it on his lap readying himself to be served. Samantha helped her mother bring the food to the table, and they all ate as if nothing had happened. She wondered whether Mitchell would speak to her about what her father had said to him once they were alone. She alternated between praying for silence and wondering what she could say that would ameliorate the heavy weight of impossibility that lay between them.

After what she hoped was a reasonable amount of time to linger at the table, Samantha made an exaggerated show of checking her watch for the time. "Well, unfortunately, we're going to have to head out," she said, turning to Mitchell. "Several decades of graft within the city government have insured that there are no good roads to the Philadelphia airport from here, not to mention that the airport itself is in a perpetual state of construction."

Mitchell brought the remnants of his breakfast to the kitchen counter and returned to the table to say goodbye. "Thank you very much for having me, Mr. and Mrs. Green." He shook hands with both of her parents. "I hope to see you again soon."

"Keep in mind our little discussion," her father winked. "Have a safe trip."

Mitchell blinked hard behind his glasses. "Thank you, sir." He picked up his suitcase and followed Samantha through the door.

Samantha switched on the radio as soon as they turned out of the driveway. Mitchell seemed preoccupied with rummaging through his small suitcase. Finally, he extracted a small, wrapped package about the size of a picture frame. He stowed his suitcase behind his seat and held the package on his lap, adjusting the ribbon and smoothing the floral wrapping paper. When he was satisfied, he turned to Samantha and said, "This is for you. Consider it another part of your belated birthday gift. I had a really great time this weekend." He slid the package toward her.

"You already gave me too much," Samantha protested. "I still can't believe that you insisted on giving me your entire collection of *Chicago* albums. You don't have to give me anything else. I am really glad that you came to visit; that's present enough."

Mitchell pushed the gift closer to her on the seat. "It's really just another small token," he said.

By now, Samantha had pulled into a parking space at the airport. "Look, Samantha, just open it after I've gone, OK?" he asked. He had wrenched his bag from behind the seat and was leaning in through the open passenger door. Samantha turned off the ignition and came around to his side of the car.

"OK," she agreed. "I'll open it later. Promise me you'll write once we're back at school. I really look forward to your letters."

"I'm not stupid," he said suddenly. The unexpected wave of his anger crested over her. "I see now that you will never think of me as anything but a friend, and that's just not what I want from you, Samantha. If I have to keep denying my feelings for you, I don't think I can go on with things the way they are between us. I can't keep writing letters and secretly hoping for something more."

She reached out to touch his arm, but he pulled it away with a hasty jerk that belied any further attempts at physical contact. "I'm sorry," she said lamely. "I'm so sorry."

Mitchell left her standing beside the car. She watched him disappear into the terminal, standing in the stale heat of the parking lot for some time. She was sorry-- sorry that she had lost his friendship; sorry that she could not love him; sorry that she could not fix this. She opened her car door and switched on the ignition. Then, she remembered the gift and picked it up gently from the seat. She slipped off the ribbon and carefully removed the tape from the wrapping. When the paper fell away, it revealed a lovely, leather- bound edition of *The Rubaiyat of Omar Khayyam*. The title was embossed in gold on the cover, and Samantha ran her fingers over the delicate filigree that surrounded it. She opened the burgundy binding and saw Mitchell's familiar, neat script on the flyleaf:

Dear Samantha,

Every so often, the world seems to be
a very unfriendly place
and life a cruel game

empty of meaning.

At these times, the greatest comfort

is the knowledge that there are

people who care about our existence

and thus render life precious.

Your birthday is indeed a time for rejoicing

the anniversary of your being

for my life is ever enriched

our having met.

Love,

Mitchell

Samantha turned the car off again and rested her head against the seat, still holding the slender volume. She was familiar with the writings of the astronomer-poet of Persia, and she flipped through the pages, her eyes alighting on verse seventy-three:

Ah, Love! could thou and I with Fate conspire

To grasp this sorry Scheme of Things entire,

Would not we shatter it to bits—and then

Re-mould it nearer to the Heart's Desire!

She knew now that she would not hear from Mitchell again. Her father had made a naïve attempt to shatter the sorry scheme of things, but it had brought Mitchell no closer to his heart's desire.

CHAPTER 43

THE FOLLOWING FALL, WHEN Samantha was a sophomore at Barnard, the liberal arts college for women at Columbia University, she met Jake. He was beginning his second year of medical school at Columbia. As with most meetings, it happened by chance. Sam had come back to New York before the start of classes to help one of her friends, Linda Levin, move into an off campus apartment. After a long day of work, the girls were starving and ready for a break. Covered in paint and tired to the bone, they collapsed onto the two remaining seats at Chock Full o' Nuts, a popular lunch counter, on the corner of 116th Street and Broadway which was famous for its signature Nutted Cheese sandwiches. The girls placed their orders, and watched ravenously as the cook spread cream cheese onto thick slices of date-nut bread. Wordlessly, Samantha and Linda wolfed down the sandwiches and coffee that, close to midnight, seemed like manna in the wilderness.

Sam barely noticed the young man seated across from her on the other side of the horseshoe-shaped Formica counter. She was exhausted, and not exactly dressed to meet anyone.

"Don't I know you from somewhere?" he asked, leaning toward Linda. *If that isn't the oldest line in the book,* Sam thought to herself. She felt even more annoyed when she looked up from her steaming cup of coffee and discovered that the voice she heard was connected to a boy who was clearly already on a date. Linda didn't seem to notice, and although equally unkempt, was preening as she attempted to place the young man.

"Why, yes," Linda cooed, "I think we were on the same student trip to Europe a couple of summers ago when I was still in high school."

The boy smiled broadly, confirming their association, and his date fumed sullenly beside him. "Jake Isaacs," he said.

"Linda Levin," she replied. "So, what have you been up to? Are you still in school?"

"I graduated from Columbia after three years, and now I'm in my second year of medical school. How about you?" Jake asked.

Linda was clearly impressed. "That's wonderful, Jake. I am a junior here."

Mercifully, Jake finally seemed to awaken to the fact that he was with someone, and stood to leave, never introducing his date to the girls. "Well," he said amiably as he stood up next to his stool, "it was nice seeing you again. Maybe I'll see you around campus."

Sam popped the last bite of her sandwich into her mouth, wiped her lips, and put some money on the counter. "I've got to go, Linda. If I don't get a shower and some clean clothes, I won't be able to stand myself."

Linda didn't seem to hear her. She had a dreamlike look on her paint-smudged face and asked wistfully, "Wasn't he nice? I really think he's interested in me, don't you?"

To Sam, Jake seemed arrogant and self-possessed. The only thing she was interested in at that moment was the feeling of renewal that comes from standing under a spray of hot water and scrubbing your skin clean. "Sure, Linda," she said, barely able to mask her annoyance. "Look, I really do need to get home. I'll talk to you soon, OK?"

Without waiting for an answer, Sam slipped through the door into the cool autumn night.

CHAPTER 44

CLASSES BEGAN, AND SAMMIE was soon busy setting up her own dormitory room, buying books and becoming reacquainted with her other friends from whom she was separated over the summer. She had not seen Linda since helping her move, and Jake did not cross her mind during the week that passed. Early on the following Saturday morning, the phone rang; and Samantha grabbed the receiver from where it was mounted on the wall before it could awaken her sleeping suitemates. "Hello," she said, dragging herself and the extra long receiver cord into the hall where the conversation would not disturb anyone.

"Hi, Sammie, it's me," Linda said in that irritating way she had of assuming that everyone could recognize her voice. "You'll never guess who just called me."

Samantha was exhausted, and she was not in the mood for guessing games. "No, you're right, I won't," she retorted, then took a deep breath and started over. "But tell me because whoever it was, you sure sound excited."

"Remember that cute guy we ran into last week at Chock Full O' Nuts? You know, the medical student, Jake Isaacs?" she prodded. Samantha knew immediately whom Linda meant, but superimposed on the mental image of his face was an angry picture of his much ignored date.

"Yeah, I remember," she said. "So, now let me guess. He called to ask you out." Samantha felt confirmed in her initial assessment of his arrogance and was doubly annoyed that her friend apparently was immune to the obvious, having been mesmerized by the possibility of going out with a medical student.

"Not exactly," Linda continued with a note of caution tingeing her otherwise ebullient tone. "He said that after seeing me the other night, he thinks I'd be perfect for one of his friends in his medical school class."

Surprised by this seemingly generous act, Samantha wondered whether her instincts about Jake were wrong. "Well, that's really great, Linda. I hope he fixes you up with someone really nice."

There was a momentary silence on the line, and Sam could hear Linda's even breathing. "Um, that's not exactly all he said, Sammie," Linda plunged in quickly, trying to sound off-hand. "He said that he would bring his friend to meet me if I would bring you along to make it a foursome."

"Wait a minute," Samantha snapped, her radar back on the alert. "He knows the perfect guy for you, but somehow his generous introduction won't be happening unless he gets a date with me? Well, I'm not interested. If he wants to meet me so badly, he should've called you for my number so that he could ask me out himself. I'm not big on go-betweens, and you can tell him that for me."

Sam could hear the whine in Linda's voice practically before she began speaking. "Oh, come on, Sammie, what's one night. You can come along and cut the evening as short as you want, but I can't believe you would deny me the opportunity to meet this guy who could be The One for me," Linda complained.

Samantha's frustration grew as she wondered how her friend, an intelligent undergraduate at one of the nation's most prestigious universities, could be reduced to a blithering idiot over the prospect of missing out on a date with someone whose only known credential was that he was in medical school. No foaming-at-the-mouth women's libber herself, Samantha nevertheless was imbued with the newly hard-won sense of empowerment that her sex had achieved by the late 1960's. She was among those young women who now saw careers in the professions as distinct possibilities for themselves, viewing her male classmates as peers and counterparts rather than academic superiors. Still, Linda was her friend, and Sam supposed she was right that she could help her out without wasting too much of her own time.

"Ok, Linda, I'll tell you what I'll do," she began, not wanting to concede too much of the point she already had made. "I have no early classes on Friday, so we can meet for a drink at The West End on Thursday night. Have Jake call me to set things up."

"Thanks. I'm so excited," Linda said. "I'll call Jake right now."

Samantha found herself listening to a dial tone. Later that afternoon, her phone rang again.

"Hi, Samantha? This is Jake Isaacs. Linda called me with your number, so I'm trying to make plans for Thursday night. Thursday's good for you, right?" Jake sounded friendly, but not presumptuous.

"Sure, Thursday's fine. Since you went to Columbia, I'm sure you know where The West End is. I thought we could meet there around 5:30 after my last class." Sam picked The West End, a popular student watering hole steps from the heart of the campus, because she knew it would be crowded and comfortable, keeping their meeting relaxed and making an early exit easy to accomplish, if that turned out to be her choice.

"That's fine with me. I'll see you there Thursday at 5:30," Jake confirmed. "I'm looking forward to it."

"Yeah, Linda's really excited, too," Samantha emphasized, implying that she viewed herself as merely a facilitator for his matchmaking. "See you then."

"See you," Jake said.

By the time that Thursday came, Samantha was tired of counseling Linda, who was agonizing over everything from what to wear to what to talk about. In subtle protest, Samantha chose to wear her favorite pair of broken-in jeans and a well-loved brown merino wool sweater with weathered leather elbow patches. She was modestly aware that the color set off the glossy, dark reddish brown of her hair and posed a beautiful contrast to the light turquoise of her eyes, but the outfit was still casual and effortless. She arrived at the West End after a leisurely walk down Broadway; and after allowing her vision to adjust to the cave-like dimness of the bar's interior, she spotted the back of Linda's head as she slid into a booth toward the rear of the room. She walked up to the threesome, and Jake moved across his seat to make room for her.

"Hi, I'm Samantha," she said, extending her hand to Jake's friend.

Linda jumped ahead to make the introduction. She clung to the arm of the young man seated beside her in an uncomfortably intimate manner and said, "Sammie, this is Alan Packer."

Alan shook hands with Samantha, and she turned her attention to Jake. "Nice to see you again, Jake," she smiled. He returned her smile warmly.

They ordered a pitcher of beer and a large cheese pizza, and Linda plunged into conversation. "My father is a doctor," she said to Alan, as if it were gaining her admission into a private club, "So I've always been interested in medicine."

"Oh, really? What kind of medicine does he practice?" Alan asked.

"He's a general practitioner," Linda said proudly. Alan's face clouded. Faster than anyone could have imagined it, the atmosphere at the table shifted.

"It's impossible to be a good GP these days," Alan admonished. "There is just too great a body of medical knowledge to master. A good doctor has to specialize."

He folded his arms across his chest, indicating that he was closed to the possibility of being refuted. Linda's eyes blazed, but she kept her mouth in a smile.

"My father reads all of the latest medical journals and keeps abreast of developments in a wide variety of medical fields. He is highly respected," she said, her voice controlled.

"I don't care how much he reads," Alan shot back. "He could read from today until tomorrow, and he would never be able to keep up with all the advancements in medicine."

Linda's mouth opened wide, her expression of anger having traveled from her eyes to the rest of her face. "You obviously have never met anyone as intelligent as my father. You're apparently so overwhelmed by med school that there's little chance that you'll finish at the top of your class like my father did. My father may not be a specialist, but he's certainly not an arrogant asshole like you!"

Alan stood up, his beer glass still full in front of him, and said, "You know what? I don't have to take this. I have better ways to spend my evening than arguing with someone who doesn't appreciate the complexities of modern medicine. I'm going home."

Without so much as offering to pay for his drink or take Linda home, he turned on his heel and was gone. Linda, Jake, and Sammie sat stunned, their mouths literally dropped open in shock.

Finally, Samantha broke the uncomfortable silence. Turning to Jake, she dripped sarcasm. "Well, I have to say that your matchmaking skills could use a little work. He was about as perfect for Linda as a glass of strychnine."

"I'm sorry," he pleaded. "I had no idea Alan could be so abrasive." Looking around at the four untouched beers, Jake chanced a smile. "What do you girls say to our downing these beers and pizza, and then I'll take you both home? No sense in our letting him spoil the party." He watched the two girls hopefully.

Taking her cue from Linda, who had accepted a slice of pizza from Jake, Samantha sipped her beer and nodded. Jake's shoulders that had been hunched up around his ears relaxed visibly. They passed the rest of the meal in innocuous, companionable conversation. Jake and Samantha first walked Linda to her apartment, then Jake took Samantha home.

"I'm really sorry about tonight," he apologized at the door to Samantha's building. Samantha had to admit that Jake had been both polite and funny throughout the remainder of the evening. His conversation was witty and intelligent without being haughty, and he was handsome. Still, Samantha was conflicted. Jake's attempt at playing Cupid had failed abysmally; and she knew that after building up Linda's hopes, Jake clearly had disappointed her friend. And, as they stood in the awkward silence that shadows the end of most first dates, Samantha was doubly uncertain because she was not quite sure whether they had even been on a date themselves or merely chaperoned the worst first date of the century.

"I'll give you a call," Jake said, squeezing her arm by way of goodbye. Before Sam could speak, he had trotted down the steps of the front stoop and begun his walk to the subway.

There were several telephone messages taped to Samantha's door when she reached her room. She wasn't surprised that all three were from Linda. Ashamed of herself for not wanting to listen to her friend dissect the aborted evening, Samantha undressed quickly and decided that she was too tired to return her friend's calls until the following day.

Linda's anger hadn't abated when Samantha called her the next morning, though. Sam felt a pang of guilt because she liked Jake Isaacs, and it was difficult to square this positive feeling with the fact that he was the catalyst to her friend's disappointment. When the phone rang again shortly after she had hung up with Linda, she was confused when she heard Jake's voice.

"Hi, Samantha. It's Jake Isaacs. I just wanted you to know that in spite of everything that happened, I had a really great time last night."

Samantha felt a smile involuntarily spread across her lips. "Well, it turned out all right, and at least nobody came to blows."

Jake laughed.

"Look," he said. "I have a confession to make. When I saw you for the first time that night in Chock Full 'O Nuts, I really wanted to meet you. I thought about it afterwards, and I didn't know how to go about it. Linda was so obviously excited about our running into each other after several years that I was afraid that when I called her, she would naturally assume that I was interested in her. I guess I was wrong to do it, but I didn't have the guts to just call her under those circumstances and ask her for your number. So, I made up that story about knowing someone who was perfect for her and suggested that both you and I come along in order for me to make the introduction seem more casual."

Samantha could not repress her amusement. "Wow, who knew I was so impressive?" she asked with exaggerated modesty. "We didn't even speak that night, yet you went to such lengths to meet me. But how did you come up with Alan?"

His tone now a little more relaxed, Jake took a deep breath and raced for the finish line. "That brings us to the worst part. Once I set up the date, I had to come up with someone to fill the shoes of the Mr. Right I had promised. When Thursday evening arrived, I still hadn't identified anyone. I live in a building almost entirely populated by medical students, so out of desperation, I stuck my head out of the door of my apartment and yelled, 'Does anyone want to go down to Barnard with me tonight to meet a couple of girls for drinks?' Alan opened his door and said he wasn't doing anything that night. He satisfied the one criterion that was most important to me at that moment; he was available. Then, we met the two of you, Alan turned out to be a real jerk and, as the saying goes, 'the rest is history.'"

Samantha bit her lip to keep from giggling again. On the one hand, Jake had lied, which she didn't like. On the other, it was undeniably gratifying that someone would go through such machinations just to meet her. While she weighed the apparent contradiction, Jake rushed in to fill the silence.

"I'm really sorry. You may not believe me, but I have never done anything like this before. I suppose I sound like most criminals after they've been caught or have confessed, but I'm a very honest person. I hope you'll give me the chance to prove it."

"I appreciate your telling me the way things really happened," Samantha said.

"Listen," Jake offered. "I have two tickets to 'Jesus Christ Superstar' for next Saturday night. My parents know the producer, so they're really good seats in the front of the orchestra section. Would you go with me?" The show, a lively addition to the new genre of rock musicals that had started with 'Hair' in the 1960's, was the toast of Broadway. "Consider it our first real date. I'd like to start over."

"OK, I'd like that," Samantha replied, guessing it wouldn't do any harm to see where this would lead.

"It's a date, then," Jake confirmed. "I'll pick you up at six so that we can have dinner before the show."

"See you then," Samantha said breezily.

"Count on it," Jake replied.

Over the next several months, Samantha and Jake developed an easy companionability. They met for study dates in Butler Library and lingered for coffee at Chock Full o' Nuts. On weekends, they took long walks down 5th Avenue, window-shopping and daydreaming about the beautiful displays. Samantha was surprised one day when Jake stopped to stare at the electric train yard in the window of FAO Schwarz. She had glanced at it in passing, but he caught hold of her hand and pulled her back in front of the glass.

"This is the most fantastic train layout I have seen in a long time," Jake enthused. She looked up at his profile, and her heart pulled when she saw the look of boyish delight on his face. "I'm a model train fanatic," he explained unabashedly.

He began to point to different train cars and sections of the track to explain their different functions and how they worked. Samantha found his enthusiasm contagious, and his eagerness to share his passion was adorable.

She asked lots of questions, and the subject came alive for her because Jake's answers were so vivid and intelligent.

Samantha loved live theater and movies, so she and Jake devoured the latest plays and films. They stood in line for two hours one evening to see the debut of the much talked about feature film, 'The Godfather.' Although it began to rain heavily, Jake insisted on giving Samantha his hooded windbreaker and would not leave the line. Jake's hair and clothes were still wet when they left the theater, but he dismissed the discomfort with a wave of his hand. Samantha spotted a nearby coffee shop. "Let's get some coffee," she said, pulling him into the vestibule.

Shaking the rain from his hair, Jake croaked in his most throaty imitation of Brando, "Now, there's an offer I can't refuse."

Sometimes, they met to grab a bite and study at her dormitory. They sat side by side, their books open on their laps, each concentrating on the text, but also keenly aware of the other's presence. One afternoon, Jake leaned over and wrote a note in the margin of Samantha's political science book: "Jake loves Samantha more every second." Samantha's breath caught in her throat as she tentatively turned her head to look at him; but he merely smiled, keeping his own eyes trained on his page.

Later, after kissing her goodbye, he held her face in his hands and, looking into her eyes, said, "You don't have to say anything right now, Sammie. I just wanted you to know how I feel." He kissed her again gently and shrugged his broad shoulders almost imperceptibly. "I'll call you tomorrow."

Samantha couldn't stop thinking about it. Jake loved her. Innumerable times, her finger traced the words he had written in her book. He loved her, and although she had not said it, even to herself, Samantha loved him. The subjects of love, relationships, and sex, she had to admit, were inextricably bound in her mind by the coarse cords of fears and judgments that her father had wrapped around her throughout her young life. *Boys are different. They all want one thing. They will do or say anything to get it. They will never be your friends and must be treated with caution and skepticism. Any girl who thinks otherwise is stupid, naïve, or both. If a boy really loves you, he won't pressure you to have sex before marriage. Any girl who gives in to those demands out of fear is a fool. After all, no one will buy a cow if he can get the milk for free.*

Jake had not pressured her, at least not yet. His kisses and caresses were deep and warm, but not insistent. When she wanted him to stop, he stopped; and he never behaved as though she disappointed or frustrated him. Still, they loved each other. Kissing Jake awakened feelings in her that she had never before experienced. Her reaction to his touch was intense, and she could feel the heat between her thighs as an aching, unsatisfied need. She wanted him, but she wanted to wait. In one of her psychology texts, she read that when a man and a woman make love, they are not alone in bed. With them are everyone from whom they learned about sex and everyone with whom they have ever had sex. Samantha had laughed, visualizing that some people's beds must be very crowded. In her own imaginary bed, only the unforgiving face of her father loomed over her and Jake. They loved each other, but she had to wait.

That summer, Jake stayed in New York to complete departmental rotations at the hospital as part of his training before taking the board examinations that follow the second year of medical school. Sam returned home to Philadelphia and began working as a salesgirl at the local branch of Bonwit Teller, the 5th Avenue specialty department store. Jake called one hot afternoon in mid-July just as she returned home from work to say that he would have one of his few days off the following Friday.

"I thought I'd get tickets to a Yankees game, and you could come in for the weekend," he told Sam. "One of my friends is going home for the weekend, so you can stay in his room in the med school's dorm for unmarried students. You can take the train in from Philly, and I'll meet you at Penn Station." Sam could hear his smile through the phone.

"Well, I'm supposed to work on Friday, but maybe I can switch with someone else on the schedule. I'd really like to come, Jake." Samantha already was mulling over plausible excuses that would allow her to miss work. Characteristically conscientious and habitually reliable, she felt like a child playing hooky for the first time.

Jake's voice became soft. "I miss you, Samantha. Say you'll come."

"I'll figure out a way to be there," Samantha said, making up her mind. But then she thought of her father. She knew that he would not approve of her going to New York to spend the weekend with Jake, no matter how innocent the arrangements. Confronting him suddenly seemed an even more insurmountable obstacle than persuading her boss to let her off from work. She felt her jaw clench and a surge of anger in anticipation of his inevitable reaction.

"I'll call you after I make arrangements," she said. She hung up the phone and went down the hall to her parents' room. She knocked firmly on the door.

"Come in," her father said. He looked up from his newspaper when she entered the room. He was seated in his favorite chair, reading glasses perched on his nose.

"Hi, honey. How was your day?" he asked, peering at her over his glasses.

"Fine, I guess, although I don't know how some women do that job for a living. The store was virtually empty, and the only customers I did have were rude, demanding, or treated me like an idiot. Eight hours of standing behind a counter! Some days, the hands of the clock barely seem to move." Samantha enjoyed her father's interest, and she could see his empathy in his nodding head.

"Well, some women have to, Sammie. That's what happens when you're uneducated and unskilled. That's why you have worked so hard to excel at school and to get into a top college. It's all about choices. You have positioned yourself to have them; they haven't. Working as a retail clerk is just a summer job for you, but it is a life sentence for them. You'll have opportunities they can only dream about." He reached out to squeeze her hand.

"Is there something you wanted to ask me, Samantha?" he asked, eyes narrowing as he looked at his daughter's troubled face.

Trying to sound nonchalant, Sam took the plunge. "I'm going to New York this weekend. Jake has Friday off, and he's getting tickets to a Yankees game."

Her father pursed his lips, and his mouth narrowed into a straight line of disapproval. "Where are you going to stay?" he asked.

"One of Jake's classmates is going home for the weekend, so he said I could stay in his room in the dorm," Samantha replied.

Her father removed his glasses slowly. He blew warm breath on each lens as he cleaned them methodically with a tissue. Samantha thought she could see the words forming in his head before he uttered them.

"Samantha, reputation isn't based on our actions alone." He spoke slowly and deliberately. "Reputation takes a long time to establish, but it can be ruined in an instant. It can be destroyed by even one instance of improper conduct, just as it can be spoiled by the appearance of impropriety. I am sure you know what I mean."

Samantha was determined not to let him win with sophistry. "So, what are you trying to tell me? Are you saying I shouldn't go because some nameless, faceless people will assume I spent the weekend with Jake? And by 'spent the weekend' I mean having sex? Are you suggesting that I should fear for my reputation because these same people might choose to make erroneous assumptions about me if I go to visit my boyfriend? Or are you really saying that you think I'd be going there to have sex? And just to clarify, were you worried about sullying Mom's reputation all those times you visited her in New York while you were dating, or are you just one perfect exception to your otherwise hard and fast rule?"

"If I have to spell it out for you," he fired back, his eyes blazing in challenge, "I think you are incredibly naïve if you don't realize that by going to spend the weekend in New York with Jake, you are putting yourself in the most difficult of situations between an unmarried man and woman. If you're planning to go with full recognition of the situation, then perhaps you've chosen to join the members of your generation who believe in 'free love.' Well, that's what they may call it, but nothing in this life comes free, and those young women are no better than whores."

"Dad," Samantha said, matching his glare, "I live away from home at school for nine months out of the year, so I am free to conduct myself according to my own choices and without your permission during all of that time. Now, because I am home for the summer, you've decided to try to reassert your control over me. Well, guess what? When I came in here, you wondered if there was something I wanted to ask you. Actually, I didn't plan to ask you anything. I am twenty years old; and thanks to all that hard work you were praising just a minute ago, I have only one semester of college left. I am an adult, and I came in here to share with you my plans for the weekend. I don't have to ask you if I can go. As a courtesy, I was informing you that I will be in

New York from Friday until Sunday. If that makes me appear to be a whore in your eyes, then I am deeply sorry for that, but I think the problem lies with your perceptions, not my actions."

Samantha watched as her father snapped open his newspaper and replaced his glasses on the bridge of his nose. The pages interposed a barrier between them, and she could no longer see his face. The print swam in front of her eyes, and she was not sure whether the tears that obscured her vision were prompted by anger or sadness. She left the room to find her mother.

Leonora was in the kitchen, wiping the counters and stacking the dishes in the dishwasher. She looked up when she heard Samantha enter the room, and stopped working when she saw her daughter's face.

"What's wrong?" she asked, drying her hands on a nearby kitchen towel. She touched Samantha's elbow lightly and steered her toward the kitchen table. "Let's talk about it."

As Samantha took the seat that had been hers since childhood, Leonora poured herself a steaming cup of coffee and returned to the table. Once seated, she lit her postprandial cigarette, blew her smoke into the air, and leaned toward her daughter with a look of concern.

"I just don't understand Daddy sometimes," Samantha began as she told her mother what had just transpired.

Leonora shook her head and gnawed at her lower lip. "It's not about you, Sammie," she began. "I'm not even sure if I can explain what it's about since the people involved are long gone, and I never knew them, but I'll try. The fact is that, as with all of us, there are things and people in your father's past that shaped him into the person he is today, including his views on men and women, sex and marriage, morality and truth, basically all of the values he holds so strongly. But he doesn't talk a whole lot about those events or individuals, not even to me, so I only can tell you what I do know."

She took a long drag on her cigarette and inhaled deeply. "Tonight, I would say you ran headlong into the ghost of his sister, Lorraine. All I really know about her is that she was what my father used to call a 'popular girl,' meaning that she loved the boys, and the boys loved her." Leonora raised her eyebrows and gave Samantha a knowing, conspiratorial look. "She made a bad, early marriage, and she died too young. She was a gifted pianist, from what your father says, and he loved her dearly. He was at least a dozen years younger than she was, and although he idolized her for her beauty, talent and free spirit, he couldn't protect her. Now, he wants to protect you. Obviously, from what he said, he isn't going about it the right way; but his motives are pure, I can tell you that. What's that old saying?" Leonora asked, leaning back in her chair and taking another pull on her cigarette. "'The road to hell is paved with good intentions?'"

"I'm sorry about Daddy's sister, really I am," Samantha said sincerely, "but I'm not her. He can't make me responsible for her mistakes, and he can't judge me by them either. I have to make my own decisions, and even if some of them turn out to be wrong, which they undoubtedly will, he has to love me in spite of them. He can't make all of my decisions for me or guilt me into doing everything he wants me to do. He's all the time talking about respect and how he wants me to respect him. How can he respect me if I don't take charge of my own life?"

"You do what you have to do, Sammie. Your father will love you until the last breath he takes. He may rant and rave or give you the stone cold silent treatment, but never doubt for a minute that that man would lay down his life for you with gladness." She patted Samantha's arm and stubbed out her cigarette with her other hand. Rising to leave, she said, "Both of us raised you to make good decisions. We trust you. Have a good time in New York."

CHAPTER 45

FOUR DAYS LATER, SAMANTHA was staring out the window of the Metroliner as it sped from Philadelphia to New York. She had been reassured by the conversation with her mother, but it didn't change anything with her father, who had indeed opted for the stone cold silent treatment. He hadn't spoken so much as a word to her since he terminated their last conversation, and she strode angrily from his room. *Happiness is a mind game*, Samantha kept telling herself as she tried in vain to superimpose the image of Jake's smiling face on the memory of her father's angry one that glared at her from the smudged window glass of the train.

Finally, the train pulled to a stop at Penn Station, and Samantha grabbed her suitcase and stepped onto the platform. There he was, just as she had imagined him. Jake stood just feet from the staircase in bell bottomed jeans and a crisp summer sport shirt. A warm breeze tousled his thick brown hair. His thoughtful eyes seemed even more intelligent since the recent addition of wire rimmed glasses. She could see him panning the crowd, and he raised his hand in recognition and rushed towards her, smiling broadly.

"Hi," he said, bending to kiss her. "Good trip? I'm so glad you're here." He took her hand in one of his and her suitcase in the other.

Sam felt immediately flooded with happiness, instantly displacing her earlier mood of anxiety and guilt. "The trip was fine, and I am really glad to be here too," she said beaming up at him.

"Are you hungry?" Jake asked. "I made reservations at this new restaurant I heard about called 'A Quiet Little Table in the Corner.' Believe it or not, every table is supposed to be just that, a quiet little table in the corner. Don't ask me how. Are you game?"

"Sounds like fun," Samantha agreed. "Let's go."

The restaurant had not advertised its atmosphere falsely: each table was surrounded by beaded curtains on all four sides, rendering each one, no matter its actual location in the room, a quiet little table in the corner. Once seated, the diners occupied their own private space, and the intimacy was affected only minimally by the discreet service as tuxedoed waiters brought food and drink through the curtains.

"Wow, they weren't kidding," Samantha exclaimed, sipping her scotch and soda. She wasn't much of a drinker, but she occasionally joined Jake for a cocktail. "This is the most romantic restaurant I've ever eaten in."

Jake looked even more handsome in the candlelight. He confided to her once that, as a young boy, his feelings were hurt when someone described his features as aquiline. In fact, the angles of his lean face had a masculine strength and exuded intelligence, much like her father's.

They sat close together on the tufted banquette, and Samantha could feel the strength of his thigh through his pants as his leg aligned with hers and brushed the thin material of her summer skirt. She tried not to concentrate on the wonderful, musky sent of his cologne or the sensuousness of his mouth as he spoke. She wondered anxiously if he could hear her heartbeat quicken or feel her temperature rise. Everything that night felt perfect. *I love him*, she confessed again to herself.

Samantha considered telling Jake about the altercation with her father. Part of her yearned to tell him so that he could console her like the best friend that he had become. But another inner voice counseled her to keep her silence because she did not want Jake to think ill of her father or conclude that he disapproved of their relationship. The voice of reason won, and she kept quiet.

Jake drove her back to the unmarried medical students' dormitory after dinner. He showed her to his friend's vacant room and gave her the key. Leaning against the doorframe, he looked down and asked, shyly, "Can I come in for a while?"

"Sure, welcome to my humble abode," Samantha said lightly, opening the door and gesturing into the unfamiliar but generic space. There was a narrow twin bed, a low dresser and a mismatched desk and chair. Looking around at the stacks of books, papers, and discarded clothing, she saw that the room's hard-working, time-starved occupant had not made much of an attempt to clean up. She laughed as she cleared a space and sat down on the edge of the bed and added, "Well, definitely humble, but just as definitely not my abode."

Jake joined in her laughter and helped her clear a few more piles off the bed and chair before sitting down next to her. "Sorry. Believe it or not, Steve's one of my neater friends. Besides, I was just so happy that he was leaving this weekend and offered you his room that I didn't think much about the state it would be in. We don't have a whole lot of time for housekeeping and...."

Samantha placed her fingers on his lips.

"There's no need to apologize," she insisted. "It's fine, really." He looked relieved and picked up her hand where it lay in her lap. He held it in both of his and leaned to kiss her. Her lips parted, and his tongue caressed her teeth and that soft, tender place at the base of her tongue. Samantha felt the surge of warmth that had become so familiar in the last few months. It traveled from her own lips where his kiss had bloomed and expanded to fill her body until she could feel it to the tips of her fingers and toes. Her arms rose to encircle his neck, and he pressed her gently down on the bed. His fingers touched the smooth skin around her midriff that was exposed when she raised her arms. Her short skirt bunched up around her thighs, and he ran his hands down her legs and whispered, "I love you, Sammie," as he slipped his fingers between her legs inside the edge of her lace panties. Her body arched against the gentle caress of his fingertips. Samantha could feel their mutual pleasure as Jake's breathing became more rapid, and he moved rhythmically against the fabric that barely covered her thighs. Then, Jake began to pull her panties off.

Samantha's pleasure quickly turned to fear. She grabbed his hand, forcefully pushed it away, and sat bolt upright. She was panting hard. "What do you think you're doing?" she demanded. She tugged urgently at the edge of her skirt and yanked at the tail of her disheveled blouse.

Jake looked hurt and startled. "Oh, God, Sam. I'm sorry. I guess I thought… I wasn't going to…I don't know, I…."

He seemed unable to get hold of his thoughts. He ran a hand nervously through his hair.

"Look, Jake," Samantha said, more calmly now. "It's not your fault. I just can't do it. I know you love me, and I love you, but I still can't do it. It just feels that if I had sex to keep you when I don't feel ready, then I would be losing myself."

"What do you mean, 'losing yourself?'" Jake demanded. "I have never pushed you to have sex with me, let alone threatened to break up with you if you didn't give in and violate some deeply held principle that you seem to be equating with your 'self.' Actually, Sammie, I want to have sex with you when you're ready and not before. Then, it will be about us; but as to what just happened, I understand that we went further than we have in the past. I wanted to touch you, to be close to you; but when you told me to stop, I stopped. I thought you trusted me and knew that I would."

Even as she listened to Jake, Sam wondered if it was her 'self' she'd be losing or whether the dark specter of her father's disapproval had reared its ugly head again. Either way, the moment was gone. Not just lost, but ruined. She looked at Jake now, and there was anger in his eyes.

"I'm just not ready," she said lamely.

Jake stood and strode toward the door. He gripped the handle and turned to look her in the eye. Biting off each word, he pronounced, "If you think having sex with me would be losing yourself, then screw you! I don't know who's been messing with your head. All I know is that sex isn't always something ugly, Sam. When it's between two people who love each other and is an expression of that love, then it's the most beautiful act in the world. I love you, and I would never hurt you. You need to think about that."

He was halfway out the door when he turned toward her again, "Oh, and just for the record, it would be my first time too. As to that other generalization I'm sure you've had hammered into you along with the one that says, 'Sex is dirty'? The equally popular if likewise stupid one that warns that all guys care about is having sex, anywhere, with anyone, at anytime? Well, just like you, I waited. I wanted it to be with the one I love, and that's turned out to be you." Before she could say anything in reply, he slammed the door shut and was gone.

Samantha slumped over her knees, covered her face with her hands, and started to sob. Her body curled into a fetal position. She had grossly misjudged Jake, and a wave of humiliation crested within her. She said she loved him; but she had built a tower, brick by brick, of nameless, faceless fears in which she had locked her trust. If she did not trust Jake, she could not love him. It was as simple and as brutal as that.

She pulled herself to her feet and went into the bathroom where she splashed her face with cold water and applied an icy washcloth to her puffy eyes. After raking a comb through her hair and straightening her clothes, Sam glared at her still red, swollen reflection in the mirror and switched off the light. She went to the payphone in the hallway and dialed Jake's number. He answered right away.

Hesitating when she heard his voice, Samantha finally mustered, "It's me, Jake. I know it's late, but I couldn't sleep. Could you meet me? I'll understand if you don't want to. I know I've made a mess of things, but…." Her voice became small.

"Give me thirty minutes," Jake said softly.

"Thanks. I'll wait for you in the lobby of the building," Samantha said. She hung up the phone and took the elevator to the ground floor. She wrapped her arms around her thin summer blouse, hugging herself in a vain effort to find comfort, as she scrutinized each pair of headlights that passed the entrance. Finally, Jake's car pulled up at the curb, and she saw his tall figure move through the door.

He took her hand and led her to an empty sitting area furnished with four vinyl armchairs and a coffee table laden with magazines. Samantha sat in one of the chairs, and Jake took the seat opposite her.

"I know it's late, but I couldn't sleep," Samantha reiterated. "I feel so ashamed." She felt the track of a tear stain her cheek, and she swiped at it with the back of her hand.

"What I said about losing my 'self,' I said out of fear. If we had sex, I was afraid I'd be doing it out of fear that I'd lose you if I didn't. I also was afraid that I wouldn't like myself for not waiting or would blame you for pressuring me into it, even though I know you never did. If we didn't have sex, I was afraid that it would be because of some false definition of what it means to be a moral person that I have internalized after years of listening to my parents. I was afraid that, at the heart of it, I didn't know what I really wanted or who I really was, and I took all of this out on you. God, Jake, I'm sorry. I didn't trust you, and I hurt you because of that, not because of anything to do with sex. I thought I knew what love is, and I thought it could exist in that climate of fear, but it can't. I want you to know that I do trust you, and I am so very, very sorry."

She took a deep gulp of air as though she had been drowning and had just broken the surface of the water. Looking into Jake's loving brown eyes was like seeing the cloudless azure sky over calm seas. He took her hand.

"Sammie, I've been thinking too," he said, looking at her intently. "I think we should get married. I've been considering it for some time, and I know it's the right thing to do. I love you, and I know you love me. Let's spend the rest of our lives together. Say yes, Sammie, please." He fitted her small hand to his palm, his long, graceful fingers intertwining with hers, and he waited.

"Yes, Jake! Oh, yes," Samantha screamed, flying out of her seat, her arms around his neck, her mouth covering his. It was the most romantic moment of her life.

But just as quickly, she heard her father's predictable reaction inside her head again. *So, I guess there goes the plan to graduate and go on to law school. You'll be pregnant within the first year! And what do you propose to live on? Jake is still a medical student and will be for two more years. Even after that, there's an internship and a residency that won't exactly rake in the dough, not to mention the long hours and little time for a personal life. Planning to ask me to kick in? I don't think so, not after you walked on my dreams for you as you walked down the aisle.*

She tried to push his voice out of her head, to let romance take over again. *Don't listen to that*, she argued to herself. *Jake's right. You two love each other. Plenty of young people make it through the tough first years. Daddy will help you, and you will complete your education. You and Jake can do it together; you know you can.*

"I'll marry you, Jake. I love you, and I will forever," she reaffirmed, staunching the tears that were flowing heavily now.

Jake pulled her to her feet and kissed her deeply and tenderly. "I'll love you forever, too, Samantha," he breathed into her hair as he held her to his chest.

The following Saturday, they were in Samantha's parents' living room sitting across from Leonora and Fred. Sam could feel the warmth of Jake's arm as it grazed hers, but they each clasped their hands in their laps and fixed their eyes straight ahead. She could hear their shallow breathing as they awaited her parents' response. Leonora's face was clouded with worry. Fred's seemed somewhere between disbelief and horror.

After an uncomfortable silence, Fred spoke, his tone tinged with barely disguised disapproval. "I understand that the two of you think you are in love and want to get married," he began. "I also understand," he continued, looking directly at Jake now, "that Samantha is only twenty years old with her whole life in front of her. Even you, Jake, are still in medical school with years of training ahead of you. If you want to become engaged, then I suppose neither one of you needs my permission or my blessing for that matter; but I don't see why, if you really love each other, you can't wait a year, until Sammie graduates, to get married."

Jake took her hand now, and they rose to their feet. "If you don't mind, Mr. Green, Sammie and I are going to take a short walk to talk things over. I understand your concerns, but I want you to know that I love your daughter very much, and I haven't tried to pressure her into anything. Just like you, I want the best for her."

Jake gave an almost imperceptible tug on her hand, and Sam followed him out into the hot summer afternoon.

Fred stared at their receding backs, the connection of their hands, and his chest heaved despondently. "I made my case," he said to Leonora. "The decision is out of my hands."

Jake and Samantha walked in silence until they rounded the corner out of sight of the house. Jake took her free hand and turned her toward him. "Sammie, I just want you to know that if you want to wait, I'll wait. I don't think your father is right. I believe you would finish school even if we got married before you graduate, but I love you so I'll wait for you, Sammie; I will."

There it was. What her father had repeated to her like a mantra her whole life. *If he loves you, he'll wait. Wait for sex; wait for marriage; wait for you.* Samantha's head throbbed like a distant but incessant drumbeat.

"A year will go by fast, Jake. It will be over before we know it; and in the meantime, we'll be studying and planning; we won't even notice the time!"

Sam tried to sound enthusiastic, as if she were not agreeing to a delay but instead was suggesting an amusing diversion. She could not make her eyes meet his.

Jake dropped her hands. "OK, then," he said, turning back toward the house. "I can wait."

His voice was resolute, his mouth a tight line. Sam quickened her pace to catch up to him as he strode purposefully, hands clenching and unclenching at his side, in a concerted effort to rid himself of his unexpressed anger. She was still a step behind him when he faced her parents in the living room.

"Mr. and Mrs. Green," he announced, "Samantha and I have decided to wait." His speech was clipped and perfunctory, belying the emotion that was otherwise evident in the set of his jaw, the stiffness of his posture, and the darkness in his eyes.

"Well," Fred said, barely able to mask his relief as he stood and extended his hand to Jake, "you'll both be glad you did."

Soon, it was fall, and dry leaves blew across Broadway and the cobblestone paths of the Columbia University campus. In her small apartment on Amsterdam Avenue, Samantha stood over Jake's seated, bowed figure brandishing a red leather bound journal. It was her precious diary, a treasured volume where she kept her innermost thoughts, concerns, joys, and despairs. She had begun writing daily during high school and had kept up the habit through her college years.

"How could you?" she demanded of him "How could you violate my privacy and my trust by reading my diary?"

"I wanted to know what you were really thinking," he offered weakly. "It's been four months since we became engaged; and other than that ring you're wearing, no plans have been made; you've refused to set a date; it's as if nothing has happened; and you don't want anything to happen. I know it's wrong, but I thought I might learn something. I felt I had to know if this is even for real."

Samantha unconsciously twisted the diamond solitaire on her left hand. It had been Jake's grandmother's and was reset in a Tiffany setting that they chose together. Her mind raced over the contents of the many pages of the journal. Samantha stood stiffly, feet apart, legs braced, as if by keeping her physical balance, she could focus attention on Jake's obvious breach of faith and prevent him from diverting attention to the words she had written in her own hand. It was not to be.

Jake seemed to derive strength from her emotional imbalance. Looking into her eyes, he gently pulled the journal from her grasp and thumbed the pages until he found the passage he was seeking.

"'I don't know what to do'," he read. "'Daddy hasn't spoken to me in two weeks. I brought up the wedding, and he refuses to discuss it. I am now convinced that when he persuaded Jake and me to wait a year until I graduated to get married, he was just trying to buy time. He seems to have expected, or at least hoped, that the issue would simply resolve itself by our breaking up before we began any serious planning. Because that hasn't happened, he now thinks that he can influence me by the weight of his disapproval. I don't know what he has against my relationship with Jake. Maybe it's nothing against Jake at all. Maybe he would feel this way about anyone I wanted to marry. But why? Why would he put me in the position of having to choose between two people I love? If it is just that he thinks I'm too young, maybe I can ask Jake to wait another year until I've completed a year of law school. If I showed Daddy that I graduated from college as promised and was enrolled in graduate school, maybe he'd believe that I'd finish law school whether or not I married Jake. I haven't discussed any of this with Jake because, I suppose, I'm afraid. I haven't been able to stand up to my father, and I haven't been honest with Jake.'"

Hearing her own words thrown back at her in Jake's familiar, strong voice, now stained with regret, made Samantha's stomach turn. He lifted his eyes to look at her face. Where she thought she would see anger, there was only disappointment.

"You've just been playing me, Sammie," he said, shaking his head from side to side. He bit his lower lip and pushed the diary across the coffee table that separated them as if he wanted to rid himself of something loathsome. "The truth is I'm not sure we're ever going to get married. I said I'd wait, and I have waited, but the thing that's allowed me to wait was my unshakeable belief that at some point, my wait would be over. After reading this, and believe me, I know I shouldn't have, I don't know what to believe. We agreed to wait a year, and now you're not so sure that we shouldn't make it two. At the end of two, what would your father say then, Sam, make it three? More importantly, what would you say? And I need to tell you Sammie, I have nothing but respect for a father who wants to protect his daughter and her dreams, but that's not your father's game. He's not trying to protect your dreams. His game is to control you to fulfill his own, and he'll go to any lengths to do it. I love you, Sammie, but we're at a point where you've got to decide if we're going to move forward and get married this spring. I'm not going to wait forever. I want a decision right now, and if the answer is no, I'm leaving; and when I walk out the door, I won't be back. I have a life to live too, Sammie, and I'm not going to live it in your father's shadow."

Samantha stood mute, her lips working, but no sound breaking the ugly silence. She suddenly remembered what it had felt like to learn to swim as a little girl, holding her breath under water and realizing suddenly that she was out of oxygen. Pushing herself to the surface, she had gulped air in an instinctual effort to survive. Gasping now, she could see that the situation had taken an unforeseen turn. The confrontation was no longer about Jake having abused her trust; it was about her having broken faith with him. It was not about his having read her private thoughts; it was about what she had written. She was not enraged by his act, as she had thought; she was unmasked.

Crossing the room, Jake placed his hand on the doorknob. "Well, your father has manipulated us right into the position he wanted us to be in." His laugh was bitter and raw. "Checkmate. Game over. Your father can go to hell," he said.

"Don't you dare curse my father," she yelled.

Her words seemed to slam against Jake's back as he walked through the door. They broke in shards and fell in the silence between them.

Jake turned to look at her one last time. Then, he was gone.

Samantha rushed to the window of her dormitory room and looked down at the darkened corner of Amsterdam Avenue and 120th Street. She heard a screech of tires just as Jake's car pulled away from the curb. The only illumination came from his taillights, and they quickly became two red periods in the distance, doubly emphasizing the finality of their last encounter.

Samantha sat in her dorm room, her back against the headboard of her bed and the telephone cord fully extended from its base on her desk. She dialed her home number and listened to the customary two rings. She rolled her eyes, as she remembered her parents instructing her as a child to allow all calls to ring twice before answering so as not to appear too anxious to the caller.

"Hello," her father's voice was instantly recognizable even though they did not speak on the phone often. It always amused Samantha that a man who made his living from words could find the telephone to be so repugnant.

"Hi, Daddy. I called because I…." Suddenly, Samantha was not sure why she had called. She wanted to tell him that she and Jake had broken up, but now that she heard his voice, she wasn't at all certain that she wanted to hear what he would say.

Plunging ahead, she said, "I called because I wanted to tell you that Jake and I had a terrible fight, and we decided to call it quits." She paused, wondering whether he would ask her for any of the particulars.

He didn't. "Well, honey, don't you worry about a thing," he said. "Jake wasn't the one for you anyway. Frankly, I could never understand what you saw in him. You'll bounce back from this whole thing more quickly than you realize."

Sam was surprised at the surge of anger she felt. He seemed almost as flippant about her broken engagement as he was certain in his belief that he knew who was right for her.

She took a deep, calming breath and tried again. "Look, Dad, Jake is a wonderful guy. He's smart and sensitive, funny and kind. The way things have turned out has more to do with me than with him. Bad timing, I guess. Maybe, I'm just too young; but the truth is that I broke his heart, not the other way around."

"Well, nobody goes through life unscathed, Sammie. You'll both get over it. I mean, he wasn't even that good looking. You can do better."

Samantha felt a new wave of shock. "Are you kidding, Dad?" she yelled into the receiver. "'He wasn't even that good looking?' I can't believe you just said that. First of all, that is completely superficial. Second, he was to me. Do you understand that, Dad? He was to me, damn it!"

Samantha could see Jake's face: the piercingly intelligent brown eyes, the laugh lines beginning to form at their corners as his generous lips curved in a ready, sensuous smile, the unruly forelock of rich dark hair that refused to stay swept from his forehead. Like any face, it was so much more than the sum of its features because it was his face, his expressions that animated it.

"If this is your idea of how to make me feel better," she continued, "then you need to know that it isn't working. I can't expect you to feel the same way I do about what's happened between Jake and me, but I did expect you to understand that I'm really upset about it. Maybe you didn't mean to, but you've just made things worse. I'm going to go now, Dad."

Her father's voice betrayed his discomfort. "Well, I'll tell your mother that you called, Sammie. Don't let all this personal stuff affect your school-work. After all, this semester's grades are the last ones that the law schools will see on your transcript. I love you."

She said goodbye, replaced the receiver in its cradle, and leaned her head against the wall. It had been three days since she last saw Jake, the indelible image of his back and the door closing behind him, the pinpricks of his tail-lights as he gunned the motor and sped away. She thought about calling him, but she could not give him what he wanted, so there was no point in hurting him further. Maybe she had done Jake a favor after all. What did he need with a little girl so hungry for her Daddy's approval? She was consumed with anger again, but this time it was displaced. She covered her face with her hands and tried to imagine her father sitting in his favorite chair, the newspaper spread across his lap. She tried to remember the hurtful, thoughtless things he had said and attach her anger to him, but her hot tears seeped through her fingers as the molten fury lighted upon a more worthy recipient: herself.

Sam's twenty-first birthday fell only a few weeks after her breakup with Jake. Despite the acrimonious end of the last telephone conversation she had with Fred, her father called her with the lilting tone of someone who characteristically chose to forget any discord between them rather than apologize.

"Hi, Sammie," he said. "Mom and I have big plans for your twenty-first! We're planning to drive into the city and make a big weekend of it. Can you be ready on Friday night at seven?"

Samantha closed her eyes, remembering two decades of poems Fred had composed for his wife or daughter on every birthday, anniversary, or other important occasion. Fred jokingly bestowed upon himself the lofty moniker "Poet Laureate of 1709," the number representing their street address; and his funny, touching, romantic rhymes were always more highly anticipated by their adoring recipients than the gifts that accompanied them. Whether the poem was for her or her mother, Sam would listen in rapt silence to her father's dulcet baritone as he read his latest masterpiece. She and her mother saved every one, penned in his neat, all-capitalized manuscript; and they read them over and over again long after the special day that was the catalyst to the poem had passed.

"I'll be ready, Dad," Samantha assured him.

Her parents took her to the 21 Club as part of a weekend-long cele-bration that also included a Broadway performance and shopping on 5th Avenue. All of the memories were unforgettable, but none more vivid and indelible than her twenty-first birthday poem:

TODAY, YOU ARE TURNING TWENTY-ONE,

TIME TO PUT CHILDISH THINGS ASIDE,

ADULTHOOD HAS OFFICIALLY BEGUN,

GRASP THE WORLD WITH ARMS OPEN WIDE.

IN MANY WAYS, MY JOB IS DONE.

MY YEARS OF TEACHING HAVE RUN THEIR COURSE;

MOMENTS OF PRIDE, SADNESS, AND FUN

FOR WHICH YOU ALWAYS HAVE BEEN THE SOURCE.

AT TIMES, I'D WANT TO DO IT ALL AGAIN,

JUST TO SAVOR MY SPECIAL GIRL.

FOR IT'S HARD TO REALIZE IT WHEN

THE YEARS FLY BY IN A WHIRL

THAT ONE DAY SOONER THAN YOU THINK

THAT GIRL WILL A WOMAN BE,

AND BLACK REPLACES BABY PINK,

FREEDOM WITH DEPENDENCY.

YET, THAT IS WHAT I WANTED FOR YOU;

TO GIVE YOU WINGS TO LET YOU FLY.

TO WATCH YOU DISCERN THE FALSE AND TRUE

TO FORM VALUES YOU WILL LIVE BY.

SO IT IS WITH SMILING FACE

THAT I REJOICE IN WHAT TIME HAS WROUGHT;

FOR YOU STAND ON THE BLOCKS, READY TO RACE,

HOLDING THE BATON OF ALL I HAVE TAUGHT.

IT WAS PASSED WITH LOVE FROM ME TO YOU,

AND AS A FATHER, I COULDN'T BE PROUDER.

I BELIEVE IN YOU, WHATEVER YOU DO;

NO FAN WILL EVER CHEER LOUDER.

HAPPY 21ST, THE WINNING HAND,

YOUR VERY OWN BLACKJACK.

BEHIND YOU, I WILL ALWAYS STAND;

AS THE KIDS SAY, "GOT YOUR BACK."

Wordsworth or Shelley need have no fear of competition from these simple, iambic rhymes, but Sam recognized from childhood that as manifestations of constant love and dedication, her father's poems had no rival. On this occasion, it was Fred who looked to Samantha expectantly, searching her eyes not only for approval but also for forgiveness. Happily, he found both.

Two months later, Sam graduated a semester early from Barnard, having met the requirements for two majors in history and philosophy. Despite the fact that she would graduate Magna Cum Laude with departmental honors in both subjects, she missed qualifying for Phi Beta Kappa, the most elite collegiate academic honor society, by only one hundredth of a point on her grade point average. That her father had cherished his membership in the academic fraternity made the near miss far more significant than it otherwise would have been.

"For a hundredth of a point, they give you gornisht, bupkes?" he ranted, subconsciously fingering his own Phi Beta Kappa Key that dangled from the gold watch chain threaded through the buttonhole of his suit vest. "What kind of an idiot made that decision? That is how Columbia University rewards all of your hard work and achievement?"

Samantha stood slack-jawed, weathering this storm. *Gornisht, bubkes, nothing,* she translated the Yiddish reflexively in her head. Despite his usual eloquence, her father often reverted to Yiddish in emotionally charged moments. *No small coincidence that the only Yiddish words I know are profanity or insults!*

"I guess they're just applying the rules, Daddy, and I wouldn't exactly say I'm being given 'nothing' in the way of rewards. I'm sorry," she added lamely, her eyes on the floor where all she could see were his shiny black wingtips pacing the carpet. She hoped that hearing the dean read her significant academic honors as she received her degree would compensate him for this failure that he took personally.

Sam had arranged for her parents to be seated next to her roommate's parents. Hannah Goldblatt had been her friend since freshman year, and their parents formed a casual friendship resulting from the bond that their daughters forged. The oldest child of orthodox Jews, Hannah had accepted the advances of a young anthropology professor whose gentile background and brooding personality were the antithesis of the type of mate her parents would approve. By graduation, they had broken up, but Hannah told Sam that her Heathcliffe, as she had dubbed him, had presented her with a parting gift. Never the student that Sam was, Hannah would nonetheless receive an honors distinction in her major, anthropology.

The graduates were instructed at the rehearsal to remain standing after their names were called so that the Dean could read any honors or distinctions they had achieved, and the audience could pay them tribute with a special round of applause. Hannah sat on one side of Sam, and another of her close friends sat on the other. The three girls clasped hands as the Dean began the alphabetical presentation of the graduates. Sam edged to the front of her chair as she heard the name of the girl who immediately preceded her being called. She fixed her eyes on the Dean and held her breath as the Dean articulated each syllable into the microphone, "Samantha Elyse Green." Sam stood and panned her eyes away from the Dean and toward her father whom she knew was seated in a center aisle seat near the front of the capacity crowd that filled the university green. Her two friends still held her hands. Then, it happened. "Danita Ann Grimsky," the Dean continued, without listing Sam's honors. Samantha stood for a moment in shock. Her knees buckled, and she landed hard back in her seat, as her two friends whispered to her frantically.

"It's a mistake, Sam. You need to remain standing," Hannah hissed. "You know, and I know that the Dean made a horrible mistake. Maybe the registrar forgot to list your honors because, technically, you graduated last February, ahead of the rest of the class. Maybe the Dean just goofed and skipped to the next name accidentally. I don't know what happened, but you should stand up!"

Tears filled Samantha's eyes. She fought to compose herself and was about to stand again when she noticed some movement at the front of the crowd. Impossibly, she saw her father making his way up the aisle and out of the commencement. She forced herself to her feet, and stared at her father's back as it receded in the distance.

It was a Columbia tradition for the faculty to form a receiving line for the graduates at the end of the ceremony. This ritual enabled students and teachers to bid each other a personal farewell. Sam made her way down the aisle, shaking hands and receiving well wishes, until she was face to face with the Dean. "Congratulations, Samantha," he said, extending his hand. Sam clasped it firmly, but she realized that the Dean already had shifted his attention to the graduate behind her.

"Excuse me, Dean Willard," she managed, "but there has been a serious mistake. I graduated a semester early, but I came back to participate in the graduation exercises with my class. I received my degree Magna Cum Laude with departmental honors in history and philosophy, but you didn't announce any of my honors, and they aren't printed on my degree either." Sam waited expectantly.

"You will have to take that up with the registrar," the Dean said curtly. "Any inaccuracies will be corrected on your official transcript, and you will be issued a new degree, if necessary."

The Dean turned to the next graduate and extended his hand. Their exchange was over, without so much as an apology.

Threading her way through the throng of people, Sam saw her parents standing by themselves on the edge of the crowd. Her mother looked around nervously, and her father was tapping his foot impatiently. Leonora smiled when she caught sight of her daughter.

"Congratulations, Sammie. We're very proud of you," she said, hugging her daughter in a tight embrace. Sam extricated herself from her mother's grasp and wheeled on her father.

"Where did you go after they called my name, Daddy? I saw you leave, and you never came back." Sam's chest heaved with anger.

"Well, when that Dean failed to announce any of your honors, do you know what that mediocrity, Hannah's father, had the nerve to say to me? He actually turned to me and patted my arm and said, 'We've always thought Sammie was such a lovely girl.' I mean, he said it as if your being a nice girl could somehow make up for your graduating without any distinction whatsoever. Can you believe that? I couldn't take it. I had to get out of there."

Fred looked at her as if his explanation were completely plausible. He seemed to believe that he had walked out in protest. Sam thought her head might burst right through her mortarboard.

"Let me get this straight," she rebuked him. "You 'couldn't take it?' What exactly couldn't you take, Daddy? You couldn't take that Mr. Goldblatt might think it is more important to be a good person than an honor student? Or was it that you couldn't take that Hannah, whom everyone knows was no great student, received honors in her major while I appeared to receive no distinction at all? Or was it that you were just plain embarrassed by the entire debacle even though you already knew that I had graduated with multiple honors, so it had to be some kind of a terrible mistake? It had to be one of these things that you 'couldn't take' because it certainly wasn't that you couldn't take that I had been denied a special moment for which I had worked for years. Let's face it, Daddy. If it had been that, then you could never have walked out on my college graduation, a ceremony that I will never, ever be able to relive or rewrite in this life."

Sam was surprised at her own intensity. Her father was dumbstruck. Her mother stood to one side wringing her hands. Sam turned on her heel and headed toward the university's famous wrought iron gates that fronted Broadway. Eventually, her parents followed in her wake; and they went to dinner and drove back to Philadelphia without mentioning it again. Fred never apologized; and years later, not surprisingly, Leonora claimed that she had no recollection of his leaving. Sam never forgot.

CHAPTER 46

SAMANTHA MATRICULATED AT Boston College Law School that fall. Fewer than ten percent of her classmates were women, a stark contrast to the homogeneous female environment that she had grown used to at Springside School and Barnard College.

There were four sections of first year law students divided alphabetically, which determined when they would have their classes. Samantha was in section A that started classes at 9:00am, and she quickly made friends with the group of students whose assigned seats surrounded hers.

Rob Ferrell was clearly the odd man out in the section. While the others were preppy, studious, and motivated, Rob was overweight, slovenly, and careless. As the remainder of the instantly close group took copious notes and cultivated a healthy dose of fear and loathing for the autocratic professors, Rob crossed his arms over his paunch, tilted his chair back on two legs, and offered a running, acerbic commentary to his colleagues that was all too often audible to the professor as well. Yet, there was something genuine about him that appealed to Samantha. She appreciated that he knew he did not fit in; but also, he knew who he was and refused to try to be anyone else.

"Are you sincerely bitter or bitterly sincere?" she asked him with a smile as she was packing up her books and papers at the end of the grueling first week.

Rob made a play of scratching his head and cocking it to one side in a parody of deep thinking. "Well, I'm just a coal miner's son from Scranton, Pennsylvania," he said self-deprecatingly and grinning broadly. "I'll have to give that one some more thought. That just might be one of those distinctions without a difference I've read about, but I'm not too sure."

"It just might be," Sam agreed, hefting her briefcase. "But while you're ruminating on that, I'm going to put in some time in the library on the lesser complexities of civil procedure. See you tomorrow."

"You do that," Rob smiled, "and I'm going to ruminate over a beer."

She left the large, tiered lecture hall and headed for the broad staircase to the library on the second floor. But when she got there, all of the tables were occupied. As she was about to give up and return to her apartment to study, she saw a woman vacating a seat at a table next to the window along the far wall. She hastened to stake her claim and began by unpacking her briefcase and draping her jacket across the back of one chair. Even before she finished situating herself, a young man in a blue suit and starched white shirt, the knot of his necktie hanging loosely around his collar, looked up from his seat on the opposite side of the table, an open tome in front of him.

"Join me," he said with a smile. "Space is pretty scarce in here today."

Samantha met his eyes that were an intense, cornflower blue. "Thanks," she said, taking her seat at the table. The young man removed his leather brief-case from the table to make more room for her. She watched as he opened the brass fasteners and removed still more books and papers, stacking them neatly in front of him.

"My name is Tom. Tom Leary," he said, extending his hand.

"Samantha Green," she replied as she shook his hand. His palm was cool and dry, his handshake firm.

"Are you a student here?" Tom asked. "I graduated from the law school last May, and now I'm a first year associate with Foley Hoag downtown. I guess I'm used to this library from having spent so many hours here doing research for the law review, so I still like to come here to get things done whenever I can."

In just two sentences, he managed to introduce the salient points of his resume: Boston College Law School grad, law review, associate with one of the most well-reputed, prominent law firms in the city. Yet, his tone was casual, his intimation offhand.

"I'm a first year law student," Samantha explained. "Still learning the ropes."

She was impressed that he had been on the law review because she already knew that only those who finished in the top ten percent of the class after first year exams were extended invitations to write for the prestigious publication.

"Look," Tom continued, "Do you want to take a break from work and go down to the student center to get a cup of coffee?" His face and his offer seemed innocent.

"Sure, let's go," Sam agreed. "I should probably leave my things at this table so I don't lose my spot."

They left the library and headed to the small snack bar at the student center two floors below. Once they bought their coffee and found an empty table by the window, Tom sat down and undid his tie completely, rolling it up and putting it in his suit jacket pocket.

"There, that's better," he sighed.

He took a sip of his coffee, looked at her sheepishly, then leaned toward her as if ready to share a secret.

"You know, it's not a complete coincidence that we're sitting here like this," he said conspiratorially.

"What do you mean?" Samantha asked.

"Well," Tom went on, "I have a friend from my hometown who also is a first year student here. We're actually rooming together. Anyway, I brought him to the law school last week for orientation, and I first saw you then. I asked him to find out what section you were in; and I've been staking out the library ever since, figuring that I had to run into you at some point. Today's the day." Tom sat back in his chair, his self-satisfied grin visible over the rim of his cup.

"You know what they say," Samantha countered warily. "There's really no such thing as a coincidence."

"Precisely," Tom agreed, undeterred by her note of caution, "and that is why I require recompense for my efforts. You must have dinner with me on Saturday night. What do you say?"

"Fair is fair," Samantha concurred. Tom's overwhelming self- confidence intrigued her. She pulled a pen and paper from her purse, jotted down her address and phone number, and pushed it across the table. "You'll need these, unless you're planning some more detective work."

Tom glanced at the paper and put it in his shirt pocket. "I don't think I'll need a detective," he said. "I believe I've already found what I was looking for." He stood, slung his suit jacket over his shoulder, and placed his hand on her shoulder. "So, Samantha, I'll pick you up at seven. Don't study too hard between now and then."

He headed for the door, and Samantha marked the self-assurance in his stride. When she returned to the library, her concentration was blurred by the memory of the intense blue of his eyes.

Samantha dressed carefully for her date with Tom on Saturday evening. Her slim black dress was simple, but its elegant lines accentuated her lithe figure, and her strappy stilettos were appropriate for dancing or anything else he might have in mind. Her lustrous hair swung freely at her shoulders, and her subtle makeup enhanced her eyes and smooth complexion. As she applied a rosy lipstick and clasped a strand of pearls around her throat, she felt a twinge of nervous anticipation. She touched a potent drop of perfume behind each ear and wrist and gave herself a final, approving glance in the mirror just as the doorbell rang.

"Right on time," she said, opening the door to Tom.

He had on another, well-tailored dark suit and a maroon and gold striped tie, a nod to his beloved Boston College. His neatly combed hair was still damp from the shower, and his cologne had a fresh, masculine fragrance that reminded Samantha of a Colorado ski run in spring.

"OK, gorgeous, let's go," Tom said, taking her hand. Samantha felt suddenly warm and excited.

Tom eased his Oldsmobile Cutlass into a parking space near Locke-Ober on Winter Place. Samantha had heard of the famed restaurant, the third oldest in Boston, but had never eaten there.

Taking her hand as he opened the passenger door, Tom explained, "I asked Quentin Mayfield, one of the partners at my law firm who's known as a real man about town, where to take you for a special dinner, and he suggested this restaurant."

Samantha noted every detail of the beautifully restored turn-of-the-twentieth century dining room, which gleamed with rich mahogany. There were intricate carvings on the front and side of the long, L-shaped bar. Candlelight reflected off of six heavy silver tureens and platter covers specially designed to be lifted by the pulleys of a hand-operated brass dumb waiter that remained in service.

A waiter, Ichabod-thin and tuxedo-clad, materialized tableside. "May I offer you a cocktail?" he asked politely.

"Two Dewar's and soda," Tom replied. Impressed by his assertiveness, Samantha could barely mask her awe when she saw the dumbwaiter rise from the bar below, bringing their drinks to the dining room. She was dizzy with her surroundings: huge plate glass mirrors, decorated ceilings, etched gold wallpaper, German silver cloches, stained Tiffany-style glass, and graceful electrolier chandeliers. The unfamiliar sting of her first taste of scotch was followed by a growing warmth that pervaded her being.

Tom surveyed the evening's array of notable characters held in thrall by Locke-Ober. "Look," he whispered appreciatively to Samantha. "There's Mayor White, and over there in the corner are Warren Beatty and Julie Christie. They just starred together in 'Shampoo'. It was hilarious. Have you seen it?"

"No, I haven't," Samantha said, smoothing her dress under her as she slid her chair closer to the table. She tried not to stare at the glitterati he had just pointed out.

Tom leaned forward and drew her attention to a magnificent bronze statue in the center of the dining room. "She's known as the Gloria Victis. You must remember to rub her foot for good luck before we leave," he said smiling. "It's a superstition here."

"Well," Samantha quipped, feeling the contagion of Tom's high spirits, "I'll definitely do that. It's like my father always says, 'It's best to be lucky and smart.' What else do you know about this restaurant?"

"Quentin says Orson Welles gulped down oysters by the dozen here," Tom affirmed, "and Caruso is said to have sautéed his own sweetbreads on the premises."

The room certainly seemed worthy of such a history. The woodwork had worn to a well-oiled, rich brown, and the wavy glass panes of the windows bent the light bathing the room in a warm glow. Beautiful damask draperies graced the windows, and each table was covered with a perfect, white linen cloth and a graceful hurricane lamp. They were immediately presented with leather bound menus. Tom reached for his, but didn't move his gaze from Samantha. She wondered again if he knew the power of his eyes, the passion they expressed or their ability to freeze her thoughts with their laser focus.

"Have I told you that you look beautiful tonight?" he asked.

She felt her face flush; and instinctively, she lowered her eyes to her menu.

"I didn't mean to embarrass you," he said softly, "but you really do look lovely."

"Thank you," Samantha said with traces of pleasure in her voice, but she was still too unnerved by the effusive praise to meet his gaze. She continued to scan the menu and was grateful and relieved when the waiter approached to take their order. They talked as they ate, taking the first, tentative steps toward getting to know each other, and Samantha was surprised to find out that Tom grew up in Scranton, Pennsylvania and had attended the same Jesuit preparatory school from which her new friend and classmate, Rob Ferrell, had graduated.

"Do you know Rob Ferrell, she asked? He sits directly behind me in Real Property. I believe he went to your high school."

"Don't know him," Tom said dismissively.

"Oh, well," she said, "he would have been a couple of years behind you anyway."

Samantha spoke of her parents, their close relationship, and how she had followed her father into the law. Tom described his widowed mother who had raised him and his two much older sisters in a small frame house next to the local parish church on the seedier side of working class Scranton.

"My Aunt Maureen lived with us, too," he added, shaking his head ruefully, "It's a lot like having four mothers."

Samantha listened thoughtfully. His background was so unlike her own. This adored altar boy, raised in a blue collar environment in a house full of women, who was the first in his family to go to college, seemed to have little in common with her Ivy League, over-assimilated upbringing. Something in his manner told her that his family had something to do with his confidence—clearly he had been raised to think he could do no wrong. Yet, she was captivated.

As they stood at the curb waiting for the valet to bring Tom's car, the wind changed directions and whipped Samantha's hair around her face. Tom raised the collar of her coat and, holding it closed against the chill, pulled her toward him. His lips were warm and lingering. The memory of his kiss supplanted any doubts she might have had.

Samantha and Tom had been seeing each other for several weeks when she met with her newly-formed study group. Everyone but she and Rob Ferrell already had left, and the two friends chatted amicably as they packed away their study materials.

"So, you haven't been around much after classes lately," Rob said.

"Just busy, I guess. Between classes, studying, cleaning my apartment, all the usual stuff, there doesn't seem to be much time to just hang out. Also," she said, turning to face him, "I'm seeing someone."

Rob shifted his considerable bulk and snapped the locks on his battered briefcase. "Who's the lucky guy?" he grinned.

"Actually, I thought at first that you might know each other because he graduated from your high school a couple of years before you, but he says he doesn't know you. His name's Tom Leary."

Rob's face went dark. "That asshole!" he blurted. "I know him, all right. He thought he was the biggest player in town. A real heartbreaker, that one."

Samantha's heart squeezed. "Maybe you have him confused with someone else, Rob. Tom's a really nice, intelligent guy." She thought again of his eyes, his kiss.

"I come from a small town, Samantha, a town that gives new meaning to the old saying, 'Bad news travels fast;' and you can take my word for it, Tom Leary is bad news. I'd be very careful if I were you."

Samantha's cheeks burned with two hot spots of outrage. "Even if you're right, people change. I'm telling you, Tom's a good guy," she insisted.

Rob's earnest face matched her anger. He bit his lower lip as if trying to keep back his words. "It's possible, Sammie, but very unlikely. Tom took out my younger sister, Rosemary, when she was a freshman in high school, and he was a senior. You wouldn't know it to look at me, but she's a beauty. They went out a few times; and then one night, I heard her crying in her room. We've always been close, so I knocked on her door and asked her what happened. She said that they'd had sex, and then he never called her again. What's worse, he'd bragged about it all over school. I confronted him the next day, and all he said was, 'Look, Fatboy, your sister came on to me,' and he actually had the nerve to laugh as he walked away. When I said he was an asshole, I should have said he was a *total* asshole."

Samantha dropped her books back onto the table. She had no reason to doubt what Rob had told her; in fact, the terrible story would explain why Tom denied knowing Rob. Still, Rob would naturally take his sister's side. Maybe, she had come on to Tom. Only Rosemary and Tom knew what really happened. "Look," she said in a conciliatory tone, "I'm sorry about how things happened between your sister and Tom, but I've got to go." Rob just shook his head, as she made a hasty departure.

Anxious to hear Tom's side of the story, Samantha drove straight to his apartment. She rang the bell, and the door swung wide.

"Hi," Tom said. "I wasn't expecting you." He still wore the navy trousers of his business suit, but he had jettisoned his tie, and the sleeves of his blue pinpoint oxford cloth shirt were neatly rolled to just below the elbow. "What a welcome surprise," he added, taking her arm and drawing her inside.

Tom took a seat on the sofa, but Samantha chose a chair opposite him on the other side of the coffee table that was littered with a half-read copy of *The New York Times*. "What's wrong?" Tom asked. "Why are you sitting over there?"

Samantha looked him in the eye and then looked down at her lap where her hands moved restlessly. She forced herself to look at his face again. His brows knit together in concern. "I spoke to Rob Ferrell after study group today," she said, her words coming rapidly now. "He says you dated his younger sister, Rosemary, and that you bragged all over school about having sex with her after you dropped her. Is that true, Tom? Is that why you lied about not knowing Rob when I asked you about him?"

Tom's smile faded with the suddenness of a light that has been switched off. He closed his eyes and cupped his forehead in his hand. "Ok," he admitted. "I know Tom and Rosemary, and I did take her out a few times, but things didn't happen the way he said. She went after me because I was one of the few guys in the senior class who was headed for college, and it was she who spread the stories about us around school. That's why I stopped calling her. I didn't have any interest in being the prize catch among the girls in my school, even if she was one of the pretty ones. When Rob accused me of seducing his baby sister, I tried to tell him what really happened; but look, I have sisters too; and if it came down to their word or the word of some guy I thought was a player, I'd support my sisters every time, so I understand where he's coming from. That's why I told you I didn't know Rob. I frankly find the whole episode embarrassing, and I was hoping you wouldn't have to hear about it from him or me. Believe me, Samantha, I'm not that kind of guy." He leaned across the table and took her hand. Samantha squeezed his warm fingers and smiled, gestures that said, *I believe you.*

CHAPTER 47

A T THE BEGINNING OF the spring semester, Tom asked Samantha to marry him. When they made their announcement to her parents, Fred and Leonora were welcoming to Tom, but Fred said pointedly over drinks at the bar of the fancy restaurant where they went to celebrate, "Samantha's Jewish, you know. I hope the difference in your religions won't pose a problem."

"Not at all, sir," Tom reassured him. "I don't think either of us is so steeped in the orthodoxy of our faith that it will become an issue."

Fred's smile looked more like a sneer to Samantha, one end of his mouth pulled high and taught, his lips pursed tightly together. This was an expression Samantha knew well; her father adopted it whenever he was skeptical at best or, at worst, completely convinced that what he had just heard was a lie. As he cut his eyes in mute communication toward Leonora, Samantha imagined how he might win a jury to his side by discrediting a witness with nothing more than the practiced twitch of the corner of his mouth, a silent scream of "*Mendacity*" to which opposing counsel could not object.

Conversation through dinner was polite, but Samantha's anger boiled to the surface when she found herself alone with Fred once Leonora had gone to bed, and Tom had started the drive back to Boston in order to make an early appointment the following morning. "What was all that about Judaism, Daddy?" she demanded. "Since when is religion high on your list of important topics?"

Fred's face flinched almost imperceptibly. "What did I say that embarrassed you, Sammie? I simply wanted Tom, and you for that matter, to understand that a mixed marriage is fraught with difficulty coming from inside and out. All I said was the truth. You're a Jew, and he's a Catholic. Why do you have a problem with that?"

"I have a 'problem,'" Samantha snapped, biting off each syllable of the word, "because this is coming out of the blue. If Judaism matters so much to you, you had the last twenty-two years to share that importance with me. Your mood dictated whether you kept me home from school for the Jewish holidays, and you chose to dress up as Santa Claus and place our gifts under a "Chanukah bush" every year of my childhood. Instead of relying on the beauty and religious significance of the menorah and the fun of the dreidel game to interest me in Chanukah, you insisted that I would be missing out on the best holiday traditions if I didn't grow up with Santa and a Christmas tree. For heaven's sake, Dad, you didn't even send me to Hebrew school or confirmation classes, and the first time I ever set foot in a synagogue was to attend a bar mitzvah when I was ten years old. Now, all of a sudden, you feel obliged to play the Jew card? What's up with that?"

Fred looked like an amazed schoolteacher. "Understanding who you are and where you came from has nothing to do with all the hokum and meaningless rules of Judaism or any other religion, Samantha. That's all I ever got out of the synagogue, and I saw no reason to inflict that on you. Besides," Fred sputtered, "I tried to join a Temple soon after I started practicing law, and I found that it was nothing more than another competition about money no different than when women show up at church and vie for who has the biggest hat. I lasted until after the first annual fundraiser. I dug deep and gave $1000- that was a lot of money back then; but my name was listed with the other *drek* who didn't have two quarters to rub together, while my law school classmate, Leonard Berger, who gave $5,000 of his Daddy's money, was considered a *mentsch*, and his name was published at the top of the list. I never went back after that humiliation. I tell you, I didn't need them and their burning bush, and neither did you!"

"Then, why now?" Samantha repeated. "If that's how you feel, why do you care if Tom's a Catholic?"

"Because if he's all about *their* rules," Fred fired back, "then he's just another blind sheep. I raised you to have your eyes open, not to be a follower of any flock. I never once suggested that we should be anything but proud of who we are and our heritage as Jews. In fact, you know that when I found out that my boyhood classmate, Aaron Levy, converted to Unitarianism, I questioned his motives and believed he was doing it because he wasn't strong enough to acknowledge who he was. I don't have a problem with Tom's being a Catholic; I only would have a problem if he tried to foist his religion on you."

"If we're supposed to be such proud Jews," Samantha argued, "then why did you and Mom act so flattered when her Aunt Rachel complimented my blue eyes and fair skin saying, 'Sammie's so pretty; she looks like a *shiksa*'"? I grew up feeling confused, Dad. I was supposed to hold my head up high as a Jew, while at the same time feeling just as proud that my looks enabled me to pass in Christian society. Look, Dad," Samantha said more calmly, "I know you feel you were denied opportunity because of anti-Semitism, and I also know that you've always wanted to live in a meritocracy where you would be judged on results rather than labels, but I wish you could understand that because you didn't raise me with the gift of the beauty of Judaism's rituals and history, I never felt that I had to wear my religious heritage like a millstone around my neck. But, you know what? I'm thankful for the gift you did give me. You taught me to question rules and to make the most of this life, not wait for some hereafter. That's a great gift, Dad." Samantha stood on tiptoe and planted a kiss on Fred's cheek.

"Ok, then, Sammie," Fred said. "If you say Tom is the one for you, I believe you and am happy for you." He cupped her chin in his long fingers; and this time, his smile was real.

The following weekend, Samantha and Tom drove from Boston to Scranton so that she could meet his mother and aunt and share with them the news of their engagement. Samantha was excited to see where Tom had grown up, but as they exited the highway and turned onto the main street of the town, she felt a slight sinking in her stomach. She hadn't expected the drabness of the clapboard buildings, the early snowfall that had turned to a gray slush crunching under their tires, and the garish, flickering neon illumination of the corner bar.

That Tom had grown up in the shadow of the parish Catholic church was no exaggeration. His childhood home shared a narrow alley with the stone edifice, and railroad tracks defined the small yard's rear boundary. As Tom pulled his car into the narrow driveway and parked behind the house, he seemed suddenly anxious, rubbing his hands together and blowing into them for warmth.

"Well, here we are," he said. "I'll get the bags."

Samantha followed him up a small flight of wooden steps to the back door of the house, and Tom opened the door and held it for her to pass into the kitchen. She couldn't imagine her own parents not greeting her at the door.

"We're here," he yelled into the empty space.

Samantha could hear footsteps from the front of the house as Tom's mother made her way back. Sam stamped the snow from her shoes and walked inside. The kitchen had an old linoleum floor with small rugs that looked like bathmats scattered about. Old-fashioned appliances lined the room's perimeter, leaving a large open area that was occupied by a lone rocking chair. The room was dark, and there were no inviting cooking smells. Sam wondered for a moment if Tom's mother had forgotten about the visit.

Bridget Leary was a small, colorless woman, as bleak as the heart of her home, and Sam was shocked at how old she looked, either aged prematurely by the hard press of life or just someone to whom the passage of time had not been kind. She wore a gray, shapeless dress the same color as her hair that was pulled back severely from her face into a chignon at the base of her neck. A black cardigan draped her rounded shoulders, and her only adornment was a large, silver cross that she fingered habitually.

She moved toward her son and gave him an awkward hug. "Hello, Thomas Anthony," she greeted him formally. "I am glad that you made it before the big snow storm they're predicting." Turning to Samantha as if noticing her for the first time, she said, "You must be Samantha."

Samantha was confused by Mrs. Leary's use of Tom's full name. She had never heard anyone else refer to him as other than Tom. She recovered her focus and extended her hand to Tom's mother. "Yes, I am, and I'm so happy to finally meet you."

Mrs. Leary's handshake was cursory and weak. Turning her attention back to Tom, Mrs. Leary gestured toward the hallway. "Let's go into the living room, Thomas Anthony. Your Aunt Maureen has stayed up waiting for you."

They followed her into the dim front room where another woman sat in a wheel chair in a pool of light provided by a table lamp with a silk, fringed shade. She bore a striking resemblance to Mrs. Leary, except that her legs were twisted with the atrophy of disuse, and her fingers curled into claw-shaped vises. Beside her, Samantha noticed a large, framed portrait of Tom, probably from his college graduation. It was the only photograph in the room, which gave it a creepy, shrine-like quality.

Tom bent to kiss his aunt's parched cheek. "Hello, Aunt Maureen," he said in a deferential voice Samantha had never heard before. "I would like you to meet Samantha."

The old woman's alert eyes seemed to devour her. "You are not a member of the One True Church, are you, young lady?" she demanded incisively and without preamble. Her bright eyes were the same intense cornflower blue as Tom's. Tom blanched, and his mother moved behind the wheel chair and placed a hand on her sister's shoulder in solidarity.

As if the heavy silence that suddenly shrouded the room emboldened her further, Maureen continued, "Thomas Anthony is a Roman Catholic, my dear, as is everyone else in this house. Do you mean to try to separate him from his faith?"

Samantha was stunned and angry. Tom seemed to await her response as much as his mother and aunt, who faced her in cold inquisition.

"Tom," she emphasized, deliberately defying their use of his Christian name, "is free to practice his faith without any interference from anyone. Whether he does so to your satisfaction has nothing to do with me."

Even as she spoke, she knew that these words should be coming from Tom and not from her. The two faces of her accusers, so alike in their small-minded intolerance, mirrored their displeasure, their mouths drawn in severe lines. The room seemed oppressively close as the radiators hissed belching heat.

"If you don't mind, I think I need some air," she said over her shoulder, approaching the door. She flung it open and went out into the cold night. She could hear Tom's voice calling after her, but she wrapped her arms around herself against the cold and continued down the sidewalk.

Tom caught up with her in the churchyard. He grabbed her by the elbow and spun her around.

"Where are you going?" he rasped between gulps of frigid winter air. "You don't even have a coat." He pulled off his sweater and draped it around her shoulders.

Tears stung her eyes as she tried to break free of him. "You just stood there," she sobbed. "You just stood there as if you were with them, and I was some alien from another planet. You never gave me the slightest inkling that they had any doubts about me, religious or otherwise. I have never felt so isolated and unwelcome in my life." She faced him, chest heaving, and the silhouette of the church hulking behind him.

"I'm sorry, Samantha," he said. "I don't know what came over them. Please forgive them and me. I think their baby boy getting married has over-whelmed the old girls."

He grinned boyishly, stuffed his hands deep in his pockets, and kicked the snowy dirt with the toe of his shoe. Samantha smiled in spite of herself.

"Come back inside before you get pneumonia," Tom urged. "I promise you've heard the last of the debate over saving my soul."

He pulled her to him and kissed the top of her head, resting his chin there for a moment. Samantha could feel her anger begin to dissipate into the cold night, even though she had witnessed the fierce hold that Tom's mother and aunt exerted over him, as if the three of them were inextricably bound by that heavy silver chain with its unforgiving crucifix.

"You will marry me, won't you, Sammie?" Tom asked.

She tipped back her head to see his face, and he covered her mouth with a kiss. She nodded and forced another smile, and they walked back to his house, the downstairs now silent and dark.

Samantha and Tom were married that summer with both a rabbi and a priest officiating. The priest had been one of Tom's teachers at his Jesuit high school, and the ceremony had a personal, interfaith quality that acknowledged both of their heritages. Samantha was pleased with the compromise, and her early doubts about Tom's adherence to the strictures of Catholicism felt assuaged.

But just as quickly, she came to realize that the scene in Tom's mother's kitchen was about far more than the church. It began to seem like there were two Toms. Her Tom, the one with whom she'd fallen in love, was smart and funny, confident and loving, and devoted to her. The other Tom, the one who revealed himself around his family and coterie of boyhood friends, was deceptive and weak, phlegmatic and distant. Samantha tried to convince herself that a man who honored his mother and aunt also would honor his wife, but all too often Tom reverted to long established precedent within his family, deferring to them and insisting that she do so as well.

They had been married only minutes when Tom's veil of independence slipped. His sister, Jan, had arrived at their wedding wearing a white dress, breaking a taboo that many viewed not only as a harbinger of bad luck but also as an intentional diversion of attention from the bride.

"Tom," Samantha whispered as Jan approached the receiving line following the ceremony, "I can't believe that Jan is wearing a white dress to our wedding. Everyone knows that it is inappropriate for anyone other than the bride to wear white. Why would your sister do something so thoughtless?"

"Shh," Tom hushed her. "She'll hear you! Who cares what color she wears? I don't know why you always have to take things so personally. Just relax, and let it go."

Turning to embrace his sister, he said audibly, "You look beautiful, Jan. I really like your dress." Jan raised her chin, basking in the compliment, and turned to Samantha just as Tom gave her an imperceptible nudge.

Samantha flushed. She had looked to Tom for support, and he had turned on her instead. Pasting a smile on her face, she hugged her new sister-in-law and relented. "Nice to see you, Jan."

Tom's expressed attitude toward religion also seemed to be changing now that they were married. He had promised his mother that they would attend Mass on their honeymoon, without consulting Samantha, even though he had not been to Mass in all the time she'd known him; and he had since insisted that Sammie accompany them to church whenever they visited his mother and aunt in Scranton. He gave his family the distinct impression that they attended church regularly in Boston, even though his only nod to Catholicism outside of their presence was to buy his decidedly non-Catholic wife a green carnation and a pint of green beer at a local Irish pub on St. Patrick's Day.

Tom had gone through both college and law school at Boston College with a close knit group of friends and still spent much of his time with them. Samantha would much later come to think of them as the "St. Elmo's Fire Brigade" in homage to the 1985 movie in which a clique of friends formed during their undergraduate days could not seem to move forward with their lives after graduation, living, working and congregating just off the campus of their youth. Tom's group of friends, mostly lawyers and mostly married, spent much of their free time together rehashing the stories of their student days with lavish embellishment in each retelling. Their young wives drifted around this tight nucleus of boy-men wearing taut expressions of approval, laughing at the preprogrammed punch lines, and bonding together not out of friendship so much as from mutual feelings of exclusion. Samantha had been popular since childhood and still kept up with friends from as far back as elementary school, so it was not the longevity of Tom's relationships that chafed. It was their exclusivity and static quality. Their hackneyed tales were like passwords that no one else knew, and their shared past was a private club to which even their wives learned quickly not to seek admission.

"You know," she ventured one evening on the drive home from yet another gathering of the Brigade, "it's just not funny anymore."

Tom looked at her blankly. "What's not funny?" he asked.

"You really don't know, do you?" Samantha continued. "I mean it was funny the first time and even the second, like that story about you and your roommate streaking across fraternity row. But by about the third time, it was just stale and expected; and if anyone did laugh, it was only to be polite. Don't you get it? You and those guys never talk about anything new. You all have vibrant, exciting lives with marriages and professional careers that should provide a wellspring of new stories to share, but you get together, and you're just frat boys again. Nothing's happened before or since that can compare to those halcyon days. Oh, what's the use? None of you will ever grow up."

Samantha had exhausted herself in this tirade. Tom's handsome face contorted with anger.

"None of the other wives seem to mind," he chided. "I'm sorry that you're so easily bored; but if you think you can drive a wedge between me and my friends, you're mistaken."

Samantha stared at his stern profile. "Just for the record," she bit off angrily, "the other wives do mind. In fact, they mind a lot. They just don't have the guts to say so."

She folded her arms across her chest and turned away from Tom. The glacial silence hung thickly between them like an unwanted passenger who had squeezed into the middle seat.

Samantha waited for a thaw; but days went by, and it never came. She felt even more alienated. The Brigade seemed tighter, their laughter louder, and their wives more Stepford-like in their voiceless forbearance. Although she despised the idea, she decided that she must launch a campaign to make Tom's present life with her more compelling than the past to which he clung with his friends.

Tom's mother rarely came to Boston; in fact, she had not often ventured beyond a safe and well-worn radius from her house that circumscribed the church and limits of her parish. So when Tom announced that she would be coming to spend the weekend with Jan and her family who lived in nearby

Braintree, Sam seized the opportunity to invite her to their apartment for dinner. All during the previous week, Sam had been obsessively cleaning, frenetically shopping, and constructing and revising the menu. It was as if, by creating a flawless meal, she could establish irrefutable proof that she and Tom were happy, that the other Tom was the imposter in their enviable life. A perfectionist by nature, Samantha felt particularly anxious when the day of the dinner arrived.

As the sun began to rise over the snow covered streets of Boston on that tempestuous February morning, Tom woke to the sounds of snowplows scraping the pavement outside and to the disconcerting sensation of an empty space in the bed beside him. He opened his eyes and pushed himself up against the headboard. "Sammie, are you up already?" he yelled.

Samantha wiped the hair from her brow with the back of her hand and grabbed a dishtowel so that she could wash flour from her hands. She had twelve hours until the dinner but had already been up preparing for two. Walking back to the bedroom, she attempted consciously to rid her voice of any signs of stress and replied, "Hope I didn't wake you, honey. Just thought I'd get started on some of the things that can be made ahead of time."

She saw him glance sideways at the alarm clock; the digital display seemed to have been magnified threefold as it flaunted the time, 7:23am. She smiled sheepishly. Tom stood and stretched as he pulled a sweatshirt over his T-shirt and pajama pants.

Padding across the floor in his bare feet, he said, "Looks like it's going to be another cold one today. Last night the weatherman predicted more snow for this afternoon."

Sam followed him into the kitchen, trying to remain calm in the face of his cavalier forecast that could doom all of her plans. Tom dipped his finger in the bowl of cake batter and licked off the sweet concoction with relish.

"My mother doesn't go out when it's snowing," he added matter-of-factly. "She's afraid of slipping on the ice."

"Well, this is different," Samantha exuded with feigned confidence. "Your sister or brother-in-law will be driving her, so they can look out for her."

"I'm just saying," Tom continued, "Jan and James don't like to drive in the snow either."

Samantha fought her anger. She stole a glance at Tom as she raised her mallet to pound the veal scaloppini. He was leaning casually against the counter eating a bowl of cereal with an expression of placid indifference.

"Well, maybe it won't snow at all," Sam managed. "In the meantime, I'm going to make the best Saltimbocca either of you has ever tasted. Saltimbocca means 'jumps in the mouth' in Italian," she added proudly.

She wielded the mallet over the defenseless veal and came down hard against the butcher block. She suppressed a smile as the crash of wood against wood made Tom jump perceptibly.

"Whoa," he commanded. "I think that recipe says 'tenderize' not 'assault.' Anyway, I think I'll just be in the way here, so I'm going to shower and go to the office for a few hours. I'll be back in plenty of time for your gastronomic masterpiece."

"Be careful out there," Samantha called after him. As soon as he had gone, Samantha switched on the television in the living room. She listened with half an ear as she stuffed each veal scallop with prosciutto ham and Fontina cheese. She gathered the ingredients for the homemade fettuccini noodles that would accompany the entrée; and as the time for the weather report approached, she carried a large colander to the sofa so that she could snap the haricots verts while watching the broadcast. She focused on the television, but she already could see the large, white flakes falling outside and sticking on the ground below.

"Boston 29 degrees with a wind chill factor of 10, so it will feel more like 19 degrees. Baby, it's cold outside," the local meteorologist was saying as he hugged himself in a mock shiver. "Snow will continue to fall throughout the afternoon; and as the sun goes down and the temperature drops, motorists should be aware of the black ice on roadways that appear to be wet but have actually iced over. If you don't absolutely have to go out, by all means stay off the highways; and driving conditions on the secondary roads are apt to be even worse. It's going to be a great night for a good book and a warm fire."

Sam angrily fired the remote at the television, scooped up the colander and the remainder of the green beans and slammed them onto the kitchen counter. She attacked the bowl of butter crème icing with her whisk and glared accusingly at each partially completed course, daring the delicacies to ridicule her efforts.

By the time that Tom returned home at five o'clock, everything was either in the oven, on the stove, or ready in the refrigerator. The table, set with their best linen and silverware, glowed in the candlelight. Samantha already had transformed herself, hair and makeup immaculately arranged and her dress and jewelry impeccably selected. She stood at the head of the table and smiled expectantly at Tom.

"Well, I guess I'd better change," he said. "Snow's still coming down out there."

Samantha opened her mouth to ask him if everything, if she, looked all right; but before the words could come, she was jarred by the ringing of the telephone. Tom reached for the receiver from the wall phone in the kitchen.

"Hello," he said. "Oh, hi, Jan." He turned his back to Samantha as he listened to his sister. Samantha's spine stiffened, and she felt a persistent throbbing in her temples.

"Yeah, it's still snowing here too," she heard him say. "No, we understand totally. We wouldn't want you or Mom to endanger yourselves to get here. After all, it's just a meal."

Samantha's eyes drifted across the elegant table and the feast that was the result of days of effort until her gaze came to rest on Tom's back. "I can't believe this," she shouted. "We all grew up in the snow, your family even more so than mine, and your sister can't even attempt the short ride over here. Take a look around you, Tom. You call this 'just a meal?' I have spent most of this entire week preparing this dinner for your mother, and it means a lot to me. If they were so concerned about the weather, they could have started out earlier, before the roads got bad; and your mother was welcome to spend the night if conditions got so bad that we couldn't take her back to Braintree. No one thought about any of that. They just waited and cancelled at the last minute without a thought to what this evening means to me."

Her chest heaved, and she had no breath to go on. It was only when she finished speaking that she realized that Tom had already replaced the receiver on its cradle. He had not even tried to convince his sister to change her mind; he was more concerned that she not overhear any of Sam's accusations than he was willing to interpose himself between his wife on the one hand and his sister and mother on the other. Shock rode in tandem with her anger as waves of emotion passed through her. She pushed past him and, slamming the bedroom door behind her, threw herself on the bed. Soon, she could feel his presence beside the bed, although her face was buried in her arms and her tears were still flowing.

"You need to call my mother to apologize," he said. "She's very upset." Samantha rolled over lethargically to look at him. His jaw was set, and his arms were folded across his chest. "I said, 'You need to call my mother,'" he bit off each word coldly, slowly articulating each staccato syllable as though he were talking to someone of limited understanding.

Samantha wiped her wet cheeks and stood up. She could not raise her eyes from his perfectly polished shoes. Tom picked up the phone from the bedside table and thrust it toward Samantha. She dialed the number robotically, just as the oven timer sounded.

"What are you crying about?" Tom snapped as Samantha returned the phone to its cradle and sagged onto the side of the bed. "It's just a meal, for God's sake. You're the one who's being selfish here, expecting my mother, sister, and brother-in-law to risk life and limb in a snowstorm because you made them dinner! You're always telling me to grow up. Well, grow up yourself, and stop making everything about you."

"It's not about the dinner, Tom," Samantha said in a small voice. "It's about how you and your family continue to make me feel that I have something to prove—that I didn't steal you away from Catholicism, that I can manage being your wife while still in law school, that I fit in with your friends, that I deserved to marry their precious Tom! You're different around them, just as you're different around your college crowd. I'm a perpetual outsider whenever you're with any of them, and it's like I don't know you at all. The dinner was just another ruined attempt to win them over."

Samantha, twisting the fringe along the edge of the bedspread, looked up at Tom, hoping to see a trace of empathy. But his face was cold.

"I'm hungry," Tom said, turning on his heel. Samantha heard him banging around the kitchen as he helped himself to dinner. She lay down in the dark and turned her face to the wall.

CHAPTER 48

F IVE YEARS INTO THEIR marriage, what had at first appealed to Samantha as self-confidence and intelligence in Tom now was revealed as arrogance and superficiality. Tom's coterie of close friends had become increasingly oppressive; what had seemed like Tom's close family ties so similar to her own had blossomed into interference and attempts to control. Sam tried to discuss Tom's unwillingness to widen his circle and his family's meddling, but Tom was vociferous in his defense of his friends and deferred to his mother or sister in any controversy.

Sam's parents had been married for nearly thirty years, and she had always looked to them as a model for her own marriage. She certainly had no moral stricture against divorce, and she understood on a rational level that two people should not be forced by either the law or their god to remain together in misery. Yet, divorce was something that happened to other people, not to her.

Now, only a day after she and Tom had decided to divorce, and he had moved out, Samantha sat curled in the corner of the sofa, her needlepoint project spread across her lap and the television playing in the background. There was something calming about the repetitive stitching and the inane TV dialogue for company. Having washed her lonely dinner plate, she sat in the only pool of light in the house, acutely attuned to any sound breaking the silence that did not emanate from the television. Divorce. She thought back to before she had been married, to her naïve conceptions of what it would take for her to end such a relationship. Like a well-schooled lawyer with no experiential learning, she ticked them off in her head. Cheating, absconding with all of the couple's money, and what was the legal term for desertion? Abandonment, that was it, "leaving without just cause." Samantha's head ached, and her fingers trembled, causing her to prick her finger with the needle.

"Damn," she cried, checking the pad of her finger to see whether she had broken the skin. She closed her eyes and breathed deeply, but that did nothing to block out her thoughts. Cheating. Money. Abandonment. As to the first, she had her suspicions-- the late nights, the blonde with whom she had seen him leaving his office building. He had shrugged her off as a paralegal working on one of his cases, but who knew? Then, there was their sex life. Their lovemaking had become obligatory and then nonexistent. The last time he touched her, he had forgone even the appearance of arousal. He had rolled over onto his back and said, "It's no big deal." Samantha had fled to the bathroom, screaming from the doorway at his impassively reclining form, "It's a very big deal, Tom. A very big deal!"

As to their money, she had happily contributed everything she earned both before and since their marriage to their joint account; but suddenly, he began talking about things in terms of what was his, not theirs. She did not care about the money exactly, but she had become attached to the things they had acquired, the things they had both selected or been given as symbols of the life they were building together. Looking around the lonely room, Samantha wondered how this house, these inanimate sticks of furniture, these glittering Waterford glasses, and the candlesticks that had been shimmering gifts of hope at their wedding had become flotsam of broken promises.

And then there was abandonment. Desertion, leaving, rejection, neglect. In a sense, she realized that the truth of the matter lay right there. What it really came down to was that the true figment of her imagination had been Tom as a loving husband. The law recognized abandonment without just cause as a physical leaving by one spouse for no legally justifiable reason. When Tom revealed what she now considered to be his true self after they already were married, he had left her in a much deeper, psychological sense. He abandoned her as a partner, lover, and friend, and he deserted their marriage long before he stuffed a suitcase full of clothes and moved out of the house.

Samantha pressed the heels of her hands into her eyes, trying to force Tom's image to retreat. *He's gone,* she told herself. *He's gone, and he can't hurt you anymore.* The house seemed suddenly cavernous and empty. She was cold and pulled the belt of her terrycloth robe more securely around her. She looked at the mantle clock. *Seven o'clock. Sometimes, Daddy works late on Thursdays.* She reached for the phone and dialed her father's office number. She knew that her marriage was over, and Fred was the one person in whom she wanted to confide.

Fred's secretary put Samantha's call through as soon as she identified herself. The phone rang three times, and then Sammie heard Fred's familiar baritone, "Hello?"

"Hi, Daddy," she said. There was a momentary pause. Samantha rarely interrupted her father during the workday. When she called her parents in the evening or on the weekend, it was her mother who monopolized the conversation, leaving Fred to complain that, even when he and Samantha finally had the opportunity to speak, Leonora hovered anxiously in the background until he relinquished the phone to her. True, Fred didn't have much to say about fashion or restaurants or movies, but that was not the measure of his feelings for his daughter. Sammie looked like him; she had his incisive mind; she shared his creativity and his love affair with words. To Fred, Samantha was his best self, tempered with an easy amiability that he had never had. "You are the eyes in my head," he often told her. "I would lay down my life for you." Fred looked at the large, brass maritime clock that sat on his credenza- 7:05pm. Something didn't feel right.

"Hi, honey," he replied. "What's going on?" *So like him,* Sammie thought. *No preamble. Cut to the chase.* Her father's voice was like a warm blanket wrapping itself around her stooped shoulders. Samantha exhaled deeply. She stood just a little taller and the heavy weight that had been bearing down on her shoulders seemed ever so slightly lighter. "

"Daddy," she began, "I've decided…. Tom and I…." She forgot all of her planned speech in a flood of grief. She began again, "It's over between Tom and me. I can't do this anymore. We're going to get a divorce."

Fred heard her crying. He felt tightness in his chest, his stomach lurched, and his temples throbbed. Although his memories of his own divorce were always there, they came to life like a crowd of violent enemies pressing against the gate of his consciousness with only his will to hold them at bay. *"Tell her,"* they screamed. *"Tell her!"*

"I'm so sorry, Sammie," he said instead. "Do you want to talk about it?"

"Not really, Daddy. Although Tom moved out yesterday, I've been alone for quite some time." she sniffed.

"You're not alone," Fred insisted emphatically. "And it's not the end of the world."

"I feel like a failure, Daddy. I feel like anyone looking at me will see the failure and won't be able to see past it." Her words caught in her throat.

"Now, you listen to me, Sammie. Everyone fails. Everyone, do you hear me? It's not whether we fail that separates us; it's what we do with that failure. Your failure will define you only if you let it. Others will see and judge that kind of submission only if you empower them to be the measure of your life's success. If you are your own judge, you will face your failures and remember every tear, every loss, every pang of regret. Then, you will learn because you will never want to feel those pains again. You are beautiful and smart, and your heart is tender. I know that I'm your father, but I am not the only one who sees those qualities in you, Sammie. Your failure lies in the bad choice that you made, but only you can decide now whether that bad choice will affect who you are and who others will see. I've told you from the time I thought you were old enough to understand that no one goes through life unscathed. Not you, not me. When it comes to love, you have felt what it is like to be unloved; but I don't think you have it in you to become bitter. I believe you'll go out and find someone who will truly see you and return your love in a way that will make this experience seem just a small part of what I hope will be your very long journey."

Samantha cradled the phone, letting the solace of her father's words wash over her. He was right. Despite the roiling sea of emotions she was feeling—hurt, embarrassment, rejection, fear, anger—she had never once felt hopeless. She had never once felt defeated. Tom's capacity to love her had been severely constrained by his greater love for himself. His self-serving, niggling kind of love had pressed down on her and had whittled away at her autonomy and strength. Listening to her father's unflagging encouragement, she was reminded of an article she read recently about the Anthurium Regale Linden, a tropical plant that persistently and inexorably seeks the light, even if it has to push and change course as it yearns for it. She understood its profound beauty when, with the improbable curve of its youthful stem and its leaves outstretched, it finally opens its flowering glory to embrace the sun.

"Thanks, Daddy. I…I love you."

"I love you, too, Sammie. I love you, too."

"Don't be so weak," the angry mob in his head jeered at him! *"Tell her! Tell her now!"* He still could hear her muffled sobs. "This weekend is New Year's Eve, Sammie. Come home. You need to be with your mother and me."

"Ok, Daddy," Sam exhaled.

"Oh, and Sammie," Fred said again, "I love you!"

A light snow fell as she drove the next day from her home in Boston to the Philadelphia suburb of her youth. Sam gripped the steering wheel with both hands and peered through the frosty windshield. She had not spent a New Year's Eve alone in recent memory. Her mother had told her that her father's lifelong friend, Chapman Stirling, and his wife were coming to celebrate the New Year, too. When Sam called and told her mother about her plan to come home, her mother encouraged her; but now she was not sure if she could abide the company of others. Samantha had grown up loving Chapman Stirling as a member of the family. Fred spoke of Uncle Chapman, as she called him, with fondness and admiration. Chapman had been his staunch friend, a fine lawyer, a college president and a mayor. Yet, Samantha felt a certain reluctance to feign happiness and social affability, even with Uncle Chapman, when she was at her lowest emotional point.

She turned onto Brook Drive, and pulled up in front of the house, a two story, L-shaped, brick contemporary designed by a disciple of Frank Lloyd Wright in 1950. There was the window of her childhood bedroom, the trim painted turquoise and white, just as it always had been. The clear glass orbs of the driveway lights burned brightly in welcome, and her tires crunched under a fresh coating of snow as she steered the car into the gravel driveway, parking to the side of the free standing garage in her customary spot. It felt like nothing and everything had changed since she was a child.

She wrestled her suitcase from the trunk and breathed in the familiar scent of pine and snow. The front door immediately swung open framing her mother and father. Their arms were open wide; and Samantha was their child again, running from hurt, into the refuge of their constant love.

"Hi, doll," her mother said, releasing her from a tight embrace. "How was the drive?"

"Fine. There was some snow, but it wasn't sticking, so I just took it slow." Sam kissed her mother's perfumed cheek and stepped into her father's out-stretched arms. "It's so good to be home."

Fred's long arm encircled Sam's shoulders and drew her into the house. "Come on in, Sammie. As long as my eyes are open, this is your home. You'll always be my baby. Don't worry about a thing." Sam sat down at the kitchen table in what was still her place.

"Want something to eat?" her mother asked. Sam smiled. Her mother's solution to anything from headache to heartbreak was food.

"No thanks. Maybe just a cold drink." Her mother placed a cold Coke in front of her. "What time are the Stirlings going to be here?" Samantha asked.

Fred seemed to light up at the mention of his old friend's name. "Around eight. We're going to have cocktails here and then go out to dinner to ring in the New Year." Never a social animal, he seemed genuinely excited by the prospect. "I haven't seen Chapman in a while. Having my best friend and my two best girls here to celebrate New Year's Eve is going to be great." Sam suddenly felt overwhelmingly tired.

"I think I'll go upstairs and unpack and take a nap before all the festivities, if you two don't mind. I guess the tension of driving through the snow has affected me more than I thought." Her parents exchanged a knowing look, but beamed encouraging smiles in her direction.

Throughout her drive home, Samantha had been sick with worry that her family and friends would make her feel like Hester Prynne, only her scarlet letter was a capital D for "Divorcee." Within the halo of her parents' understanding, she felt that brand begin to fade to a less livid shade; and she had the nascent sensation that healing was possible.

"You take all the time you want. This is your home," her father repeated.

At eight o'clock on the dot, the doorbell rang signaling the arrival of the Stirlings. Fred answered; and the two tall men, with their lanky physiques and silver hair, still looked like brothers as they embraced and their wives traded greetings. Chapman hugged Sam's mother and turned to Samantha as the closely knit group walked toward the living room. "Sam, I was so happy when your parents told me you would be here tonight. It's been too long. I've heard nothing but wonderful things about you. I understand that you landed a great job after law school and that you are a young star at your firm." His smile was so warm and genuine that Sam began to relax.

Sam realized that she had been sitting with her arms crossed against her chest in the recognized, closed body language gesture of self-protection. She unwound her arms and reached for her glass from the cocktail table in front of her. Her father loved playing bartender, and his Beefeater Gin martinis were legendary among family and friends. Sam took a sip of her drink and replaced the glass on her coaster. "I'm enjoying my work. I am part of a new section of the firm establishing an energy and environmental law practice. It's exciting to get in on the ground floor of a new legal discipline. Because all of the laws and governmental regulations are new, there are no established experts in the field, so I find myself breaking ground instead of trying to succeed in an area where my age and my sex could be a liability." Chapman and Fred nodded their understanding and agreement. She felt competent and accomplished for the first time in months.

"Sounds like a wonderful opportunity," Chapman concurred. "Your Dad and I expect great things from you." He sat back in his chair, and the cordial conversation continued to swirl around her. The hors d'oeuvre tray was almost empty, so Leonora rose to replenish it. Fred collected the martini glasses with the help of Chapman's wife, Elaine; and they followed Leonora into the kitchen so Fred could make another round. When all three were out of earshot, Chapman leaned forward toward Sam and covered her hand with his.

"Look, Sam, while your parents and Elaine aren't here, I want to share something with you. I know what you're going through. Your father isn't one for opening up about his feelings, but he told me about you and Tom, and I just want you to know…" Chapman paused and looked her in the eye for a long, serious moment. "I want you to remember something. I was there for your father when he got divorced, and I stood by him. He went through some very hard times, but he went on to make a beautiful life for himself with Leonora and you. You're a strong, smart, beautiful girl, and all of us here tonight will stand by you. You'll get through it, and you'll go on and make a wonderful life for yourself just like your Dad did. Remember that whenever you have even a scintilla of doubt about your future." He squeezed her hand and withdrew it just as her parents and his wife reentered the room.

Samantha was floored. Her father had been married before? The shock of Chapman's revelation seared her brain. *Remember that?* How could she remember something she had never known? What hurt more was that, if it were true, her father had chosen not to reveal it even when he knew that she was laboring under the weight of her own failed marriage. Sam clenched her hands, then opened and closed them into fists several times in a vain attempt to rid herself of anger and betrayal. She fought with the muscles in her face to return Chapman's supportive smile. *Maybe I misunderstood what Chapman said,* she thought. *Maybe I'm confused. Surely, Daddy wouldn't have lied to me all these years. But Chapman would have no reason to lie. He acted like it was common knowledge. He was kind to me. And if Daddy did lie, why did he do it? He had to know I wouldn't judge him for his divorce. He had to know that what I would care about was the lie. And if he lied about that, what else has he lied about? Did he lie to Mom too, or does she know?* Samantha's eyes drifted to the silver-framed family portrait on the mantelpiece and the three smiling faces in it. In place of their home in the background, she imagined another, unfamiliar house; her mother replaced by a stranger, Samantha eradicated from the tableau. *Another wife, another life, and I might never have been born.*

Listening to the pleasant timbre of their voices, she found it difficult to sit still there, as if nothing had happened. Her mother rose again, this time to clean up before they left for dinner. Sam grabbed some empty plates and glasses and shadowed her to the kitchen.

Sam looked at her mother's back as she scraped the plates and placed the glasses into the sink. How had everything changed so suddenly? "Mom," she began in a hoarse whisper. Her mother did not turn around as the torrent of words poured forth. "Mom, I need to ask you something." Sam impulsively grabbed her mother's shoulders and spun her around to face her. Soapy water dripped from Leonora's hands, and confusion and concern mapped her face.

"When you were in the kitchen earlier, Chapman told me something, at least I think he did, but I can't believe it. He wanted to comfort me about the divorce; and the next thing I knew, he was telling me that he had helped Dad through a similar situation. He said that Dad had been married before, Mom. He said that he had 'stood by him' when he got divorced. That's not right, is it? That can't be right because Daddy would have told me." Sam seemed to run out of air. Her mother reached out to touch her face, but Sam flinched.

Looking furtively from her daughter to the swinging door that separated the kitchen from the dining area and living room, her mother said, "Chapman is telling the truth, Sam. Your father was married before. He never told you because he wanted to start over, first with me and then with you. You have to understand that in our day, there was a great stigma attached to divorce. It was perceived as a mark of failure both in the eyes of God and man. Your father isn't used to failing, Sam. It didn't seem appropriate to tell you when you were a little girl; and as the years passed, it seemed less and less important. I'm sorry that you're upset, honey." Leonora turned back to the kitchen counter and began washing a silver tray, as if her explanation settled the matter and relegated it to its deserved level of insignificant history.

Sam was reeling. Her mother had known. She had been a silent accomplice in this strange mendacity. "What do you mean, 'It seemed less and less important?'" she hissed. "I can tell you it's important to me! Whose opinion were you really worried about? Mine? Or everybody else's? It was just an image thing, wasn't it, Mom? That's always what drives you. You couldn't stand for even your own daughter to know anything that might make you and Daddy seem less than perfect? Do you know how hard that is to live up to? Do you know how hard it's been to think I've failed in your eyes only to find out that protecting your precious image was more important to you than my pain?" While Samantha ranted in a hysterical whisper, Leonora kept eying the door. Even now, she seemed more afraid that they would be overheard than worried about the maelstrom around her.

Leonora shook herself in an unconscious gesture, as if rejecting this distasteful confrontation. When she spoke again, her expression was closed, her voice low, and her eyes dark and indecipherable. "Samantha, I taught you a long time ago that we do not air our dirty linen. What happened in your father's past has nothing to do with you. It was over before we met, and I never asked him about it. In fact," she said with the hint of a prideful smile, "I thought it was very honest and courageous of him to tell me at all."

She looked off into the distance, remembering. "We were on our first real date. He came to see me in New York, and he brought it up because he thought that one fact, his being divorced I mean, might affect whether I wanted to see him again. Can you imagine?"

Without waiting for Samantha to reply, she concluded matter-of- factly, "Anyway, this whole thing has had no bearing on the wonderful husband and father he has been." She dried her hands on a dishtowel and removed her apron. "I am sure Chapman was just trying to help," she sniffed, "but he really had no business…."

"Everything is always someone else's fault," Samantha interrupted. "Of course, you would focus on Chapman and how I found out rather than on what I found out. You know what, Mom? I don't feel like dinner. I think I just want to be alone."

"Oh, please come with us, Sammie," Leonora coaxed, reverting to her familiar maternal tone. "It's New Year's Eve, and we were counting on your joining us. We don't want you to be alone tonight. Why don't you go wash your face and fix your makeup? Then, we can all go out and have a good time."

"I can't, Mom. I just can't. Please say I'm sick or something, anything. I need to be by myself."

Sam pulled her coat from the closet in the kitchen hallway and yanked the back door open before her mother could say another word. A gust of frigid air smacked her cheeks, rousing her as she got behind the wheel of her car. As she backed out of the driveway without a thought to her destination, she forced herself to drive carefully in the wintry night.

Sam pulled into the well-lighted parking lot of a coffee shop that was staying open late for New Year's Eve. She closed her eyes as hot, sticky tears glued her lashes against her cheeks. *We don't air our dirty linen.* So ingrained was this maxim in her psyche that Samantha realized it hadn't occurred to her to ask any of the logical questions that now wouldn't stop forming in her head. *Who was she? What did she look like? When were they married? Where did they live? How long were they married? Why did they divorce? Were there any children?*

Then, it came to her. It was a lie of convenience, a conscious erasure. *'Daddy never lies'. How many times has he said that? How many times has he told me that an act of deliberate omission is the same as a lie? But he not only lied, he lied to me!*

Samantha sat up straighter and wiped her face with the back of her gloved hand. The loving, ever-protective image of her father floated, ghost-like, before her. "Who are you?" she entreated him with a silent scream. "Tell me who you are!"

CHAPTER 49

I T HAD BEEN ABOUT two years since her divorce when Samantha flew to San Francisco to represent her law firm at a trade association meeting of grocery retailers. She was to make a presentation to the Board concerning legislation pending in Congress that was important to the industry members. Her speech was the last agenda item of the meeting, and she had noticed a handsome blonde man seated across from her at the Board of Directors' table throughout the day. He had wonderfully warm blue eyes that seemed to transcend the staid, professional atmosphere. Following her remarks, she offered to remain behind to answer any questions of individual interest to the directors. The friendly stranger was among the small group of people who moved to the front of the room for her Q and A session. He hung back as they dispersed one by one to find their mates for the evening. When they were alone, he extended his hand, and introduced himself.

"Lars Swinton," he said.

Samantha shook his hand, and he slouched comfortably in a chair, commenting insightfully on several of the points she had made. For a while, they spoke informally as she packed her briefcase.

Handing her a file folder, he asked, "Would you care to continue this discussion over dinner?"

Only then did Samantha realize that the room had emptied completely except for the two of them. It was the mid-seventies, but she still was one of only two women practicing law at her firm. He stood there smiling at her; and the prospect of eating alone just to avoid the appearance of impropriety grated on her, especially since she was certain that her male colleagues, given the same situation, would not give the matter a second thought. Had one of them been asked to dinner by a client of the opposite sex to discuss his presentation, there would be no question about the appropriateness of his accepting. How were things ever going to change for her or future generations of women if she were not entitled to the same presumption of professionalism?

"Sure, that would be nice," she said, trying to keep her tone neutral. "Let me just stop at my room to drop off my things and freshen up, and I'll meet you in the hotel lobby in about fifteen minutes."

"Great," he said. "I'll meet you by the front door."

As the elevator rose to her floor, Samantha debated about changing her clothes, but she decided that she should remain in her well-cut, navy blue blazer and calf-length, muted Scotch plaid skirt. Once in her room, she ran a brush through her hair, freshened her lipstick, and checked herself in the mirror. Her attire was a compromise between the IBM "dress-for-success" look popular among the few women professionals of the day and the business casual look that would not arrive until two decades later. It was casual for her, but the association was known to be relaxed, especially at conventions, and the trend-setting city by the bay was far less stuffy than Boston. Her associate,

Mark Erickson, who was senior to her by only three years, wore a pumpkin orange cable knit sweater and khakis to the Board meeting. But the closest her comfort level would permit had been to shed the otherwise obligatory black, gray, brown, or navy suit and silk bowtie in favor of the separates. She gave herself an ironic grin when she realized that she could put her compact of blush powder away. She already had the natural flush of a young woman anticipating her first date with a new and exciting man. Her heart beat faster with hope, as she admitted to her reflection that, putting her professional rationalizations for accepting his dinner invitation aside, she was attracted to and intrigued by Lars on a personal level.

Descending in the elevator, Samantha realized that the last time she visited San Francisco she had been with Tom. She did not know it at the time, but it was to be their last trip together. They had argued intermittently throughout the weekend, and she remembered his hasty departure from a cable car after one particularly angry exchange. She had to force her way through the other passengers to disembark, and in her urgent leap from the last step, she caught her heel and fell flat on her face. Besides her torn stocking and wounded pride, she noticed that the gold setting of her engagement ring had bent when she instinctively extended her hand to break her fall. She came to think of that accident as symbolic; her marriage broke at about the same time. She shook her head to rid herself of these memories and hurried out of the elevator toward the hotel entrance.

Lars waited for her beside the large revolving door leading to the sweeping, semicircular driveway. Indicating to the doorman that he wanted a cab, he directed the driver to take them to Fisherman's Wharf. "Since neither of us is going to be here very long, I thought we'd soak up some atmosphere," he told Samantha, and she was charmed by his unaffected desire to do the touristy things that San Francisco had to offer.

Their destination was Scoma's, a renowned seafood restaurant overlooking San Francisco Bay. Nestled by the water's edge at the end of an alley amid the fishing boats of Fisherman's Wharf, it boasted unparalleled views of Alcatraz and the Golden Gate Bridge. As they walked past the restaurant's receiving station, they could see men offloading fresh fish and local Dungeness crab. They ate abalone, one of the restaurant's specialties, and their conversation never waned. He seemed genuinely interested in learning about her; but his questions were not too personal, as he restricted himself to the subjects of her family, her education, and her law practice. He explained that he was born in Minneapolis but moved to Charlotte, North Carolina as a very young boy. There, he attended a private school, followed by Brown and the University of Virginia Law School. As the evening wore on, Samantha was surprised by how comfortable she felt.

They walked around the Wharf for a while and took the cable car back up the hill. It was a beautiful night, cool and cloudless; and Lars wrapped a protective arm around her, shielding her from the autumn breeze as they shared the same safety strap. Somehow, his proximity seemed natural, and she was glad when he asked if she would like to stop for a nightcap at the Top of the Mark at the Mark Hopkins Hotel.

The view from the bar was spectacular, twinkling stars suspended over city lights. Samantha ordered an Old Fashioned made with Old Granddad bourbon and muddled fruit, just the way her father had taught her. She sipped her drink slowly, not wanting the night to end. Feeling the intensity of Lars's stare, she turned to meet his gaze. "This is such a lovely setting," she said. "I think this is one of the most beautiful cities in the world."

"It is," he agreed. He looked out the large window and back at her. He bit his lower lip and then seemed to make up his mind to share his thoughts with her. "Samantha, I know we've just met, and there's really no reason for me to tell you this at this time, but I want us to be honest with each other, and I would never want you to think that I had kept something of importance from you."

Samantha felt an unwelcome surge of fear. She tried to remain impassive so that he would not be dissuaded from continuing by her reaction; but she felt a prickly unease about what he was about to reveal.

"I've been married before," he said, never moving his eyes from hers. "I don't know how you feel about that; but if it bothers you, at least now you know." He remained leaning forward in his chair, waiting.

Samantha felt an almost giddy sense of relief. Her divorce was something that she did not discuss comfortably; but Lars's statement was short and forthright. He made no excuses; he asked for no sympathy; he exhibited no shame. She immediately was enamored of his honesty.

Just as she was about to reply, Lars continued. "There's something else, Samantha. I have two children, a son and a daughter. Eddie is ten, and Anika is nine. They are a very big part of my life. So, if you don't date divorced men or men who have children, I will understand. I just thought that you should know from the beginning." He took a sip of his drink and cupped the glass with his hands, all the while watching and waiting for her response.

Samantha was stunned momentarily, buying time by taking a sip of her own cocktail. First, he called this dinner a "date," dispensing with any vestiges of her illusion that they were merely two professionals enjoying each other's company. Second, the date meant enough to him that he was thinking ahead to a relationship, and he wanted it to be based on honesty from the beginning. So far, so good. Then, he hit her with the big one; he was a divorced father of two.

Another scene crowded her mind. She remembered when her divorce had just become final, and she had gone home to seek solace from her parents. She recalled her father telling her that she was so fortunate to have deferred having children with Tom. Having children together meant that you were never totally free of your ex-spouse, he had said. You could divorce each other, but the children were an unbreakable connection between you. "You are totally free," he had insisted. "You can go forward as if this unfortunate chapter in your life never happened." She looked across the table at Lars. She knew then that her father was wrong. Her marriage and divorce from Tom marked her life every bit as much as did Lars's. Her father, who had so adeptly closed the door on his first marriage, would not be able to recognize or value the devotion on the face of this earnest man speaking of his children. He would see only Lars's failed relationship and the baggage he retained from it. To Samantha, however, Lars was to be commended, not condemned.

She touched his hand and said, "Thank you for your candor. I don't have any rules about selecting the men I date, unless it's that I think I should stop dating fellow lawyers. Having grown up the daughter of a litigator, I've concluded that more than one lawyer at the table is one too many. It makes for way too many arguments."

"Well, as you know, I don't actually practice law." His voice trailed off.

"Oh, well then," Samantha grinned, "I suppose I could make an exception in your case." She squeezed his hand, and he smiled back at her.

The following day after the conference concluded, Lars and Samantha took a walk around the Embarcadero. Samantha felt a lightness to her step. She liked Lars, and she forced from her mind the thought that they would both soon be leaving for their respective homes. She didn't know what would happen after that; but for now, she dared to enjoy herself.

"Samantha," Lars asked, bringing her back to the moment, "have you ever been married?"

368

The question jolted her. She knew that it was simple enough and one that he was bound to ask, but she felt gnawing embarrassment as she considered her answer.

"Yes, I have." *Well, at least it's out there,* she thought. *The cat's out of the bag; the jig is up.*

"You would've had to have been," Lars stated matter-of-factly, linking his arm through hers.

"What do you mean?" Samantha asked.

"A girl like you? Beautiful, smart, sexy. There's no way you wouldn't have been snapped up by somebody. His loss, my gain. That's what I say." He smiled, giving his shoulders an easy, dismissive shrug, as if he were stating an indisputable fact.

Samantha felt the tension leave her body. Maybe she couldn't see herself quite the way Lars had described her; but she knew she had tried to make her marriage work; and she was tired of feeling ashamed. Lars took her hand, and they continued their walk in friendly conversation. She hadn't felt this free and unburdened in some time. She realized that she was happy.

When they returned to their hotel after dinner, Lars asked, "Can we meet for dinner again tomorrow night?"

"Sorry, I already have plans," Samantha replied with genuine regret. "Just before I flew out here, I won an administrative law case against the Department of Energy for another association member, Don Pinter. He asked me to dinner as a thank you."

Visibly disappointed, Lars said, "Maybe, we can meet for drinks afterwards."

"Sure," Samantha said. "I'll call your room if I get back at a reasonable time. Anyway, I'm staying an extra day in San Francisco after the meetings are over. When are you leaving?"

"Well, I can stay too, and we can drive up to the wine country," Lars offered with a smile.

"It's a date," Samantha agreed.

Samantha had never met Don face-to-face. What she did not expect was that he had planned the dinner at an inn outside the city, nourishing the hope that good food and great wine would result in his having a very lucky night. It was not until, at Samantha's insistence, they returned to the hotel lobby in the small hours of the morning that she saw Lars waiting for her. He was slouched sleepily in the corner of one of the overstuffed sofas, his newspaper long discarded, when she touched his shoulder gently. "Hey, Sleepy, what are you doing up?"

"I think the questions as to what we're doing belong to me," he said, rubbing his face. He looked from his watch face to hers. "Rather late to be returning from dinner, isn't it? You said you'd call me in my room when you got back, but I couldn't wait up there any longer. By the way, where's your boyfriend?"

Samantha was tired and already felt like she had dodged a bullet. She didn't feel like explaining herself when all she really wanted was the feel of her pillow beneath her head and the safety of her locked room. Nevertheless, Lars's glib remark was contradicted by the look of concern in his eyes.

"Very funny," she said mirthlessly. "Just for the record, he's not my 'boyfriend,' and suffice it to say that a client who is literally overreaching doesn't exactly make for a professional dinner. Seriously, I'm just glad to be back, and all I want to do right now is go to sleep."

"Sorry," he said, pushing himself to his feet. "I guess you're not used to my sense of humor, but I think you should know that your boyfriend is married." They were now in front of the bank of elevators, and Samantha stabbed at the *Up* button.

"I'll ignore that second boyfriend reference, but I have no reason to care whether he's married or not because he doesn't interest me personally at all." She punctuated her last three words with three additional jabs of the elevator button.

The doors finally opened, and they both boarded the elevator. They reached Samantha's floor first, and Lars held the door open for her to pass. "Good, then I'll see you in the morning." She could see him yawning as the doors closed.

The next day, Lars rented a car, and the day was perfect for the drive from the city to the Napa Valley. Samantha found out just before their departure that a group of association members had planned the same excursion, including the presumptuous Don Pinter.

During the forty-five minute drive to Napa Valley, Samantha expressed worry that they would run into the convention group on a similar excursion. Lars, showing no concern, teased her relentlessly about the probability of this occurrence and, what would likely be even more deliciously awkward, the likelihood of finding her spurned love interest, Don Pinter, among them.

Sensing that he had teased her too much, Lars said, "I just think you should be prepared." His words were belied by a mock look of concern and a tone to match. "You have your career to think of, and you might want to give some thought to what you'll say when someone inquires as to why one married member of their group takes you to a romantic, mountain top getaway on one night of the conference and another very eligible single one squires you to the wine country after most everyone else has returned home."

Samantha had turned the corner past worry and was now moving rapidly toward defiance. "Look, I told you before that married or not, Don Pinter and I never went on a date. I accepted the dinner because I thought he was a client celebrating a victory with his attorney; and as soon as it became clear that he had something else in mind, I was out of there. He's the one who should be embarrassed, not me. As to you and I being seen together by other association members, I planned this vacation day before I ever met you; and what I do with my free time is my business."

She folded her arms across her chest and leaned against the car door, watching his profile shift to an amused smile. Beyond him, through the window, she saw the sign for the Robert Mondavi Vineyard. Lars turned down the long driveway and parked in front of the building fronted by a sign advertising tours, tastings, and sales.

"I thought we'd start here," Lars said, consulting his map marked with the locations of the various wineries. "Robert Mondavi is one of the best."

They entered the building and were greeted by a smiling receptionist. "If you hurry, you can catch the tour group that just left," she said. "They couldn't have gotten further than the end of the building, and then you won't have to wait."

"Let's go," Lars said, extending his hand to Samantha. As he pulled her along, he saw the last of the tour group round the corner; and he stopped in his tracks. Wheeling on Samantha, he whispered urgently, "That's them! The association members are just ahead of us."

Samantha, who no longer found even a residue of humor in Lars's routine, challenged him. "You're lying."

She brushed past him and strode forward, determined to catch up with the group, whom she was certain was comprised only of strangers. Lars caught up with her just as she spotted Don Pinter on the fringe of the crowd around the guide. She decided that the best thing to do was to approach him before he spotted her, a clear sign of her innocence.

"Hey," she said, touching his sleeve. "Isn't this a great day to learn about wine?" She smiled broadly. She saw Don's eyes slide from her to Lars beside her and took satisfied note of his overt unease. Going in for the kill, she continued, "You know Lars Swinton, don't you?"

Lars stepped from behind her and extended his hand to his stupefied rival. Don offered Lars a weak handshake and stammered something about wanting to overtake the tour group that had moved on with the guide. When they were out of earshot, Lars leaned casually against the wall and said admiringly, "Nice one!"

Samantha took him by the arm and led him toward the group. Over her shoulder she grinned, "Nothing works like being confident of your innocence. Now, can I please learn something about wine?"

After a gorgeous day in the valley, feeling sun-kissed and wine-sated, they drove back into San Francisco. At one particularly beautiful spot, Lars parked along the side of the road where a windswept bluff overlooked the vineyards below. They stood in the serene, tall grass, leaning against the car and admiring the view, the only sound that of the breeze lifting their hair and rustling the leaves on the trees. Lars gently brushed a strand of Samantha's hair from her forehead and leaned in to kiss her. She closed her eyes. His lips were warm and tentative, as if he, too, knew that this momentary touching would change things between them. She had locked her heart away for the past two years; but now she could feel it fluttering against the walls of its captivity, like beating wings demanding freedom. The twin sentries of fear and self-protection immediately crossed their swords to warn her that her guard was down; but when she looked at Lars, she couldn't help but smile.

"I hope this doesn't sound crazy," Lars said when they returned to the car, reaching for her hand and entwining his fingers with hers, "but I think something important is happening between us. I have to tell you that I'm as surprised as you must be about the feelings I have for you after so short a time. I've been happy with my life since my divorce, Samantha. I didn't think I needed anything or anyone else. I have my kids, my business; I date whenever I want to; but these last few days with you, I've come to realize that something's been missing. I'd given up on the possibility of finding someone…." He looked out the window at the panorama of the vineyards. "Someone like you."

"I know," Samantha said. "But I don't see how we can make it work. I mean, we live so far apart, and we both have such demanding careers. How will we be able to see each other? How will we find out where this is going?"

"I get to Boston frequently, Samantha," Lars insisted, squeezing her hand. "We can make it work if we try."

"And there's the fact that you're a client of the firm," Samantha continued defensively, listing all the obstacles she could think of. "We may be able to bridge the geographical distance between us, but we'll have to see each other in secret, at least at the beginning, if I don't want to jeopardize my position at the firm."

Lars laughed at her seriousness. "Look, Samantha, you're worrying way too much. Your private life belongs to you, and your firm doesn't have to become involved in it. Besides, a little intrigue can be exciting; and when they do find out, you just might get points for your outstanding judgment!" He winked at her, and she joined in his laughter in spite of herself.

"I want to try, Samantha," he said sincerely, steering the car back onto the highway. "Please say you'll try."

"I will, Lars," she agreed. She laid her head on his shoulder for the remainder of the ride back to the city.

As she prepared for her departure the following morning, she repeatedly mulled over what he had said when they parted the night before. He had said all of the right things, but the minute that Samantha was alone, her doubts reasserted themselves with an even greater force than before, as if her momentary lapse had precipitated a stronger defense. Then, as she was leaving her room, suitcase in one hand and briefcase in the other, she saw a small envelope that had been passed underneath the door with her name handwritten across the front. She set down her baggage and slid her fingernail under the flap. She removed the paper and saw that one sentence had been written on it, "You pulled the string that held my mask and exposed my heart. Love, Lars."

She refolded the note carefully and returned it to the envelope, safeguarding it in the secure pocket of her purse. She could feel the beating wings of her heart again, this time pressing so firmly against the barricade that she could almost hear the creak as it opened ever so slightly.

"This one may be a keeper," she whispered to herself and pulled the door shut behind her.

CHAPTER 50

WHEN SHE WAS SAFELY back in Boston, Samantha called her parents to fill them in on her trip. She enthused about San Francisco and chatted excitedly about her successful presentation before the trade association. She tried to sound casual when she mentioned Lars and the various restaurants where they dined and the vineyards they visited, focusing more on their atmosphere, cuisine, and wine in an effort to make her companion sound merely like a business associate. As she spoke, it was difficult to conceal her excitement; but she was trying to proceed with caution and wanted to make up her own mind about Lars without her parents' inevitable exertion of influence, positive or negative. Truthfully, she wasn't sure her mother was buying her blasé representations.

"Well," Leonora said with undisguised amusement in her voice, "it sounds as though you had a wonderful time in more ways than one. Let me put your father on. He's standing here, champing at the bit, anxious to talk to you."

The next voice Samantha heard was her father's. "I thought I'd never get a chance to talk to you. Your mother simply monopolizes the phone when you call," he complained good-naturedly. "What's this I hear? Have you met somebody?"

Samantha tried the same tack on her father that she had taken with her mother, making her voice light and her descriptions devoid of emotion. "There was this man at the conference, and he and I were the only single people there, it seems. He had some questions after my presentation on the first day, and he suggested that we continue discussing them over dinner." She launched into details about the Wharf, abalone, and anything else she could think of that skirted personal details about Lars or her burgeoning feelings for him.

"But your mother seemed to indicate that you saw this fellow more than once," he said, insisting on directing the conversation back to Lars.

"Well, yes," Samantha admitted, "We took a walk one afternoon; and coincidentally, we had both planned to stay an extra day in San Francisco after the meetings were over, so we decided to drive up to Napa Valley. Daddy, the wine country is incredible. It is so picturesque, and the weather was so beautiful, and I learned so much about making wine. Did you know that white and red wines are made from the same grapes? The red color comes from the tannin in the grapes' skin that is left on in the process of making the reds and…"

"No, I didn't know that, Sammie," her father interrupted, "but you must have liked this Lars if you spent that much time together. What's he like? Do you plan to see him again?"

It was no use. She had always been transparent to him. "Yes, Daddy, he is very nice. He is really smart, but he's also very funny. He runs an extremely successful business that was started by his Dad, and he says he gets to Boston often, so yes, I do think we will see each other again."

She hoped her honesty would satisfy him without prompting a demand for further details. Yet, her voice undulated with enthusiasm, and her heart quickened at the thought of seeing him again.

"Sounds like the thunderbolt to me," was all he said.

"'The thunderbolt?'" Samantha queried.

"Don't play dumb, Sammie. You know, the inevitable, the thunderbolt! When both of you are struck by the feeling that you have seen the future in each other's eyes." Samantha thought of Lars standing on the bluff, the kiss that she could still feel on her lips, his note still folded in her purse, and the almost audible sound of the unlocking of her heart's confinement. Every day since their parting, the dream within her that he had revived, the hunger that she thought had died with the demise of her marriage, grew stronger and more urgent.

"Ok, Dad, maybe it was 'the thunderbolt'," she conceded. *How wonderful that he still believes in such a concept! I've been afraid that my belief went the way of Santa Claus and Tinker Bell, but I was wrong. How can you want something so much and yet be so afraid of being played the fool one more time? Maybe it's all about taking another chance, standing in the storm, face upturned and arms spread wide, daring lightning to strike, unafraid.* "Maybe it was," she repeated, this time with more conviction.

"You know, Sammie, I've always told you that nobody goes through life unscathed," her father repeated, as if reading her thoughts. His voice was soothing, like an extra blanket against a winter chill. "We all make mistakes. You have every right to seek happiness, and I hope you find it."

She allowed him to tuck the mantle of comfort more tightly around her while, at the same time, she decisively shrugged off the old cloak of shame that she had worn since her divorce.

The holidays were fast approaching, and Lars decided to give a Christmas party. He asked Samantha to fly to Atlanta to be his hostess. With the exception of one weekend when she went to New York to interview law students for her firm's summer associate program, Lars had come to Boston to see her every week since their first meeting in San Francisco. If she accepted his invitation, it would be her first trip to Atlanta. When she thought of it, she was both excited and apprehensive because she also would meet his children for the first time. Lars had purchased a house within biking distance of the home that he used to share with his ex-wife and children. He had done so in order to minimize the impact of his divorce on his son and daughter, allowing them to move freely between the homes of their parents at their own discretion. She was so delighted with Lars's frequent visits that she had not really considered that he was able to come to see her so often because his children stayed with their mother. She did not ask nor did he volunteer how much time they typically spent living with him. However, he had made a particular point of telling her that, over the party weekend, they would be with him. During this heady time of new love, Samantha imagined Eddie and Anika as adorable sprites and their father as a doting patriarch. When he spoke of his children, his face shone with pride and his obvious determination to shoulder lightly the arduous responsibilities of parenting them without a partner.

Although they did not talk much about his ex-wife, Lars did not vilify her; and for this, she admired him. "I suppose I found her fly-by-the-seat-of-your-pants attitude fun in the beginning," he had reflected, holding himself accountable for his youthful misjudgment. "She came from the world of country clubs and second homes, whereas my father's idea of a school vacation was giving me the choice of either working in his stores or going to summer school. She collected people, but I was taught to satisfy the high standard of the man in the mirror. I thought she'd provide a counter-point of lighthearted- ness to my life. She's not a bad person, just irresponsi-ble; and nothing made that clearer than trying to raise children with her. She loves Eddie and Anika; that's for sure; but love alone doesn't instill confidence or motivation or the value of hard work. When I realized the effect her incon-sistency was having on them, I knew she couldn't change; so I knew I had to. I mean, what good could come from her insisting on taking the children out to dinner on the night before an exam and then berating them for failing the test? Kids can't thrive in an atmosphere where they feel beloved one moment and reviled the next."

The only thing missing from this storyline in Samantha's mind was a new mother to complete the broken family unit, a benevolent and loving woman who would provide the stable environment that they craved. She imagined herself as their angel of rescue; and in turn, the three of them would save her from her loneliness by returning her love and appreciating her compassion.

Upon arriving in Atlanta, Samantha was pleasantly surprised by its beauty, with its gently rolling hills and wooded neighborhoods. Lars lived in an area called Buckhead, which boasted one lovely home after another on spacious, manicured lawns. When they pulled up at his former wife's house, the door burst open immediately, indicating that the children must have been waiting for them. A gangly boy, all arms and legs in motion, raced toward the car followed by a towheaded girl, small for her age, trying to master roller skates. The boy slid into the back seat behind his father and began talking amiably, apparently unperturbed by meeting his father's girlfriend. The girl, clearly more reticent and skeptical, skated around to Samantha's window, as if to get a better look before seating herself next to her brother. Samantha chattered innocuously to Lars and the children as they drove the short distance to his house. She got along well with children, but she was painfully aware that she cared deeply about this first impression. Her own voice echoed in her ears as she self-consciously monitored it for just the right level of interest and enthusiasm. Now that Eddie and Anika were flesh and bone, they seemed to her like Charon, the ferryman at the River Styx; only these two children could transport her across the river of Lars's approval. If she could not win them, she could not win him.

Young Eddie insisted on carrying Samantha's suitcase to his room, which would serve as the guest room for the weekend. Lars placed the children's small overnight bags in Anika's room, which they would share while Samantha was visiting. Anika dawdled at the front door until Samantha suggested that she show her around the house. Pleased with her new role as guide, Anika conducted a tour, proudly explaining that her father had designed an addition to what had been a two bedroom house, constructing a third bedroom and bathroom for her brother, as well as a game room and swimming pool. Samantha noted with amusement that, even with all the renovations, the kitchen had not been modernized, a testament to the fact that this house was, at its heart, the home of a bachelor who did not cook. The doorbell rang announcing the caterers; and while they prepared for the arrival of the guests, Samantha, Lars, and the children went to their respective rooms to dress for the party.

Not long after Samantha stepped from the shower and began to apply her makeup, she heard a hesitant knock at her bedroom door. She cinched the belt of her robe and asked who was there as she hurried toward the door, while at the same time casting an anxious glance at the clock on the nightstand and noting that the first guests would be arriving in less than a half hour.

"It's me, Anika," said a small voice. "I was wondering if you could help me? My dress... it's...." She sounded on the verge of tears. Samantha opened the door to find Anika standing in a Christmas dress that was much too small, the hemline falling several inches too high above her knees.

She could see the child's desperation in her moist eyes. "Well, don't you look pretty!" Samantha took her hand and pulled her into the room, shutting it behind her. The dress was a deep green velvet trimmed with ecru lace and small red flowers at the collar and cuffs. "You look just like Christmas!" She saw a glimmer of hope return to Anika's eyes.

"I guess I've grown a lot since last year," Anika apologized. "My mother never thinks of things like that; and when I told her about Dad's party, she said this dress would be fine." She pulled again futilely at the dress.

"Would you mind if I just take a look at your hem?" Samantha asked, trying to sound casual.

She flipped up the edge of the dress as she spoke and was relieved to see two inches of material that could be let down. She cast another surreptitious look at the clock and calculated that there might just be enough time to alter the dress and finish her own preparations, although she had not begun to dress or fix her hair. "You wouldn't happen to know whether your father keeps a needle and thread around here, would you? Dark green would be best, but black thread will do."

Anika's face brightened, and she raced out of the door and down the hall. In moments, she was back with a needle, black thread, and scissors. She stood shyly by the bed in her slip and sock feet as Samantha began to rip the stitches of the old hem, stopping every so often to smile at the child reassuringly.

"Voila," she exclaimed, when she completed her sewing, snipping the end of the thread and turning the garment right side out. "Try this on for size."

She handed the dress to Anika who slipped it over her head. It now fell to an appropriate length. "Perfect!" Samantha pronounced.

"Thank you, Samantha," Anika said, skipping from the room, then adding, "You'd better hurry. I can see cars coming up the driveway."

Luckily, Samantha had never been one of those women who need hours to get ready. She always believed in the natural look when it came to makeup, adorning her fresh face with the barest powder and lipstick and her eyes with just a hint of shadow and mascara. Her hair had a lustrous shine and softness, and she swept it from her face with a pretty rhinestone clip. She hummed to herself as she hurriedly stepped into her burgundy crushed velvet dress, a form-fitting sheath that showed off her slim figure and shapely legs. Her shoes, strappy spiked heeled sandals, were no concession to comfort, but they added three inches to her height. She had just finished putting on her jewelry and brushing her hair when she heard footsteps down the hall and Lars's voice at the door. *So, this must be what the juggling act of wife, mother, hostess, and professional woman is like,* she thought with awe, starting to understand the symbolic balls that so many women had to juggle every day.

"Ready?" he asked, tapping the door lightly.

"Ready," she said, exhaling a calming breath, flinging the door open wide, and putting on her best accessory, her smile.

"Wow," he exclaimed. He took her hand and spun her around admiringly. "You look great. And, hey, thanks for fixing Anika's dress. She told me all about it. That's the kind of thing about her mother that used to drive me crazy. She'd rather spend the day entertaining some stranger that the Junior League asked her to squire around town than see to it that there's food in the house or that her kids have clothes that fit."

His face clouded over, and Samantha pressed her fingers gently to his lips.

"It's ok. I didn't mind at all. Besides, all of that's over now. Smile!" she coaxed. "Tonight, we're hosting a party, so let's enjoy it."

She watched the worry lines in Lars's brow smooth and his eyes crinkle in a grin. She slipped her hand into Lars's warm grasp as he ushered his children to the foyer to greet their guests. She was grateful that, except for the hole in her heart, her break with Tom had been clean. Here, with Lars, that hole was finally healing.

When Eddie and Anika assumed their places at the front door beside Samantha and Lars, they looked like a family. A perfect second chance for them both.

CHAPTER 51

T WO MONTHS LATER, SAMANTHA looked out of the car window as the familiar scenes of Boston glided by. Lars was driving slowly, listening to Samantha recount tales of her years as a law student, taking note of the places that had been important to her, restaurants, the park where she studied, stores where she shopped.

"There," she said, pointing to a garden apartment complex with a large sign emblazoned Spring Hill. "That's where I lived. Just over there."

Lars pulled to the curb and followed Samantha's gaze. For the first time in a long time, Samantha wanted someone to know about her. That apartment was where she wrote her law review articles. It was where she learned to cook. It was where she lived with Tom. It was where she believed her life had fallen apart. Somehow, it no longer hurt to think about that. It was a part of her past, but getting to know Lars had kept it in the past where it belonged.

Lars turned toward her and covered her hand with his. Samantha had seen that look before, first in Jake's deep brown eyes and then in Tom's duplicitous blue ones. Her own eyes, frequently admired for their translucent, aquamarine color, widened. *Don't be a sucker*, she admonished herself. *It's too soon.* Yet, in an instant, there it was, the L word. Her mind raced. *How had it happened?* One moment they were sightseeing through the annals of Samantha's youth, and the next minute they had fallen through the wardrobe like the children in *The Chronicles of Narnia*. He said, "I love you," and now Samantha found herself in that strange but familiar territory where everything was expectation but nothing was sure.

"You don't mean that," she insisted. "You haven't known me long or well enough to say something like that." Her voice sounded harsh and accusatory yet wary at the same time.

"I know how I feel, Samantha, and I want you to marry me," Lars countered. "I've never felt with anyone what I feel with you. I wasn't looking for this…for you. I was happy with my life, with my work, and my kids. I was even happy causally dating the nice, attractive women I've met since my divorce. They were honest, no strings relationships, and I preferred it that way. I even liked coming home to the quiet of my house, reading or listening to music, and just being on my own. I thought I didn't need anyone else; meeting you changed all that. I suddenly realized what I've been missing, a true love, a companion, a friend. Someone with whom I can share my life.

My God, he does mean it, Samantha realized. The door to the inner chamber of her heart swung slightly wider, permitting a little light to shine on the dark prison of her longing. What she had come to think of as a sleeping dragon lurched awake, breathing its flames of hope and desire until they lodged like a hot ember in the back of her throat. She burned with a deep desire that she hadn't felt since it had been shattered by broken promises.

"Look, Samantha, I just wanted to tell you how I feel," he repeated. "You don't have to say anything about it right now. Hey, we're still going to see your parents in Philadelphia next weekend, right?"

Samantha was grateful for the change of subject. The dragon slunk back in its cell, omnipresent but momentarily quiet.

"Sure, we're still going," she smiled. Her parents, initially so excited about Lars, had cooled considerably once she told them about his children.

"That's a deal-breaker, Sammie," her father declared as a statement of fact. "Why in the world should you take on that burden? You have everything going for you and no extra baggage. I'm sure he's a great guy, but there are lots of great guys out there who don't have kids. At a minimum, they represent divided loyalty for him and, worse still, a thankless responsibility for you. I'd give that some serious thought if I were you."

Nevertheless, she harbored hope that Lars's easy humor and obvious intelligence coupled with what she had come to think of as exceptional kindness and generosity would win them over. "Don't worry, they don't bite," she quipped, trying to sound offhand.

"If they do, I'll bite back," he retorted with a grin. "Besides, I've never subscribed to that adage about marrying the family or that other one about how if you want to see what your girlfriend is going to look like in thirty years, you should look at her mother. I only have eyes for you."

He kissed her neck and gently nibbled along its curve. Samantha pushed him away playfully and laughed. "Seriously, I'm looking forward to meeting your parents. I know how important they are to you, and I want them to see that I'm crazy about their daughter."

Samantha hadn't introduced her parents to any men since her divorce. She assumed an air of nonchalance when she told her parents that she would be bringing Lars home with her, and she was likewise blasé when she invited him. Yet, in the late 1970's, long after free love had become commonplace and living together an accepted alternative to traditional marriage, meeting the parents still invested the relationship with a seriousness that belied the demise of time-honored mores. Despite her conscious effort to minimize the significance of this first meeting to all parties, her father had looked at her knowingly, reminding her about the "thunderbolt;" and Samantha knew that her father sensed her growing feelings for Lars and considered him as something more than a casual boyfriend.

The following Friday, the beginning of the three day Easter weekend, Samantha took the train to Philadelphia, borrowed a car from her parents, and picked Lars up at the airport. Just as she had done when Lars visited her in Boston, she resumed her personal travelogue, pointing out her father's office building, her high school, and various other significant landmarks along the way home, chattering nervously along the way. Lars smiled indulgently, and she wondered whether her prattling was a welcome distraction to nervousness of his own. She felt both relief and heightened tension when she turned into the driveway.

Entering the house, Samantha tried to picture the spotless living room as if she were seeing it, as Lars was, for the first time. She was struck by the plethora of photographs of herself as a child, making the room a shrine to a beloved little girl who no longer existed except in a series of Kodak moments as indelible as her parents' memories. Lars walked over to a table and lifted one of the frames to examine the picture, a shot from her high school graduation, more closely. Her parents beamed at him as if her commencement had been yesterday, and Lars returned the picture exactly to the spot where he had found it, his face awash with understanding.

"Samantha says you have children," her father said when they sat down later for cocktails. Samantha felt her spine stiffen and her jaw set as a rush of defensive adrenalin shot through her; but when she looked at Lars, he remained slouched in his chair, relaxed and without the slightest indication of the body language of the accused.

"I have two," he confirmed, looking her father squarely in the eye. "A son, ten, and a daughter, nine. I spend as much time with them as I can. They are really great kids."

"How much time exactly?" her father asked, continuing his line of questioning as if he were cross-examining a witness.

"Well, I have joint custody with their mother, but they are free to come and go between our two houses whenever they want. Even though I couldn't live with their mother, I still want them to feel that their lives have been disrupted as little as possible by the divorce. It's never easy when parents split up; but the burden of that should not fall on the children, if it can be avoided." Lars spoke calmly and evenly.

Her father sipped his martini, giving himself time to process this information. Samantha couldn't read him—his inscrutable expression could just as easily have signified that he was satisfied with the answer as it could that he was disenchanted. Samantha shifted in her seat, wondering which way the pebble would drop. To her surprise, her father changed the subject to sports, and he and Lars found common ground in their love of all things athletic. Their only point of disagreement was their friendly competition as to whose baseball team, Lars's first place Atlanta Braves or her father's beloved Phillies, would win the pennant race.

Samantha hoped that she had misjudged her father and that he had been swayed by Lars' personality, just as she had been. But the following morning, Lars went out for a run. Without preamble, her father launched his closing argument. "Samantha, you will never come first with that man. I can see why you like him, but he's wrong for you. As I told you before, he's got too much baggage. If you were to marry him and a decision on any matter, big or small, came down to a choice between you and his children, you would always lose. You may admire his dedication as a father, but he will inevitably put their interests ahead of yours. I know you have opened your heart to this man, but I think you are blind to what your role as a stepmother would be. I don't think you have given any thought to what you would be taking on or to how you would feel after assuming all of the burdens without the natural benefits of motherhood. Marriage is hard enough, as you know, without a ready-made family in which you and your husband start out life together as potential adversaries. You should break things off with Lars before they go any further. There are plenty of other fish in the sea."

The answer to his accusation was on the tip of her tongue. The words sat there like a bitter pill, but she forced them back. She thought angrily, *You were divorced when you met Mom! You still wanted the same things in life that Lars wants, that I want. Why were you entitled to a second chance, but he isn't?* But her words died unarticulated because she knew what he would say without asking the question—he hadn't had children.

"Look, Samantha," he continued, as if speaking impersonally, "A childless marriage can end with a clean break, and hopefully both parties can start over with new partners. Whenever there are children involved, blood will out; and the new spouse is an ineludible outsider. A relationship cannot withstand that kind of pressure. You've already been hurt and disappointed once; why subject yourself to that again?"

Samantha looked at her father; and the expression on his face seemed to say even more than his words; but Lars could return at any moment, so she decided not to confront him. "Ok, I get it," she snapped.

Lars returned from jogging to find Samantha and her parents huddled in the kitchen. He was drawn by the low murmurings of their conversation, and their serious expressions were apparent as he entered the room. Wiping his face on the towel that was draped around his neck, he smiled tentatively, looking from one to the other. "I hope I'm not interrupting anything."

"Actually, we were just discussing marriage and step-parenting," Samantha's father said, refusing to let the subject drop. The air in the room instantly seemed to become heavy and close, the way it does before a rain-storm. Lars ran his fingers through his hair and inhaled deeply as he took the remaining chair at the kitchen table. Letting his breath out slowly, he turned to Samantha, emphasizing that what he was about to say was for her consideration, not a matter to be decided by her parents.

"Samantha. I'm not ashamed of the fact that I have children. They are extremely important to me, and they always will be. I made a mistake when I married their mother. I was young, and what I took to be her fun-loving joie de vivre turned out to be irresponsibility and values fundamentally different from my own. I moved on, and I made a life for myself that has included my children as much as possible. Do I wish I'd met you years ago and that I had an uncomplicated past? Sure I do, in certain ways; but who I am today is a product of what I've been through, just as you have been shaped by your past. Truthfully, I'm not sure you even would have liked me back then." He gave a short, self-deprecating laugh. "The point, as I told you before, is that I want a second chance. I never thought I'd say it or find it, but I believe you are the love of my life, and I think we can get it right this time. I hope that you and my kids will form your own relationships and that they will turn out to be something positive in your life rather than a liability. I know you would bring something wonderful to theirs. It's your decision, Samantha. If you can't give me that second chance, I think it would be a tragedy for both of us; but it's up to you whether you're willing to try."

Samantha knew then that she would marry Lars. She saw strength in his resilience; he was a phoenix who had risen, as she had, above the ashen ruins of a relationship to soar again. He neither denied his past nor denigrated it. Instead, he chose not to dwell there, carrying forward only those aspects from which he had learned and emerged stronger. He had become happy with himself. Now, they could be happy together. They were not two damaged people seeking solace; they were human beings whose missteps were far exceeded by their sure-footed progress on life's journey.

CHAPTER 52

S AMANTHA COULD HAVE HAD any type of wedding she wanted. Even Emily Post and the other mavens of etiquette had rewritten the rules on wedding propriety to resolve such contemporary, commonplace issues as the wording for invitations from blended families and proper attire for brides taking a second trip down the aisle. Gone were the days when only virgins could wear white; in 1979, the white wedding gown could signify anything from a *tabula rasa* to a mere nod to tradition. Samantha thought of her marriage to Lars as a new beginning for both of them, and she fantasized about their children someday perusing their wedding album, admiring all of the photographs of their parents as bride and groom. She wanted to look like a bride because she felt like one, but she could not shake the feeling that she was not entitled to all of the trappings. It never occurred to her that her many friends and coworkers who either attended her wedding to Tom or knew him wouldn't have wanted her to be embarrassed. To the contrary, they had shared her grief when the marriage dissolved, and they joined in wishing her joy now that she had found happiness with Lars. She had yet to learn that her guilt was self-imposed, and it was a burden only she could put down.

They were to be married at noon in the perennial gardens of the venerable Lyman Estate in Waltham, Massachusetts, a National Historic Landmark dating from 1793. The mansion, also known as The Vale, was built in the Federalist style as a summer home by shipping magnate Theodore Lyman. Samantha fell in love with the landscaped grounds, the Victorian library, and the oval parlor that retained its original, hand-carved woodwork. When she first saw the magnificent ballroom with its crystal chandeliers, Grecian columns, and marble fireplace, she knew immediately that this historic room was where she wanted to marry Lars. They and their family and friends would have cocktails in the garden and then dine al fresco on the covered veranda overlooking the manicured landscape of the grounds, followed by dancing to the music of a seven-piece orchestra in the ballroom.

Because of the daytime ceremony, she decided on a tea length dress, mostly of white with a delicately embroidered neck and hemline. Looking at her reflection in the bridal salon's full-length mirror, she was every bit the bride. She still subscribed to the superstition that it was bad luck for the groom to see the bride prior to the ceremony on the wedding day and wouldn't even describe her wedding dress to Lars. Nevertheless, she rushed home to call him after making her selection. As soon as he answered, she exclaimed, "I found my dress today. It is so beautiful. I know you're going to love it!"

"I'm sure I will because I love the girl who'll be wearing it," he said, the warmth of his voice wrapping itself around her. "Listen, I want to ask you something about the wedding arrangements. I've been thinking about it, and I have a great idea."

Samantha kicked off her shoes and put her feet up on the ottoman that matched her favorite chair. She rubbed them gently, thinking that she must have walked miles today inside the finest stores and bridal boutiques trying to locate the perfect dress. As she massaged her arches and wriggled her toes, the pain subsided; and she felt satisfied that her efforts had borne results. "What do you have in mind?" she asked.

"Well, we haven't discussed our wedding party," Lars said. "You know, groomsmen, bridesmaids, a best man, and a maid of honor."

Immediately and almost instinctively, Samantha had a vision of her attendants at her wedding to Tom. There had been four, a beloved childhood friend had fulfilled the role of maid of honor, and the three bridesmaids had been two college friends and a classmate from law school. Tom's best man and all three of his groomsmen were part of the Brigade, the clique they had formed in college, all of whom then marched in lockstep to law school. Samantha wondered whom Lars would want and whether his choices would affect hers.

"What I was thinking was that I would ask Eddie to be my best man, and you could ask Anika to be your maid of honor. It would make them feel a real part of the wedding, and it would make us a real family right from the start. What do you think?"

Samantha was stunned. She liked both of the children very much; and they seemed genuinely happy that she and Lars were going to be married; but she had close relationships with many friends, and while she had not made up her mind which ones she would ask to be in her wedding party, it had not occurred to her to ask the nine year old girl who would become her step-daughter. She had visions of staying up late the night before with other young women who would share her excitement, with whom she had memories, who understood her. Lars was asking her to give that up because it would make his daughter happy. He was oblivious to what the wedding party meant to her.

Stalling, she asked, "If Eddie were your best man, whom would you ask to be groomsmen?"

"I wasn't going to ask anyone else," Lars replied. "If my son and daughter were to witness my vows to you, that would be all I would ever need." His voice had a wistful, wishful quality.

Samantha opened her mouth to speak and then closed it again. One by one, the ephemeral images of her friends clad in beautiful bridesmaids' gowns vanished from her mind like puffs of smoke. In their place, her father's face appeared, silently admonishing her. *You'll never come first, Sammie. He will always put his children ahead of you.* She squeezed her eyes shut. It was not her first wedding, after all, she reminded herself. She had done the whole nine yards the first time around. The only thing that really mattered was marrying Lars. *Screw Emily Post and her updated revisions.* Real life was more complicated than what could be solved by a few simple rules. Even the time worn warning that when you marry the man, you marry his family took on a whole new meaning in her case. If she married Lars, and marry him she would, then she must face that he was a package deal.

Her head began to ache. Recently, she had read an article on stress in which the author said that the simultaneous occurrence of three or more of the ten most life-changing events could induce at the least a heightened level of anxiety and at the most an accompanying physical illness. Samantha thought ruefully that she was about to experience at least four of them: a new marriage, becoming a parent in a ready-made family, moving to Atlanta, and joining a new law firm. Her father insisted that her share of these transformative responsibilities was disproportionate in comparison to Lars's, but Lars was the head of a family-owned corporation that was based in Atlanta, and his children were there, so setting emotion aside, it made no sense for Lars to move to Boston. Samantha understood the logic of her decision, and she resonated even more strongly to the feeling behind it. It was all about the second chance that she craved.

So, she set aside her picture perfect image of her wedding party and agreed that Anika would be her only attendant. If having the child as her bridesmaid would set the tone of family unity that Lars anticipated, then she would sacrifice a fleeting fantasy for a more important reality that could pervade her future relationships with her stepchildren. She would do it even though she had her doubts.

Samantha was no fool. No matter how friendly and affectionate she was to Eddie and Anika, she knew that they had to wonder how their life would change with a stepmother in it. She knew, too, that they would not forever remain the malleable children that they were now. She speculated on what would happen to their relationships when, in the fullness of time, she meted out discipline or disappointment, both inevitable parts of parenting.

She knew as well that Lars had two choices with regard to his children when his marriage to their mother disintegrated. Like many other fathers in the same situation, he could have become an absentee parent having little or no contact with them. Courts in the late 1970s increasingly granted sole or joint custody to divorced fathers, but birth mothers more often than not were the custodial parents in the absence of proof of unfitness. Moreover, most divorced fathers neither wanted nor fought for custody because their futures were greatly simplified if they did not shoulder the responsibility of children. They were much more free to date, travel, or commit to a new relationship if contact with their children from a previous marriage were limited to visitation or custody at specific times. Lars had decided against this easier and more widely accepted course, opting instead for joint custody. As a result, all of their getting to know each other as husband and wife would be colored from the beginning by the need to construct or modify other intimate familial relationships existing under the same roof.

Samantha tried not to worry about these obvious repercussions of her marriage to Lars. She saw herself and her new husband creating a stable home for Eddie and Anika where there previously had been none. She imagined gratitude and appreciation. She saw only that, unlike her own father, Lars was open about his mistakes. While her father had a great deal of difficulty ever admitting he was wrong and certainly had never acknowledged his divorce to Samantha, Lars accepted personal responsibility for his actions. While her father repeatedly broadcast warnings that Lars's past portended ill for Samantha's future, he had chosen to present himself to her for so long as a person with an unblemished history that she had begun to wonder if he believed his own lie. She loved the two men in her life fiercely; but respect, that elusive commodity for which her father had fought his entire life, was something that Samantha knew Lars had earned by virtue of his unwavering integrity with regard to what her father devalued as mistakes that were better off buried.

Instead of the steamy, airless days typical of July, their wedding weekend was unseasonably clear and spring-like. Samantha handed her car keys to the hotel valet and turned to look at Anika in the passenger seat.

"Let's give the porter all of our things except the garment bags that have our dresses in them," she said. "That way, we'll be sure the gowns make it to our room."

She draped Anika's bag over her arm and lifted the hanger of her bag high to keep the hem of her dress from brushing the ground. Anika followed her to the reception desk.

As she signed the registration card, Samantha chattered amiably to Anika. "Tomorrow morning, we have a hairdresser coming to our room, and a manicurist who will do our nails. You can pick any color nail polish that you like, but I suggest a shade that will go with your beautiful lilac dress."

Anika smiled but said only, "I think I want to wear my hair in a French braid."

"I'm certain the hairdresser can do that," Samantha assured her. "It's going to be so much fun!"

She opened the door to the room that they would share for the night and hung her dress in the closet. She walked over to the window and looked out over the cityscape. *Starting tomorrow, I will have a new life with Lars,* she thought, hugging herself at the prospect. *Starting tomorrow, all of the successes and missteps that brought us here will be overshadowed by the wondrous fact that we are together in this moment and for all the years to come.*

The following morning, Leonora paraded into the room, followed by the hairdresser and manicurist. Nimbly bowing the wide satin streamers at Samantha's waist, she surveyed her daughter approvingly in the full-length mirror. "You are a beautiful bride, Sammie," she said, as the hairdresser fastened a white gardenia in her hair. "As my father used to say, 'You look like a dream walking.'"

"Thanks, Mom," she said smiling at her reflection. Turning to Anika and handing her a white wicker basket filled with gardenias and deep, velvety blue violets, Samantha said, "Anika, I want you to wear this locket for the ceremony. It was given to me by my grandmother, Netania, who has since passed away. I think you wearing it will bring us luck." She fastened the delicate gold chain around the young girl's neck and laid her hand reverently over the heart that was inscribed with her monogram.

"It's beautiful," Anika sighed. "Thank you so much, Samantha." Ever since Samantha altered Anika's dress for the Christmas party, the quiet girl's reservoir of self-protection had begun to evaporate.

"Well, let's get this show on the road," Samantha said, kissing her cheek. She picked up her own bouquet, a spray of white gardenias, roses, and camellias, and walked toward the door.

Standing at the top of the aisle with her father, Samantha squeezed his arm and could feel all of the tension recede from it, as they began walking toward the arbor where a beaming Lars with Eddie beside him and Anika, who also smiled broadly, awaited them.

Having exchanged their vows, Lars stomped decisively on the crystal glass that the rabbi placed beneath his black patent leather formal shoe. Their assembled family and friends yelled, "Mazel Tov!" For Samantha, it was a moment; it was forever.

Everyone moved toward the garden for the commencement of the reception. Samantha saw the bandleader rushing toward her. "What's he doing?" she asked Lars, pointing out the distraught, balding little man.

Before Lars could reply, the bandleader was upon them, breathing and perspiring profusely. "I'm terribly sorry, Miss Samantha," he said, wiping his brow with a copious handkerchief, "but we didn't have time to learn the song, 'Could I Have This Dance.'" He looked crestfallen as he began to ring his handkerchief and look down at his shoes. Lars had proposed to Samantha by slightly altering the lyrics to this recently released love song, crooning, "Will you wear this ring for the rest of my life?" Since then, it had been their song and the obvious choice for their wedding dance.

"What do you mean you didn't have time to learn it?" Samantha demanded. "You've had the contract to play at our wedding for months, and learning that song was a condition of your employment." The more she castigated him, the more the man stared dejectedly at the floor.

Lars placed his hand on her arm and was gripped by a flash of inspiration. "You must know 'I Left my Heart in San Francisco,'" he insisted. "Don't worry, Sammie. You and I actually have two songs, so everything will be fine. Remember, San Francisco's where I was struck by the thunderbolt."

The bandleader, clearly relieved, nodded his agreement like a bobblehead doll and quickly withdrew to his place with the other musicians. Moments later, as the dulcet tones of the Tony Bennett sound-alike filled the room; Lars led his new bride to the dance floor.

Halfway through the reception, one of the senior partners at her law firm, fueled by several drinks too many, embraced the microphone for an unexpected and seemingly interminable toast to her skills as a lawyer and his wishes for her future. Samantha's smile never faded as she joined him at the foot of the stage. She hugged his neck as she simultaneously disengaged his hand from the microphone. He relinquished it sheepishly and returned to his table. What most of the guests would remember was not his inebriated rambling but Samantha's toast, a poem she had written Lars, inspired by the end of loneliness and the promise of a new beginning. As she looked up from the pristine, white paper on which she had written it, she saw only two pairs of blue eyes: Lars's were fixed on her; and there, too, were her father's. His love of the written word had put poetry in her soul.

Today we say for all to hear

    Vows we made long ago

Exchanging rings which will make clear

    What our hearts already know.

That from almost the very first day

    A feeling incomparably strong

Grew within us till each would say

    To you I truly belong.

And through the years of hope and strife

    Embers of our dreams survive

To find in the partner of our life

    A force to keep them alive.

What before was aching need

    Endless and unsatisfied

Can now flower from the seed

    Of promises we have ratified.

Life alone could never be

    What two can surely fashion

For all is possibility

    With loving and compassion.

We begin, July twenty-second,

    As songs start with a hum

Responding to a love that beckoned,

"The best is yet to come."

CHAPTER 53

SEVERAL MONTHS AFTER SAMANTHA and Lars returned to Atlanta from their honeymoon along the Amalfi Coast, Lars burst into the kitchen. They had begun their married life together in the small house he had purchased after his divorce. Dropping his newspapers and briefcase on the floor and breathless with excitement, he could not contain himself. "Sammie, I've got great news! We're moving. I found a great piece of property, and I want us to build a house. It's over six wooded acres, and we'll have plenty of room to design whatever we want. What do you say?" He looked like a small boy who had been offered his choice of anything he wanted from the candy store.

Samantha untied her apron and wiped her hands on the dishcloth. "Well, Dreamworld," she replied affectionately, using the sobriquet he had been given in high school, "how could I say anything but 'yes' to that? Let's go see it right now."

They got in the car, and on the short drive, he explained how he found it. "So, there I was in the dentist's chair, and he's complaining that his wife knows no bounds when it comes to designing and building a house from the ground up. He kept saying, 'She's going to make me go broke.' He started encouraging her to look at resales and is thrilled that she found one that satisfies her. He said, 'At least I know what I'm getting myself into, but now I have to liquidate the other property before I can buy the house.' I went to look at it right away, and I think I can work a tax free exchange with him so that he gets his house, and we get this gorgeous piece of land."

Lars pulled up at a dirt driveway leading to a hilltop site that would be totally private when the deciduous trees leafed out in spring and summer and that would boast magnificent views throughout the year. He held her hand as they climbed to the summit, and he began to step off imaginary plans for their new home. "The living room can face the pool here," he said, throwing his arms wide, "and our room can be at this end where it's even more private. Oh, Sammie, don't you think it will be wonderful?"

This is what I love about him, Samantha thought, drinking in his youthful zeal. She took his face in her hands and kissed him tenderly. "It's fabulous, Lars," she enthused. "And what's even more amazing is that I found someone who dreams so big to dream with me."

Plus, Samantha had a secret of her own, and there couldn't be a better time than now to tell him. "Lars, I'm pregnant." She smiled tentatively, waiting for his reaction. In the seconds that it took her to utter those words, the sky did not fall; the earth did not stop turning; but when Lars encircled her in a gesture of pure happiness, a cosmic shift occurred as if the mere utterance had made real the fact that she was to have a baby of her own.

CHAPTER 54

NICHOLE CHARLOTTE SWINTON was born on a beautiful summer day and was immediately surrounded by the love of her parents, two eager siblings, and her grandparents, who had flown from Philadelphia to Atlanta for the birth of their granddaughter. She was named for Samantha's maternal grandmother, Netania, and Lars's paternal grandfather, Charlton. "It's fitting. After all," he agreed, gently caressing the soft, brown down that covered his new daughter's head, "she's part of both of us."

"After nine months of talking and singing to her in the womb, she already seems to know me," Samantha said, cradling Nikki in her arms, as the alert newborn looked her directly in the eye.

Nikki grew up like a sunflower, firmly rooted to the ground, but inexorably drawn to the light. She developed the breezy self-confidence that came from knowing that, despite their age difference, Eddie adored her; and Anika admired and respected her for her extraverted, natural leadership. Because of their shared interest in Nikki, Samantha believed that she, Lars, and the children truly were building a family.

Nikki's first few years flew by, and thanks to her parents' loving attention, she began to develop a love for books, sports, and the arts. A natural talker, she soon understood the purpose of the telephone; and Samantha encouraged her to call Leonora and Fred frequently to share her escapades. Fred, who had never loved the telephone, had from the beginning made an exception when it came to talking to his granddaughter.

"Then, what happened?" he prodded her to prolong their conversation. "Well, of course, you won the race!" he enthused. "You come by your runner's legs and endurance directly from me. And incidentally, that drawing you made of your house that your mother sent me is now framed and hanging in my office. You show real artistic talent, Nikki. I'm so proud of you!"

Beginning at the age of five, when Nikki was old enough to fly by herself on a commercial airline, Samantha sent her to spend a week with her grandparents every summer. She learned to cook at Leonora's elbow, and Fred was the first to place both a tennis racquet and a paintbrush in his cherished granddaughter's hand.

"She's got *allemen*, everything," Fred exclaimed repeatedly, resorting both to Yiddish and English, as if one language were not enough in which to extol the virtues of his granddaughter. "She's going to be a force to be reckoned with."

Witnessing the closeness between her mother and her grandparents, Nikki learned to confide in Samantha. Practically since Nikki could put words together in a coherent sentence, she would regale her mother with a seemingly endless monologue about her thoughts, her daily activities, and anything else that would keep her mother by her bedside each night. Soon realizing that she had to devise some means to ensure that her very busy child would get enough sleep, Samantha invented the game she called "Two Things" that gave Nikki the freedom to choose the subjects they would discuss each night but limited her to two. Nightly, when Nikki hopped into bed and Samantha tucked the covers under her chin, Samantha sat down on the edge of the blanket and asked, "What are your two things tonight?"

Now entering the sixth grade, Nikki said without hesitation, "Well, Mom, I want to talk about the first day of junior high tomorrow. I'm excited, but I guess I'm also a little scared," she admitted.

"You have nothing to worry about," Samantha reassured her. "You are the best girl in the whole world, and you will make lots of new friends and learn many exciting new things. Besides," she winked, gesturing to the other twin bed in the room on which a brand new, much more grown-up outfit was laid out on the coverlet, "You can't miss with that new skirt and top from Limited Too. You will look every bit the sixth grader that you are."

Nikki sat up in bed and hugged her mother. "You're the best, Mom. Thank you for taking me shopping for new school clothes again this year."

"You're welcome. So, what's your second thing?" Samantha asked.

"Did you hear about Nancy?" Nikki asked. Nikki and Nancy had been inseparable friends since kindergarten. "Her Dad's company trans- ferred him to their London office, and Nancy won't be coming back to school this year." Samantha could hear her daughter's sense of loss in her inflection and see it in her eyes. At twelve, the absence of a best friend with whom to share so many impending changes could seem devastating.

Without hesitation, Samantha squeezed Nikki's hand and reassured her. "Nikki, we will go to visit Nancy to celebrate your thirteenth birthday next summer. We will celebrate you and Nancy becoming teenagers with afternoon tea at Brown's! You can count on it."

Nikki lay back down against her pillow, her eyelids closing heavily but a smile upon her lips. As she drifted off to sleep, she muttered, "You really are the best, Mom."

Samantha and Nikki made the trip to London the following August. Neither would ever forget the shared experiences of Big Ben, the whispering gallery at St. Paul's, or Shakespeare's Stratford Upon Avon. As she matured, Nikki would realize that the trip was so much more than the sites and the reunion with her friend. She came to realize that her mother had kept her word at a time in her life when she was vulnerable and needed to know that there were some things in life that she could count on never changing, and her mother's promise was one of them.

Throughout her high school years, Nikki and Samantha remained close. Samantha taught Nikki to appreciate sports, books, and art, just as Fred had taught her. Nikki lettered in both cross-country and track, and she expressed her passion for words as editor of the school's sports magazine.

Samantha and Nikki often would read a book at the same time in order to discuss it or attend special art exhibits at the High Museum. When Nikki was a sophomore, she and her mother took a weekly oil painting class together, followed by dinner at their favorite pizza restaurant. Before long, Nikki's room was full of exhibit posters and coffee table books ranging from Vermeer to Picasso, along with a shelf of her favorite fiction, including all seven volumes of Harry Potter. Samantha not only read them, but also she enthusiastically took Nikki to see each of the films based on the book series as soon as they were released.

Before she taught Nikki to drive, Samantha carpooled her to and from school every day, introducing Nikki first to tapes and later to CDs of her favorite music that they would blast appreciatively through the car's stereo system. Nikki learned to love to sing along with the Beatles' "Twist and Shout," delighting her mother one day by climbing on top of their minivan to perform her own reenactment of Ferris Bueller singing the iconic song. She also embraced the Beach Boys, Brian Adams, and the Eagles, along the way to forming her own musical tastes. Later, having learned to play piano and keyboard, Nikki would often preview for Samantha the songs she wrote for her band with which she performed as lead singer. The two of them would call Fred and play Nikki's latest composition over the phone. "You girls are keeping me young," Fred exclaimed. No one was more elated than Nikki when her grandfather called her a few days later and sang a few of her lyrics back to her, laughingly concluding, "It must be a good song if an old guy like me can't get it out of his head!"

Even after leaving for Wellesley College, Nikki continued to speak to her mother almost every day, while managing a strong independence encouraged by Lars. Her dorm room was covered with what she affectionately referred to as "smooshed faces" photos of her cheek to cheek with her parents and grandparents. Fred was a frequent visitor to Wellesley and loved to take his granddaughter out for an expensive dinner or a shopping spree on Newbury St. in Boston. At twenty-two, Nikki had her father's ambition and forthright integrity, combined with her mother's articulate intelligence and open heart.

Fred had been diagnosed with prostate cancer almost a decade earlier; and despite the care of specialists, his health began to fail in Nikki's senior year. Samantha was concerned that he did not have the stamina to travel from Philadelphia to Boston for Nikki's graduation in May and then again to Atlanta in July for the big celebration she and Lars were planning to mark their wedding anniversary. "You choose, Sammie," Fred said reluctantly, admitting his increased frailty. "You know how important both events are to me, and I would be at both Nikki's graduation and your anniversary party if I could, but I just don't feel up to that much travel in so short a time."

In her mind, Samantha knew there was no contest between the two events. Nikki was so many things, as Fred so often stated; but in the lexicon of all things important to Fred, academics came first; and Samantha could no more suggest that Fred forego watching his granddaughter cross the stage to collect her degree with honors than she could miss that moment herself.

"Come to Nikki's graduation, Daddy," she said without hesitation. "Nikki and I both want you there." So, he came and sat alongside Leonora, Samantha, Lars, Eddie, and Anika, in the front section where Nikki had reserved seats so that he could have an unobstructed view as she mounted the stage. He stood with the rest of the family as her name was called, followed by an alphabet soup of honors and awards. Nikki's smile was blindingly radiant as she caught the shining eyes of her grandfather, one of his elbows supported by Samantha and the other by Leonora. Looking at Nikki, Samantha thought of her as a gift, not just to her and Lars, but to Frederick as well. Catching Samantha looking at him, Fred put his arm around Samantha and smiled. "She's our posterity, Sammie," he said, and as her father stood beside her, Samantha believed him.

CHAPTER 55

SIX MONTHS LATER, SAMANTHA sat in a chair pulled up close beside her father's bed. At the onset of his cancer, despite his advanced age, they all thought he would beat it. He thought so too. Even the doctor had told him at the initial diagnosis that he'd be just as likely to die in ten years of something else. He related this prediction with a smile, as though he were letting her in on an inside joke. "I'm a tough old bird, Sammie. Even the cancer won't get me." But unpredictably, his physical health began to decline precipitously, although his incisive intelligence refused to leave him.

"Will you speak about me when I'm gone?" Fred asked, tightening his grip on Samantha's hand. The web of veins bulged blue against the taut translucence of his skin. She could see his bones working as they squeezed harder, more insistently. He lay in a bed that smelled of sickness no matter how often the sheets were changed. His still alert blue eyes implored her, brooking no silence; yet she was riveted to the floor as surely as if nails had been driven up through the floorboards piercing her shoes and the soles of her feet.

Ask him now, she screamed soundlessly.

She thought of him as trapped, a firefly in a jar. His mind still glowed brilliantly, but his body was so diminished that he could no longer stand on his own, and she could see his bones beneath his aged skin. Only the aureole of silver hair and the warm smile that appeared in his rare painless moments remained of the towering presence that had always been her Daddy.

Samantha willed herself to ignore the cold, waxy feel of his hand. She conjured once more the warm, secure clasp that always had embodied strength and safety for her, the protection of those long, artistic fingers that completely enveloped hers. Seeing her healthy, creative fingers interlaced with his now gnarled and bony ones was terrifying; she wanted to pull him back from the abyss with all her strength, but she knew she could not. Instead, she covered their entwined fingers with her free hand, cheating the image of death if only for a while longer.

"Of course I'll talk about you when you're gone, Daddy," she replied weakly. Then, mustering a stronger tone, she scoffed, "But you're not going anywhere. You're getting better. Soon, you'll be strong enough to get in your wheelchair, and then you can start practicing to walk with your walker again. Then, we'll be dancing." She feigned enthusiasm and squeezed his hand as she spoke. She knew she had to look at him, but she wondered if he would see the deception in her eyes. *Does he know I'm lying? And more importantly: what if this is my last chance to ask him?* She moved closer to the bed and perched on the edge of the mattress, being careful not to disturb his frail and skeletal body. Gently kissing his forehead, Samantha set her face in a smile and looked at her father for as long as she could.

"I wish you were right, but that's not what I'm talking about," he said, still gripping her hand. "I'm asking about my funeral. Will you speak about me then, Sammie? Will you?"

As his eyes bore into her, he saw what he had always seen. She was naturally beautiful and inherently likeable. At fifty-three, she still had the lithe body of a woman in her thirties; her face remained unlined; and her chestnut hair retained its natural, burnished sheen. Her blue eyes radiated intelligence and kindness, a rare combination; and her smile was genuinely warm and sincere.

Fred's gaze fell upon a silver picture frame on the table by his bed, a photograph from a happier time captured within its borders- a younger, still robust version of himself smiling and beside him, Samantha, in her doctoral robes, her smile virtually identical to his, holding her leather-bound law degree. *That was a proud moment*, he thought. *Becoming a lawyer just like her Daddy! That was something!* His eyes cut back to his daughter's face. He watched her and waited, a sea of emotions breaking across her beautiful face. Her lips parted, and he looked at her expectantly, but she said nothing. Instead, she picked up the frame, fogged the glass with her moist breath, and polished it with the sleeve of her silk blouse, making sure to replace it at an angle where he could see it clearly.

Don't go yet, Daddy. Oh, God! Please stay with me just a little while longer.

During the last two weeks, since she had left Atlanta to help her mother care for him, Samantha had often felt greedy, unwilling to give her father up to the natural forces of life, when she already had basked in the warm radius of his protection for much longer than anyone would have predicted. He was eighty-nine, and she was an adult with a grown child herself. Shouldn't she be able to let him go?

He was asking her to deliver his eulogy. How circular life was. For her whole life, she had been the one asking things of him. Daddy always said that she was his baby. She asked, and he delivered. And at the end of the unbroken circle, he was the one who could no longer perform even the most mundane and personal physical acts for himself. He could not sit without help; he could not wash or dress or read or complete his favorite crossword puzzles. He now required her care much as she had once needed his.

She looked at his broken body uncomfortably folded into the fetal position in the hospital bed that occupied the space in front of the fireplace in the living room. The bed, foreign and unfamiliar, was the only thing new in a room otherwise unchanged since she was a little girl. As she scanned the room, her eyes came to rest once more on her father.

I could tell him I know.

"It's time to make you a little more comfortable, Daddy," she said instead, as she assumed her position behind his head. She despised being the herald of his pain, but seeing him curled in helpless discomfort was even worse. For Samantha, who was petite and slight, even her father's reduced weight presented a challenge. She positioned herself at the head of the bed and locked her elbows under his armpits. "Ok, on the count of three. One, two, three!" She closed her eyes, pulled as if she were in a tug of war with the Angel of Death, and expelled her breath. He moaned; but when she opened her eyes, she was pleased that her efforts had raised his head to near the top of the mattress; and she was able to plump his pillow and smooth the sheets under his spindly legs. Her arms ached, but she fought off the desire to rub them. She had achieved a small victory. The Angel of Death would win, but not yet, not now. "There, that's better!" she pretended eagerly. As she carefully perched on the edge of the mattress, he gripped her hand again.

"I asked you a question, Sammie. Will you speak about me when I'm gone?" Their blue eyes locked, and there was no avoiding his query this time. The unrelenting clasp of his hand and the unflinching bore of his eyes reproved her silently for her hesitation. *Who better, Sammie? Who better?*

"I will, Daddy. I will speak about you when you're gone."

Like you, Daddy, I can put the pretty words together, but do I really know you at all?

CHAPTER 56

B ECAUSE FRED'S PHYSICAL THERAPIST was at the house, Samantha and her mother were able to take a rare break from their toil as caregivers to have lunch at the William Penn Inn, one of Leonora's favorite restaurants, located in an eighteenth century period home in the Pennsylvania countryside. The white colonial façade loomed at the end of the tree-lined driveway. The Monet dining room was beautifully appointed with Monet paintings in an elegant, open setting. Frederick and Leonora had dined often at "William Penn," as they affectionately called it, and were friendly with the maître d'.

Since Leonora dedicated herself to her husband's care, she had lost a significant amount of weight; and her clothes suspended from her protruding shoulder bones like they were drooping from a hanger. She had always been interested in fashion, but now she frequently left the house without makeup in old, ill-fitting garments that expressed a blatant hopelessness. Without her life's companion, she rarely indulged in what had been one of her favorite pastimes, dining out in fine restaurants. Lars often kidded Leonora about her champagne taste. "You'd eat nails if they were served in a five star atmosphere," he teased.

Samantha had coaxed her mother into this lunch date and was glad now that she had. As they sat across from each other, two chilled Beefeater Gin martinis, their glasses fogged with frost, sat on the gilt-edged charger plates in front of them. Leonora mustered a rare smile; and for the first time in ages, she looked polished and fresh. Her Escada suit jacket, a deep blue boucle with sapphire jewel-toned buttons, sagged on her frame, but her hair was freshly cut in its perpetual pixie style, and her makeup was immaculate, down to the perfectly applied red of her Chanel lipstick.

Samantha raised her glass and said, "To Daddy."

She took a sip of her cocktail and plunged ahead. "Mom, I've been thinking a lot about Dad's eulogy." Leonora stiffened perceptibly, but Sam persevered. "God, I pray every day that he'll get better, and I'm not saying that it needs to be done with any urgency, but he's asked me to deliver it, and there are some things I wanted to ask you about, you know, about whether you wanted them to be included."

Leonora sighed heavily. "Like what? You know everything there is to know about your father." Her voice was calm and conversational. Only because Sam knew her so well did she notice the flicker of wariness in her eyes.

"Well, for example, I was looking at some of the obituaries in the Philadelphia Inquirer, and I saw that a lot of those pertaining to the men Daddy's age include their military service during World War II or the Korean War. I was wondering if you wanted me to mention Daddy's service record." There was no mistaking it now. Leonora looked shaken.

"What do you know about your father's service?" Leonora asked reflexively. She made a show of aligning her silverware and smoothing the tablecloth in order to avoid making eye contact with her daughter.

"He never talked about it much," Samantha said cautiously, "but he told me back in elementary school when I first studied World War II that he had volunteered for the Navy after the bombing of Pearl Harbor. He didn't pass the physical because of some minor abnormality in the formation of his rib cage, what he called a 'chicken breast,' so he joined the Army instead. He said that he became a part of the OSS and parachuted behind enemy lines into Czechoslovakia."

"That was a long time ago," Leonora replied breezily with a wave of her hand. "I don't think your father regards that as a really important episode in his life. Perhaps, we should just leave that out."

"Not important?" Samantha's voice rose to express her shock. "Daddy told me that he finished out the war as a lieutenant colonel in the Army. How can you say that he doesn't consider his service to his country important, especially after what happened to the Jews?"

Leonora's face became a kaleidoscope of warring emotions: sadness, confusion, defensiveness, and finally, resignation. She rested her elbows on the edge of the table, hugging herself as she leaned toward her daughter to speak.

"Sammie, remember that New Year's Eve years ago when you were going through your divorce from Tom? Remember that visit from Chapman and how he told you that night that your father had been married before?"

Sam felt suddenly hot and uncomfortable. Her palms began to sweat as she conjured the memory of her parents' living room-- the snow falling outside; the tall, distinguished scion of that eminent family who had been her father's lifelong friend; his revelation that had been the first visible crackling in her father's pristine veneer of honesty.

"Honey, are you listening to me?" Leonora asked as she covered Samantha's hand with her own. Samantha's eye's snapped back to attention at her mother's tone, which had become urgent.

"You said you couldn't understand why your father might think that whether he served in the military was unimportant. Well, I'm trying to tell you." Leonora sounded almost impatient now.

"Wait a minute," Samantha demanded, something that her mother said having become lodged in her brain like a seed taking root. "What do you mean 'whether he served?' Daddy not only told me he served, he said how and where. Besides, what has any of this got to do with what Chapman told me that night?"

All these years later, Samantha still could not refer openly to her father's previous marriage. It lay between them, an unarticulated secret.

Leonora shook her head almost imperceptibly, and a small, wry smile played at the corners of her mouth. "Oh, my lovely, brilliant daughter," she sighed. "Don't you see? Your father was still married to his first wife when the war broke out. There was still a military draft in place, but some married men were exempt. Of course, many married men volunteered, but married men with families, well, they rarely took them. You see, such men already had responsibilities. They..."

"What are you saying, Mom?" Samantha interrupted, beginning to panic. Part of her wanted the answer; part of her wanted to flee from that germinating moment of recognition.

"Samantha, there was a child." Leonora slumped back in her chair as if she had been exorcised. "Your father had a daughter, Lydia, and so he never served in the military. He became a civilian employee of the United States Armed Forces who worked stateside as a cryptographer. You know what a genius he is at deciphering any kind of code, word games, crosswords. He applied that skill in service to his country. Sitting straighter, she added defensively, "Your father served in his own way, and he has nothing to be ashamed of."

Samantha covered her ears, hoping to block out what she had just heard. Her mother's mouth continued to form words, but all Samantha could hear was a roaring, wavelike din inside her head. She splayed the fingers of one hand in a stiff-armed gesture toward her mother, trying to stop her flow of words. *Daughter…Lydia…Crosswords.*

"A daughter," she stated, with deadly calm, "He had a daughter, and her name was Lydia. I guess neither of you thought that was a 'really important episode in his life' either. I have a sister whom I never even knew existed, and neither of you bothered to tell me until long after I had a child of my own?"

Leonora frequently used her active imagination to create complex scenarios out of bare boned facts that she would pick up from the newspaper or the eleven o'clock news. The unemployed man who had a lazy eye and a stamp collection was a serial killer. The woman who kept fifty-seven cats and five years worth of unread magazines was the secret heir to a multi-million dollar fortune. Now, Leonora tented her fingers and tapped their tips together, clearly satisfied that she had already plowed this fertile ground.

"Well, it occurred to me that you needed to know now that Nikki has graduated from college and will be meeting so many new people, dating more young men. She might somehow get involved with someone genetically related to her. You know, Samantha, you hear about such cases all the time where two young people fall in love only to find out that they are cousins or something." Leonora lifted her chin awaiting Sam's acknowledgement that she had done the right thing.

"I don't believe this," Samantha fumed. "You're worried about some ridiculous hypothetical situation involving your grandchild and a possibly nonexistent 'half-cousin' or whatever you would call this person? You can't just drop a bomb and then walk around the crater like the only thing that's important is the remote possibility of fall-out affecting a distant planet. Daddy lied to me. He lied about being in the Army; he lied about what he did in the service; and most importantly, he lied about the very existence of something and someone that are part of the essence of who he is and the life he's led, his first marriage and his daughter. Don't you see that? How many other lies has Daddy justified concealing as unimportant episodes? You're not going to stick to that ridiculous explanation are you?" Samantha demanded. "First of all, we don't even know if Lydia married or had children. For that matter, we don't even know her last name, neither the name she went by when she was single nor any married name she might have assumed. We don't know where she lives or if she's still living. Yet, somehow, you've been brooding about the possibility that our children might meet, marry, and produce children with birth defects? Really, Mom, there are times when your thought process completely eludes me."

"It could happen, Samantha," her mother insisted defensively.

"So, based on what even you would have to admit is an extremely thin possibility, you decided to rock my world. Not because the burden of a big lie became too much for you; not because Daddy's so sick that you decided you both needed to make peace with a terrible choice you made long ago; not because of anything that bears even a remote relationship to a concern for truth; but simply because you have watched too many episodes of *Dr. Phil* or *Court TV*. What I'd really like to know is what you expect me to do with this information. It's clear to me that you thought you could purge yourself, and everything would just go on as before. Words have meaning, Mom; they can hurt or heal; but they aren't vacuous. Perhaps you've heard the expression, 'There's an elephant in the room?' Well, there's one gigantic elephant in the room, Mom, and it's too big to ignore."

"I don't know what to say, Samantha," Leonora sighed into the silence. "I suppose there always has been an elephant in the room; it's just that only your father and I could see it."

Samantha managed a wry smile at the image of an elephant train led by a mammoth female, a family marching in intimate succession. Her frustration dissipated, replaced by a mischievous desire to make her mother laugh and the fleeting thought that she actually might succeed in making her point through humor when anger had so obviously failed. "You might not think this is funny," she began, "but when I was on the Atlanta Metro a few weeks ago, this man farted. I was standing right next to him, but he thought he could get away with it because it was one of those SBDs."

"What's an SBD?" Leonora asked.

"A 'silent-but-deadly,'" Samantha laughed. "Anyway, the subway car was packed, and everyone grimaced and looked around accusingly because there was no escape from the stink. So, I'm crammed in with all the others, holding on to my bag with one hand and a strap with the other, thanking God that I was getting off at the next stop. The train mercifully came into the station. I pushed my way through the crowd and out the door onto the platform, and I see the guy who had been standing next to me squeeze between the doors just as they were closing. He looked furtively from side to side; and not recognizing anyone else from the train, he jumped back on to the next car just as the doors shut. He couldn't stand his own stink!" Samantha chortled, reliving the memory; and she could hear Leonora who, unlike her father, had a stated aversion to what she called "bathroom humor," giggling in spite of herself. "See, the thing is, we all have to own our own stink, Mom. It's just like you and Daddy always told me, 'Don't do anything you wouldn't want someone else to see because, whether you know it or not, someone is always looking.'"

She doubted that Leonora was capable or desirous of understanding the metaphor. The elephant, the fart, and Lydia all were still in the room.

Leonora looked around furtively at the other diners. She self-consciously began fussing with her appearance, patting her hair in place, pinching her wispy bangs into the ageless pixie cut that she had worn for the last half century, adjusting her jacket so that the back of the collar stood up to frame her face, and pulling on the cuffs of her crisp, white blouse so that they peaked out of the jacket sleeves.

"Honestly, Samantha," she said finally, "I don't think you understand. When I met your father, he was already divorced; and his wife had taken their daughter and fled to Florida with another man. Despite this unanticipated physical separation from Lydia, he said he still intended to be a part of her life. He and your grandparents, Walter and Ruth, actually made a trip to Florida to see the child, but they were prevented from doing so."

"But Daddy's a fighter," Samantha argued. "He would have fought for his right to be a father to his daughter. There has to be more to it than just his being tricked out of custody. You said yourself that he loved her. That kind of love doesn't stop just because two parents get divorced." Samantha's voice was hard and accusatory. She was thinking with absolute certainty of her father's love for her. And, as a mother, she was thinking about the unfathomable depths of her love for her own child. The thought of losing her daughter in a divorce settlement and not fighting for her was utterly unthinkable.

Her mother's tone bristled with defensiveness. "You can't possibly understand. It was 1944; things were different then. Fathers didn't have many rights when it came to a custody dispute over a child. The assumption was that a child was always better off with his natural mother unless there was proof of her unfitness. I know what you're thinking. She was having an affair. Your father could have dragged that through the courts; but then it would be public, tarnishing not only her reputation, but his and the child's as well. And even then, he may not have won. Also," she said, lowering her eyes now, "I think he was thinking of me. It was difficult enough telling my mother that I wanted to marry a divorced man, but telling her that I was considering taking on the obligations of a child, well...."

Her voice trailed off as she pursed her lips in disapproval. "Besides, I was pregnant with you by the time the adoption papers came, and I would have had to take on all the responsibilities of being a stepmother just as I was learning to be a mother. Even so, I told your father that the decision was his to make. In the final analysis, he just wanted to start over. He'd been hurt, no, humiliated; and he didn't want to burden me with any of the vestiges of his former life. You and I became his life, Samantha."

"Mom, we each get only one life. There are different chapters, but they are each part of a continuum that together makes one book. If you rip a chapter from the binding, then the whole story comes apart. This is like finding a missing Shakespeare play. It changes his entire body of work. Don't you see? Daddy made his decision; but no matter how deeply he's buried it, it has affected everything; and I mean everything that he has done since. All of his joys and all of his fears have to have been colored by a choice so big."

Samantha thought of her father confined to his hospital bed in the middle of the living room; the hospice nurse seated in a chair beside him. Everything he had said to Samantha in those precious, deathbed conversations seemed now to glare in a different, sharp-edged light. *Over and over again, he had asked me to fix him. Surely, he had meant for me to find some way to spring him from the confines of the bed that had become his prison. Yet, was he not also asking more of me? Was he not begging me to absolve him of the greatest sin of his life, the new life that he had purchased at the expense of his own firstborn child?*

"There aren't any real do-overs, Mom," she said, thinking of how she would explain the complex rules of a game to Nikki when she was small. "There are sometimes second chances, and maybe we even get it right the next time, but the first round score stays on the record. If we're lucky, there may even be forgiveness; and if we're exceptionally fortunate, we may yet forgive ourselves." Samantha slumped back in her chair, now silent and spent.

"Are you all right, Sammie?" Leonora asked, leaning towards her and covering her hand. "You seem lost in thought." Samantha shook herself forcefully as though she could throw off her troubling reflections in much the same way that she would arrest the grip of an assailant.

"Sorry, Mom. I'm ok," Samantha managed. "It's just that there's been so much to take in. I don't know what to think right now."

Leonora opened her purse and put her reading glasses away. She reached inside for her compact, opened it, and carefully reapplied her lipstick, then checked her image in the mirror before putting away her cosmetics and snapping the clasp on her bag.

"Your father is the same man you have always known, Samantha," she said conclusively. "Nothing I have told you today alters that. I have given you information that I thought it best you have, but it was never my intent to cast aspersions on your father's good name. You are a grown woman and an intelligent one. You may not understand your father's past actions, but you must respect him and believe that he made the right decisions." She stood to leave, and waited for Samantha to join her.

Samantha almost couldn't believe what her mother was saying. She wanted her to take a lifetime of knowledge about her father, add to it the inestimable revelation that he had lied to her repeatedly, severed relations with his daughter, and concealed that fact for the remainder of his lifetime, then simply discard that information, and assess his character, his life, based solely on what she knew before. On top of that, her mother seemed almost to derive pleasure when she described what she characterized as her father's sacrifice of his relationship with his daughter. *I think he was thinking of me,* Leonora had said, as if she'd won some competition. Samantha looked at her mother who only moments before had seemed so selfless and saw only vanity.

"How can you be so cavalier about Daddy's actions?" she demanded. "You're acting as if my opinion of Daddy shouldn't change, as if you've revealed nothing more significant about him than that I have been mistaken all these years about his favorite color. Well, all his lies add up to a whole lot more than whether he prefers blue to red! I can't believe you don't see that, and you're equally dismissive about your own role in what happened, your own selfish desire to break with Daddy's past. Let's face it, Mom. You wanted him, but you didn't want all of him, by your own admission. You didn't want to deal with the parts that were messy, only the tidy parts like his education and his lifestyle that fit so neatly into the kind of life you wanted to lead." Samantha stopped abruptly as her mother, already so physically diminished, seemed to shrink even more. Just as quickly as her anger had risen, Samantha's feelings oscillated back toward empathy when she remembered Leonora's unflinching resolve to care for Fred at home and her refusal to employ anyone to help her beyond the physical therapist and the volunteer hospice nurse. There was as much truth in these acts of unsung heroism as there was in the accusations that had just left her mouth and had so clearly punished her mother.

Then, just as acutely, Samantha's thoughts veered toward her father and the image of him, bedridden and awaiting Malach Hamavet, the Angel of Death. Never a religious man, he had nevertheless taught her that there have been many literary explanations; but the one that was the most vivid to Sam was the image of the Angel of Death bestowing her cold kiss as she sucks out our very soul. Perhaps, she was a beautiful apparition after all; and it was not

Malach Hamavet who terrified her father and deprived him of sleep, but the ledger she carried, the Book of Life in which, according to Jewish law, all of our earthly deeds have been recorded and the date of our death inscribed. If so, maybe she hovered over Fred's bed forcing him to consider the evidence on his page? Did her long, tapered finger point to the image of his little girl, forever four years old at their parting, and demand an accounting?

Perhaps, Samantha thought, *the Greeks had it right in describing their mythological hell. Prometheus, who was damned for eternity for the sin of stealing fire, would have his heart eaten out only to regenerate and be eaten again in perpetuity. Sisyphus, mighty king of Corinth, would perform his endless, unavailing task of pushing a boulder up a steep hill in Hades, only to have it always roll down again when it neared the top. So, what hellish punishment does Daddy fear for abandoning his child? Has he kept the thought of it at bay all of these years only to have it plague him now that he is so near to death? Maybe his damnation is to be forced to view his forsaken daughter's innocent face for all time without end.*

Recoiling from this horror, Samantha thought again of Malach Hamavet's ledger and the many wonderful acts of kindness, generosity, and honesty it must surely also list beside her father's name. She drew a ragged breath, realizing that the ledger that she had envisioned so starkly in black and white was not a mathematical exercise to which she could assign values or reach a final tally.

Rising and pushing her chair away from the table, she saw again the image of her father in that bed waiting, just waiting, on and on. "Let's get home, Mom." She hurried to the door propelled by a sudden urge to see him.

Leonora stood slowly. "What are you going to say about Daddy when he's gone, Samantha?" she asked.

"I don't know at this point, Mom," Samantha admitted. "I honestly don't know."

CHAPTER 57

A S SHE WALKED FROM the car to the front door of her childhood home with her mother trailing behind, the trees were beginning to lose their leaves; and the first to fall crunched under Samantha's shoes. Through the living room window, she could see a lone lamp burned in the living room illuminating the silhouette of her father's still form in the hospital bed. Samantha turned the key in the lock and announced herself cheerfully as she pulled the door closed behind her.

"We're home, Daddy," she called.

She shrugged out of her coat and kicked off her shoes in the kitchen, a habit formed long ago in homage to her mother's fastidious housekeeping. She padded across the floor that was warmed by radiant heat, making her way through the dining room to the living room. She pasted on a smile. Kissing the top of her father's head, she pulled a chair up close to the bedside and spread the newspaper across her lap. She had decided to ask him about his past, but not before she felt certain that he was having a good day- a day that was defined by minimal pain and, at best, a glimpse of her father's former humor and intelligence that so often now were clouded by a chemical haze from his many medications.

"How about catching up on the world, Daddy?" she asked, perusing the paper in front of her. "What will it be? News or sports? There's an interesting article here about the al-Qaeda network in Afghanistan."

When her father did not respond, Samantha lowered the paper to look at him. A single tear coursed from the corner of his eye when she reached for his hand.

"What's the matter, Daddy?" she asked.

Her father's eyes were unblinking, staring into space. "Is it because of what I've done?"

"What do you mean, Daddy? We don't have to read now if you don't want to. You can just rest. I'll sit right beside you." She held his hand in one of hers and stroked it with the other.

"No," he continued, his voice strengthening, his face a painful mask of guilt and terror. "I'm asking you if all of this is happening to me because of what I've done!"

All the years of silent conspiracy between her parents distilled in an instant into one question of horrifying clarity. Her mind reeled backward to the third grade. The spelling words were posted around the perimeter of her classroom all week to aid the children in memorizing them for the test each Friday. Their teacher believed in an honor system and did not remove the words from the walls on test day when she called them out from the front of the room. Habitually, Porter Malden, a raffish eight-year-old, would glance surreptitiously at the placards containing the words she announced before he copied the answer on his test paper. Samantha told her father in righteous indignation, but he only smiled and shook his head ruefully.

"He will be caught, Samantha. If not now, then later. You may never know about it, and it may be years from now, but he will get caught. That's the way it is for cheaters and liars. In the end, they always get caught; and they always pay."

Her father's strict moral code had made a deep impression on her, but now she, too, wondered how he reconciled his own actions with it. *Here's my chance*, she thought. *I can ask him.* The father she knew and the Frederick Green she had never known could in minutes be reconciled, or instead, her worst fear might be realized- his explanation might be weak or self-serving; and then, her diamond of a father would be devalued by a massive inclusion previously invisible to her naked eye. She leaned toward the bed, and her lips parted; but his grip on her hand became tighter.

"Is this all happening because I'm ninety-five, Sammie?" His eyes were wild with fright.

In that moment, Samantha bit down hard on her lip, unaware that she had drawn blood. She looked into her father's stricken face and wondered if finally getting answers was worth the anguish she saw there. Fred had retreated to a vacuous recess of numbness, and Samantha wasn't willing to risk the emotional cost to both of them. Coward or heroine for remaining silent, she would never know; but she stood and smoothed his hair back from his lined forehead. Over and over, she repeated the comforting gesture until the creases smoothed and his eyelids fluttered shut.

"No, Daddy," she soothed. "You're not ninety-five. You're eighty-eight, remember? You're not even close to ninety-five. You're going to rest now. You need to rest in order to get better. Then, everything will be just as it was, ok, Daddy? I will be right here while you sleep."

"I want you to stay, Sammie," he said as he drifted off, "I want you to stay."

"How long do you want me to stay, Daddy? I will wait right here," Samantha promised.

"Forever," he whispered. Samantha wiped the errant tear from his cheek, but she knew he would never get better, and only God or oblivion, not the absolution of his beloved daughter, would grant him peace.

CHAPTER 58

S AMANTHA TIPTOED AWAY FROM her vigil at her father's bedside and opened her computer. She sat in front of it, staring at the monitor, her fingers poised over the keyboard. She had seen the pop-ups advertising the websites where you could search for anyone from high school classmates to lost loves, but never thought she'd need to use one. This is crazy, she thought, as she typed in the first variation of Lydia's name. Lydia Green. Even as she typed it, she knew that there was slim chance, based on the minimal information she had, that she would ever locate her sister. All she knew was that Lydia was born in Philadelphia some time shortly before World War II. When her mother moved to Florida, Lydia was taken there; but Samantha had no way of knowing whether she remained in Florida or if she now lived somewhere else.

She listened as the computer buzzed and whirred, finally posting a list of Lydia Greens currently residing in the state of Florida. Scrolling through them, Samantha realized the hopelessness of her search. She clicked the "back" icon on her computer screen and returned to the homepage of the website. This time, she typed in *Lydia Miller*, based on what her mother had said about the adoption papers—she must have taken his name. But this search yielded a similar result, pages of names with no way of distinguishing between them, even by eliminating the married from the maiden names. Samantha bit her lip, rested her elbows on the desk, and cradled her face in her hands as she leaned closer to the screen. All those names, all within the appropriate age range, all living in the only place to which she could trace her, but Samantha knew her sister could be one of them or none of them. The cursor continued its rhythmic blinking, and Samantha's hand hovered over the mouse. She had the power to move it but not the knowledge. She closed the window, and the names faded instantly from view.

Samantha rocked back on her chair and wondered why she was search-ing at all. She snapped the laptop shut, grabbed her car keys, and headed for the door. Passing her mother in the kitchen, she said, "I need a break, Mom. I'm going out for coffee." She squeezed her mother's shoulder and added, "I won't be long."

Samantha liked the local coffee shop that still managed to compete with the ubiquitous Starbucks, one of which had opened a few years ago across the street. Perkfection had a double-sided stone fireplace, overstuffed furniture, distressed tables, and worn Navajo rugs. As she took her latte to a small table by the fire, she stared sightlessly into the middle distance. Picking up her steaming cup, she thought, *Lydia could be anywhere.* She glanced around at the assortment of women occupying other chairs. *Any of them could be my sister*, she thought. She closed her eyes, cupping the coffee mug with both hands, and allowed the warmth to pervade the solitary chill inside her. *Any of them. And if I could find her, what would I say? What would she say?*

Samantha imagined what it would be like if Lydia were sitting right there, across from her. It was a strange vision. In it, Samantha stole furtive glances at her chimerical companion, searching for physical resemblance to herself, her father. *Would she have blue eyes and straight brown hair, like Daddy and me, or would she be tall and lean like Daddy and look even more like him than I do… or be nothing like him? Oh, what difference does it make,* she thought, banging her cup on the table more forcefully than she realized and briefly drawing the attention of the middle-aged women at the adjoining table. *I don't care what she looks like. What I really wonder is whether Lydia remembers her father, our father, at all? If she does, would not those fractured childhood memories have been inevitably stained by the taint of his abandonment, by the lies and half-truths her parents and grandparents presumably must have told her?*

She imagined her sister as the physical embodiment of her alter ego, yet she could not concoct a conversation between these two less than complete selves that would make the other whole. What did either of them know of the other's father after all? Shared DNA would identify him as the same man, but was there anything else the same?

Samantha shook her head violently, and the phantasmagoria of her sister finally opened her mouth to speak. *All I remember of my father is a tall, smiling man who told me bedtime stories about a cast of characters he created, mostly centering around a clown, Coco or Dodo- something like that. Then, one day he was gone.* The apparition was haunted by a wisp of a memory.

Bobo, Samantha corrected her. *The clown's name was Bobo, and he had an elephant named Bozzy. There also was one monkey named Lulu who could fly, another called YoYo with a talent for yodeling, a frog named Croaker, and his own personal superhero, Curly the Corkscrew. I heard those stories almost every night too. My father was there for me. He never missed a single piano recital, school play, field hockey game or teacher conference.* Samantha stopped, suddenly embarrassed.

Her pale companion's cheeks burned, two angry red spots. *Of course not,* she snapped. *Everything he took from me, he gave to you.*

There was nothing more to say.

Samantha's eyes flew open as she grabbed her car keys in frustration, almost knocking her coffee mug to the floor. She sped home and fumbled with her key in the lock.

"Hello," Leonora said, pulling the door open from the inside, her greeting breathless. She explained, "I was coming downstairs, and you know I can't hurry anymore." She had been forced to use a cane for the last two years since falling and breaking her hip. She had lost her balance while bending to extinguish a partially smoked cigarette in a frugal effort to preserve one more puff. No small concession to her vanity, the cane was a sleek English walking stick topped by a silver handle in the shape of a Labrador retriever's head. Samantha had presented it to her father, hoping that he might condescend to use it because it fit his sartorial image, but her gift had come too late, and now Leonora had incorporated it as an accessory to her personal style and basked in the attention it garnered.

"I've been thinking," Samantha began, dropping her keys in the bowl on the foyer table. "In fact, I can't stop thinking about it." She could hear her own deep breathing in the silence that ensued, and she pictured it traveling like a current between them. She did not attempt to mask her angry look, and her mother's eyes widened. Leonora had quit smoking cold turkey at the doctor's insistence after her accident, but her newly acquired habit of chewing on the end of a drinking straw that she cut to simulate the shape and length of a real cigarette provided inadequate compensation.

"Thinking about what, honey?" Leonora asked, suddenly anxious, reflexively putting the faux cigarette to her lips.

Samantha exhaled audibly again. "I can't get it out of my head, this thing about Daddy. I mean, it's like I never knew him at all," she exclaimed, her heartbeat quickening and the toe of her knee high boot tapping nervously on the hardwood floor.

"What are you talking about, Samantha? Of course, you know your father." Leonora spoke with a certainty that brooked no further discussion.

It suddenly hit Samantha. Her mother had to have been an integral part of the entire series of decisions; first, she accepted and, in fact benefited, from her husband's failure to maintain a continuing relationship with his daughter; second, it was a short leap from this choice to encouraging him to agree to the adoption; third, Leonora not only acquiesced but also she participated in the conspiracy of silence to keep the facts of her father's first marriage and child from the daughter they raised together. It all began to make sense. Leonora said herself that times had been different. Divorce was uncommon; to many, it was a taboo, to all, a failure. She claimed to have only a vague memory of whether she had even told her family that her fiancé had been married before, and was absolutely sure that she had never mentioned the child. To Leonora, this withholding of information about Frederick Green from her family, this little white lie, bore no more weight in the pantheon of veracity than her admission that she shaved three years from her age the very first day when she met Fred at Scaroon Manor and did not reveal her true age to him until many years after they were married. *My God*, Samantha thought in disgust, *Mom's driver's license still perpetuates that lie*! Once her parents started down this slippery slope, they gained acceleration in their descent.

Leonora's face softened, and her eyes clouded with the unfocused look of one who is gazing down the long, broken road of the past. Retrieving the story that she had long ago accepted as fact, she again offered Samantha the same explanation, the only explanation that she knew. "I suppose I always considered that your father did what he did for me, really," she sighed, "He didn't want me to have to deal with the often thankless job of being a step-mother. I also think he wanted to start over. He wanted our marriage to work, and he wanted a fresh beginning with me, and then you. Can't you understand that?"

"So, you're saying that you regarded this as some kind of favor?" Samantha's incredulity was manifest. "Let me get this straight. You're say-ing that Daddy's decisions and your complicity or even encouragement were some kind of perverted wedding presents to each other? He didn't want to burden you with the undesirable responsibility of helping him to raise his daughter, and you wanted to relieve him of the living reminder of his past? That's sick, Mom, just plain sick! How selfish could you be, and how deep in denial could Daddy have been that he could convince himself that there was nobility in his abandonment of his daughter? Oh, and pardon me if I don't thank you for your generosity in depriving me of a sister, and excuse my ingratitude for suddenly finding out at this late stage of my life that, thanks in large part to your conspiracy, I don't know my dying father at all!"

Samantha's head ached with a pulsing throb that felt as if only the flesh and bone of her cranium prevented a bloody geyser from spewing out of the top of her body, leaving her a lifeless puddle on the floor. Unconsciously, she pressed the flat of her palm firmly against the crown of her head, as if she were clamping the lid onto a pot that threatened to boil over.

"I can't talk to you about this anymore now," Samantha rasped. Her mother started to protest, but Samantha could not make out her words as she pushed past her. She went into the small den and sank back into the armchair, grasping her knees to her chest. *Does anyone ever really know anyone else,* she demanded of the room soundlessly, *or are we really each just here together alone?*

CHAPTER 59

ONLY WEEKS AFTER SAMANTHA flew home to Atlanta following a profusion of promises to her father to return as soon as she could, she received an urgent call from her mother. "You'd better come, Sammie," Leonora said, her voice a monotone devoid of emotion. Samantha's breath caught. She had spent a lifetime trying to interpret Leonora's and, for that matter, Fred's communications, because neither of her parents had ever been able to deliver bad news in either a timely or direct manner. Despite her repeated protests that finding things out later rather than sooner did not serve their stated purpose of protecting her and often had a worse impact than if she had been included in the information loop, they persisted in their reticence. Instinctively, Samantha knew that her father's condition had deteriorated. Still, for once, she was going to make her mother say it.

"What's going on, Mom?" she asked, trying to remain calm but insistent. "Is Daddy worse?" *Say it, damn it,* she screamed silently. *Stop treating me like a helpless child, and just say it! He's dying. I know it, so just say it! Stop pretending that he's going to get better because he isn't. You've never told me to come before, and you wouldn't now except for one thing, he's dying!*

"Hospice is here, Sammie, and they've told me not to give him any more food or water. Not that he's asking for any. He's just sleeping. He's very peaceful, actually." She sounded almost wistful, as if she wanted to curl up next to him and close her eyes too.

She still won't say it, Samantha thought, stifling her anger. *I know that hospice comes only when someone is dying.* Samantha pictured her mother. Leonora had become a shut-in herself, no longer taking pride in her appearance, losing interest in her clothes, her makeup, shopping, dining out, all the things that she had always loved. It was Fred for whom she had dressed and with whom she had shopped and traveled. Without him to bolster her self-confidence, she had morphed into a handmaid and nurse, padding around the house in old sneakers and a pair of Fred's socks, sometimes even forgetting to eat.

"It's strange," Leonora mused, "Daddy has been grumbling incessantly about his teeth and his ears. He always hated going to the dentist, and then all he could talk about was that his dentures don't fit right, and he kept asking me when I was going to take him to the dentist to have the fit corrected. When he wasn't asking me about that, he'd go on about his ears, how he had a ringing in them, and why wouldn't I take him to a doctor who would stop the ringing? I didn't know what to say, Sammie. I can't stand it that he might have been thinking that I was refusing to help him, but I didn't know how to tell him that he couldn't go. Now, he's just sleeping, and I wish he'd say something, anything, even if it's to complain that I'm not helping him with his teeth or his ears. Oh, God, if he goes thinking I wouldn't help him…." Her voice trailed off, and Samantha could hear a strangled sob over the phone line.

Samantha's anger escaped from her like so much air from a deflated balloon. She wanted to reach across the phone line, wrap her mother's frail body in her arms, and draw her anguish into her own strong body so that she could bear it for her.

"Daddy knows you would do anything to help him. And you know that he's tried so hard to get better, Mom. He wanted so much to get better; but he can't, so maybe we have to be strong enough to let him go." Her mother's sobs were like a torrent now, as Sammie tried to comfort her. "Let me help you, Mom. Please, let me. You know that peacefulness you've been talking about? Dad is at peace because he knows that you won't be left alone. I'll come back right away, and I will help both of you."

She could hear commotion in the background, the sound of unfamiliar voices, curt, professional, but she couldn't differentiate the muffled cadences into words. *The hospice workers*, she thought. "Hold on, Sammie," Leonora said, "They're calling me."

Leonora's voice, an otherworldly calm taking possession of her, came back on the line. Her next words were disturbingly loud and clear over the background of muddy intonations. "That's it, Sammie, he's gone," she said.

No! Samantha yelled wordlessly. *I was supposed to be there when it happened. I was supposed to hold his hand and speak to him softly so that he wouldn't be afraid. How could this happen? How could he go and leave me without my greatest counselor, my staunchest friend?* But then she stopped, the cacophony of words just stopped, and she realized that it wasn't about her. She could not succumb to her grief when her mother waited on the other end of the silent phone line and Nikki was unaware that her grandfather, who had always said that she and Samantha were the eyes in his head, had just closed his forever. *No*, she thought resolutely, *I have to be strong for them.*

"Mom," she stated firmly, "I will be on the next plane. We will handle all the arrangements together. I will tell Nikki, and she and Lars, Eddie, and Anika all will come."

"Thank you, honey," Leonora said. "Always remember; your Daddy is so proud of you."

Samantha disconnected the phone, then picked it up again and began dialing.

CHAPTER 60

THE FLIGHT TO PHILADELPHIA was a blur. All she could remember was repeating to herself over and over again, "He's gone." Lars sat beside her, holding her hand. Eddie and Anika were in the row behind them, and Nikki was taking the train from Washington where she had matriculated at Georgetown the previous fall. Nikki had howled a primal wail of gut wrenching grief when Samantha called her with the news, the same shriek that still lay buried deep in Samantha herself. In the ensuing days, Nikki pulled herself together, finding solace in her many happy memories of her grandfather and strength in her desire to honor him, even in death.

When they arrived in Philadelphia, the others went to the house, but Samantha went directly to the funeral home where she had promised to meet her mother to make the funeral arrangements. A cold October wind whipped her hair across her face as she stood on the threshold of Joseph Levine & Sons. She had a vague recollection of coming to this same funeral home as a child when her grandfather, Walter, died, but mostly she remembered passing it innumerable times making the drive along Broad Street to and from her father's office. She pushed open the plate glass door resolutely and stepped into the plushly-carpeted lobby. The thickness of the carpeting absorbed her footfalls, and the overstuffed furniture looked straight out of some elderly person's living room. She realized that this was intentional, designed to evoke emotions of comfort and security when anyone who came here was feeling anything but. She smoothed her hands over her windblown hair, sat, and then stood again, seeing no one and unaware of how to make her presence known. Hearing a door open and then close behind her, she turned to face an obsequious looking man of indeterminate age who moved noiselessly toward her with his hand extended and his face a caricature of empathy.

"I am Richard Rubenstein and I would like to express my sincere condolences at your loss," he simpered, pumping her hand up and down. Samantha wondered how many times a day Mr. Rubenstein delivered this greeting and how many years he had spent practicing and refining it until it conveyed the proper measure of professionalism and concern.

"I am Samantha Swinton, she replied. "I am here to meet my mother, Leonora Green, to make funeral arrangements for my father, Frederick Maier Green. Is she here yet?"

She withdrew her hand from his moist one and surreptitiously wiped it by unbuttoning her coat. It seemed uncomfortably warm in the room.

"Why, yes, Mrs. Swinton, your mother is waiting for you in my office. Right this way," he gestured toward the door through which he had entered. "The three of us can go down to the casket room where I will leave you alone for a few minutes to make your choice."

Samantha wanted to dislike this insipid little man, but she knew that years of absorbing the grief of total strangers had rendered him colorless and vapid. It wasn't his fault; he simply was a casualty of his profession. In some way, she supposed, he must have wanted to help people. She couldn't hate him for providing a service, no matter how distasteful she found his sweaty hands, the nasal timbre of his voice, or his clichéd black suit.

She followed him down a dimly lit hall until they came to another door. Turning the knob, he stepped aside for her to enter. She saw the back of her mother's head. Although her hair had always been fine, Samantha felt a wave of shock pass through her when she realized that she could see Leonora's scalp in the soft light of Mr. Rubenstein's office. Leonora was seated in another overstuffed chair, her form looking diminished within the folds of the upholstery. She sat slightly stooped, worrying a tissue, and staring down at her hands that fidgeted in her lap as if disconnected from her otherwise still body. Samantha forced herself to stand ramrod straight and walked purposefully into the room. The sound of her heels clicking against the polished wood floor seemed startling after the carpeted silence of the other rooms. She crouched next to her mother's chair until she could meet the level of her eyes.

She covered Leonora's hands with her own and said, "I'm here, Mommy. We'll make all of the arrangements for Daddy together, ok? He trusted us to do everything in a way that he would have liked, and that's just what we'll do."

She drew her mother to a standing position; and turning to Mr. Rubenstein, she continued, "We're ready to go to the casket room now." He gave an almost imperceptible nod and led the way.

The casket room was a cavernous space lined with platforms. On each one, a different type of coffin was displayed. They ranged from the very simple to the highly ornate, from common pine to exotic woods, from ordinary muslin interiors to the finest silks, and from conventional iron hardware to silver or gold. Although no tags were in plain view, Samantha was certain that the prices reflected the variety, ranging from the one that belonged in the pauper's grave of English fiction to the gilded model that cost the proverbial king's ransom.

Leonora seemed to stagger, leaning heavily against Samantha's shoulder. She had a wild-eyed look of confusion on her face, but she said nothing. Samantha placed her hand firmly under her mother's elbow to steady her. She steered her to a polished walnut coffin with a smooth, ecru colored silk lining.

"This is the one, Mommy. This one is understated but elegant. It reminds me of Daddy--the warm woods of his office, the perfect fabrics of his shirts and ties."

Leonora slowly raised her arm and ran her hand along the glossy surfaces. Her fingertips caressed the silk pillow on which her husband's head would rest. A trace of a smile lit her face.

She turned to Samantha and took her face in her hands. "You're right, Sammie, this is the one."

Turning to Mr. Rubenstein, she added, "Didn't I tell you my daughter had excellent taste? Didn't I say she would know exactly what to do?"

"Yes, you certainly did, Mrs. Green," Mr. Rubenstein confirmed. "Now, shall we return to my office to discuss the service?"

Seated once again in one of the overstuffed chairs and having signed the necessary paperwork, Leonora raised her eyes to meet Mr. Rubenstein's. "My husband was not a religious man," she began. "He would not have wanted some rabbi he didn't know saying some mumbo jumbo over him. I mean no disrespect; only that's what he called it, 'mumbo jumbo, hokum.' You see, my husband believed in this life, Mr. Rubenstein, the one he knew about for sure. He believed in being a good man. So, we'll want a graveside service; and although I'm no public speaker, I will be speaking and Samantha, of course, and anyone else who wants to may say a few words. So, if we're clear on that, my daughter and I will be going now."

Leonora's voice seemed to resonate from a well of strength when she spoke about her husband. She offered her hand to Mr. Rubenstein who lapsed comfortably into his practiced empathy. Leonora linked her arm through Samantha's, and they walked together toward the door.

"Will you speak about me when I'm gone?" Samantha remembered well her father's question, and the time had come to keep her promise. She was seated in her father's favorite chair in the living room of her childhood home. All of the indentations in the leather were his; she felt like the little girl she once was who had slipped her tiny feet into his shoes. She slid back against the seat and grasped the armrests, straightening her spine and pushing herself to her full height; yet she still was engulfed by the chair that, after so many years, would conform only to her father. She tapped her pen against the blank page of the legal pad that rested in her lap. How many important pieces had she written in her life? There had been countless essays, writing samples, articles, and legal briefs; but this would be the first eulogy. *How do you sum up a life,* she wondered? *What do you say to encapsulate a person, especially your father?* The tapestry of forte and foible inextricably linked to form the fabric of a life was as difficult to describe as Joseph's coat of many colors. Then, it came to her. She did not need to detail all of the things that constituted her father's life. She had only to talk about the *greatest* thing.

He was with her again as her pen danced across the page. He was the angel on her shoulder confirming that what she wrote was good and true. After all, he had said it himself, so how could she be wrong? He had been sure at the end of his life that he knew what was the *greatest* thing. Samantha felt the thrill of his certainty as she wrote, for he had lived long and well and had come to the end of this life confident in that knowledge. There could be no better way to leave this life than that.

Samantha looked down at the pages in her lap. They were filled with her words, his words, and fear no longer gripped her. She had written what should be said of her father, and she took comfort in that. They were not the words of platitudes that he would have abhorred; in fact, what pleased her most was that the man she described was so real. He had been saint and sinner, lover and lothario, selfless and selfish; but most of all, he had been human.

CHAPTER 61

THAT OCTOBER DAY DAWNED clear and crisp, the last of the autumn leaves still clinging to the trees, their less stalwart siblings crackling beneath Samantha's feet as she made her way to the limousine that would carry her to the cemetery. She had dressed carefully in her black crepe suit and pearl gray silk blouse. Her beautifully handcrafted gold necklace had been a honeymoon gift from Lars on their trip to Italy. She was the picture of sober appropriateness. She smiled to herself as she recalled how her father was always impeccably dressed. She now carried that banner; so if funereal black were required, then she would wear the finest.

She laid her head back against the glove leather of the seat and closed her eyes. She felt for her purse that lay on the seat next to her and gave it a comforting pat, knowing that her eulogy was tucked safely inside it. Lars sat next to her, a warm presence, and he squeezed her hand, offering his silent support. Nikki and Leonora sat across from her. Each stared sightlessly out the window, bookends of grief. Eddie and Anika followed in a sedate black sedan rented for the occasion.

The small cortege wended its way through the tree-shaded paths of Roosevelt Memorial Park and came to a stop beside a newly groomed gravesite. Everything was in place. A small enclave of chairs faced the casket, its polished wood surfaces catching the thin autumnal sunlight. Leonora led the small procession to their seats. The intimate group of mourners might have seemed paltry to an observer, particularly for someone who had lived the better part of a century; but Samantha knew that, in the end, a funeral was for the living. Occupying those few chairs were the people her father had cared about the most, those for whom his passing meant a permanent void in their hearts. And for Samantha, these were the people who would be the most support. To her right sat his wife and grandchild; to her left she was flanked by her husband, Eddie, and Anika; and reaching forward from the row behind Samantha to lay a gentle, comforting hand on her shoulder were her closest childhood friends who had known her father almost as long as she had. Conspicuous by his absence was Chapman Stirling, who had died five years before. Certainly, there would have been others if her mother had chosen to notify them, a few of Fred's surviving childhood friends and many comrades in the legal profession; but intuitively Samantha and her mother had known that this celebration of a life was not about the number of those in attendance or the grandiosity of the arrangements. It was about the loss of a husband, father, and grandfather and the long shadow he had cast and would continue to cast across the lives of his precious few. It was, above all else, a celebration of family.

Even the hushed voices silenced as Leonora stood and turned to face the group. "I've been a lucky girl," she began with a smile that was at once girlish and shy. "My grandfather used to say, '*Ich hoffe er wird dich auf seinen Händen tragen.*'" She scanned the upturned faces of her family and friends and, turning her hands palms upward, she explained, "That means he hoped I would find someone who would carry me around in his hands. Well, I met a man who did just that. He loved me with all of his heart, and we were fortunate enough to spend fifty years together."

She reached out and touched the arcing lid of the casket lovingly. "We had a wonderful life. We raised a beautiful, accomplished daughter who gave us many moments of pride, and she has given us a wonderful son-in-law who has treated us like his own parents. Their daughter, our granddaughter, has been, as her grandfather used to say, 'the light in his eyes.' She, too, is beautiful inside and out and is our posterity. We saw the world, and we made a home. As I said, I have been a lucky girl."

Leonora kissed her fingertips and rested them gently at the head of the casket. Turning back to the audience, she looked at Samantha with an expression that asked, *Have I done all right?*

Samantha rose and, taking her mother's elbow, steered her back to her seat. She leaned to kiss her mother's cheek and whispered, "That was good, Mom. Daddy would have liked that very much."

Just then, the sun glinted off the polished walnut surface of the casket reflecting the tears that had pooled in her eyes and trickled down her cheeks, leaving tracks in their wake. "Daddy would have loved that, Mom," she corrected herself, enfolding her mother in a protective embrace. She could feel their two hearts beating in unison, the simultaneity of life and love.

Straightening, she saw that Lars had risen to speak. Never having been a natural public speaker, he had forced himself to learn to address groups because giving speeches and conducting meetings had become an integral part of his business. Samantha's heart squeezed because she knew that like an accomplished actor's stage fright, the feeling of trepidation never left him; it was merely cleverly disguised.

Lars cleared his throat. "Frederick Green loved a good argument," he said with a grin. His family laughed softly as the truth of that declaration hit home. "I think we got closer over the years because, as you all know, I can argue with the best of them; and he was definitely the best. I'll miss that."

He looked down at his shoes, and his chest heaved, but he raised his eyes to meet Samantha's. "But what I learned most from him was what it means to be a family man. He was definitely the best at that too. I want to thank him for that; and I hope that to my wife, my children, and some day my grandchildren, I can embody the same sense of family that he taught me." His eyes squinted against tears as he took his seat.

Samantha cast a surreptitious glance at Nikki. She had told her that the choice of whether to speak was entirely hers, and neither she nor Leonora had applied any pressure to her to do so. "Everyone grieves differently," she had reassured her daughter. "No one expects you to do or say anything unless you want to. You don't have to make up your mind until the last minute. Just do what feels right."

The moment had come. Nikki stood and moved to the front of the group. Her shiny, golden hair caught the chilly autumn breeze, and she tucked it firmly behind her ears, an expression of resolute determination clouding her delicate features. Her sunny beauty was only slightly diminished by her charcoal grey winter coat. She bit her lip and exhaled slowly, a gesture so like her own that Samantha was riveted. The scenery faded. There was only Nikki and the lingering presence of the loved one she had lost. Rather than facing the others, Nikki directed her face and her words to the man for whom they were meant, her grandfather.

"Granddad, I guess you know that I learned journal writing from Mom." She withdrew a small, leather-bound book from her coat pocket and began to turn the pages as she spoke. "I write about happy times, and I write about things that make me sad, so I wrote about you."

She looked down at the page, and Samantha thought that she would begin to read; but as she held the open diary, she spoke directly to her grandfather. "You were with me through so many important times in my life so far. You watched me win at cross-country and track meets, and you were my Santa Claus. More recently, you saw me graduate from high school and begin college. Now, you're gone, but there's something you don't know. You still are with me. You'll be with me when I graduate from college, when I start my career, and when I get married. You'll be with me when I have children of my own. So, don't worry, Granddad, you'll be with me always."

She swiped at a tear that escaped from her brimming blue eyes and bent to kiss the wood that separated her from where his head rested in its final peace. Her back was straight and her chin held high, and the faintest hint of a smile lighted her lovely face as she walked back to her seat.

Lars slipped his arm around Samantha's shoulders and drew her close. He kissed the top of her head, resting his chin there. "She's strong, like you," he whispered. Samantha snuggled briefly into the folds of his coat, the spot she always had regarded as her safe place, and then she rose.

Each pair of eyes was locked on her, and the expectancy weighed heavily as she unfolded her paper and began to read. Her words were heartfelt, and her tone had just the right mix of love and respect, the two things her father had craved throughout his life:

Frederick Maier Green, April 7, 1912 to October 11, 2001. How to describe an extraordinary life? What was the greatest thing?

Is it that he was the consummate academic who, through scholarships, earned the highest degrees with honors from the finest universities?

Is it being elected to the Student Council in college to represent your peers?

Is it over sixty-five years of law practice marked by professionalism and unquestionable and unwavering ethics?

Is it that he was an artist, a runner, a dancer, a "walking dictionary" or a man with an encyclopedic knowledge of a wide array of subjects?

That he was the "poet laureate of 1709?"

That he was the author of countless Bobo stories to the delight of both his daughter and granddaughter?

That two generations knew the adventure of trips to his office highlighted by lunch at the Colonnade or another favorite restaurant that made both of us feel like a partner in the family firm?

Is it that he used his incomparable vocabulary and intelligence to become master of the crossword puzzle and the cryptogram?

Is it that he inspired us throughout our education and our lives to offer our best and never doubted that, at our best, we were capable of excellence?

Is the greatest *thing any one of these things, or is the whole of this extraordinary life truly greater than the sum of its parts? Clearly, the answer is yes. We are here to celebrate the wonderful life of Frederick Maier Green, and it is a blessing that, as the Bible says in 1 Chronicles,*

'He died in good old age, full of days…and honor.'

In closing, I would like to tell you what was, although I did not know it at the time, the last meaningful conversation I had with my Dad. I was helping him with some physical task which, regrettably, he could no longer perform for himself, and he looked up at me and smiled and asked, 'Isn't love the greatest thing?' And that was when I knew with certainty that he knew how much I, and each of you, loved him, and I knew how much he loved each of us.

So, when we seek to describe the extraordinary life of Frederick Maier Green spanning almost nine decades, we can say that he experienced and embodied the greatest thing, and in his own words, the greatest thing is love.

Samantha folded the page and stood for a moment, her head bowed. Her father was gone. She thought she would look to her mother or Lars or Nikki, but she had in that instant no instinct or desire to seek the approval of others. Even as she placed a single, yellow, long-stemmed spider mum, her father's favorite flower, upon the glossy surface of his casket, she did not wonder whether her words had been right. She knew. Her heart was light with the winged freedom of knowing.

Chapter 62

IN THE MONTHS SINCE Fred's death, his daughter and granddaughter both called Leonora almost daily and made sure, more than ever, that she had a visit to or from one of them to which she always could look forward. On one such day, Leonora admitted plaintively to Samantha, "I just can't do it, Sammie. I know I have to go through your father's things, but I just can't do it. Would you and Nikki do it?" Leonora let her hand trail across the papers still neatly stacked on his desktop. "I'm sure you could figure out what to keep and what to give away. Some of this probably should be thrown out."

"Don't worry, Mom," Samantha reassured her. "Nikki and I will do it the next time we come to the house. Just leave it for a couple of more weeks until we're there with you," she added reassuringly.

Samantha and Nikki arrived together for their planned visit. As Samantha looked around her parents' room, she realized that Leonora had kept Fred's closet, his desk, everything, exactly as it was. Nothing had been touched.

Samantha exhaled slowly. "We'll go through Daddy's things, Mom," she said resignedly. "If Nikki and I work together, it shouldn't take that long. Don't worry about it. Tomorrow, you can go out for the day, and when you come home, it all will be done. I promise."

The following morning, Samantha and Nikki agreed to start with Fred's closet. "Nikki, let's work fast. Then, we won't have to think about it too much," Samantha said, patting her daughter's shoulder encouragingly. "You make the list of Goodwill donations as I call out the item, fold it, and put it in a bag, OK?"

"Sure, Mom," Nikki replied, taking the pen and pad from her mother. "Granddad had such beautiful clothes," she remarked, caressing the sleeve of a cashmere coat. "He always looked elegant."

Her eyes got a faraway look as she laid her cheek against the soft hand of the fabric. "This coat still smells like him," she sighed wistfully. She buried her face in its folds.

Samantha turned away, biting her lip. "Funny how something like scent can live on," she agreed, gently taking the coat from its hanger. "Come on, honey. Let's get this finished before Grandmom gets back." As Nikki bent her head to commence her list, Samantha also furtively breathed in the familiar smell of her father's cologne before consigning the beautiful garment to a large, black plastic bag.

They worked systematically until the closet was empty and then moved on to Fred's desk. "This is going to be more difficult," Samantha admitted. "We're going to have to go through every drawer carefully to determine what Grandmom may want to keep, what we'd like to have, and what should be discarded. Why don't we each take one drawer at a time until we're finished? You start with the top drawer, Nikki."

Nikki pulled the drawer out completely from its runners so that she could set it on the floor and more easily remove its contents. Samantha watched as her daughter sat cross-legged on the rug and examined a Mont Blanc pen, a smile of memory in her eyes. She held it up to her mother and said, "Mom, I think I'll keep this pen. I remember watching Granddad use it to solve so many puzzles."

She laid it lovingly aside and resumed sorting the remaining contents of the drawer. Samantha began to sort the items in the second drawer, making piles to distribute later. They worked steadily and silently, until, after an hour or so, the quiet was broken by Nikki's startled voice.

"Who's this, Mom?" She held up a small, worn black and white photograph with a deckled edge, the image of a young but unmistakable Frederick Green with a little girl on his lap, their faces pressed together and their arms entwined, locked in a moment of perpetual happiness. Samantha looked at her daughter, surrounded by the jumble of her grandfather's belongings, yet so focused on this one, powerful object. Samantha laid down the papers she was holding and reached for the photograph. She had never seen it before, but she was certain she could identify it. Her daughter's face was a sea of confusion as Samantha sat down next to her on the carpet, still holding the picture.

I'm going to tell her the truth, she realized abruptly. "That," she said, "is Granddad with his daughter, Lydia."

"What?" Nikki yelled, erupting to her feet. "What did you just say? Granddad had another child? You had a sister that I never knew about?" She ripped the photograph from her mother's grasp and bore her eyes into it accusingly. Tears coursed down her cheeks. "Mom, why didn't you tell me?"

Samantha mentally recoiled from her daughter's strident tone, the belligerent shield that always had been her defense against the assault of anguish, but she willed herself to look Nikki in the eye when she replied.

"Look, Nikki, I didn't find out that I had a half-sister until long after I was a grown woman. An old friend of Granddad's, Chapman Stirling, mentioned Granddad's first marriage to me when he was trying to console me about my divorce. He presumed that I knew Granddad had been married before, although it was a shock to me. Much later, Grandmom told me he had a daughter and that his ex-wife and her new husband had adopted her. Granddad never saw her after that."

"What did Granddad say about it?" Nikki demanded. Her eyes still had not left the blissful image.

"I never asked him about his previous marriage or his daughter, and he never told me," Samantha said. She pursed her lips and shrugged her shoulders, physically expressing her consternation.

Nikki slumped back onto the floor, still clutching the photograph. "Oh, my God!" she exclaimed. "He always said, 'Granddad never lies,' but Granddad was a liar." She swiped angrily at the tears now streaming from her eyes.

Samantha took her daughter's face in both of her hands and tilted her chin so that she was looking her squarely in the eye. "Yes, he lied, Nikki, but he's still my Daddy and your Granddad. He's still the man who is so much a part of who I am and who you are. The man whom I believe would have given his life for either one of us. The demanding, funny, razor-smart, loving man who made us believe we could accomplish anything. No matter what else he did, he's still my Daddy, Nikki, and your Granddad."

Nikki wiped her face on the sleeve of her shirt and covered her mother's hand. Sniffing audibly, she managed a small smile. She squeezed her mother's fingers tenderly, comprehension dawning across her beautiful features. Shaking her head, she said, "You didn't want to know the real story? By not asking him, you could write his history in your own mind and make it consistent with the father you knew. Because of everything else you know to be true about him, you didn't want some other truth to compromise your version of Granddad. You wanted to protect your belief that he's innocent; and you know what, Mom, even if that's a selfish motive, then that's OK." Samantha watched as Nikki purposefully released the photograph into a pile of papers to be disposed of.

"You know," Samantha said, "I think you're right. There were so many times I could have asked him, times that I almost did ask him, times that it seemed like he was on the brink of telling me, and then just as quickly, those moments were gone. I could have pressed him. I could have given voice to all of those questions swirling in my head, but something always held me back. I realize now that I didn't want to know that man, that other incarnation of Frederick Maier Green who had given up a daughter he loved. I could never imagine an explanation that would have been acceptable to me. That act was so antithetical to the father I knew that it was beyond my ability to reconcile. I knew my Daddy and the man he was to me, and in spite of and because of all that he was, I love him."

"You know," Nikki said, her voice soft now like the chenille throw still draped on her grandfather's favorite chair, "we'll never know why Granddad took his silence to the grave, but he undoubtedly took his pain too."

She picked up the Mont Blanc pen, gave it a long, hard gaze as if it held some oracular response, and slipped it into her purse, securing it inside the zippered compartment. Snapping the clasp and closing it decisively, Nikki returned her attention to the drawer.

CHAPTER 63

I T DID NOT SEEM possible that almost a year had passed. An entire winter, spring, and summer had relentlessly paraded their days until fall arrived, with its palate of colors, Indian summer afternoons, frosty mornings, and heralded the first anniversary of her father's death. Observance of Jewish ritual required that they keep a parent's headstone covered for the first eleven months, and just before his first yahrzeit, unveil it.

There had rarely been a day that Samantha had not thought of him. Every time she saw a tall, sartorial gentleman with a shock of silver hair, a determined hand attempting to solve a crossword puzzle, or a grandfather and his granddaughter holding hands, their heads together in a shared moment, Samantha's breath would catch or her nose begin to sting, a warning that tears were not far behind. Yet, she didn't cry.

Now, it was time for the unveiling. Samantha brushed her hair and put on the jacket of her new suit. She headed to her car and drove to the cemetery.

The slam of her car door broke the stillness. The wind lifted her hair and her hemline as Samantha stood to survey the rows of neatly manicured graves. Samantha shielded her eyes from the still-bright October sun and scanned the landscape, dotted with darkly clad strangers, for some sign of her mother and Nikki. She had told Lars, Eddie, and Anika not to come, as the wound was no longer fresh; a scar had begun to form. She spotted Leonora seated nearby on a stone bench, her head bowed, her lips moving soundlessly. Nikki stood over the grave. Even the rhythmic click of her heels on the stone pathway that made a perfect grid among the graves seemed an affront to the peaceful quiet as she made her way toward her mother and daughter. She stopped beside Leonora and put her hand on her shoulder. Leonora covered her daughter's hand with her own.

"It's lovely, isn't it?" Leonora asked. With her free hand, she brushed a leaf from the brass marker just beyond her feet. "You know, I practically had to drag your father here to pick this gravesite. He was adamant that, as he put it, 'dead is dead,' and he had no interest in building a monument to himself. Still, I think he deserves a beautiful resting place like this. Maybe I'm just a silly old woman, but I couldn't bear it if I had to think of him in a place that was…."

"It's beautiful, Mom," Samantha reassured her. "In fact, it's serene." She sat down on the bench next to her mother and began to notice the details of her surroundings for the first time. The bench was granite and sat just inside a boxwood hedge, which outlined the neatly clipped rectangle of grass enclosing not one but two gravesites, the left already occupied by her father and the right, waiting like a patient, anonymous sentinel, for her mother. A tombstone carved of the same white granite and engraved with their family name rose at the head of the grave giving it the appearance of an oversized bed, with the footboard represented by the brass marker Samantha had designed. Her eyes came to rest on the relief of words.

"Frederick Maier Green...Beloved husband, father, and grandfather," she read. "'...Isn't love the greatest thing?'"

She reached out to touch the raised lettering of his name and let her fingers come to rest on his final words. The metal was warm; and she pressed her flesh against it, remembering the safe, strong feel of her father's hand. She felt she could almost touch him. If she could, she would smooth his brow and say, "Let your demons go. Banish them forever. Rest in peace."

Samantha reached for three smooth pebbles at the base of the recently pruned hedge demarcating the parameters of the gravesite. Keeping one, she handed the others to her mother and daughter.

"What's this for?" Nikki asked.

"It is a Jewish custom to leave a pebble on the top of a headstone. One explanation is that the stone is as a reminder to later visitors that someone else has been to the grave of their loved one. A more religious explanation is that the stones help keep the soul where it belongs," Samantha explained. She moved to place her pebble on the marble top. Her outstretched hand stopped in midair. Her fingers closed around a small, slightly charred object that glinted in the sun, a gold cufflink with the scales of justice embossed on the scratched surface, its corner broken off. She turned toward Leonora and Nikki, with her palm open now, her face a question mark.

Camarado, this is no book,

Who touches this touches a man,

(Is it night? are we here together alone?)

It is I you hold and who holds you,

I spring from the pages into your arms—decease

calls me forth.

> *Walt Whitman, Leaves of Grass, Book XXXIII. SONGS OF PARTING, So Long!*

ACKNOWLEDGMENTS

I owe a debt to my passionate early readers: Natalie Bolch Morhous, who enthusiastically engaged with me in lively debate over sometimes daily phone conferences during the years that this book was conceived and birthed, Melanie Bolch Isbill, whose creativity is a constant source of inspiration, and Jordan Bass Bolch, whose unflagging belief in me and innumerable artistic and imaginative contributions provided me with the necessary motivation and perseverance to fulfill my lifelong dream of making this book a reality.

To my husband, Carl Edward Bolch, Jr.: I wish to express my deepest love and gratitude for his constant encouragement until I put pen to paper or, in this case, fingers to keyboard. Carl was, in fact, my master editor; and this book would not have been possible without him. The final result, while my own, is the product of our endless, often animated and always meticulous discussions that give truth to the Delphic pronouncement that it is always a challenge to have two lawyers under one roof!

To my "first readers," Nina and William B. Schwartz, III, Marcy Bass and Carole Basri: Many thanks for sharing in the excitement of this project and your willingness to apply your rigorous standards and inestimable talents and intelligence to my work.

To the pro: Rebecca Shapiro, Managing Editor at Columbia Magazine and former assistant editor at Random House. Your detailed edits and comments were invaluable to the process.

Abiding thanks to my college friend, Anna Quindlen, who took the time to read and comment on several early chapters. Your statement that the writing was "lovely, lyrical, completely resonant," spurred me on many times!

A grateful shout out to Richie Schwab for his dedication to the details of cover design and publication. You were an invaluable part of the team!

Lastly, a special recognition to my grandchildren for whom I hope this book will provide the impetus to fulfill their goals and the confidence to dream big as long as their eyes are open!

7/19